HARVEST OF THORNS

Harvest
of
Thorns

Shimmer Chinodya

BAOBAB BOOKS

First published in 1989
by Baobab Books
A division of Academic Books (Pvt.) Ltd
P.O. Box 1559, Harare, Zimbabwe

© Shimmer Chinodya 1989

Reprinted 1995

Cover design: Maviyane-Pike, Harare
Typeset by the Mouse House, Harare
Printed by Mazongororo Paper Converters, Harare

ISBN 0-908311-18-4

Studio Four

Shimmer Chinodya was born in 1957 in Gweru and educated at Goromonzi High School and the University of Zimbabwe, where he studied literature and education.

Harvest of Thorns is his fourth novel following *Dew in the Morning* (1982), *Farai's Girls* (1984) and *Child of War* (written under the name of B. Chirasha, 1985).

He began writing *Harvest of Thorns* in 1984, a few months before he left to attend the Iowa Writer's Workshop at the University of Iowa, USA. Part of the manuscript was presented as a thesis for an MA in Creative Writing which the University awarded him at the end of 1985.

Chinodya has also published several children's books in drama, folklore and poetry under the name of B. Chirasha. A serialization of *Dew in the Morning* has been broadcast on radio.

Part One

Chapter 1

The day he came back, and she walked in obliviously from the shower-room with soapsuds on her hands and found him sitting in his big brown boots on the sofa, she cried so much the neighbours rushed in thinking she had received news of death; after they had gone and she could talk she looked at the ropes of dried meat hung on a strip of newspaper and fished into her long skirts to send Peter to the butcher.

And on that same morning of the day he came back he fixed a plate on the stove she said she had paid an electrician to repair and he said "You shouldn't throw money to the sharks" and went out to help Peter water the cabbages in the garden while she watched them from the window trying to reclaim from the shaggy-haired man in brown boots the Benjamin she once knew who had repaired a burnt-out pressing iron element with a piece of tin foil and operated the old gramophone on a car battery and disused transformer until his father took it away to sell it.

The afternoon of the day he came back he went out with Peter to the shops and she stood at the window watching them; Peter hobbling on his crutch beside him, the stump of his leg jiggling in his shorts, his face flashing and him striding on and she thought how tall he had grown, how broad now his shoulders, how sunburnt his face.

And on the night of the day he came back he knocked on the cracked green door and it opened and she let him in and he blinked in the light and said, *"Manheru."*
  She bolted the door and brought him his food and a bowl of water and sat on the sofa opposite him.
  "You shouldn't have waited for me," he said, glancing at the little yellow clock on the display cabinet that ticked three.

"I just thought you'd want to talk," she said. His hands and mouth worked nimbly at the sadza and meat. *The last time he ate so fast he was seven,* she reminded herself, *he was seven and he was rushing off to school for the first time . . .*

His eyes skimmed over the cracked glass picture frame on the wall and the shelf where the bibles stood. He grabbed the mug of water and slurped down a mouthful.

"We're all fine here," he heard her say. "I'm so glad you came back alive, Benjamin."

He braced his hands on the table to cut off a belch. He looked up and saw her face watching him, waiting.

Suddenly seized by a panic of bright lights he stood up and said, slowly, carefully mouthing each syllable, "Good night."

Hardly hearing her reply, he stepped into the spare bedroom. For a moment he swayed in the sleep-suffused dark. He groped for the switch. In the yellow neon burst Peter sprawled in pyjama shorts on the bed, his chubby face half buried in a pillow. Benjamin planted himself carefully on the edge of the bed and, pushing the door back, began to undress. He took Peter's full leg in his hand and moved him to one side, brushed down the switch and pulled the thin blanket over his chest.

He thought he heard Peter chuckle in his sleep, dreaming perhaps. He turned his head from the roof where the light from the main bedroom formed little crosses on the corrugated asbestos. On the other side of the wall a bed creaked, a voice coughed. He heard another sound, the neighbour's toilet flushing or a car washing through a puddle in the street perhaps; his mind plunged swiftly to sleep.

4

Chapter 2

When he woke up the sun was already three hours old, blazing on the township scene. He whipped open the thin curtains and looked outside. A group of young boys were playing football in the street. An ice-cream man and a firewood vendor were jangling their bells from opposite ends of the road. Young girls sauntered from the grocers with loaves of bread or packets of milk, neat little green packages of meat and bottles of paraffin, frugal tots of cooking oil and bunches of choumoellier. A mother with a blanket round her waist was slapping a naked child playing with a garden tap. The child was screaming wildly and stamping her feet.

He yawned, got up and put on his clothes. Peter came in.

"I didn't hear you come in," he said. "I'll make the bed."

"I still can, and will," Benjamin replied.

"There's a visitor with mother in the kitchen. She came on the early morning train. A young woman."

"A relative of ours?"

"I don't think so. Mother doesn't seem to know her either. She's young and dark, kind of pretty. Judging by her looks and her luggage she's coming from the country. She brought an old suitcase with her. Mother has been trying to make her talk but she's been very quiet."

Benjamin shrugged and went out to the kitchen. Peter followed him. The young woman sat on the floor in the kitchen. She looked up briefly as Benjamin came in, shook his hand when he offered it and turned her eyes to the wall. Benjamin said "Good morning" to his mother and went out with Peter to clean the chicken coop.

There were eight hens in the coop. They cleaned and replenished the food troughs, and cleared the droppings.

"Do you know her?"

"No," Benjamin grinned. "Do you?"

"Not a clue," said Peter, the flash in his brother's eye puzzling him. Slowly, his face too broke into a grin.

Benjamin went to take a shower, changed his clothes and sat in the kitchen for breakfast. The young woman was still sitting on the floor. Mrs Tichafa poured out the tea and Peter sat on the stoep.

"So," said Benjamin by and by, "have you introduced each other?"

Mrs Tichafa's eyes widened in disbelief, her immediate suspicions confirmed. But she controlled herself and let him play his game.

"Mother, this is my wife. Her name is Nkazana. Nkazana, this is my mother. And that is my brother Peter."

The two women shook hands again and said, at the same time, "I'm very happy to meet you."

Benjamin grinned the grin of one who enjoys a novel situation he has created. Suddenly his mother laughed, the quick short laughter that dispels nervousness and incredulity without removing the shock. On the stoep Peter sat and watched. The bride looked up and smiled.

As usual the afternoon omnibus was full – there never seemed to be enough buses in the townships. Had it not been for the one-legged boy waving frantically at the side of the road, the driver might have shot past without stopping, gaining a minute on his ailing schedule. Peter and Nkazana found seats at the front and for a while Benjamin stood in the crowded aisle, braving the sharp turns as the bus swept round corners.

At the fourth stop several people got off. Benjamin eased himself on to a seat, lit a cigarette and opened the window to look outside.

A lot of the small four-roomed houses were being extended. Everywhere there were mountains of brick and sand on the side of the roads. Some of the houses had been finished – these had a sprawling, squashed look even where the extensions were newly painted. He noticed TV aerials perched on the roofs of several houses – symbols of the new progress – contrasting starkly with the billowing smoke from chimneys and the gravel roads that erupted into clouds of dust behind them. Looking at the aerials he remembered the excitement that had swept through the township when the first television sets appeared a decade earlier. He smiled at how, thinking the aerial was all there was to a television, he had wondered how it was possible to watch pictures on those thin sticks of metal.

He saw the grounds where he had played football with his mates as a young man, now bared of grass. Before water restrictions, the place had been green and he and his friends had run about and rolled in shirtless, sweat-glazed glee, shouting "Sticken!" or "Handsball!" or "Penelet!" or "Rough!" They had their own teams then – their Dynamos and Caps United. One Saturday morning he had scored seven goals and the members of his team had lifted him high on their shoulders and called him Pele.

He remembered too, furtively selling cigarettes outside the beerhall, running away from patrons who knew him and might report him to his parents. Now there were two new beerhalls in the township and one large new school with rows and rows of flowers and neat gardens.

The bus hurtled out of the stuffy, smoky atmosphere of the township and the sky became clear as they drove through a patch of forest. Earlier on, as a boy, he had trapped birds here with the sticky gum they chewed up out of flower buds of certain trees – a sour but delightful pastime requiring not only strong teeth but large reserves of saliva and optimism. Once, a strange man had chased him and a friend out of the forest and the sharp thorns stabbed into their feet as they fled. Later he had had a terrifying dream in which the pursuing man had hanged himself in the tree in which he, Benjamin, had set his traps. At his approach the fleeing birds had beaten up a fury in his face and he had heard the bloated corpse creaking above him ... The dream had been so vivid that he had fretted it into a living experience. Now the forest was wrecked to a grassless thorn bush, criss-crossed by aimless footpaths.

The idyll was dead. He was startled by the sentimentality of his reminiscences.

He was jerked back to the present by the towering haze of the fuel tanks ahead of them. At the height of the war three of the tanks had gone up in flames, hit by guerrilla fire. The site had blazed for days; after the flames had been doused the whole area had been declared a curfew zone and soldiers had been brought in ... Now the place had been reconstructed and there was no trace of the damage.

Amazing, he thought, that certain areas could completely heal, while some festered on like stubborn wounds and others, like the suburbs on the hill, chose to remain untouched by war. He looked at the faces of sparkling glass, pinewood, stone, at the marble driveways and blue swimming pools and gleaming cars in half-closed garages, at flawless lawns tended by black garden boys in khaki and black maids still pushing white babies in prams – after the war and only months after independence.

"There is the Tauyas' house," Peter pointed, with the smile of a visionary, to one of the mansions. "They were among the first blacks to leave the township after independence. They lived at the end of our street."

"Who else moved out?"

"The Mubis. You remember the Mubis? They live around here. And that big house over there belongs to the new black mayor."

"Is that all?" Benjamin asked in a queer tone. "Is that all?"

They got to the city centre during the lunch-hour rush and entered a small shop where Benjamin bought three maternity dresses for Nkazana, a bright red T-shirt and white sports shorts for Peter.

Then they went on to the supermarket to buy groceries. The white girl sitting at the till raised her eyebrows when she saw them line up their three trolleys in front of her.

"Are you sure you can pay for all this?" she asked, looking first at Nkazana, then Peter and settling on Benjamin's boots.

"Why are you asking us that?" Benjamin demanded, snapping into English. "Do you think we can take things if we can't pay for them?"

"Just making sure," said the girl. "Some customers find they don't have enough when they're at the till."

"Do you ask that to every customer?"

"Hey, I'm sorry," the girl attempted a smile.

The Indian manager came down from his glass office. "Any problem here?"

"I just asked if they could pay for these groceries and he started shouting," the girl explained unhappily.

"Oh, I think what the madam meant . . ." the manager began.

"Don't explain for her!" Benjamin erupted at the manager. *"Madam, madam, madam!* I'm not your *pickaninny."*

The flustered cashier got down from her seat and slipped off to the back.

"I'll serve you myself, sir," the manager said, with the low voice of one who has learnt never to confront trouble. "It was a mistake. We always try to respect our customers in this shop, sir."

He got behind the till and started banging at the register, pushing the goods down the trough to the packer.

"If you don't like Zimbabwe go to South Africa," Benjamin yelled.

The manager took a deep breath and quietly held out his hand. Benjamin slapped the money on to the counter and stomped out after the packer ferrying their goods to the pavement.

"See what I mean?" Benjamin fumed outside the shop. "We've been so good to them they think they can still treat us as they used to!"

A taxi pulled up and they climbed in with the bags.

"They didn't learn a thing from the war," Nkazana said, the first full sentence Peter heard her speak.

Thoroughly flustered now, he frantically loaded himself and his crutch into the back seat beside her. His head hit the spine of the door as the taxi swerved into the street.

"I want to talk to you about Nkazana," Mrs Tichafa told Benjamin in her bedroom that night, taking advantage of the breeze of tenderness brought by the groceries he had bought her. "I want to be sure what you want to do about her."

"What's there to be sure about?"

"Do her people know she's here?"

"What difference would that make?"

"Anything can happen to a pregnant woman! Besides, her people would need to know."

"In the bush hundreds of girls had babies without anybody knowing."

"This is a different situation! What if something should happen to her?"

"If something happens it happens . . ."

"Oh, Benjamin. Whatever you did out there has . . ."

"What do you think I did? Shoot birds with a catapult?"

She gaped at him.

"All right, all right. I just walked around with my gun. Nobody fired at me and I didn't fire at anybody. I didn't see corpses and didn't touch any. I'm clean. There are no vengeful spirits after me. You don't have to take me to a n'anga or to a priest. Is that what you want to hear? Does that satisfy you? Does that make you happy?"

Her eyes quivered, stewing in horror.

"Why don't we just not talk about it, mother?"

"If only your father were here and I didn't have to face all this alone. I just hope she doesn't have complications."

"What are hospitals there for?"

"But you'll be good to her, Benjamin, won't you? Promise you won't hurt her. She's just a stranger here until we let her people know she's here."

"Her people died in the war," Benjamin said.

Nkazana was a long time in the shower. When she came out Peter was already asleep in the kitchen. She carefully skirted his blankets and stepped into the sitting-room. The muted weeping in the main bedroom was over. The house was quiet. She lingered over a sofa, in the midst of the silence, thinking about how his mother had come out to the kitchen to offer her condolences and, with tears raining from her eyes, fled to her bedroom.

Benjamin popped his face round the doorway of the spare bedroom and said, with a conspiratorial wink, "You aren't going to stand there all night, are you?"

In the kitchen Peter started a rattling snore.

In the main bedroom Benjamin's mother coughed on her creaking bed.

Benjamin popped his face round the doorway again and said, "Switch off the lights when you come."

She made one last triangle with her wet towel and stepped into the spare bedroom. She pushed the door open: it mewed and a yellow tongue of light licked her arm, washed her face. The door croaked shut behind her and she was standing in the light, facing him. He was lying on his back in his trousers, on the bed. His chest was clean and shiny and ribs furrowed the sides of his body. There were swirls of hair in his armpits. Stacked against one wall of the room were suitcases and cardboard boxes. Her own suitcase stood in the middle of the room, on the green floor. It almost did not look like hers, the battered plastic and wood thing she had packed just the night before, in the moonlight.

"You better unpack your things," Benjamin said.

She knelt over the suitcase, popped it open and removed the blanket on top. She put bottles of lotion, a mirror, combs and a toothbrush on the side-table.

"What's that you're knitting?" Benjamin turned over to watch her.

She held up the woollen things.

"How much longer will it be?"

"Several months," she said.

"Does it hurt?"

She smiled over her suitcase and shook her head.

"Do you feel it move?"

"Not yet."

"Did you have trouble getting here?"

"I asked for directions at the station."

On the other side of the wall his mother sniffled and coughed. Nkazana thoughtfully shut her suitcase and stood it next to the stack against the wall. She tied up her hair in a scarf.

"Why must you do that?"

"What?"

"The scarf."

"Blanket wool gets into my hair."

"It makes you look old like a mother."

"I'll soon be one."

"The switch is near the door . . ."

She flicked the room into darkness. For a few seconds he could not see her in the dark. He heard her movements.

Gradually, he made out her small figure sitting on the floor.

"What are you doing?"

She coughed.

"There is space for you here, my shy bride."

"You didn't invite me there."

He sat up on the edge of the bed and reached down to her. He put his hands under her and hauled her over. She lightly tugged back but slipped up beside him on the bed. The feel of her small, supple body in his arms flooded him with tenderness. He heard his mother sniffle again in the next room. Nkazana heard her too, and she pushed his hand from her face, fighting off the dregs of grief she had swept to the corner of her soul. He peeled off her dress and ran his hand over the soft hill of her motherhood, kneading her skin with his fingers, like a child intrigued by a big breathing thing found on the ground.

"Does it hurt?" he asked again. He did not know what to say. His voice was tremulous, quavering over the moist caverns of her silence, his mouth searching hers.

Her arms eased on to him. Her breath was warm on his neck.

Chapter 3

When he woke up she was already out. He stretched himself, yawned, put on his clothes and went to the kitchen. She was beating the doormats and Peter sat on the doorstep, helping her. He shot her a smile, and grinned at Peter.

"Helping your wife with the housework, eh? Where's mother?"

"She's gone off to town," Nkazana replied, adjusting the print cloth round her waist in a motherly way which amused Benjamin.

"She took the dresses she sews," Peter said.

"Does she get many customers?"

"It depends on the time of the month."

"Do you want warm water for your bath?" Nkazana asked.

"Warm water is for pregnant women."

"Ba'mnini Peter had warm water."

"Are you pregnant too?" he grinned at Peter and then wagged a finger at him. "Getting warm treatment, eh?"

He went into the shower-room and turned on the tap. The thick cold rope of water beat the languor out of him. He felt good. When he came out of the bathroom there was no one in the house. The bedroom had been swept, the bed neatly made and his freshly ironed jeans laid on the pillow. He changed into the jeans, fished an old corduroy shirt from his suitcase and as he sat on the bed to tie his boots he saw through the window Peter and Nkazana coming down the street. Nkazana was holding a loaf of bread and a packet of milk and Peter was talking animatedly to her. Every now and then Nkazana looked sideways at Peter, shot a hand to her throat and laughed. They seemed locked in a fervent conversation.

"So her mother found the letter and read it . . ." Benjamin heard Peter say as they came round the path. "She tore up the letter. I tried visiting her at her home but her mother wouldn't allow her any visitors. Her mother is the kind who have boiled up tea-leaves ready for suspicious-looking visitors. Anyway, when I met the girl later she said I was a bit too young for her, that

I should wait another year until I was fifteen and in Form Two at least. Can you imagine a Grade Seven girl telling me that?"

Nkazana laughed again. Peter lowered his voice as they approached the kitchen.

"She said I could try her younger sister who's in Grade Five if I wanted ..."

"And what did you say?"

"Me having a girl in Grade Five! She's so young she'd cry if I asked her her name."

Beside himself with laughter, Benjamin went out, passing between them, to brush his teeth.

"What is it, *M'koma* Benjamin?"

"A friend told me a joke last year."

"Are you going somewhere?"

"Yes."

"Can I come with you?"

"I don't walk with *Skuzapos* like you."

"Is it on business?"

"Nothing to do with you."

"Won't you have tea before you go?" Nkazana asked.

"That's for pregnant women too."

He combed his hair, put on a checked jacket and strode down the road. An omnibus was at the terminus loading passengers but he tucked his trousers into his boots, lit a cigarette, and marched on ahead of it. He liked to work his muscles and to feel the wind rush into his face. It was amazing, he thought, how a few weeks of idleness could weaken a body.

He met people he knew, childhood mates, distant relatives and even one of his teachers. He knew they would know about him and he detected the sly interest in their eyes as they shook his hand, slowly, feelingly, their eyes scanning his face, his clothes, his boots – devouring every second of him as if he were a creature from another planet. Their questions buzzed like flies in his face. He responded briefly, knowing they would turn round to stare after him as they might stare at a one-legged man in the street.

He took a short cut through the thorn bush, past the tree about which he had dreamed the birds screeching into his face when he found the dead man; round the Light Industrial Site and over the little brown river from the shoe factory which reeked of decaying leather. Across twin railway tracks baking in the sun, past the high fenced prison into the besieging hordes of vegetable vendors and stranded passengers in the market place where his own mother plied her trade.

Once, the market place had been an appendage to the town, a vast dustbowl in winter and a swamp in summer. Now most of it was tarred and there were men working on sheds to keep commuters dry. He crossed the street and walked to the demobilization office. As usual, there was a long queue waiting outside and around the building. The people were roughly of his age group and there some women too. They all looked tough and hardened – their skins were noticeably sunburnt. They wore denim or corduroy or khaki with camouflage caps or cowboy style hats, thick boots, pieces of uniform scattered among them as if half a dozen fatigue kits had been flung among them to share. To the quick eye of a passerby, the women did not appear very different from the men. They wore the same clothes and carried themselves with the same gait. They walked to go forward, to get where they wanted to go, their heads craned out over tightly T-shirted busts and their behinds thrust out behind them. Some of them had big, braided hair, while others, like the men, had huge afros with twists of dreadlocks. A few even had closely cropped or shaved heads.

As the line slowly moved forward the ex-combatants smoked, played draughts or chatted quietly. Across the road, on the other side of the street, chauffeured cars stopped to drop suited gentlemen at the entrance of a hotel.

After a few minutes a military truck pulled up with a screech outside the demobilization building to let off a couple of officers. A sudden hush descended on the place; the combatants opened out and the officers, brisk in their crisp uniforms and shimmering shoes, clonked down the hallway. Slowly the hubbub resumed and the line crept forward again.

Benjamin smoked sparingly in the line, looking to see if there was anybody he knew. The people around him seemed at once familiar and strange. He did not recognize any of them but their faces spoke to his like the voices of long unseen relatives. He borrowed a newspaper from the person in front of him. There were pictures of villagers building a clinic on the front page and a story about a bus crash and various articles about political rallies. He paused over strikingly beautiful profiles of women wearing indigenous hairstyles. On the other half of the page was, as if to balance the scene, a picture of a rural mother holding a baby with measles. He flipped to the vacancies section. The jobs advertised in big letters were for managers and accountants and directors and the ones in very small print were for mechanics, engineers, secretaries and the like. He folded the paper neatly and gave it back. He glanced at the large posters in the hallway:

JOIN A BUILDING BRIGADE
FORM A FARMING CO-OPERATIVE
START A STUDY GROUP
JOIN AN APPRENTICESHIP
JOIN THE NATIONAL ARMY

There were seven officers behind the counter at the end of the hall. The officer on the extreme left, a hefty man with a huge waist towards whom the queue snaked, listened to all the cases and directed the arrivals to the relevant booth. As he approached him Benjamin extinguished his cigarette and felt his pockets for his papers.

"I've come to fill in my demob pay forms."

"Which assembly point are you from, comrade?"

"Freedom Cliff."

"Your name?"

"Benjamin Tichafa."

"What was your war name?"

"Pasi NemaSellout."

"What is your code number?"

"X-one-five-three-B."

"When did you leave Freedom Cliff?"

"Last week."

"Have you got your discharge papers with you?"

"I left on urgent family business."

"Do you have discharge papers or not?"

"No."

"Have you got a pass from Freedom Cliff?"

"No."

"You'd better talk to Comrade Ngano."

The hefty officer stepped to the next booth, consulted his colleague and waved Benjamin over. The second officer was a short wiry fellow with blood-shot eyes, a stunning contrast to the corpulent first. His diminutive features belied the steely strength beneath his new uniform. Benjamin could tell at once he had not been long out of the bush.

The diminutive officer fetched Benjamin's file from the rack behind him and examined it. His forehead creased into a puzzled smile.

"Why did you leave Freedom Cliff without a pass, comrade?"

"The commander was away at the time."

"But you know the rules, comrade. You know after the ceasefire you were supposed to remain in the camps. We can only give demob pay to combatants with their discharge papers in order."

"So?" Benjamin asked drily.

"So there's nothing we can do about your case. We have to screen all people carefully . . ."

"But you have my particulars."

"I know. You see, comrade, we're having trouble with people who come forward claiming they were combatants when in fact they were ordinary civilians. The army has already lost thousands of dollars paying out these false claims. We've had to tighten up our screening process. I can see your file is in order but without discharge papers there's not much I can do."

"But officer . . ."

"Now, now, let's get this straight. Do you realize you could be charged for leaving Freedom Cliff without official permission?"

Benjamin stared blankly at him.

"To be honest with you, if I were you, comrade, I'd keep a low profile for some time. What did you intend doing?"

"I want to join the new national army."

"Even if your papers were in order that would take time. The recruiting office has a long waiting list. They are taking people with special skills first. Mechanics and so on. What certificates do you have?"

"I was about to write my 'O' levels when I left for the war."

"So you have only a Junior Certificate?"

"Yes."

"Did you see the posters in the hallway? You could try joining the building brigades or the farm co-operatives. You could even join a study group if you wanted to further your education."

"I really wanted to join the national army."

"Why?"

"Because . . . it's what I can do."

"Have you got a family to look after?"

"Yes."

"You can register at the recruiting office if you want but I wouldn't promise anything. There's a limit to the numbers the army can take right now – with the government building schools, roads, hospitals and all that. As I said, if I were you I'd look at the posters in the hallway."

Benjamin picked up his papers and shuffled out of the building. The streets were alive with the lunch-hour rush. Girls in rainbow-coloured skirts were pouring out of offices and flocking with men wearing jackets and ties to restaurants that exuded rich smells of hamburgers and chicken. Black men in flashy cars stopped to pick up mistresses waiting, newly perfumed and lip-sticked, on the pavements. A briefcase knocked him on the side and when he turned round he faced a young black man in a blue suit. The young man scowled at him and strutted on.

Benjamin side-stepped into a bar at the street corner. There was classical music playing and elegantly dressed couples sunken in velvet sofas, nursing tots. People looked up at him when he came in. They made him conscious of his clothes and he wondered if he would be asked to leave. But there were several black couples in the bar and he suddenly remembered all places were supposed to be multiracial now.

He stepped to the bar and ordered a bottle of Castle. The waiter placed a glass beside the bottle but he picked up the bottle and drank it down without a break and asked for another one. The waiter looked at his boots and reached under the counter.

Chapter 4

To his mother he was fiercely laconic.

For Nkazana he alternated periodical silences with a playful banter that sometimes even had his mother laughing, but always he was generous in his own brusque way.

Peter he handled with a mixture of camaraderie and ruthlessness. When he came back from wherever his mother imagined he had spent the day and found the garden had not been watered, he would scold Peter and take him out, even if it was dark, to do it. "Who do you think will do the work here?" he would say. If the boy came home after dark he would ask him when he was planning to study, or he would make him take out his books to examine them, "You think Form One is a joke, eh!"

When she saw Benjamin doing things together with Peter, like gardening or homework, Mrs Tichafa felt a muted joy, but when Benjamin lashed out with unpredictable fury at Peter's faults, and the laughter froze in the house, even she trembled helplessly.

Benjamin went out alone. Nkazana he only accompanied to shopping trips sometimes; her domain was quickly established. Peter he rarely took to the places he went or people he saw. Mrs Tichafa was naturally surprised when she came back one evening and learnt the two had gone out together.

"But didn't they say where they were going?" she asked Nkazana.

"No, mother," Nkazana replied, looking up from her knitting, "they didn't say. They just left."

"What time did they leave?"

"Just after lunch. I was in the shower and when I came out they were gone."

Mrs Tichafa lifted the curtain again and looked out into the street. It was nearly midnight. The road was deserted.

"Just where could they be?" Mrs Tichafa said, closing the curtain. "You must be tired, Nkazana."

"A little."

"Do your legs still hurt?"

"A little."

"Does the medication they gave you at the clinic help?"

"Yes."

"Don't work too hard, Nkazana. Take a rest whenever you feel like it. I'll try and come home earlier from the market to help you. Don't wash blankets or do anything like that on your own. You had better go to sleep."

"I'll sit with you a little longer."

"I'll get you a blanket, then."

Mrs Tichafa fetched her rug from the bedroom and wrapped it round her. "Don't let the chill get into you," she said. "It could affect the baby."

Nkazana continued her knitting. Mrs Tichafa sorted her rags for half an hour then looked again through the window. She buttoned her coat and opened the door. "I'll just step out and look around. I won't be long. Bolt the door when I'm out and don't open to anyone."

She shuffled out of the house. It was a windy night: winter was approaching. The chilly May draught made pieces of paper scuttle like rabbits across the street. It whipped her long skirts around her. It was never easy walking in those ankle-long skirts. For twenty years she had lived in those skirts and though she no longer regularly went to church she could not bring herself to doff them. They had become as much a part of her body as her prematurely grey hair. Her light-skinned legs had become white, almost like a white woman's, under the constant cover of those skirts. She had developed over those two decades a subconscious fear of the sight of her naked legs. To put on normal dresses that showed her sun-starved calves would be like stepping out in the nude. Besides, what would the neighbours say? What would the church people say if she suddenly appeared in shorter dresses?

She waded down the windswept streets in her skirts, scanning the half-lit alleys on either side of her. Now the lights had gone off in most of the houses. The voices she heard were muted, distant, respectful of the night in a strange way.

She had never imagined the streets could be so quiet. She hadn't walked the streets at night in a very long while, so now some of the houses looked new to her, though she had lived here twenty years.

At the end of a road, ahead of her, a huge poster she had not seen before showed life-size members of a healthy, happy family all beaming over a loaf of bread and a brand of margarine which was being advertised. The husband in the poster had a corpulent waist and a handsome beard. The two children, a boy and a girl, had shiny skins and looked so alike you could think they were a real family. The mother, who was cutting the margarine, wore an afro wig and a short cotton dress. Her face was the colour of Fanta and her plump shiny legs the colour of Coke. The wife looked as if she had been using skin lightening creams for a long time.

She hurried past the poster to the other section of the township. Where could they be? At the township hall? Maybe they were at a film or a disco but she didn't know what weekday nights the township hall opened. She suspected Tuesdays or Thursdays because that was when she saw hordes of youth walking down the road and that was when Peter sneaked off sometimes and came back after nine. She always scolded him severely when he came home late, but he grinned in a way that nipped the anger off her voice. He always had an excuse.

She took the road towards the hall but halfway down it she saw the empty dark shimmer of the windows. There were no gusts of cheering voices, no raucous clank of music. She knew they could not be there. She turned, aware of the futility of her excursion, in the direction of the beerhall. That too, she discovered as she approached, was closed. This surprised her. She had always imagined the beerhalls stayed open all night, that at any time there would be people fighting and shouting and bleeding in the street. The silence made her afraid and suspicious. She hurried past the beerhall. Somewhere behind her she heard voices.

"It's a woman."

"She's wearing long dresses."

"Aren't those dresses worn by church women?"

"Yes, the Gospel something . . ."

"What's she doing at this time of the night anyway?"

"Don't let their dresses fool you."

She hurried on, angrily, gripping her skirts in her hands. She did not turn her head until she got home.

Nkazana was still up, knitting. Mrs Tichafa tried to hide her anger but her lips were twitching.

"No trace of them," she muttered.

Sensing her mood, Nkazana bunched up her knitting and stood up. She was just about to step into the bedroom when a car stopped in the road outside. Doors banged, the car sped off and footsteps approached. Mrs Tichafa opened the door a little and peeped out. They heard the grating of Peter's crutch on the stone path.

"Hold yourself like a man," said Benjamin's voice, irritably.

He paused at the open door, surprised by the stony reception, then eased Peter in. Peter crumpled into the nearest sofa, his crutch clattering to the floor in front of him.

Peter looked a mess. His eyes were glazed and hung half open. The house was full of the smell of him. Benjamin picked up the fallen crutch and stood it against the wall. He didn't look at anybody.

Peter became sick. Benjamin held him by the shoulders and turned his face down. Peter threw up again, then sat up. His face was knotted, his red eyes blankly surveyed the room. Nkazana brought a pail of water and a mop. Benjamin took the mop from her and cleaned the mess. He made Peter rinse his mouth into the pail and then carried him to the spare bedroom. He laid him on the bed and went out to empty the pail.

"Why did you make my son drink?"

He picked the fallen crutch and propped it on the wall.

"Answer me, Benjamin!"

He sat down opposite her and instinctively lit a cigarette. He pulled twice on the cigarette and extinguished it into a matchbox. He had not smoked before in the house.

"You made him drink!"

"I didn't."

"How did he get into that state? He's never come home like that before."

"I'm just as surprised as you are!"

"Don't lie to me!"

"If you won't listen to what I have to say there's no point in talking."

"Aren't you ashamed to drag your crippled fourteen-year-old brother into a beerhall?"

"We weren't in a beerhall. We were at a friend's house."

"Beerhall or house, what difference does it make?"

"Are you going to listen or not?"

"Lies, lies, lies. That's all I've heard from you since you came back. I was out there half the night looking for you two!"

"You shouldn't have bothered."

"I cannot understand your movements, Benjamin. You've been here weeks now but you just come and go as if this were some ... some ... some kind of

waiting-room or train station. I can't even talk to you. You never say anything ..."

"Do I always have to tell you where I'm going?"

"Does Nkazana know?"

"She knows I went to drink."

"I was out there looking for you and you know what two boys called me?
They called me a streetwalker."

"I don't blame you for not wanting me back here."

"I never said that! All I'm saying is you ought to let us know where you're
going. You could tell Nkazana at least."

"She knows."

"She knows, eh? She knows every time you disappear without a word. She
knows what's on your mind, what you're planning."

"Do you think I'm just sitting on my butt?"

"But don't you understand, Benjamin. People are watching us and they see
all these things happening. I wish you knew what they are saying about us."

"Neighbours are all the people you've ever cared about. You seem to live
your life for them."

"We don't live on an island."

"Yes, but when a house comes crashing down on the people who live in it
it's the same neighbours who laugh and gloat on the ruins."

"Since when did you start preaching?"

"I thought I was the elder son in this family."

"What right have you to say anything against anyone? You couldn't point
a finger at me, Benjamin. You know very well I wasn't responsible."

"A man is always blamed when a marriage breaks up."

"You are defending your father, then."

"I'm not defending anyone. I'm merely stating the facts."

"If your father cared so much why hasn't he come to see you? Do you think
he hasn't heard you're back?"

"You drove him out."

"Did I?" Mrs Tichafa glared at Benjamin, then looked appealingly to
Nkazana. Nkazana continued her knitting.

"You knew about Muchaneta long before she took him away," Benjamin
said, "but you didn't put up a fight. You made him think you didn't care."

"What did you want me to do? Turn myself into the scandal of this
township?"

22

"You are the kind that would offer their enemy the other cheek instead of hitting back."

"What about you? What do you care for anybody? I don't know what it is I did in this world to deserve this. First you disappear from home. Then your father packs up. Then your sister runs off with a man I haven't seen. Now you come back to tear apart the little I've tried to hold together. You, who have brought me nothing but misery, finding fault with me! You want Peter to be a wreck too. That boy will be taking *mbanje* next."

"I didn't *see* he was drinking."

"You think I'll believe that?"

"We were at a friend's place. You know Mabeza. I went to school with him."

"He got arrested for attacking a policeman."

"Peter is friends with Mabeza's young brother."

"You'll drag him into politics too."

"Are you going to listen or not? When I told him I was going there he decided to come with me. I said fine. They live on the other side of town so we went there by bus. We spent the afternoon playing cards and listening to records . . ."

"And drinking . . ."

"Look mother, you know I drink. Peter knows I drink. So what's the point of hiding it?"

"So you got him to drink too."

"I didn't! I was drinking brandy with Mabeza. Peter and Mabeza's brother were having coke, or so we thought. They were in another room. We didn't realize they had been pouring brandy into their coke until later, when Peter got sick."

"Why did you come back so late?"

"I was waiting for him to get better."

"You shouldn't have taken him with you in the first place."

"So I'm not supposed to even move around with my own brother?"

"Not if you are going to be visiting people like Mabeza."

"Mabeza is my friend!"

"How come he never visits you here?"

"Because this house is too good for people like him, that's why. Look, you'll never understand who he is or what he means to me so why don't you just leave him out of this?"

"Who are you to talk to me like that? Who are you to criticize anything I say?"

"Just because things have gone wrong in this family doesn't mean I wasted my life. There are millions in this country who are having it good because we went out. You just don't happen to be one of them."

"I can't understand your bitterness, why you are so hardened. You keep trying to blame me for your failure. Look at your friends who finished school and started working. You'll never ever catch up with them!"

"Do you know what this war was about?"

"This whole family is damned by all the blood on your hands."

"That's all you can think of. We'd have killed traitors like you during the war."

She swivelled her eyes at him, trembling with rage.

"I hate to talk like this in your presence, Nkazana," she fumed, "but his heart is hard as a rock. He's my son and he's your husband and I must not hide anything about him from you."

Nkazana packed up her knitting, reluctant to be drawn into the conflict, but the broken voice of the older woman made her stay where she was.

"Yes, Nkazana. You must know."

"Tell her!" Benjamin banged out to the toilet.

Outside, in the false neon dawn, a cock crowed. On the other side of the thorn bush the shoe factory yawned. Peter's drunken snores intensified in the spare room. In the toilet Benjamin struggled with the recalcitrant cistern.

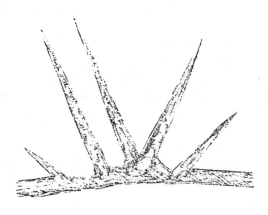

Part Two

Chapter 5

Back in the mid-fifties, when she was still a lean, strong-limbed, black-kneed, hoe-blistered, tender-eyed, braid-haired, bra-less, knee-skirted, scout-belted, *mariposa*-shoed, country-humble girl of eighteen, just completed Standard Three and living with her elder sister married to a dip-attendant who worked on the farms neighbouring the reserve where he lived, Shamiso Mhaka had one day accompanied her elder sister to the district office in the town nearest to their village to get a birth certificate for her sister's two-year-old son.

The two sisters had got off the bus at the town market place, bleary-eyed, their skins brushed with dust after the jolting, dirt road drive through farm and village country. She had stood carefully on the pavement, clutching the bag full of nappies to her knee, while her sister went up to the vegetable stalls to ask for directions to the district office. They had crossed the road, arm in arm, darting through the honking traffic, sidling on to the wet pavement peopled by mealie cob vendors, self-employed cobblers, window-shopping idlers and suspicious looking city slickers, weaving through the crowd until they found a cafe.

They went in and found two red chairs and a green table to sit on. Her sister loosened her baby and brought him round to breastfeed him, pushing her huge cream-coloured breast into the boy's mouth. They noticed the white man at the counter pointing at them and saying something frantic they could not hear in the blaring music, and then a young black man wearing kitchen whites came over and told them that the Greek owner of the shop would not have women breastfeeding their babies in his shop, and besides, they had to buy something if they wanted to sit on the chairs.

Her sister plucked the breast out of the baby's mouth with alarm, squirting a jet of milk over the green table. The baby's lips twisted into an ugly scream. Thrusting the boy into Shamiso's arms, she strapped the carrying cloth on her back, wiped the milk off the table with her palm and, fumbling through the nappies in her bag for her purse, hurried to the counter.

"Toffees," she said, slapping a tickey on the counter in front of the Greek's face.

"You sit here, you buy more," the shopowner said, ignoring the tickey, gesturing fiercely.

She turned her head, looked round the cafe, pushed the tickey forward and said, "Two Fanta and two Strong buns."

"One'n'six!" the Greek shouted.

"Hwe?"

"One shilling and sixpence!"

She took the tickey, put it in her mouth and counted out on to the counter twelve huge brown pennies stamped with the face of the Queen of England.

"Gimme the tickey!" shouted the Greek, picking up the pennies.

She put the wet tickey on the counter. Shaking his head, muttering, the shopowner slid the tickey across the counter, into the till, snatched two bottles from the fridge, popped them open, tore off two big yellow buns from an uncovered rack on the counter and tossed them into a wobbled plastic plate.

"Next!" he shouted, drumming the counter with greasy black fingers.

She picked up the drinks and hurried back to her screaming child.

"We'll have to drink fast," she said to Shamiso, plugging the baby's yelling mouth with a bottle, glancing back at the counter and biting into her bun.

Back on the street, Shamiso bumped into an old white lady. The lady's white-haired husband stepped out and angrily shook his stick, shouting a string of insults.

"Don't you know you should step off the pavement when you see white people coming?" her sister hissed when the couple went off. "You nearly got us into trouble!"

They eventually found the district office outside the town without further trouble. But the place was crowded. A long line of people snaked from the narrow door of a yellow government building to the very gate. There were mainly men in the line. Some people were standing, others kneeling: the women preferred to sit on the tarmac yard, shuffling forward every few minutes when the line heaved.

They joined the line near the gate.

"We'll never get done today," the older woman said, surveying the line, shading her eyes with a hand in the squinting sun.

28

Cars kept coming in and out of the gates, driven by white men who honked at the line and sat stiffly at the wheel, staring ahead as they swept past. Black men in government khakis strolled across the yard, carrying files, newspapers, tea cups, oil-drenched, aromatic packages from the restaurant across the street and sometimes even flowers, in what seemed an endless routine.

Towards four o'clock Shamiso's sister stopped one of the messengers in khaki and said, "*Mkwasha,* what time does the office close today?"

The man shot a hand to his face, glanced at his huge shiny watch and said, "Very soon. Thirty minutes from now."

"Is that before the sun sets?"

"Oh, yes," he said, a small laugh twinkling in his eye.

He was a young man, probably twenty-three or twenty-four with a smooth, dark complexion. His hair was neatly barbered in the style of the *English cut,* with a small *bibo* parted on the side and sideburns sliced off to a clean shave. He had bright black eyes and a straight steep nose. Starched and creased to an intimidating point, his khaki trousers fitted his slim, neither-short-nor-tall frame very well. There was about him the breezy smells of carbolic soap, shaving cream and hair oil.

"Did you want anything?" he asked, surveying them, his lips parting into a brilliant flash of well spaced teeth.

"We need a birth certificate for my child," she said. "Do you think we can get it today?"

"You'll probably have to come tomorrow," he said, glancing at the line and again at his watch.

"*Iii, Mkwasha,* we came from far away, by bus."

"In the reserves?"

"Yes."

"Oh," he said, the sound coming out more like "*Ooouu.*"

"So, *Mkwasha,* I was going to ask you if you could do something for us. . . so we can go in before the office closes."

"That can be done if you give me your daughter, *Ambuya,*" he laughed, pointing a flirty finger at Shamiso.

Shamiso shyly looked away. Her sister glanced at the sun and said, "Please, *Mkwasha* . . ."

"Very well, I'll try," he said. "Wait here."

He went across the yard to the other door, came out with a trayload of tea cups, disappeared behind the building and then returned a while later with a bundle of dirty looking, brown government files.

"Come with me, *Ambuya*," he said.

She hauled the baby back on to her back; Shamiso picked up the napkin bag and they followed him up the line into the building. People in the line looked suspiciously at them as they passed and a male voice brashly muttered, "Must be the girl he's after" but the young messenger did not turn his head.

It was cool inside the building. A fan whirred at the counter, whipping cold air round the room. Men and women sat on benches along the side of the room, waiting their turn to step out to the counter, where an amazingly young white man sat writing. Behind him in the room were stacks and stacks of brown and green files, and black men in khaki shuffled among the stacks, clipping, stapling, pushing and packing files on the stacks along the thin corridors. The young messenger moved a little closer to the counter and stood waiting to be noticed. The white man looked up and saw Shamiso and her sister standing the middle of the room.

"Well, Clopas . . ." said the white man.

"This woman she is needing help, Baas," Clopas explained in English.

The white man's head shot up. He sniffed the air suspiciously and screamed over his shoulder at the grey-haired man sweeping the floor, "Dust! Sprinkle more water on the floor, *Madala*!"

"This woman is needing help, Baas," Clopas repeated, pointing at Shamiso's sister.

"What does she want?" said the white man.

"She is needing to have a bath certificate for his child, Baas."

"*What!*"

"A bath certificate for his child, Baas."

"Who needs a birth certificate?"

"This woman, Baas."

"But I thought you said *his* child, Clopas."

"Yes, Baas. This woman is having a child."

"Is this woman a *he* or a *she*?"

"She, Baas."

"Then why did you say *his* child?"

"Mistake, Baas."

"I thought you said you passed Standard Five."

"Yes, Baas," Clopas said, smiling.

"They taught you English at school, didn't they?"

"No, Baas."

"What? Did they teach you English or did they not?"

"They did, Baas."

"Then say *yes*. For God's sake speak *proper* English! If the Queen heard you she'd send you to the gallows!"

"Yes Baas."

"All right, Clopas. What's the problem?"

"This woman she is for to wanting to have a bath certificate for *her* son, Baas."

The young white man laughed again and shook his head. A snicker ran down the line. Clopas grinned.

"Why isn't she in the queue with all the others?"

"S'begging your pudding Baas."

"Begging my *what*?"

"Pudding, Baas."

"*Pardon*?"

"Yes Baas. Pardon, Baas."

"I wish my mom could hear this. She thinks our cook speaks rotten English! I said why isn't she in the queue. The queue, Clopas, the *line*?"

"She's coming from away far, Baas. To the reserves."

"So?"

"She needs for to climb buses."

"What?"

"Climbing buses. Back to the reserves, Baas. If she no get bath certificate then is nowhere for them to sleeping, Baas."

"Has she got everything with her?"

Clopas turned to Shamiso's sister and snapped in Shona, "He needs to have your husband's registration certificate and the letter from the clinic where the child was born. Do you have them?"

Shamiso's sister fished for the required documents in her *doek* and gave them to Clopas, who handed them over to the white man. The white man smoothed the heavily folded papers and squinted over them.

"Was this child born at the local hospital?" he asked.

Clopas translated the question to Shamiso's sister who seemed to have already grasped it and readily said, "Yes."

31

"Does she live in this town?"

Clopas quickly translated, got a response and relayed it back.

"No Baas, she living in the reserves."

"Then why was the baby born here?"

Clopas translated again and then explained, "She staying here in town with his hasbend a long time ah go, Baas. But now she is staying for the reserves."

"Where is her husband? Why didn't he come too?"

Clopas translated again and said, "Her hasbend is at working, Baas, at farm with other Baas, so he can't coming."

"You people keep leap-frogging from place to place and make our work difficult. That'll be the day you learn to stay in one place!" He plucked a form from a pile and filled it in quickly. Then he said, "That's all. She can come back for the birth certificate tomorrow."

"Tomorrow, Baas?"

"Yes, tomorrow. Don't you know the District Commissioner has the half-day off today?"

"Oh, yes, Baas."

"This certificate is useless without the District Commissioner's signature. Only the D.C. signs birth certificates. O.K?"

Clopas turned round to explain. The two women's faces fell, but the white man threw the half-done certificate into a tray, glanced at his watch and said, in a half-tried *chiraparapa* accent, *"Wena buya tomorrow, Mfazi."*

"Couldn't he just sign it for us?"

"He sometimes signs but I don't know why he didn't today," Clopas explained. "He's a *mambara*, this one. Doesn't take a minute to break his wires. I don't know what his mother said to him, or perhaps his girlfriend – she sometimes comes and spends the whole morning drinking tea and talking to him, *"Tswiri-tswiri-tswiri, Ntwi, Ntwi, size, oh, dali, dali ..."*

The two women laughed.

"You can come for the certificate early tomorrow."

"But where will we sleep tonight?" said Shamiso's sister. "We know nobody in this town."

Shamiso took the baby, who was now sleeping, and held him in her arms.

"There's only one place you can go to *Ambuya*," said Clopas, running a finger through his hair, "but it's not really safe."

"Where's that?"

"The waiting-room at the train station."

"We might as well go there before it gets dark."

"But as I said it's not safe," he said, with a seriousness that told familiar town stories of knives and thefts and rape. "You can come over to my place if you like."

Shamiso's sister considered for a second, then shook her head slowly, "No, *Mkwasha*."

"*Honest,*" Clopas said, painting a saliva cross on his forehead. "If you want I can leave my room to you. I have friends I can sleep with."

"No, *Mkwasha*. Thank you very much. The waiting-room at the train station will do."

"Very well," he said. "I'll show you how to get there."

At the gate he pointed out the roads to the station, which was not far.

"Can I ask you one thing, *Ambuya*?" he said, stopping them as they turned to go.

"Yes, *Mkwasha*."

"Is this girl really your daughter?"

"Why would you ask that?" she laughed.

"You're much too young to be her mother. You look so alike anyone can see you're sisters. I could swear there was nobody between you."

"You may be right."

"May I know your name?"

"Does a *Mkwasha* ask his *Ambuya* for her name?"

"Well. Maybe I should call you *Maiguru* then."

"I am a married woman. My name is Mai Zimofa."

"And what is your sister's name?"

"That is not for me to tell you."

"But she can tell me herself, can't she?"

"That is up to her."

"What is your name, *vahanzvadzi*?"

Shamiso looked up shyly and told him.

"I'm Clopas Tichafa," he said, offering his hand, "and I'm pleased to meet you. You're sure I can't give you a place for tonight?"

"No. But thank you very much."

"Very well, then. Have a good night. I'll see you tomorrow."

He turned and ran across the tarmac yard.

"Isn't he a kind man?" the older woman said as they waited for the traffic to ease before they crossed the street. Shamiso patted the baby on her back and quietly straightened her skirt. They pushed through the five o'clock crowds towards the train station.

At the waiting-room they found a corner to sit in. By six o'clock the place was already crowded. Men, women and children sat in clusters round mounds of luggage, eating and drinking, shuffling to the toilets, unpacking blankets from suitcases. Mothers changed babies' napkins, fetched water from the tap in tin mugs, chided playful children who strayed from familial clusters. Men strapped boxes with strips of elastic rubber, rearranging, repacking, moving the luggage. A stale smell hung in that waiting-room – a smell of toilets and trapped people and coal smoke from the train engines. Every half hour the concrete floor vibrated as a train thundered into the station and the crowd reared, only to settle down again as the incoming train turned out to be a goods train.

Shamiso went to buy two more Fantas and two pieces of *chikondamoyo* cake from the vendor outside the waiting-room. It was already dark outside and the street lights were on. The vendor, a young man with very tight-fitting green trousers and a blue shirt with a large collar asked her her name and laughed as she turned and ran back into the waiting-room, the bottles clinking in her hands.

A sudden hush descended on the waiting-room. Half a dozen people fearfully scuttled out just as two policemen, one white and the other black, entered the waitin- room. The white policeman wore a brown uniform with long sleeves and full trousers and the black one had on short sleeves and shorts. They charged into the waiting-room, their eyes darting everywhere, scanning the crowd. In the middle of the room they seemed to find the person they wanted – a dishevelled man huddled on the floor with a thin blanket wrapped around him.

"Him!" the white policeman pointed.

"You've been sleeping here for a whole week," the black policeman charged, snatching the blanket off the man.

"I've nowhere to go, my son," the man wailed.

The black policeman looked up at the white one, "What do we do with him, Baas?"

"He can go to jail," the white one barked. "This waiting-room is no fucking boarding house!"

The man kept shouting, "I have nowhere to go" and wriggled like a madman as they dragged him out to the waiting jeep, loaded him in and screeched off.

The hubbub in the waiting-room resumed, rising from a low, fearful pitch.

A chill wind swept into the waiting-room through the open doors. The travellers dozed, yawned, waiting for the train.

Shamiso clutched the baby in a thin blanket and huddled next to her sister. She was about to fall asleep when she saw Clopas, the man who had helped them at the district office, come into the waiting-room! He clutched something under his arm and was looking around him as he walked down the waiting-room. For some reason Shamiso raised her hand and smiled. Clopas noticed her, waved excitedly and came over.

She shook her sister awake and said, "That man is here!"

"Who?" her sister started, but Clopas was already there, crouching on his heels on the floor in front of them, smiling.

"Good evening," he said.

He had changed into a light green polo-neck pullover and brown trousers. He still wore the immaculate brown shoes he had had on that day.

"I brought you a blanket," he said, handing over the brown packet he carried under his arm.

Shamiso's sister clapped her hands and accepted the packet. "That was very kind of you," she said, adjusting her *doek*.

"I saw it was getting cold and I didn't remember you carrying a blanket so I thought to bring you one of my own," he said, "and there's a flask of hot tea in there."

He pulled the strap of his silver watch and smiled at them.

"You must live near here, then," Shamiso's sister said.

"I live in a township two miles from here."

"And you walked all that distance!"

"I have a bicycle," he laughed, "and besides, I was visiting a friend of mine who lives near here."

He was uncomfortable on his heels, struggling to maintain his balance. His eyes met Shamiso's and he said, "I hope you will be comfortable."

"Thank you so much," the older woman said.

He stood up, said, "Good night," and strolled back towards the door.

"It almost smells new," Shamiso said, sniffing at the pink blanket he brought them.

Her sister opened the flask and tasted the tea, "Just the right amount of sugar," she laughed. "I wonder how he knew."

"Isn't he a nice man?" she continued as they snuggled in the blanket, sipping the tea. Around them the crowd rushed to their feet as another goods train rumbled into the station.

The District Commissioner did not come in until ten o'clock the next morning and they finally had the precious certificate signed at noon.

When they went to give the blanket and flask back to Clopas he asked for their address. After hesitating, Shamiso printed it out on a piece of paper and they went down to catch the bus back to the reserves.

Four days later, children from the local primary school brought the Zimofa household a letter in an unusual looking cursive addressed to Shamiso Mhaka.

"It's him, isn't it?" her sister said, pointing to the looped 'S' sweeping across the face of the envelope and the crimson heart drawn into each bottom corner.

"Who?" Shamiso asked, turning over the envelope suspiciously.

"Who else? The messenger from the D.C.'s office."

She turned the letter over and over, on her knees.

So far, in all her life, she had received four letters, scribbled out on coarse green counter paper by country boys from across the river whose enthusiasm had mysteriously fizzled out when they did not get a reply.

"Aren't you going to read it and find out what he says?"

She tore the letter open along the narrow edge and turned it over, on her knees.

"What does he say?"

She pulled the letter out of the envelope. It was written on thin pink sheaves of paper, laced on the edges with pictures of flowers. There was a pair of crimson hearts on each page. A green box was drawn round the address in the corner.

"Look at those flowers," her sister said. "I wonder if he drew them himself."

Shamiso Mhaka read the letter. The handwriting was unusual, like that of one of her teachers at school, she thought. The letter was in English but there were some Shona words, too. She read it slowly, pondering every word.

36

Dearest, Daleng Shamiso Mhaka, I hope you no sarpraised by riciving this missive but I just decision to send you one because I have importent news and this news I am keeping for to myself for some time. I love you very very very much. The day I seen you in the line outside my job I know I have found a pritty wife. You are the prittiest girl ever meet and to say pritty is telling god lie because you prittier than the word pritty. Your skin is like the mupichisi frute. Your eyes like black diemonds. Your lips is maroro chaiwo. When I met you that day I can't telling you I love you because I think you sister is your mother and I don't want you to thought I rush too fast. Now you know. Please please please please please please please reply because I cannot sleep at night thinking about you. I want to marry you and to call your Mrs Clopas Wandai J. Tichafa my wife. Yours in hope, Clopas Wandai J. Tichafa. P.S. If I can meeting you any place any time please telling me this . . .

"Well?" said her sister.

"He wants to marry me," Shamiso said. "What shall I do?"

"Do you want him?"

"I don't know."

"What a queer man. Saying that in the very first letter!"

"What shall I tell him?"

"Just wait. Don't write him yet."

Once, in Standard Three, a boy from the same village had pinched her breasts and she had swung viciously at him with a ruler.

Another boy had been bold enough to come and stoop at the kitchen door and ask for her but her sister's husband had asked him where he came from to do things like that. That same young man had followed her to the township one day and she had told him she could not marry anyone because she was a witch, just to put him off, but the young man had perhaps believed her because he did not follow her again after that.

Many boys had made passes at her but she had ignored them. Before she came to live with her sister, her mother had called them both to warn them against men. Men were wicked, she had said, because they gave you children and then went off to live with other women. Especially handsome city men. And handsome city men who drank beer were the worst because beer washed their brains out of their heads and made them look pregnant while their wives and children starved. An ugly man was better because few women would look at him. A poor honest man was even better because few women would want him. But a kind-hearted, good-looking man who had a reasonable job and did not drink and went to church every Sunday was best if you found one.

She thought about these things and did not know what to do. She liked this man Clopas. But she couldn't just tell him that.

"If you tell a man you love him straight away he will think you are a fool," a friend had told her at school.

A week later, another letter came from him. Her sister was away visiting her friends. Her heart jumped when she saw his handwriting and the crimson hearts on the envelope. She opened it at once. She was afraid he might be angry with her for not replying.

I was surprise you do not replying my letter, he wrote. *Everyday I come back from job expecting letter under my door and is not even a little emvlope and I take off my jackit and sits in my sofa thinking why are you not writing. Please please please write to me. My life depending on you, Shamiso. Every nights I woke up thinking about you and everybody at work says what's wrong Clopas are you ill or has eneone died at your home or you brather or sister is not well? but I can't talk because I want to make sure first. My heart is swolling and paining with love for you. I can't even do job propery because of you and the Baas is scolding every day. Please seve my life and my job by marry me. I love you better than myself. Please please please reply. Please Shamiso. Yours in saspence, for bitter or worse. Clopas Wandai J. Tichafa. P.S. Greetings to your sister's baby son and if only you say yes then I can say Maiguru to her please.*

When her sister came back Shamiso showed her the letter. Her sister read the letter. She smiled and shook her head.

"What a man!"

"Should I write him now?"

"No, wait."

At night she thought about him. She could not sleep. When she washed clothes she thought about him. When she cooked she thought about him. When she minded the baby she thought about him. One day she burnt the meat and her sister's husband laughed and asked if that young man from the line had come again that afternoon.

38

After a week, another letter came from him. She ran to the path to meet the children who brought the letter. She opened it at once. A photograph fell out of the letter. It was a picture of him, wearing a black suit and a white shirt and a black bow-tie. He was smiling right into the camera and had two *sheds* in his hair. She went weak inside, looking at the photograph.

I am hereby sent you a camera fotopicture taken me by my best friend Jeshua so that you can remind and thinking of me all times. Perhaps you have fogotting me and I'm sending this fotopicture for you to put on top your pillow so you can dream about me when your eyes falling sleepy. I still love you over than and will not stop scripting until the world stops and all the enjels come and God "says" every-body to Heaven or to Hell but I'm cokesure a butifull girl like you is going to HEAVEN stret away. S'true God, Shamiso I love you more each day. I will go on scripting even I buys all the written peds and emvlops at Bright Bookstore and even the postmaster say no, Clopas, you finishing pestej stemps for others because my heart says you the woman for me and I must not sarenda. Please please don't think I'm stubbon because I love you. You are a good woman and I want to marry you. Our old ansestors said The forest gives when you are tiring but I em not tiring yet. Please please write me a letter ndapota zvangu. Ndapota please please please. Please send me your fotopiktcher too so I can put it on the wall near my bed, and not think of you too much. Every morning cars nearly footing me because I'm thinking about you too much. Perhaps you have not write because you think I am too olds for you but I am a young man only twenty four years of old and ready to start family. But I can't starting family without you, Shamiso. Otherwise you think I's joking and I'm having many other girlfriend but I say to you I never jok on this matter. I am being a stead man without fulling around and looking at silly town girls who is after beer and money chete. Sometimes you think I says this because I have job in town and house and you are from reserves but I tell you no, it is love only. Perhaps you thinks I am a bed man because I live in big city but again I say no, I do not know the mouth of a beerhole and I do not touch cigaroots and I do not play cards or betting horses. I have small house and small education but my head is not small. Every month I banking money at Post Office Saving Banker and I can keep well you and our children if you becomes my wife. So please Shamiso hear mercy for me and consider all my proposing and please please write me and cool my heart and say you love me too and agree, Yours in tears Clopas Wandai J.

Tichafa. P.S. Say hello to your sister from her suffering Babamnini and hello too to Babamkuru, I hope you have speaking to him about me sometimes . . .

"He must have a book he gets all these ideas from," said her sister. "You write him now, but say you are not very sure and need more time to think about it. Don't encourage him too much."

Dear Mr Clopas Wandai J. Tichafa, she wrote, in Shona, *I have received all your letters and read what you wrote in them. I can't say anything now because I have not yet decided and need more time to think about it. Shamiso Mhaka.*

This letter was followed by a barrage of protests and pleas from him. She tied up all his letters into a bundle after reading them and would afterwards take them out to read them before she went to sleep. The thought of him sitting up all night bleeding his thoughts on to paper filled her with pangs of guilt and pity, a pity edged with her own excitement. Finally she wrote, without consulting her sister:

Dear Mr Clopas Wandai J. Tichafa, I have thought about what you said. I accept you. Yours, Shamiso Mhaka.

She put the letter in an envelope and sealed it but did not post it. A week after she had written it another long letter came from him and after reading it her sister said, "He seems really serious about you."
"I've already told him."
"What did you say to him?"
"That I accept him."
"But why didn't you tell me?"
"I haven't posted the letter."
"What *exactly* did you say to him?"
She told her.
"Was that all?"
"Is there anything else I should have said?"
"No. It's just right. Send it off."

Two weeks later, on a Saturday morning, he visited her at her sister's home.
Her sister accompanied her to the township to meet him. When he got off the bus, jubilantly immaculate in a black suit, white shirt and matching

black tie, clutching a small package of groceries in one hand and swinging a black umbrella with the other, Shamiso's heart thumped up a terrific roar. She shook his hand limply, and suddenly the green crimpolene dress and the new canvas shoes her sister had bought for her seemed inadequate. She dabbed at her forehead with an orange handkerchief which had rolled itself into a nervous ball in her palm. Flanking him, they trudged up the dusty road past the shops and the bottle store. She fretted about the dust swirling up in their faces, the scorching midday sun, the clusters of people gaping at them from the shops, the donkeys bathing in the ash and shambling across the road in front of them, the cattle lowing, the stinking he-goat parading his shameless act with a female, the blank-eyed herdboys who sprawled in the sand at the side of the road and stared miles after them, the tottering old women in unwashed skirts who ought to have died ages ago but stepped over to the side of the road and greeted them with slow, faltering voices. She fretted for his nose, fearful that the smell of cowdung and *muhacha* trees and the pit latrines would overwhelm him. For his sake she suddenly hated everything, the grass huts and squatting trees and *chidongi* ridden October fields.

Her embarrassment at the world she had lived in all her life made his voice echo in her ears so that when she tried to respond her voice was shaky.

Her sister's home seemed ten miles away from the township that day, though it was only half a mile. When they approached it she was glad that she and her sister had recently repainted and decorated the walls of the huts with black and brown clay and cleared the yard, that the path leading to it was wide and the cattle pen out of the way.

Her sister's husband was waiting for them, having put off a Saturday afternoon's work in the garden. A diminutive, gentle-eyed but firm-principled man with an Adam's apple that stuck out prominently in his throat (he was lead baritone in the village church choir and part-time catechist), he spoke affably with the visitor in the cool sitting-room of the brick and zinc house while the two women prepared food in the round pole and dagga hut that served as the kitchen. Once out of Clopas's presence Shamiso's frayed nerves settled considerably, though she made a conscious effort not to spoil the cooking. While her sister presided over the pots, she carried the water and plates to the sitting-room.

"Oh yes, sometimes there are long queues at the District Office," Clopas was explaining when she came in.

"Getting *situpas* has always been a problem," the other said, and the two continued with the surprising ease and familiarity of long acquaintances. With eyes held down, Shamiso unfolded over the small coffee table the white and green table-cloth she had sewn in her Standard Five class, and laid two knives, two glasses and two forks next to the plates.

Kneeling, she planted the jug of water on the table and hurried out of the room, back to the kitchen.

Her sister was scooping out the brown rice mashed in peanut butter and shaping it into a formidable hill with her cooking stick. She dished the chicken and gravy, making sure that the drumsticks, *chikanganwahama* and neck went into the guest's dish. Everything ready, the two sisters carried the covered plates to the sitting-room. Kneeling one behind the other, they placed their loads on the table.

The man of the house prayed, *"Lord, we thank you for this visitor within our walls and this food you have given us today and we ask you to bless the food so that it can make us healthy and give us the strength to praise you all the days of our lives. Amen."*

"Amen," said everybody.

"But there're only two plates here," the man of the house said to the women, "aren't you joining us?"

"Go ahead and eat," his wife said, leading the way out. "We have to feed the children."

"Were we supposed to eat with them?" Shamiso asked, as they settled to their own plates with the two children, in the kitchen.

"We could have done so but it's not always proper on the first occasion," her sister said. Reaching for the pot to peel out the crisp thin cakes at the bottom of the pot, she laughed, "Besides, you don't want him to know right away that you like eating *makoko*!"

Rice and peanut butter with chicken and gravy was Shamiso's favourite dish, but she did not eat much that day. As far as she could tell the food was perfect, the rice just solid enough, without sticking to the fingers, and the chicken tender and brown in thick rich gravy. Once after she had come to live with her sister, a woman from the village had sold them a suspiciously huge cock that had turned out to be at least five years old and absolutely unchewable even after five hours on the fire: thank God there had been no visitors on that occasion! This one was all right, but she worried if the pepper was not too strong. What if he didn't like pepper at all?

"We forgot the drinks," said her sister.

Shamiso fished into a bucket of water and brought out a Coca-Cola, a Canada Dry Cream Soda in a twisted bottle, and a Fanta Orange, dried them carefully with a dish cloth, put them on a tray with two fresh plastic glasses and a bottle opener and shuttled to the sitting-room.

"I'm the only child in our family," Clopas was saying in the sitting-room. "All the others died at birth or when they were very young. My father died three years ago."

She paused outside the sitting-room and that mention of his family hit her like a strange, rare fact. She went in, knelt, placed the drinks on the table.

"So you really insisted on deserting us, *Mainini*," the man of the house said, and Clopas beamed conspiratorially, but she was already on her feet, facing the door, making her escape as gracefully as possible.

"What church do you go to?" she heard her sister's husband ask the visitor, just as she went into the kitchen, but did not catch Clopas's reply.

She fetched herself a Fanta Orange. Coca-Cola irritated her stomach and she had heard that if you left a penny or shilling in a glass of it for a long time the coin might disappear. Cream Soda had a nice taste but the green colour almost nauseated her. When she returned to the sitting-room to collect the dishes later she noted with relief that three-quarters of the food had been eaten and only the Coca-Cola was unopened. He likes Fanta too, she concluded, knowing her sister's husband drank Cream Soda.

"You don't look like you have eaten, *Mainini*!" the man of the house bantered and she laughed for the first time that afternoon as she took away the dishes.

After washing up the dishes she delivered the tea – together with a pot of boiled water and an unopened packet of Ellis Brown instant coffee, in case he didn't drink tea.

"How long have you been working at the dip tank?" Clopas was asking when she came in and the man of the house said, "Eight years."

"You've kept your job!"

"It's the only thing a black man can do in this country. Thank you, *Mainini*. Aren't you going to stay a while, *Mainini*?"

Clopas beamed, but again she hurried out.

When she returned later to collect the tea things her sister sent her child to call out the man of the house and as soon as he was alone with Shamiso, Clopas said, "Why did you not come to eat with us?"

Wondering if he really expected an answer to that question, she went on packing the tea things. Her sister's elder boy returned with another message from his mother saying that *Mainini* Shamiso could wash the tea things later.

"I have to catch the bus at five o'clock, Shami," Clopas said, looking at his watch, when the boy left. And then he added, laughing, "But I wish I could stay for the weekend."

"Do you work on Sundays?" she asked. The mere prospect of his intention to stay sent a stab of panic through her. He told her no. She was still kneeling next to the coffee table and he sensed it. She rose awkwardly and sat on the edge of the sofa, opposite him. Outside she heard her sister and her husband walking in the garden inspecting the tomatoes and her sister saying, "They are still green, *Baba* Manuel."

Shamiso slipped back a little on the sofa.

"Your sister and her husband are such nice people. Have you always stayed with them?"

"I've been with them three years."

"A pity I didn't meet your parents."

"You will sometime."

"When are you coming to visit me to see where I live? Next week?"

"We'll see."

"Do you have any pictures of yourself I can take with me?"

She had two pictures, one in which she held her sister's babies and another which a shopowner at the township had snapped without warning her. In both pictures she had worn a *doek* that her sister had said made her look older than she was. She herself did not like the blank expression on her face and the way her lips hung open as if she had been caught about to stuff her mouth with pumpkin. Pictures made her nervous. She feared he might not like either of them so she said, "No".

He talked to her for a while and when it was time for him to go he asked for her sister and her husband to be called and he thanked them for their hospitality and they in turn thanked him for coming and for the groceries he brought. After a short prayer from the man of the house, they accompanied him to the bus stop. Just before they got there, her sister and her husband turned back home, leaving the two of them alone.

"I brought you something," Clopas said, putting a necklace with a dazzling yellow chain and a gleaming chocolate coloured stone round her neck.

"Thank you," she said, admiring it.

"I wish I could stay all weekend, Shami," he said, putting his hands on her shoulders and pulling her towards him. Suddenly his face plunged down towards hers, lips pursed. She pulled away and stepped back.

"Please Shami," he said, in a strange new voice, his mouth hanging in a quivering grin.

She turned her face away. He tried to gather her into his arms and she swung off and panted, "Your bus has come!"

He turned and saw the last passenger get into the bus. For three seconds he stood rooted to the spot, staring into her face. Then he tore off towards the road, frantically waving his arms. The bus started moving. He let out a sharp, herdboy's whistle and, his tie flying, his coat-tails flapping and the soles of his shoes flashing in the sun, he sprinted for the door. The bus stopped and he scrambled in. Staggering in the aisle as the bus pulled off, he had no chance to wave out to her.

"Now he's trying to be smart and you have to watch him," her sister said after eagerly listening to her communique. "Asking for that on the very first visit! I didn't let *Baba* Manuel touch me until after he married me."

Shamiso went to bed wearing the necklace he had given her but sleep did not come easily. Her mind wandered along the borders of joy and disappointment. Everything had gone well, almost. He had liked her sister's husband, their home and the time spent with them. Everything had gone well until he tried to hold her.

Three days later, he wrote again.

Dearest, Daling Shamiso, I was very happy to came to your sister's home and meeting her housebund. It was such a supper time talking to my new Babamkuru and knowing he is a good kind Krishian man and the food was very very delishous and everything was very very smat. I would like to thanking you and my good Maiguru for that. I hop that when we get married we shall be eating good food like that all-ways and meny meny vistors will be coming to our home because they know Mrs Clopas Wandai J. Tichafa is very good cooker. I hop you like the little gift I brout for you and don't think I don't love you becaus it's a small gift I only say to you one days I shall bringing something to show really how I love you my Shamiso.

Anhow I have a small small complains to make that disappoins me at my visit to your sister's home and please Shami don't think I am being stubbon in this its a small thing and that complains is this that in my visit I spoke to you only ten minutes, peheps eleven minutes and foty fife secends as accoding to my Renova ristwatch but please Shami when I tried to hold you in my arms why did you rifus? And to rifus to give even a small small kiss for to make me happy in my jenny. Please Shami dont you love me eny more? And please Shami I need to see your figger very soon otherways I would die of dizaya and if you have a fotopicture of yourself send it so that I can satisfy the hunger of my eyes with your pritty legs. I hope that you will be eble to visit me this weekend and you can telling me the time of your bus so that I ricive you at the stetion. Sorry about such complains my Shami and I hop you dont think I am complain-complain all the time. Greetings to Maiguru and Babamkuru and the children not forgetting you my darling and tell them job is fine lonelines only. Write to me as soon as you finish reading this and kiss your letter twenty times before you post it, Yours forever Clopas Wandai J. Tichafa.

"What do the words 'figger' and 'dizaya' mean?" Shamiso asked.

Her sister gave the letter a good shaking, flung it in the air and erupted, "Those are words a man uses to court a prostitute in a beerhall, not a decently raised girl like you. I told you he was trying to be smart!"

Dear Mr Clopas Wandai J. Tichafa, Shamiso wrote in her laconic Shona, *I was not happy about your last letter. All along I thought you were a decent man and I did not think you could even think of things like that. Please don't waste my time if you are not serious about me. I am prepared to end this relationship if that is the kind of person you are. Shamiso Mhaka.*

There followed a string of protests, profuse apologies and promises. He would never make another such request until the right time came, he swore. He did not know how these thoughts had come to him; the devil must have injected them into his mind while he slept or it must have been because he missed her so much, and he hoped please she didn't think he was a vulgar man to talk about her figure and her legs because he really thought she was very very pretty and was it wrong for a man to admire the beauty God had given to his beloved? To prove that he meant what he said he would not ask her to visit him until after he married her.

Forgiven, he came at the end of the month to arrange for the marriage.

After that, things moved with an incredible swiftness. With his friend

Joshua as his *munyai* he visited Shamiso's parents at their rural home to start the proceedings. Every person who was there – Shamiso's slender, well-preserved mother and her wizened, asthmatic father, their hefty, overalled, eldest son on a weekend off from the mine, the large-boned, stern-faced aunt from the hill across the river, the father's jovial, sun-grilled younger brother summoned from a hundred miles away in the middle of manuring his fields to preside over the negotiations, the usual handful of neighbourhood elders turned out as unofficial advisers or observers to swell this formidable ensemble – everybody – was impressed by the prospective *mkwasha* and his *munyai* right from the start.

First, the *mkwasha* and his *munyai* were both impeccably dressed in black suits which made them look like twins. Second, they bought drinks for everyone – crates of cool drinks for the women, Castle Lager for the men (sold by a sympathetic liquor outlet through the back door: blacks were only allowed to drink opaque beer at that time), brandy (obtained the same way) for the master of ceremonies, cigarettes and snuff for those who required them and sweets and biscuits for the children. Third, they did not take part in the drinking of the alcohol they had brought.

By the time the actual proceedings began every belly was blissfully full of rice and chicken; the tongues of the in-laws were loosened and their minds expansive from the drinks, the atmosphere in the hut auspicious with the smoke of a dozen cigarettes. Leaning his adze on the wall next to him, with nothing but a twinkle in his eye to bear witness to the spirits inside him, the father's brother ground his molars and opened the negotiations.

The *mkwasha* and his *munyai* were brought in and after a round of hand-clapping and inquiry into the well-being of each of their hosts, Joshua launched into their quest, accentuating his richly symbolic litany with a frequent clapping of hands. The in-laws listened in silence, nodding their heads with the slow manner and restrained enthusiasm of those called in to glimpse a massive, freshly slain beast about to be carved.

After a round of whispered consultations the in-laws asked for the *vhuramuromo* so that they could hear the visitors' mission. This was paid, and they asked for the *makandinzwa nani*. This paid, they then inquired if "our daughter is still herself or has been wounded and is limping on one leg." The *munyai* swore she was all right and the aunt was called upon to testify and she too agreed the daughter was all right. The question of pregnancy and, consequently, the claim of damages, thus removed and the marriage firmly established as the objective, they moved on to *zvibinge*. The father demanded a goat because, he said, the *mkwasha* had "climbed the mountain without first scaling the hills".

Conversely, the master of ceremonies demanded a goat too for having been skipped in the preliminary consultations, and the aunt from the hill across the river followed suit with demands for a cockerel for having been let in late on the arrangements. The beasts were promptly promised and they got on to the business of *kununga mari*. First the aunt picked a blue ten shilling note and a brand new two'n'six from the wooden plate; Shamiso picked seven and six and, because she didn't have a younger sister, her two cousins had to pick too. The elder cousin picked the remaining five shillings and the *munyai* had to put another four shillings and sixpence for the other cousin.

Satisfied by the prompt payment of these preliminary dues, the master of ceremonies went on to announce the *roora*. The *danga* was to be four head of cattle, at least one of which was to be a cow for the mother, and twenty-five pounds cash. Then there were the *nhumbi* for the parents; a black suit for the father, of a similar texture to what the *munyai* was wearing – the old man carefully explained – though the jacket didn't need to have as many pockets and the collar was to be small, preferably, and the shoes could be brown or black, size seven, with laces or without, and the hat had to be brown with the yellow feather of a bird stuck in the band and, yes, a walking stick with the face of a man carved on it, not like the walking stick of the *Mapostori*, but something more traditional so that (this last bit he mumbled righteously to himself) people would look at him and know he had raised and married off his second daughter too. For the mother they had to buy a dress made of cotton – nylon easily caught fire, she said – and she didn't really mind the colour as long as it wasn't red or yellow or blue or some other too bright colour that might attract lightning or cause her to be too conspicuous among her peers, so long as it wasn't that material with permanent folds in it girls wore to the township, *tererina*, yes, . . . so long as it wasn't *tererina* and it wasn't too bright and was a decent dress for a woman of her age, and she was to have a warm coat for the winters, and brown shoes and a black shawl for her shoulders.

The *munyai*, who was writing a list of the required items, looked up and asked if all the cattle, apart from the mother's cow, had to be live, or they could be substituted for with cash. The master of ceremonies consulted at length with the father and announced that two of the cattle had to be live, that is, the mother's cow and one other, and the other two could be substituted with a cash amount of fourteen pounds each. The father let it be known that once the in-laws bought the clothes they could take their bride with them and bring the rest of the things later, bit by bit. If later they decided they wanted a formal wedding, they would be free to discuss further arrangements.

This seemed like a fair arrangement to the *mkwasha* and his *munyai* who pledged to bring the clothes the very next weekend. Not having any further questions, they thanked the in-laws and retired to the hut to which they had been assigned to sleep, while the in-laws resumed, with great gusto, their drinking and talking.

Chapter 6

And so, five months after that trip to the District Office she became Mrs Clopas Wandai J. Tichafa, packed up her battered green suitcase, hugged her mother, buried her wet face in her sister's shoulders and went to live with him in the township.

The township consisted of rows of blocks separated by narrow, dusty roads and small gardens. Each block was long like a classroom block, divided into six compartments. Each compartment had a wide, half-walled in verandah and two green doors leading to separate rooms. Each compartment housed two people, one in either room, sharing the verandah. Ranged in front of the block were the toilets, one serving every two blocks, and great big washing sinks of concrete with overhanging water taps. Their room had a three-quarter bed with a padded white headboard, a wardrobe with a strip of mirror, a chair of heavy dark wood, a small transistor radio, a blue sofa with orange armrests, and, behind the door, a green cupboard with rickety legs where he kept the cooking utensils.

The first few days she swept the room, polished the concrete floor, cleaned out the cupboard, washed the cooking utensils and rearranged them, scrubbed the walls and the windows, scraped candle wax off the headboard and beat down the cobwebs in the corners and when all the wood surfaces were gleaming she laid out on either side of the headboard the doilies and flowers of dyed feathers she had brought. In the display cabinet she folded orange and green dishcloths into little pyramids among the plastic tumblers.

After this she moved out to the verandah. She cleared the old ash from the disused fireplace, swabbed the concrete floor with soap and water and polished it, beat out the door mats. She tried to wipe the soot off the charred, smoke-blackened walls but stopped when cakes of black paint peeled off and left brown scars on the walls. This completed, she cleared the weeds in front of the verandah and reinforced the ridges round the aloes growing against the front wall.

Then there were pillowcases and sheets and blankets and curtains to be washed in the great big sinks, loads of clothes that took hours to wring out and hang up on the wire fence to dry. She worked alongside other women who greeted her cheerily but could not, largely because of her reticence, involve her in their conversation beyond a few interested questions. Afterwards she would sit for whole afternoons pressing the washing with a metal iron full of hot coals.

The heavier tasks disappeared under the robust attack of her industriousness, and soon when she woke up in the mornings she began to think what there was to do and look around her for the less obvious things she had overlooked. There was always something to do – buttons to sew on and primus stove to wipe – some dusty little nook that had escaped her notice. But these became easier, more routine tasks and she found herself with more time to spare. She began to take siestas in the afternoon. She would sleep for an hour and then go to the toilet block to take a shower (if somebody was already there she waited). Refreshed, talcum-powdered and Ponds Vanishing-Creamed, she would breeze out in a billowing cotton dress and rubber slippers, wearing the necklace he had given her, to the nearby shopping centre, weaving her way through crowded vegetable stalls, truckloads of cabbages and mangoes and towering pyramids of purple sugar cane, pavements strewn with cobblers' shoes and weavers' baskets; dodging barbers' elbows, carpenters' planes and n'angas' leopard skin headpieces, idling curiously past photographers who waved her in from their stalls till she got to her favourite shop, where the light-skinned girl behind the counter already knew her and got her what she wanted – half a loaf of bread, a pint of milk, one shilling and six pence worth of meat, a bunch of choumoellier, and, if she had not already bought these from the trucks outside, two large mangoes or guavas.

Back home she would braid or comb out her hair before putting the meat on the primus stove. Sitting in the blue sofa with the orange armrests, installed regally in the centre of the room, watching in the mirror her hands meticulously working at the crown of her hair, she was filled with a joy that quickened deep inside her when the man on the radio said, "The time is four o'clock": and then she would go out to the verandah and see troops of school-children in khaki and garden green uniforms march down the road and spill into the hedged alleys, the melting sun hover yellow over the township, the roads thicken with cyclists and cars, the air cloud with smoke from a hundred little fires. If she was lucky she saw the cob-yellow bus stopping at the bend with the shed of brown brick before rushing off to the town, and then the town siren would go off at five o'clock.

He usually arrived at five minutes past five.

He would ring his bicycle bell three times as he wheeled up to the verandah and she came out to meet him. And he would hand her the package he carried, undo his trouser clips, chain the bicycle to the verandah and, whistling volubly, follow her into their room.

"Jeeeeesus!" he would say, swinging his head round the room, "you've been working yourself to death again, Shami!"

He would take off his shoes and put on his slippers and recline in the sofa to listen to the news, eating a mango she had washed for him. While she cooked he chatted to her, telling her what had happened at work during the day and some of the interesting people he had met – so that the world of his work pieced itself together vividly in her mind as if she spent the day with him, participating in his acts of kindness and helpfulness.

Then she lit the candle and served the food and they ate together from the same plate, with their hands, like man and wife and he would urge her to have bones that crushed easily when he found she liked them. Afterwards he made them tea, his excuse being that he made it a dozen times during the day and making one last pot for his wife would not hurt him, whatever the general opinion on such matters. This tea they would have with scones he bought at the bakery on his way back from work, with butter and marmalade.

After listening to the eight o'clock news they would go to bed. She remained so quiet, especially liking the tenderness of his hot face buried in her neck afterwards, the wonder of his ruptured breath steadying and stilling inside him, the smoothness of his moist back drying under her fingers. The stillness of him curled up over her made her burn to say something back, a kind word, to his ear. She liked, too, the conversation they had lying together in the darkness, while the streets outside chattered with bicycles and drunkards and the voices of passers-by; when, in the warm nest of his arms, the nestlings of his thoughts would crack out of their eggshells to peck delicately at the audience of her breast. It was then that he told her what they had to do and the things they had to buy, the people they had to meet and the places to visit, the wedding they would have. And slowly, the streets outside died, leaving her to the world of his embrace in which the only sound was the gentle stir of his snoring, the ripple of her own mind sliding with him into sleep.

Late one night she woke up to a loud noise of people fighting in the next room. She recognized the voice of the man who lived there, shouting and panting and, she imagined, throwing furniture at the woman who was screaming for mercy. Her mind racing, she sat up in bed. The noise shot to an unbearable pitch and she almost yelled to the man to stop the fighting. Suddenly, the shouting crashed to a halt, the noise shattering into moans and whispers. Incredulous, her heart thundering inside her, she dived back into bed and whipped the blankets over her head.

"Does the man who lives next door have a wife?" she asked Clopas the next morning.

"No," he said, jerking his tie into place, "why?"

"I just wanted to know," she said, and he went out, with a puzzled smile, to unchain his bicycle.

On some evenings she heard different voices in the room and when the noise started she lay still with a finger in one ear, hoping that Clopas would not be woken by the noise. When she was alone in the mornings she thought about it and then her heart would nibble at itself about the earring she had swept up from under the bed while cleaning up and the woman in a short dress with stretched hair and painted mouth who had come up to her when she was beating up the doormats and asked if a man called Kedmon was at home, though the woman could not confirm if the man's name was Clopas. She had insisted he was slim and light-skinned, but she wasn't sure where he worked. Was Shamiso living with him, she had asked. She must have come to the wrong place and maybe she would call again later.

Clopas had shaken his head in great wonder when Shamiso told him about the woman. The blocks in the township were so alike, he had said, that it was common for people to confuse one for another.

The first weekend she had there he bought her new dresses and took her to down to the country to introduce her to his mother. His mother, she found, had given Clopas his lean features and straight nose and smile. His smooth dark skin and straight forehead had come from his father whose picture he had shown her. Clopas's mother was an obliging, industrious old lady, neither given much to talking nor demanding like other mothers-in-law. She gave Shamiso a large tin of peanut butter she had made for her and insisted, contrary to the common practice of mothers-in-law of staying with their *mrooras* for some time after the marriage, that Shamiso return to town with her husband the very next day. Shamiso was very touched by this widow who was satisfied with three visits a year and incidental packages of groceries, who chose to live her own life and not look to her young son for sustenance as other mothers did. By the time they left her Shamiso had made a pact with herself to·be good to her, and visit her often with presents.

At weekends Clopas would have her sleep late into the mornings.

She would feel a pang of alarm at waking up at eleven and finding the sun ablaze outside. While he went out in a T-shirt and shorts to water their small vegetable garden with a can she would sweep the room and prepare a late breakfast of liver and eggs. Then in the afternoon Joshua and his wife Mukai, who lived in the other township across the main road, might visit them. Joshua worked as a hand at a milling company and his pregnant, straight-headed wife who already had one baby, immediately assumed the role of Shamiso's sister. Shamiso, who was already favourably predisposed to Joshua for making her marriage possible, quickly became friends with Mukai. Sometimes when the men went out to watch the soccer matches at the local stadium the two women would stay together crocheting, talking, or going to the market place, going to watch swarms of *Mapostori* baptizing their new converts in the local river while goods trains thundered past over the bridge, or traditional *ngquzu* or *shangara* dancers performing in swirls of dust and applause at the edge of the township.

She discovered Clopas did not really belong to any church, and, alarmed at the unaccustomed prospect of spending half her Sunday in bed, she would go with Mukai and her child to the local Catholic church. At first she found the Catholic rituals strangely different from those of the Dutch Reformed Church to which her sister and her husband went. The kneeling and the liturgy she slowly got used to, but she staunchly pursed her lips against the wafer. Later when Mukai gave birth to another baby boy the men had, decked out in celebrant suits, accompanied their wives for the baptism, and afterwards they had made two more appearances, before the soccer games claimed them once more.

Sometimes when there was a big match in another city Clopas and Joshua would catch a morning bus or train to see the match, returning in the evening. One evening they did not come back on time. After checking with Mukai, Shamiso sat alone waiting, terrified stiff, wondering what had kept them. Clopas had never been away so late. At three in the morning, she was considering going to the police station to ask if there had been any bus or train accidents when the two men came in, singing jovially as they always did when their team won. Joshua did not stay long, but when he went away she noticed it seemed difficult for Clopas to stay on his feet. Even more amazingly, Clopas, apart from trying to fondle her in his friend's presence and scarcely touching the food she had left him, stripped his clothes and flung them to the floor and rolled into bed. Then she noticed the strange smell about him, filling the room.

"Do our husbands drink beer?" she solemnly asked Mukai the following day.

"Didn't you know?" the other said, amazed. "Do you think there are any men who don't drink these days?"

One night they woke up to a loud rapping on the door. It was pitch dark outside, around four o'clock in the morning when the street lights went off. Clopas got out of bed first, tripping on his trousers, knocking his knee against the sofa as he stumbled towards the door.

"Who is it?" he gasped, his hands frozen on the latch.

"Spekshen!" a gruff voice barked.

His face shot back to Shamiso. She sat up in bed, in her petticoat, groping for matches on the headboard. She lit the candle. The faint yellow light flickered in the room. He opened the door and three black policeman in greenish khaki tunics trooped in, their blinding torches criss-crossing the room.

"Good morning, *Madzishe*," Clopas coolly greeted them.

"Spekshen!" the one with the gruff voice barked again, his shadowy face darting round the room. "Who lives here?"

"Me and my wife," Clopas told him.

"Do you live with anybody else, your relatives or friends or people like that?" He flashed his torch under the bed and on Shamiso's face.

"No."

"Is this woman your wife?"

"Yes."

"Where's your *chitupa*?"

Clopas fished for his registration certificate and held it up to the policeman's torch.

"Say your RC number off by heart!"

Clopas recited the number.

"So you come from Makondo Village," said the policeman.

"Are you from there too?" Clopas ventured.

"Yes, homeboy," said the policeman in the same professional gruff voice. "Do you have a marriage certificate?"

"I just got married."

"Do you have a marriage certificate or not, homeboy?"

"No, but I am married."

"That's no proof this woman is not a whore you picked up at the beerhall," said another policeman, flashing a beam at Shamiso's face.

"She's my wife, *Madzishe*," Clopas tried to keep his voice steady. "I have just married her. I paid *lobola* for her."

"We need to see your marriage certificate, homeboy."

"My *munyai* lives in this town."

"Listen, *munin'ina*. We too have our *munyais* but we had to get marriage certificates to live with our wives. You think the white man understands about *lobola* and *munyais*?"

"You know the rules, homeboy."

"I understand, *Madzishe*."

"We didn't make those rules, *munin'ina*. We're only doing our job."

"This woman's presence in this room is illegal, homeboy."

"Let me explain, *Madzishe*."

"*Aika*, homeboy, don't waste our time. You need to get a marriage certificate to live with her in this town and even if you do get that certificate you have to move out to the married section. You *know* this section is for bachelors only."

"I understand, *Madzishe*."

"Then do something soon if you want to stay out of trouble, homeboy. Get a marriage certificate and move out of here."

They marched out of the room. Their boots crunched on the verandah and down the steps to the next compartment. They rapped on other doors.

"*Mazibhurakuwacha!*" Clopas cursed. "You'd think they were white men themselves, marching into people's bedrooms like that."

He reached over to look at his watch. It was a quarter past four. He put the watch back on the headboard and stared into the candlelight, scratching his armpits. A bug fluttered off the candle stub and scorched its wings in the flame.

"Can we get a house in the married section?" Shamiso asked, sitting up still, against the pillows, with the blankets up to her chin.

"It should be possible to get one," he said, flicking the dead bug off the headboard with a finger, "but the rent is higher."

"Will they throw me out if they find me here again?"

"They shouldn't be back for another month, at least."

"Maybe I could go and stay with your mother while you find another house?"

"No," he said, blowing out what was left of the candle and climbing back into bed in his trousers. "We'll work out something."

That weekend he took a bus to the mine where Shamiso's brother worked to ask him to witness for them in his father-in-law's place. Fortunately, the brother happened to have the day off on Monday, and was able to accompany Clopas back to town. Joshua had got a workmate to report him sick at the mill – his foreman wouldn't give anyone the morning off on Mondays, he said – and the four of them, Clopas, Joshua, Shamiso and her brother, met at the district office mid-morning for the swearing.

The District Commissioner was out and Clopas's young white boss filled in the forms. Had Joshua been the ... the ... *munway* for the two, he asked, and Joshua said Yes Baas, had he met Shamiso's brother and father and all the family, Yes Baas, had Shamiso's father agreed to the marriage, Yes Baas, and what was the *lobel* charged, four cattle Baas, one live and one live other Baas, and what about the other cattle, were they to be butchered and delivered as meat, No, No Baas, or they had to be draped in black for some ceremony, No Baas, all right, all right, four cattle and what else, money Baas, cash eh, Yes Baas, how much, fifty pounds – eighty pounds, twenty-five pounds Baas, anything else, clothes Baas, what clothes, clothes for the father and mother Baas, a suit for the father Baas and – all right, all right, we can't go into those in detail, gosh you people are real merchants when it comes to marrying off your daughters, aren't you, anything else, Yes Baas, *zvibinge* Baas, what's that, *zvibinge* Baas, how on earth am I supposed to know what that is, just custom Baas, and how much were those, two goats and a cock Baas, Oh forget it, that's enough, and this man is the *mfazi's* brother, is he,

Yes Baas, show me your *situpa* first, Here Baas, so your name is Tar-r-irai
Ma-ha-ka, Yes Baas, say your RC number by heart, 1675346 Chi Baas, OK
let's get the spelling right, and you're standing in for your father, aren't you,
Yes Baas, did Clopas give you any cash for taking your sister, No Baas, it's
all for the old man, eh, Yes Baas, you're this *mfazi's* real brother, aren't you,
Yes Baas, not her cousin or uncle or nephew or brother-in-law but *real*
brother, eh, Yes Baas, and you allow Clopas to take your sister, Yes Baas, you
trust him, eh, Yes Baas, you don't think he just wants to uhm uhm with her,
do you, No Baas, and if there's any trouble later you or your father won't
come buggering the DC will you, No Baas, all right, sign your name here, if
you can't write just put a big X, Yes Baas, where did you learn to write, at
school Baas, all right, now the *munway* must sign here, me Baas, yes you Cob-
head, you're the *munway* aren't you, Yes Baas, can you write, Yes Baas, then
sign your name here, Yes Baas, got yourself a pretty *mfazi* eh, Clopas, Thank
you Baas, didn't tell her you were a clerk here, did you, No Baas, can I sign
now Baas, No Clopas, *you* don't have to sign this, Clopas, this is not a marriage certificate, Clopas, it's just *permission* from the DC for you to get married, Clopas, you understand, Clopas, Yes Baas, to get a marriage certificate
you need to go to a church, Clopas, and get a minister to marry you, Clopas,
not to marry you *himself*, Clopas, but to marry you to this *mfazi*, Clopas, Yes
Baas, OK Clopas, Yes Baas, you won't say "Mistake Baas" later, will you,
Clopas, No Baas, and if you don't have a church you better get one, Clopas,
Yes Baas, I'll give this to you once the DC signs it, Clopas, Yes Baas, look
after your *mfazi*, eh, Yes Baas, that's all and you can all go now, Thank you
Baas, Thank you very much, Baas.

"I hope I made the point clear to you, my children," Father Utsvene said,
straightening the papers and shifting the bottle of ink to a safer distance in
front of him, "I must emphasize that God will not take it lightly if you come
to his holy house just for the convenience of this certificate. I realize you
need this certificate to get a house, but I hope you won't turn your backs on
God once you get it. This certificate is just a piece of paper which, without
your honest dedication to God, cannot bind you truly to each other nor to
God Himself. I therefore urge you to remember this house in which God is
going to unite you as man and wife, to remember this house and to respect
it. God does not ask much from you, just this respect. Of the one hundred
and sixty-eight hours in the week he asks for only two hours of your time.

You are a young couple away from your parents, away from your people, cast in this city of snares, and I advise you to make this church your home, to make its inhabitants your people, with whom you will share your problems and your joys alike. Make this house the well from which you will draw the drink of wisdom that will quench your thirst. Do you have any questions before we begin?"

The four looked at each other and shook their heads.

"All right. Come out, all of you, and stand here."

Clopas and Shamiso stood in front of the table, flanked by Joshua and Mukai, their witnesses. Father Utsvene read from his book for a while, and then asked them the questions, *Do you, Clopas Tichafa, take this woman as your wife, etc., etc. Do You, Shamiso Mhaka take this man as your husband, etc., etc.*

Afterwards the priest made them hold hands and asked for the rings, and it was discovered then that the young couple had overlooked that aspect. This caused momentary panic but the priest said it didn't matter, the rings could come later, and proceeded with the signing ceremony. First Clopas signed, and then Shamiso, followed by Joshua, and when Mukai took the big nib to sign a drop of ink splashed into a radiating blue sun at the centre of the certificate. The priest merely smiled reassuringly, put the spoilt certificate aside and plucked a clean one from his sheaf. He cleaned his nib with a handkerchief and began the signing afresh. The couple turned this little mishap to advantage: Clopas was able to write his name with a better flourish on the "s" than he had been able to the first time round, and Shamiso brought her letters firmly on the line. The witnesses performed without further accidents and then the priest shook their hands and smiled and made them embrace in front of him in that empty church, and suddenly it was over and they were going out into the bustling Saturday streets, laughing in a bunch, going to eat the rice and chicken Shamiso had prepared that morning, and to drink minerals and listen to records on the gramophone Joshua had brought.

Chapter 7

Two months later when the same three policemen made another routine early morning check, it was another couple they found in room 8, of Block B, Section 3, and not Mr Clopas Wandai J. Tichafa of Makondo Village and his supposed spouse. From the nervous couple – the man's eyes trembled and the woman's hands shook in the torchlight – they learned that Mr Clopas Wandai J. Tichafa and his wife had left that Monday for the married section.

Later that morning the women in Section 3 gathered to protest, with the furious clamour of hens after an eagle's swoop, the humiliation of being invaded in that naked, marital hour and vented their wrath on the prostitutes who tarnished their cause, while the men among them mumbled curses against the tyranny of unpainted walls, high rents, crowded toilets, supervised relationships and the problems of acquiring marriage certificates. Across the road in the married section Clopas was pruning the guava and banana trees in the yard of, and Shamiso sweeping inside, their new house.

And later when the policemen were docketing the evictions, and while the women in Section 3 were tying up bundles of their possessions and enquiring about the schedules of rural buses, Clopas and Shamiso were contemplating when and how they would furnish their empty house.

It was like any other house in the married section, semi-detached, with a kitchen the width of a corridor, a small sitting-room, a bedroom large enough to contain a three-quarter bed and wriggling space and a slightly smaller second bedroom referred to by the municipality, which rented the houses, as the "spare" room. An extension jutting out from the middle of the block contained a separate toilet and a shower room shared with the neighbours. He liked the banana and guava trees and the garden patch: she liked the separate toilet, the whitewashed walls, the shower room and tap they had to share with only one other neighbour. Together they liked the tarred roads and the combined space of three rooms. But the echoes in the empty, unfurnished rooms that smelt of cement and the rainwater which collected into a seasonal puddle round the house depressed them. It was to this house that their visitors came, relatives from both sides who stayed nights, days and sometimes weeks while they sought work in the town or treatment at the general hospital, families in transit whose children temporarily livened the childless house with their voices.

Eighteen months after the marriage Shamiso was still not pregnant and the relatives began to talk.

Sometimes when she dozed in the afternoon between chores she would wake up with a dull throb in her head and a faint languor in her limbs. In the shower she would carefully examine the texture of her skin. On some mornings she woke up with a stale taste in her mouth and lay still, listening to her womb. In the evenings she would watch the slice of the moon grow in the sky, and her heart waited with a flicker. But always, with amazing timeliness, the washing out came.

"You shouldn't give him hot water to bathe in," Mukai said, needlessly, because Shamiso knew Clopas always took a cold shower in the morning even in winter.

When they visited her family at Easter her mother gave her a yellowish powder that looked like crushed grass, to be taken with a bowl of porridge every morning. For a month she chomped secretly through the bitter bowl. Still, her womb gave.

Then Mukai brought her a similar looking powder from a woman she knew. This one she only had to take for a week, once a night, stirred in a cup of warm water, before she went to bed. It didn't taste offensive but left a clinging feel to her tongue which toothpaste could not remove. She worried that he would taste it on her, or one day stumble upon the twisted concoctions slipped away in the corners of the cupboards. But he never rummaged in the cupboards unless he had to. That was her territory.

He didn't speak about it but she could feel his worry. Sometimes when they lay in bed, awake, on the days her womb gave, she could almost feel something like a cold, spiky fish lying between them. Her period became the slow drip of mourning. He was still very nice to her. It was the unspoken fault inside her, inside *him* perhaps, that made him sullen. The prospect that he might be the problem rarely struck him, and when it did, he nervously routed it from his thoughts.

Sometimes at night he would lie very still, his eyes smouldering with a glow that made her panic. She imagined the powders accumulating in a sticky lump inside her, clogging her tubes. She began to have odd dreams which she could not remember in the mornings.

The morning she dreamt about the house full of broken dolls with missing limbs, she plucked the courage to see the nursing sister at the local clinic.

The black nursing sister welcomed her into her office with a matronly smile and asked her a number of questions – how often they had sex, what positions they took, how soon she or he got up to walk afterwards, if he bathed before going to bed and with cold or hot water, what kind of work he did and what he did at home, if she had problems with her cycle or had had an abortion. Shamiso thought most of the questions unaskable, and had even imagined that the older woman was making fun of her for being so young. But the sister assured her that these were routine questions and she need not feel embarrassed about answering them.

"I wouldn't worry too much about it at the moment," the sister said. "I don't see anything abnormal about you or what you and your husband do. I think you should just give it more time."

She had meant to tell him about the visit but did not do so just to avoid having to say the things the nursing sister had said.

Several days later he surprised her when he said, with an abrupt laugh, "Are we ever going to have any children in this house?"

Then he told her there was a man who could help them, a doctor who lived at the edge of the township. She thought he was taking her to some kind of clinic, but when they turned on to a house with a pair of buffalo horns propped over the threshold, her suspicions were immediately roused. There was no time for questions; the door opened and a plump, middle-aged man with a shaved head welcomed them in. The man wore a black vest and green trousers with yellow lines on each flank, similar to those worn by ice-cream men or bus drivers. He chatted casually to them when they sat down in the sofas, as if he had known them for some time. The room was surprisingly well furnished, with a large gleaming display cabinet and a table size stereo. The only unusual thing was an oxtail stuck on the wall above the stereo.

After some minutes the man disappeared through a green door into the "spare" room. He was in there a good fifteen minutes, during which they heard him sneezing, belching and mumbling behind the door. He came out of the room clutching a worn leather bag, his shoes removed and his thick neck heavily draped with black, white and red beads.

"It's not going to be easy," he said, sucking phlegm down his throat with a load rasp. He scratched the shiny dome of his head. "The problem seems to be bigger than I thought, but it's something that can be contained. It's not easy to explain and it's something from both sides – you understand me..."

Clopas looked at Shamiso, whose face was blank, and nodded vaguely at the man.

"It's not easy to explain, but this – thing – is not a spirit or a person or a spell but just a wandering thing, an obstacle that found a weak spot in your path and lodged itself there. Now this thing is nothing terribly serious, but it is very very elusive and given the chance it could complicate things and cause more problems, but as I said it is a thing that can be removed. There is a chance I can remove it and enable you to get what you seek. I know you have been seeking what you are seeking for over a year and a half, now, but you have worked in vain. The problem is not with either of you, but just this thing; in fact I don't see anything lacking in your bodies. Many times you have got close to what you seek. You have seen the signs and the symptoms that made you think you have it in your grasp and then..." he swung a curled finger across the air between them and clicked his tongue, "it's snatched away. Three months after you lived together you came so close to it that for three weeks you thought you had it, but this thing snatched it."

He paused briefly, not to search their faces for acknowledgement, but merely to let his words sink through to their minds, before continuing. "It's a small but tricky problem. There are other things I see about both of you, but I won't worry you with those. Your father died a few years ago of stomach pains," this he said to Clopas, "and your legs once swelled up inexplicably when you were a young girl," this to Shamiso. "But I am not the kind that reaps profit out of the terror of his patients. This problem is a problem of its own, unrelated to the things I mentioned and as I said we may be capable of dealing with it. I am not saying yes, you will definitely get what you seek, but I have been able to help most of those who came to me with similar problems. And I'm not saying once you get what you want now this bad thing will be removed forever. This thing could work with the forces of darkness to bring harm to you and your offspring but life wouldn't be life without obstacles, would it? As I said I don't believe in stirring terror into my patients and I never cure the unseen. My task now is to get you what you want now and whether or not to return to me later for further help remains your choice."

He dug into his old bag and brought out medicines. The powder he poured and twisted in a strip of khaki paper was to be sprinkled over hot coals and the smoke carried into every room to cleanse the air. The greenish leaves he wrapped up in a newspaper were for her bath water and the thick yellow oil in the vaseline bottle was to be rubbed over her whole body and especially her belly after the bath. The greyish water with a floating layer of black leaves she would have to sip twice a day. She was not to travel outside the town for as long as possible, at least not until she got what she sought.

"You don't have to pay me now," he said after administering the potion. He closed his bag and dug into his nape with a finger. "I only take payment after my patient is satisfied that he or she has been cured and my patients decide how much they want to pay me."

With that he dismissed them, cutting off Clopas's effusive attempts at thanking him. He stood up to open the door for them, and saw them to the road.

On the way back home, Shamiso did not say a word. She cooked in silence but did not herself eat. After washing up she went straight to bed.

"Why didn't you just tell me you were taking me to a *n'anga*?" she demanded bitterly. "I've never ever visited *n'angas* in my life."

He's worth a try, Shami. Several people spoke highly of him."

"If this is the only way to get a child then I'd rather die childless."

She jerked round and lay on top of the blankets, covering her face with her hands and facing the wall. She heard him go out to the garden, and half an hour later he came into the bedroom with a dustpan full of burning twigs. A pungent smell stirred in the room, the air thickening quickly with white smoke. He coughed madly at the centre of the room, holding up the sputtering pan, but she lay still, without making a sound, on the bed. After a while he went out through the sitting-room to the spare room. "You ought to try the medicines, Shami," he began again, sitting on the bed when the smoke cleared.

"You try them!" she panted fiercely. "You know him! He's your doctor, not mine!"

"But don't you want a baby?" he yelled, his composure snapping suddenly. "Don't you even want to give this a try?"

Through her fingers she saw the shadow of his face flutter angrily on the candle lit wall.

"He's your doctor," she shrilled.

"I only took you there because I heard he could help," he trembled with rage.

"I never thought you could waste money on people like him."

"It's my money!"

"You can kill me if you want but that won't make me drink a *n'anga's* medicines."

He stomped into the sitting-room, banging the door behind him. She heard him slump into the sofa, in the dark. She lay on the bed for a long time, staring at the walls. The darkness caved in on the room as the candle slowly flickered out. She lay in the dark, listening for his movements, but the sofa only squeaked once or twice and he was still. Then her eyelids dropped and she fell asleep there, on top of the bed.

When she woke up the bed was unpressed beside her and the curtain was flushed red with sunlight. The reek of smoke still lingered in the air. She got up and walked out to the kitchen. His bicycle was not in the sitting-room where he parked it. The toilet door was ajar. She checked the bathroom; that was empty too and the voice on the neighbour's radio said, "The time is ten minutes to ten."

His eyes were dull and his *shed* displaced when he came back in the evening. She greeted him curtly and pumped up the primus stove to make him tea. Smiling briefly at her, he wheeled his bicycle into the spare room and went into the bedroom to remove his tie and shoes. The medicines were still on the headboard where he had left them.

"At least he knew what your problem was without your telling him," he began again.

"How did he know about my legs?"

"So he was right then. You never told me about it."

"Didn't I?"

"And he knew about that time you thought you were pregnant too."

"You told him that."

"The only time I ever talked to him was yesterday, and I was with you!"

"How did you know where he lived?"

"I told you the office-cleaner told me about him and gave me the number of his house. Honest, Shami, I only met that man yesterday."

"Did your father have stomach pains when he died?"

"Yes."

"Did you tell the man that?"

"You were in the room with me," he retorted.

She washed the cups and put a pot of water on the primus stove, for the *sadza*. He went out into the sitting-room to get the radio, switched it on and sat on a chair in the kitchen while she cooked.

"Are you going to try the medicines now?"

She continued pensively with the cooking.

It was only after they had eaten that she said "What if they harm me?"

When he came home the next evening, the level of the greyish water had dropped by an inch and he detected an odd oily musk about her when he climbed into bed next to her.

"You should know what to say to my parents if I die," she said.

Chapter 8

There were two of them, a man and a woman, and when they came upon her from behind, while she was beating doormats that Saturday morning, they were like shadows from the sky. The man wore an olive-green suit with a yellow shirt frayed on the collar and a bottle green tie. The woman wore an ankle-length cotton dress and a *doek* of matching material. At first she thought they were relatives she had not been told about, or travellers strayed to the wrong door, but they stood firmly on either side of the doorway, smiling, and she saw the books in their armpits.

Clopas came out in his Saturday T-shirt and shorts to see who they were and she stepped over for him to shake hands with them.

"We have been sent by God to your house," the woman said. "May we come in?"

They sat on the chairs in the kitchen.

"God has sent us to your house to help you find him," the woman said.

"What church are you from?" Clopas asked.

"Our church has no label," the man said with a flourish. "We are not the Roman Catholic Church or the Anglican Church or the Assemblies of God or the Lutheran Church or the Methodist Church or the Dutch Reformed Church or the Church of Sweden or the Presbyterian Church or the Church of Christ or the Apostolic Faith Mission but just God's Church. We are the Church of the Holy Spirit and we worship God directly."

"God has revealed to us your problems," the woman said. "He has revealed to us that there is a young couple in this township who have had a problem for a very long time, a problem that has baffled them and led them into all sorts of evil paths. He has guided us here this morning, leading our steps to your door. He has revealed that couple to be you."

"He has revealed to us that this problem is threatening to destroy your happiness and now He would like to give you that one thing only He, and not any man of flesh, can give. He says come now, and He will give you the thing you so desire and happiness and rest."

"May we pray for you?" the woman asked.

Shamiso and Clopas glanced at each other and nodded.

"Lord Jesus," the woman prayed. "Thank You for leading us to this House and for bringing us face to face with Your children. Thank You for driving the devil from their door and giving them the strength and courage to let us in. Thank You for giving them the wisdom to listen to Your revelation. Lord Jesus we pray You now to help our brother and sister to stand in front of You now so that You can enter their hearts . . ."

"Amen," the man cut in.

"Enter their hearts, Lord Jesus, and we ask You now to give them rest. We urge You now to turn them away from this danger in front of them, and Lord Jesus I beg You, I *challenge* You Lord Jesus."

"Amen."

"I challenge You to show Your power, Lord Jesus."

"Amen!"

"I dare You to show Your power and give this couple here, today, *now*, what they want, Lord Jesus."

"To make them see Your great mercy and kindness, Lord Jesus. And Lord Jesus we ask You now to make them consider Your church, Lord Jesus, to give them the courage to give their hearts *totally* to you Lord Jesus."

"Amen."

"Thank you Lord Jesus. Amen."

"Our Sunday service starts at eight in the morning," the man said. "We would be interested if you could come to pray with us."

"Of course we know you might be going somewhere else . . ."

"We sometimes go to the Catholic Church," Shamiso told her.

"It really doesn't matter what church you go or belong to," the woman smiled. "All we're asking is to invite you to pray with us this Sunday."

"Our church is near the cattle market stall."

"We'll come," Clopas said emphatically. "We'll be there."

"Praise the Lord," the man and the woman said when they left.

At the end of the sermon, when the Overseer called for those to whose hearts God had spoken and on whose rib-cages He was knocking with His key of Life, Clopas Tichafa felt a tightness seize his body. His right hand unfurled from his side, as if possessed by a power of its own, trembling, and slowly climbed up to his head. He barely heard the Overseer's voice: "Yes, I see that." His eyes were squeezed shut but not completely. Through his blurred vision he saw another hand sticking up straight over the forest of heads in front of him. The Overseer's voice spoke again, an urgent reverberation, and his hand inched up boldly over his head. With his other hand he clasped the bench in front of him for balance, his body was swaying. His toes gripped through the soles of his shoes for the floor. The tendons behind his knees grew taut. There was a shuffle in the aisle ahead, the flash of a dress from the women's side. He opened his eyes. The Overseer's face bathed in a bright beam of sunlight. He turned his head round and through his floating vision he saw the men on his right leaning back for him to pass through. The voice of the Overseer drowned in the roar in his ears. He stumbled out of the pew, brushing past the leaning-back bodies, into the aisle, through the dusky corridor of men and women to the sunlit front where figures knelt around the Overseer. His knees sagged to the floor. A hand touched his head. He shut his eyes fully to stall the gallop of his heart, to slow the rush of his breath. The voice of the Overseer spoke above him. A hand touched his head again. And then the voices of the men and women behind him swept into song; his mouth opened. The words of the song trickled like half-remembered litanies from his lips.

A hand helped him to his feet, alongside the two men on his right. He saw the profile of the woman beside whom he had been kneeling, next to whom he now stood, the strange familiarity of her dress. He was stunned to recognize his wife, right there next to him, beside him. As the singing surged on, the whole congregation thronged up from behind them, among a flourish of "Amens!" and "Alleluyas!" to shake their hands.

The second Sunday they returned home after the evening prayers, a stormy night when thunder cut off the street lights and the Overseer gave them a ride up to the corner of their street, she rushed off from the table, cupping her hands to her mouth, and retched for ten minutes in the toilet.

Chapter 9

A Malawian tailor with a stall at the shopping centre sewed the ankle-length dresses for her, out of the material she chose from among the rolls lined up against the walls.

The maternity dress (ankle-length too) he bought for her at an Indian shop they had to walk down into from the pavement; it was like a warm cave reeking of new cloth. The bearded Indian trader (he was so dark she almost mistook him for black) accepted a small deposit and took down his RC number and the name of the place where he worked and then laughed and poked at her belly with a finger and asked if she had eaten "too many beans".

He said they could have the dresses in two weeks.

At the clinic the nurses wound a sticky strap of black plastic round her arm above her elbow and pumped a black tube (shaped like a tiny pumpkin) that made the strap tighter but didn't hurt. They gave her two plastic cups for her urine and stool – the young nurse stuck the name tags on them without wrinkling her nose. Then they weighed her, wrote in the answers to the questions they asked her on a khaki card and told her to eat plenty of fish and cabbage and oranges, and to come again in a month's time.

He brought sacks of oranges for her and frozen bream the size of her arm, and he peeled and cut the oranges for her. He read everything the nurses wrote on the khaki card, pondering aloud the nursing sister's scrawl, and when he came back and found her watering the garden or washing the blankets he said, with anguish, "Oh Shami! You don't have to do it!"

But it was nothing, really. She did not feel any different, at first, not until the weight shifted decisively to her belly: just a sourness in the mouth some mornings, and a sudden craving for *matemba*. There was the craving for him too, as if (this she never told him) the tickling thing inside her needed to be constantly pushed back firmly into place. It was nothing, just a feeling that made her confuse eating and love-making, and sometimes brought the words *matemba* and *Clopas* in one breath.

If there were no *matemba* at the township shops he would take a bus to the hillside township after work (if it wasn't a Wednesday or a Friday, the days they had evening prayers at the church) and if there were none available there either he would send for a hefty packet from the neighbouring reserve. He knew a bus conductor who fetched and delivered for a small commission.

At the church he joined the church choir, as one of the tenors. Everybody complimented his voice. As a boy, he had sung at school and in the village choirs at harvest contests. She sang alto in the women's fellowship group which met on Thursday afternoons. In the evenings the two of them sang and prayed together before going to bed. It was this spiritualism that saw them through the sexless tension of the last weeks of her pregnancy when she changed into this ballooned-out creature with a faceful of pimples and a sad elephantine gait; enabling him to endure the brooding moods of this self-absorbed new being he now loved, pitied, feared and waited for to become the Shamiso he had known.

"I was a man caught in the jaws of the devil," he was to testify many times later, in front of the congregation, "a prisoner bound with the chains of sin and cast in the deep dungeons of darkness. I was a Jonah whom the shark swallowed and almost never spat, a Saul on the road to Damascus whom the lightning struck at the very last minute, a Legion possessed by a thousand demons. I was born in sin of parents who trusted the practices of darkness and did not know His Light. I was a child in sin and young man in sin. My stomach was the devil's gourd and my lips were the devil's pipe. I squandered my weekends in revelry, soaking my soul in the scented sweat of cunning creatures of the night. Yes, I looked healthy and felt healthy but my lungs were chimneys. My liver was a floor mop. I was a rotting man. Yes, I knew there was God and I knew there were His churches but the God I knew was the God of Christmas and Good Friday Holidays and even then I did not know Him at all. I went to church to please those who knew me, to satisfy my lust by gazing at the bodies of women. Yes, I was a young man in sin. I made friends in sin. I courted in sin. Then I decided to change, to mend my ways. But it was not God speaking to me yet. I was still a man in sin. I met, in sin, the woman who was to be my wife, and though He gave me a good woman, I married her in sin. We were married in a church that condones drinking and smoking and the playing of drums; by a priest who did not

71

search our souls first to save us from peril. A collared priest who rushed us through the banns and tried to blackmail our souls over to God by signing that piece of paper for us. And when God saw this he decided to punish us. Yes, he decided to punish us to make us turn back to him. He punished us with childlessness. We tried everything. We visited the houses of men who dabble in magic, where the horns of warthogs and the skulls of hyenas meet you at the door and serpents hiss in your ears. Men who wear the skins of leopards and civet cats to consort with the devil in strange languages, behind closed doors, and then, inspired by the devil with a few bits of information about our lives, tricked us out of a fortune with subtle threats and smiles. We were given herbs and oils and potions whose smell alone would overwhelm even the most accustomed user but in our blind determination we used them. Yes, we went through all that, but God saved our lungs and our skins and our stomachs from harm, because he had a purpose for us. When he saw that we were on the verge of destruction he sent us two messengers from this congregation, two good people to whom he revealed our fate. Two blessed people who brought us here, to His House, where he knocked on our hearts and we heard Him, and opened to let Him in. And to show us his strength he gave us what we wanted. Immediately. Yes, he gave us fertility."

Having begun with a rich punctuation of "Amens!", "Alleluyas!" and "Praise the Lords!" the congregation were gripped by silence as the testimony progressed. Women clicked their tongues and some wept; men shook their heads. Even the Overseer stared in awed absorption from the pulpit. And if somebody else stood up to testify after that, there was a pause, an anti-climax. Lacking the vigour of Clopas's testimony, the new voice was invariably a let-down.

His wife listened in her pew, among the other women, her head held low, her heart thumping with the terror of recognition, trembling at the things he revealed fully now in the tent in front of the congregation. Things that had been kept from her. Things that had, at best, only *hinted* themselves to her. But then she was emboldened by the courage of his confession, dared by his passion to crush her bitterness and delve into her own soul, to testify.

She did not testify half as often as he did, and to cut down on dramatics when she did, she made it a point not to come directly after him. Her confession was, typically, concise. She was brought up in a church-going family, she said (discreetly leaving specific church names out of it), but she had not really known God in the spiritual sense until two members of the church

72

came to her house to tell them God wanted their souls, Praise the Lord. Yes, she had used medicines given by a *n'anga* (she referred to him specifically as that) and before that had even used herbs given to her by people she knew (no names), herbs which she hid from the sight of her husband, a secret which had tormented her conscience. She had now turned her back totally on such people and was glad God had answered her prayers for a child and she would praise Him in this house for the rest of her life, and wanted the congregation to remember her in their prayers, Amen!

Chapter 10

She gave birth to a baby girl at the township clinic, half a mile from their house, after only two hours of labour. When Mukai came to tell him about it at work, Clopas gave a shout of joy, asked for the rest of the afternoon off and went by taxi to take her home. Holding the delicate white bundle in his arms, Clopas Tichafa led his family up the stone path, into the house. Mukai cooked and Joshua came later; Muchaneta, the young woman from next door whose soldier husband was away on patrol, sat with them in the bedroom.

In the evening the people from the church came and sat in the sitting-room. They sang a song and the Overseer prayed, standing at the centre of the room, in the halo of the candle-light. Then the women slipped into the bedroom, one after the other, with their gifts of nappies, woollen suits, bootees, shawls and they plunged to the side of the bed and flung their hands round her and shook her limp hand and peered over the cot, carefully poking at and babbling over the little face. She was a big baby, they all said, and she was going to be dark – don't let that pink flush fool you, not *dark* dark but smooth dark, Muchaneta pointed out, like his father, and the nose was her father's too, but the lips were *hers*, definitely, as for the eyes and forehead, well – you couldn't be too sure yet – the way babies' heads changed their shape those first few weeks you'd think they were made of plasticine, and she was going to gave a good head of hair, no, don't worry about the seeming baldness, that would fill out, and my, look at her fingers, how long and shape-ly they are, she was going to be a finely tall lady, *katepi chaiko*, and the way she held her hands together as if she was praying, the peaceful look on her face, she was going to be a great singer, like her father, and what was her name?

"Esther," Shamiso sighed blissfully, stretching back on the pillows against the headboard.

"Yes, she looks like her father," Mukai and Muchaneta agreed after the church people had left.

Her sister and her mother came to see the baby and one week later his mother made her pilgrimage. When the baby was old enough to travel they went to his mother's place to formally show her the baby. But because he felt guilty for not having made, after that dazzling first appearance at his in-laws', any further instalments towards his *roora*, she had to go alone to show the baby to her parents.

When she returned, after a week during which the house seemed so large and empty to him, they made love, sometimes even while Esther clawed about with her hands and the pink balls of her tiny feet, lying on the bed right beside them as if silently urging them (her mother mused) to make her a little brother or sister.

Six months after the birth of Esther she was again pregnant. This second pregnancy was difficult from the start. Pimples swarmed over her face. Her feet swelled. Her appetite revolted at foods she had previously liked. The nursing sister advised her to cut down on salts and to eat plenty of fruits.

"It's going to be a boy," Muchaneta assured her, hanging her husband's camouflage uniform on the line to dry. "Boys are always more difficult."

The baby was three weeks late. After a protracted five-hour labour she delivered – on a blazing October noon – a huge, hairy boy with alert brown eyes and a loud, listless cry. The nurses assured her he had hair on his back because he had stayed too long inside.

"This one is an exact cross between you," Muchaneta said, sitting again at the head of the cot as she had done fifteen months earlier, "What is his name going to be?"

"Benjamin."

"Is that a Shona name?"

"It's from the Bible."

"Just like Esther. Are you going to get pregnant again soon?"

"I can't stand the idea of going through all that pain again soon!"

"Then you had better get on the pill. I used it for some time after I had Kurai and if my husband wasn't away half the time I'd still be using it."

"Our church does not allow us to use the pill. Besides, the pill causes lots of problems. I wouldn't like to get pregnant for two years, at least."

"Then you'll have to apply sanctions in the bedroom," Muchaneta giggled.

Her third and last child, Peter, a frail-looking pink smudge in natal clothes, did not come until six years after Benjamin; a miraculous six years in which she used no contraceptives and many eventful things happened; after repeated appeals to his *mkwasha* to pay the *roora*, Shamiso's father died and two years later her mother followed him; her sister's husband began a long painful invalidity after paralysis struck his legs (a jealous junior did it to take his job, every person in the district maintained); Clopas's mother lived long enough to see Peter crawl and then bade them farewell after a brief illness. At the District Office Clopas's young white boss was promoted to District Commissioner following the retirement on pension to Great Britain of District Commissioner Richard Winston Carrington, Esquire (lance-corporal in the First World War) after twenty-five years of illustrious service in the Department of Native Affairs of both The Federation of Rhodesia and Nyasaland and Southern Rhodesia; Clopas was promoted from tea-boy to the chief messenger and allocated a bicycle with a silver 'On Her Majesty's Service' badge on the carrier for use on government business. The Tichafas' friendship with Joshua and Mukai slowly died after the latter declined repeated offers of conversion to The Church of the Holy Spirit; Clopas Wandai J. Tichafa and Shamiso (Mhaka) Tichafa had a big church wedding with bridal robes, suits, flowers, and a three-storey cake (the bridal troupe was chosen from the congregation and daughter Esther held up the bridal dress – a pity their parents had not lived to see this magnificent wedding and the bride's sister got tied up with her invalid husband, everyone said); Muchaneta's husband was killed two months after the wedding when the military truck in which his unit was travelling hit a tree: the Federation of Rhodesia and Nyasaland broke up; Ian Smith signed the Unilateral Declaration of Independence and Mr Clopas Wandai J. Tichafa was appointed the new deacon at The Church of the Holy Spirit.

Chapter 11

For those of us who saw the traumas of our country from the doors of township houses, peeking through the restraining skirts of our mothers like young Benjamin, the 'sixties are a special period. Every generation has its sentimentalities, its nostalgias; for us the 'sixties were both an end and a beginning.

Those were the days when – to keep pools of rainwater from washing away our houses – we went with our mothers in the dark to steal whitewash from the hills municipal trucks dumped at the road sites. We beat down the whitewash into hard pavements to keep the water away. We never thought that was stealing; everybody was doing it. We waded in the flooded roads, pushing ships of khaki paper, or if it was dry, we chased passing trucks in clouds of dust. The houses had no electricity, or if they had, the municipal lights went out at eleven, plunging the township into a mass of black. In the thorn bush we trapped birds with *urimbo* or shot them down viciously with catapults, churning palmfuls of *mpafa* in our mouths. We yelled obscenities at couples we caught in a delirious tangle among the thorn bushes and when our voices cracked or we were hissed away or threatened we went to sit at the edge of the road counting and claiming for ourselves the Zephyr Zodiacs, Morris Oxfords and Fords from the traffic that streamed past.

To Sub A we took chattering bundles of counting sticks, oversized uniforms and mucous-smeared, curious, large-eyed faces; for the teachers we brought mealie-cobs, melons, avid folk-stories and burning summaries of what we learnt at Sunday school. We rattled through our times' tables, quacked at genders and plurals and pluperfects, writhed over adverbial phrases, puffed at mental arithmetic, recited the Student's Companion from cover to cover and hummed poems about Bongwi The Baboon, fumbled through dictations and for Christopher Columbus and David Livingstone we sang songs after break. We staged plays of Noah and Shem and Ham, fought in the corridors when our teams lost; played *pada* and *butterscotch* and munched shallots at the garden, squabbled to carry books to the teacher's house, and in winter picked pennies from the ground in the cracks on our feet.

Then December came and flew home with our report cards and flocked out to catch the *ishwa* and *madumbudya* and *tsambarafuta* swarming out of the anthills and we dreamt of rice and sweets and balloons at Christmas. On New Year's Eve we smashed dustbins with rocks, shouting "Hep-hep- Hure! Hep-Nyu-yeee!"

Those were the days when there were loudspeakers at the centre of the township which were tuned to the radio station and you didn't have a radio in your house unless your father was a businessman or a fireman or, maybe, a teacher. During the day a voice would interrupt the music to call out the name of a lost child or a stranded visitor from the countryside for their people to come and collect them, or perhaps the voice might announce a special game or contest or tell people to stay indoors because a hailstorm was coming or certain prohibited meetings were being called. In the evenings men came out of their houses and stood between hedge fences or at the edge of the roads to listen to the eight o'clock news.

Yes, those were the days of the mobile bioscope, when the nights belonged to Mataka and Zuze and the Three Stooges and cinema was so alive you could smell cowboys' gunpowder off the big white screen.

Days of blind hope and resilience; households were run on a handful of change; you ate from the same plate with your brothers and sisters, wrestling with your hands for the meat – at night you wrestled for blankets with visitors from the country who came to look for work or school places while your father brooded over school fees' invoices in the candle-light.

As we grew up, things changed, slowly. We had scorned the poverty we did not see in our ignorance of it, wearing our clothes till our bodies showed through, but we began to notice clothes that stole our souls. We saw bell-bottom trousers, 'Satan' denim jeans, platform shoes, bold, bright shirts with large, raised collars, checked jackets, massive belts. Dresses crept up women's thighs and women were so much taller, suddenly; we heard of gogo shoes and hot pants. A strange disease afflicted the heads of the women. It made them rip off their hair and don wigs which, when oiled, looked like the fur of drowned cats. Dislodged from the heads, the disease crept over their faces. They scrubbed it out with sponges and fought it off with creams and

78

lotions. The creams wiped off the disease and the lotions left their faces with a bright, healthy shine. Dislodged from their faces, the indefatigable infection went down to their legs and settled there: they fought if off with pulling socks. Then, alas, the disease returned – in a vicious new form, a charry ashiness that settled permanently on their faces.

We were busy scavenging empty bottles and bones to get money for Chunky Charlie Comics or to pay for Teen Time at the township halls. The Beatles came to us too – everybody sang "Don't let me die . . ." Jim Reeves and Elvis Presley and Dolly Parton came too from across the bridge to contend with our Harare Mambos, our Safirio Madzikatires and Spokes Machianes. Later Hendrix and Otis came, with 'feeling', and many many more were to follow. With a swagger and a certain brashness of speech, young men took to rock and roll and refused to comb their hair. We heard of a new word, 'hippies'. Older men and women were seized by a passion for long coats, frilly swishing dresses and smooth, long strides. On the radios we heard a flood of new foreign songs. *S'manjemanje* from the south rushed in to the rescue, but *mbakumba, shangara, m'chongoyo, ngquzu, and jerusarema* were dead before we knew them.

Then we saw other things happen too, in the schools and in the churches and in the streets; in people's houses, in the shops and at the market place, on the buses and trains. Manners died with a hiccup. The young went wild. Hordes of youth left the country to seek out tricky fortunes in the towns. Men shunned the countryside. Against the onslaught of schools and churches the respect for *bira* and *kurova guva* faded, *midzimu* were demoted to the rank of ghosts and evil spirits; traditional healers were spat at. Churches preyed on the confusion and reaped massive harvests from the townships – every other family belonged to a church. Birth, registration, school, marriage, death, you went through the church at each stage of your life.

Religion cushioned poverty and radiated on the faces of the meek, but a mysterious tension creased the faces of teachers and priests and parents. A certain hardness seized their voices but their bitterness lashed at some malady beyond the decay of manners and the rebellion of the young. It showed in the football stadiums. Football was not just football any more. Teams were no longer just teams but armies of power and identity. People fought after a match. It showed on the streets. Men wore their beards long, put on loose fitting shirts of print cloth and leopard-skin hats and shook hands in a brusque way. People were stopped by voices in the dark. Questions were asked. Houses were stoned and men slept with knobkerries under their beds. Certain words took on fierce new meanings. Old songs shed their innocence and acquired a sarcastic edge. Even the innuendos of old stories changed. Hare was not hare any more and lion was no longer just lion. The arrogance was in the voices of some priests, too.

Men shunned the streets and in the darkness of their houses listened furtively to crackling voices on muted short-wave radio stations. The anger was there in the voices, in the air. We sensed it, we saw police reserve men patrolling the streets at night, but in our youth we did not know what it meant.

Cushioned from this danger and freed from the shackling connections of their past by their new faith, the Tichafas raised their children.

She had always wanted three babies, one of either sex at least; the sequence did not matter. When she found her womb answered her prayers and she did not have to worry about birth control, she rejoiced.

As soon as the babies' crowns were strong enough to withstand the spirits prowling in the air, she would take them to the church to be baptized. She held up the baby, swathed in white cloths while her husband stood beside her, holding the bibles under his arm. The Overseer reached down and dipped his finger in the silver bowl and touched the baby's forehead. The baby gave a scream as the water touched it. Making soothing sounds, she would clasp the white bundle to her breast while the Overseer prayed.

When her children were old enough Mrs Tichafa took them to the camps. There they learnt the rites of the church.

At home she taught them to pray. They prayed before eating, they prayed when they went to bed. In the morning, when they woke up, they prayed before going to school. Even when somebody brought them a packet of biscuits from the grocer's they prayed before opening it. They were not allowed to play table soccer at the shops or to watch games at the stadiums or films at the hall. They were not allowed to dance. Whenever they saw somebody dancing in the street they would yell "Daughter of Satan!" or "Son of Lucifer!" Whenever a perfumed woman with a made-up face and plaited hair passed them in the street they hissed "Eve!" Whenever a bell-bottomed youth passed them whistling and smoking a cigarette they gasped "Gehena!" And when, on their way from school, their route took them past a beerhall and they saw drunken couples necking in the trees they chanted "Everlasting fire!" When they saw their friends at school reading comic books they whispered "Damnation!"

They kept an eye on each other too, so when Esther saw Peter switch on the radio when there was no gospel programme on the air she shrilled "Judas!" He in turn, on seeing her talking to a boy at school snapped "Pillar of Salt!" Each one of them was on guard and tried to outspot the other.

The Overseer was a big man with a healthily light complexion and a broad, clean-shaven face. He wore dark suits and spotless shoes and drove a green station wagon with curtains on the windows. He lived with his family in a sprawling eight-roomed farmhouse renovated with funds from the ten percent monthly tithe paid by members of the congregation. He was a busy man, always off to visit this or that member of his flock, to see the sick, to console the bereaved, to congratulate the successful or commiserate with the desperate, to conduct the financial business of the church – paying the bills, banking the Sunday service collection of payments from numerous individual pledges, endlessly negotiating a regular lease for the church plot with the municipality. Because he was a busy man he drove very fast. Because he drove fast he did not always see members of his congregation flagging a ride at the side of the road; once the bonnet of his car tossed a child on to the grass. Through God's grace, the child was neither hurt nor bruised.

Mrs Tichafa rode once in his car on a trip to a fellowship camp. She *did* think the car moved a little fast, but her anxiety was relieved by the church songs he played on the tape recorder. Humming with the other women in the car in accompaniment to the music, she forgot her fear and was surprised they reached the camp an hour before the bus carrying the men and the rest of the women.

The fellowship camp meetings were held in various places at various times, once every three months, at least. At Christmas and Easter these usually extended into two-week marathons and when they came back their bodies were numb and their voices hoarse from singing. All the women and girls in the church wore ankle-length skirts and *doeks*; the men wore suits and the boys trousers and school blazers – the only bare legs to be seen were those of the unwashed youth from the township who sometimes lined up along the fence of the plot to yell and whistle insults at the worshippers.

During the week they would preach to crowds in the streets or go from house to house talking to people about the power of the Holy Spirit. Sometimes they were listened to, sometimes they were ignored or asked to leave, but always there was a soul out there waiting to be found and brought to the fold.

These street sermons were very dramatic and often took on apocalyptic dimensions, as if the preachers were vying with each other in a desperate exercise of well-intentioned exaggeration.

Mr Tichafa's confession, for instance, steadily took over and succeeded in kindling his past into a beast of draconic proportions: "Before He found me I did *anything* for money. I lied, I cheated, I stole. I lurked in the bushes behind houses and robbed the drunk and the old. I gambled at cards with men like me who did not care about losing their salary if it could bring them more, and if I didn't win I slashed my rivals with knives and cast them into ditches. Yes, I *killed* for money!"

Once the Overseer showed in the township hall a film he had taken of a seaside fellowship camp in South Africa. (The camp had taken place before the conversion of the Tichafas.) A lot of people came to see the film, even people who did not belong to the Church of the Holy Spirit. The Overseer, who had shot the film himself with his own movie camera, kept the audience informed of what was happening at each stage. The film first showed the congregation singing in a park, around a jubilant man whose sight had just been restored to him. Then the congregation colourfully flocked down to the beach where they caught fish washed ashore by the waves. The audience gasped to see every person in the film holding a huge wriggling fish in his or her hand.

"Those fish were just washed up by the waves," a voice remarked from the back, over the whirr of the soundless film track.

"Who said that?" the Overseer demanded, stopping the film and switching on the lights. The people in front twisted their heads to the back.

"The man wasn't really blind, either," another voice added, again from the back.

A momentary silence fell in the hall, then an excited murmur trickled across the hall. Mr Tichafa, the new deacon, leapt to his feet and took cursory steps towards the back of the hall.

"Who said that?" the Overseer demanded again. "You better own up, whoever you are, or we'll pray to God to break your arm or leg for saying that!"

A sudden loud sharp laughter crashed over the murmuring and three youths swaggered towards the door.

"You could be crippled for life!" the Overseer panted after them, but the deacon was hurrying the offenders out already and safely closing back the steel doors.

The Overseer switched off the lights and resumed the film.

Certain men drove into the township and slept in houses guarded by hordes of men and youth who slept in the gardens. After they left mysteriously in the mornings, meetings were held in the streets, voices sang and shouted in the night.

One day a man came to the Tichafas' house selling membership cards for a political party.

"We're church people," Mr Tichafa told the man. "We're interested in the spirit, not the flesh. If it is God's will to change a government, then He will change it Himself, in His own time."

He would have gone on to talk about the problems of serving two masters at one time, and the importance of salvation, but the man quietly picked up his bag and left.

On Sunday mornings men began to go around the township telling people to gather in the township square for a march into the city. The men wanted everybody to come, including women and children. When she heard these men coming Mrs Tichafa hid herself and her children in the wardrobe and under the bed. Mr Tichafa rolled himself into a jute sack and wriggled against the wall like a bag of sweet potatoes. They left their doors wide open, so that when the men came banging on the doors, kicking everything in sight and shouting if anybody was home, they left thinking the occupants had already gone. As soon as the men had left the Tichafas would sneak out of hiding, their bibles tucked safely under their clothes and their children stuck to backs and armpits as they scuttled across the half-deserted streets to their church where they stayed all day.

The singing of the crowd marching into the city was so thunderous it could be heard even on the outskirts of the township where the Church of the Holy Spirit was. The Overseer's sermon was interrupted by the din of the crowd roaring, "Power!", "Heavy!" and "One man one vote!" The "Alleluyas!" and "Amens!" from the congregation were drowned by the wail of police sirens, by the crash of the erupting crowd as the tear-gas landed, by the dull thump of batons beating bodies. Sometimes shots rang out there and a momentary silence struck the congregation, but always the singing of hymns would resume.

In the mornings scores of people would be snatched out of their houses and taken away by the police; at dusk the streets would teem with police reserve men.

Chapter 12

Children had been pointing at him and his sister and whispering things about them and their church. When the two boys who had been tracking him all through the break followed him into the toilet, he guessed they wanted to do something bad to him.

"Sellout!" the boys hissed.

"Lick the urinal!" the other said, stepping forward.

He swung round to face them.

"Sellout!" they hissed again, edging towards him to cut off his escape.

He made a rush for the door but his foot slid across a pool of water and he crashed to the floor, landing on his back.

"Lick it!" the boys hissed.

He tried to get up. They each grabbed him by the leg and heaved his head at the urinal.

"Lick it!"

He kicked out furiously, spitting at their faces. A crowd quickly gathered in the toilet. He kicked out furiously, ducking his head between the legs of one of the boys. They wrenched his head out and pushed his face against the urinal. He clamped his lips between his teeth as his face squashed against the slimy yellow tin foil and slid up. A jet of water streamed down and washed his face. The boys dropped him to the floor.

Laughter filled the toilet. He leapt to his feet and charged blindly towards the door. The boys were already out, vanishing down the corridor. He swiped at his nose and mouth and bunched his lips. A finger poked at his back. Another face sneered in front of him.

"Sellout!"

He hit out at the face with balled fists. The boy plunged back among the hisses of the spectators. Suddenly it was quiet. The crowd had fled. Only he was left there, him and this sobbing boy fingering his bruised face.

"Stop it!" a teacher yelled from behind him, grabbing him by the hand. "Why are you fighting?"

"I didn't do anything to him," the bruised boy blabbered, a big blob of blood bouncing from his nose.

"Why did you beat him?" the teacher demanded. "Why did you do it? What's your name?"

"Benjamin Tichafa," he stammered.

The teacher took him to the deputy headmaster's office. A grave man with a bald head, the deputy questioned him repeatedly but the more questions Benjamin was asked, the more he shut up into himself. He could not tell them about the two boys in the toilet who started it. He was too ashamed about it. Naturally, the deputy decided Benjamin had beaten the other boy for no reason and punished him. His punishment was to scrub the toilets after classes.

As soon as he got back home his mother, who had heard about the fight from Esther, asked him about it but he refused to talk. When Mr Tichafa came back from work and heard the story he asked him why he had done it. Again Benjamin refused to talk. His father took off his belt and whipped him on the legs.

"They called me a 'sellout'," he eventually yelled.

"What's a sellout?" his mother asked.

"It's nothing to beat another boy like that for," Mr Tichafa fumed, threading his belt back into his trousers.

Benjamin locked himself in the spare room and refused to eat. He fell asleep on the mat and did not wake up until Esther came in after they finished eating to tell him he had to be there for prayers. She came in slowly, afraid he was angry with her for having told their mother about it but he came out quietly and sang as if nothing had happened. Even as they lay on the mat afterwards, he said nothing. He just lay there facing the wall until he heard his parents snoring in the next room.

The police came one morning, banging on their doors. It was still dark, just after five. There had been trouble in the township. A beerhall had been set on fire.

Mr Tichafa jumped into his clothes and opened the door. Five policemen stood in front of him, their torches shining into the house. Their truck was parked in the road. Two of them carried guns. They marched past him into the house. Their boots crunched on the floor.

Mrs Tichafa came out of the bedroom, tying her robe. She was shocked to see the men.

"There must be some mistake," she said.

"We want Benjamin," said one of the men.

"But what has he done?" his father gasped.

They all heard the window in the spare bedroom open. They heard him try to jump out. Two policemen rushed into the spare bedroom. The other three rushed out round the house. Mrs Tichafa screamed. The men did not fire. He was stuck in the window. They dragged him down and handcuffed him. Peter climbed out of his cot and stood staring at the men. Esther stood in her pants and wept. The house smelt of sleep and wet blankets, the stale morning smell.

"But what has he done?" Mrs Tichafa asked, sweeping Peter into her arms.

"You had better come with us," said the policeman.

They all climbed into the truck. Benjamin sat between two policemen. His mother and father sat on the opposite bench. Their neighbours came out of their houses to watch. The truck swerved and lurched down the street. The city was a blaze of lights ahead of them but the lights looked dead. Dawn was a purple glow hovering over the matchbox houses of the township. The police camp was alive with people. Men in vests and shorts were marching round a government flag, exercising. The truck swept round to the entrance.

They climbed out of the truck. A burly sergeant with a smooth looking face sat at the counter waiting for them. Mr Tichafa knew the man. He lived in the same street in the township but he wasn't smiling. Mr Tichafa wanted to greet him but he did not try to.

"Is this the boy?" the sergeant asked.

"Yes, sir," one of the corporals answered.

"Are you his parents?" the sergeant asked Mr and Mrs Tichafa.

The questions surprised Mr Tichafa. He knew the sergeant knew Benjamin was their son. The sergeant had even borrowed their wheelbarrow once when he was building a chicken coop.

"Yes we are," he said. "What has he done?"

"Your son took part in burning down the beerhall."

"There must be some mistake!"

"What time did he get home last night?"

"Why, around seven o'clock."

"What time did he leave school?"

"What time did you leave school, Benjamin?"

Benjamin did not look up. He did not answer his mother's question. He said nothing.

"Answer the question, Benjamin!" his father shouted.

Benjamin said nothing.

"He usually finishes school at three," his mother said.

"Do you know where he was between three and seven?"

"He was collecting manure for the school garden."

"Did he bring home any manure?"

"I don't know," his mother said, "I didn't see it. But how do you know all this? What proof have you he did it?"

"There are people who saw him."

"He wouldn't have tried to escape through the window if he knew nothing about it," said one of the policemen who had brought them in.

"He wouldn't deny it if you asked him. He was among the first three to light up the beerhall. He helped pour out the petrol. The other boys have all confessed."

"Did you *do* it, Benjamin? Did you burn that beerhall?" Mr Tichafa asked his son. He looked at the policemen and at the sergeant. He looked worried. He looked ashamed.

Benjamin said nothing.

"This is a serious case," the sergeant said. "Young boys like him burning down government property!"

"But how, *Saijen*?"

"These boys were used by older people who are organizing the illegal demonstrations. The older people are hiding behind these boys so the law can't get them."

"But we're church people," Mrs Tichafa wept, "we'd never encourage our son to do things like that."

"Superintendent Twinkleton was going to have these boys thrown into jail right away. You know how white people feel about these things. I had to talk to him . . ."

"Thank you, *Saijen*," Mrs Tichafa said.

"Had I known my son was doing this I'd have *killed* him, *Saijen*," Mr Tichafa hissed. "Oh, Benjamin! Benjamin! How can you shame us like this? We know all these men here and not once have we picked a quarrel with any one of them. Your mother and I have never ever been inside a police camp. To think *you* could bring us here like this!"

"Burning government property, or any property, for that matter, is a serious crime. The law cannot let such acts go unpunished."

"Please forgive him," Mrs Tichafa wept. "He's only a child. If he did it, it was only because he was tricked into it."

"There's no question he did it," said the sergeant, with some impatience. "As to the forgiving part of it, I'm afraid that's only possible in church. The law must take its course. People like him are sent to reform school for years."

"Please don't send him to a reform school," Mrs Tichafa wept. "He's only eleven. Oh, what will our neighbours say?"

"If he did it and deserves to go to a reform school then to reform school he'll go!" Mr Tichafa swore. "I won't bring up the devil in my household."

"I talked to Superintendent Twinkleton. Because of their ages we're letting the boys off with serious warnings. But if your boy is ever involved again in this or any other illegal demonstration at any time we'll lock him up. He's on our records now."

"Thank you, *Saijen*."

"Having said that," said the sergeant, "the boy must take his punishment."

The sergeant unlocked the handcuffs and took Benjamin into the next room. They all heard him tell Benjamin to put his hands on the table. They all heard the cane strokes slashing one after the other. They all heard the sergeant inhale as he raised the stick and gasp as he brought it down. They all heard Benjamin gasp as the blows struck.

The corporals looked at the wall. Mr Tichafa cracked his knuckles in his palm. Mrs Tichafa moaned.

"You can take him away," the sergeant said when he brought him back, "but remember what I said."

He walked as if his back was on fire but his face was dry. He did not look at any one. He did not look up. His mother took his hand and marched him across the tarmac square to the gate. The men in shorts and vests were still marching round the flag. Their shorts and vests were green and their calves were tough. Their faces were beaded with sweat.

The sun was coming up and there were cars and buses on the roads, black men rushing to work, on foot and on bicycles.

People were rushing to work as if nothing had happened but Mr Tichafa thought they all knew. He thought the people would look at the three of them and *know* they had been in a police station. He thought the people would look at them and know they had never been in a police station until that morning. He thought people would look at him and his wife and know at once that their son had disgraced them. He still felt he was in the back of the truck, with the policemen. He still heard the policemen's shoes crunching beside them.

Mrs Tichafa held Benjamin's hand and cried into a handkerchief. Inside her heart, she was praying. She still hoped it had been a mistake. It never occurred to her that the boy had already taken the due punishment or that the sergeant had exaggerated his mercy.

Mr Tichafa marched on in front of them. His eyes were ablaze. When they got home he closed the doors and unbuckled his belt.

Benjamin knelt alone on the floor in front of the pulpit.

The whole congregation was behind him. The Overseer was in the pulpit above him.

He could feel the sea of dark faces behind him. If he raised his eyes a little he could see the Overseer towering above him in the pulpit. The Overseer wore a black suit and a white shirt and a white tie. He was so high up there in the pulpit he looked like God. Perhaps God looked like that except in the pictures he smiled and was white and had a beard and wore a robe and there were sheep frisking over his lap.

He knelt on the floor for a long time. Grains of sand ate into his knees. His limbs ached.

"The devil is trying to invade this church through one of our young people," the Overseer was saying from the pulpit.

The pulpit gleamed. It was the colour of gold. Women polished it every day. Some women polished their faces like that. They smeared polish over the pulpit and rubbed it until it shone like a mirror in which you could see your face. He had looked at his face on the pulpit one morning when the Sunday-school teacher was out with the class doing a sketch and there was nobody looking. His face had looked queer – almost like somebody else's face. He hadn't looked long because he feared God might be watching him.

The Overseer read from the Bible. He read verses about children and sin and punishment. Benjamin knew some of the verses. He knew many verses by heart but his favourite book was the Psalms. The Psalms made him think of shepherds and rivers. Some of the Psalms were like the poems they recited at school. They made him wonder what it was like to be meek and blessed. He had gone down to the country and looked after his grandmother's sheep once. There weren't any taps there and when he was thirsty he had drunk from the river. The water had a cloudy grey colour but the banks of the river were green.

He and Esther knew many verses. Sometimes they stood together in front of the congregation, in the space where he was kneeling now, and recited verses to the congregation. His mother smiled when they did that. Once when he recited many verses his father had bought him a new pair of shorts at an Indian shop. The shopkeeper had said the shorts were too big but his father said they were all right.

The Overseer spoke for a long time. He told the congregation about the burning of the beerhall, about the police, about *him*. The Overseer seemed to know everything. Perhaps he had been there, seeing it all. Perhaps it came to him in his dreams while he slept.

Benjamin was afraid. He felt he had burnt down the whole city. He had burnt down his father's house. He had burnt down the church. He had burnt the pulpit. He had killed a person. That person's face was on the pulpit.

Benjamin listened to the Overseer's words. His heart filled with fear. He wanted to scream. He wanted to shout. He wanted to run out of the tent into the bush. He wanted to pray. He did not know what to do.

"Open your heart to Him, Benjamin," the Overseer said, "just open your heart and he will drive out the devil."

The Overseer climbed down the pulpit. He climbed slowly. Benjamin saw his black shoes, his trousers, his hands. The Overseer put a hand on Benjamin's head.

"Open your heart, Benjamin," he said, "just open your heart and He'll come in."

Benjamin's heart roared. His ears filled. His eyes swam. His lips clenched. He wanted to open but he did not know where. He wanted to open but he did not know how. Tears squeezed from his eyes.

The Overseer put out his two hands in front of him.

"Take His hand and walk with Him," he said.

The Overseer sang a song. He held his hands out. The congregation joined in. Their voices were like thunder. They sang like they did when they took a dead person to the township cemetery. He did not want to die. He lifted his arms. He touched the Overseer's hands.

"Walk with Him!" the Overseer said.

His knees lifted from the floor. The congregation sang more loudly. His whole body was trembling.

Chapter 13

Six months later, on a cold howling Sunday morning, Mr and Mrs Tichafa left early for the service, taking Esther with them. Benjamin and Peter remained at home. Peter had a very bad cold and Benjamin stayed with him, looking after him. Thirteen-year-old Esther would have remained too, since she was the eldest child, but there was a special Youth Week of Witness she could not miss.

Before they left Mrs Tichafa prepared a light lunch of buttered bread and a flask of tea. (The second commandment forbade work on Sundays and any normal cooking was construed as work.) And so off they went, Mr Tichafa in his black Sunday suit and white shirt and grey tie and his wife and daughter almost identical in their long dresses. At thirteen, Esther was almost as tall as her mother.

Left at the helm of the Tichafa household, Benjamin managed well enough. At lunchtime he poured out the flasked tea and arranged the bread in thick slices as he had seen his mother do. After eating he washed out the cups and plates. They sat in the sitting-room and turned on the radio.

"What station is that?" asked Peter, with the inquisitiveness of a six-year-old.

"Just listen and say nothing," said Benjamin, fiddling with the knobs of the radio. An assortment of sounds whirred in the air.

"But those aren't church songs, Benjamin."

"Shut up or get out."

"I'll tell mother."

"If you do, I'll tell her I caught you eating peanut butter."

Benjamin found a pop music station. He turned the radio loud and locked himself in the spare bedroom.

"I can hear you," said Peter. "You're dancing"

"Oh, shut up."

"I'll tell mother you were a son of Satan while she was away."

"And what will you get for telling?" asked Benjamin, swaggering out of the bedroom and twisting recklessly in front of the blaring radio.

"The devil will roast you up in hell, Benjamin."

"Let him try."

"What's that book you're reading?"

"None of your business."

"Isn't that the book father beat you up for last week?"

"This is a school book. I'm studying."

"School books don't have black and white pictures all through them," Peter sneezed.

"How do you know? Have you ever been to school?"

"I know. I heard father say so."

"Judas! You're always telling."

"What will you give me if I don't tell?"

"I'll buy you toffees."

"Have you got money?"

"Look," Benjamin flashed a bunch of silver.

"Where did you get the money, Benjamin? Have you been playing *chaputa* in the street?"

"Do you want the toffees or not?"

"I do."

"You promise not to tell?"

"I promise."

"Here," Benjamin tossed him a coin.

Peter made for the door.

"Where are you going?"

"To the grocer's."

"Wait, I'll take you there."

They locked the doors and went out to the grocer's to get the toffees. It was bitterly cold outside. When they came back Peter was sneezing badly. Monstrous black clouds scrambled over the sky. The wind whined down the street, sweeping up little whirlwinds of dust, whipping fleeing children to their mothers' doors.

"I'm cold, Benjamin."

"Put on another jersey."

"I'm freezing."

The boy's teeth were chattering. A worm of mucous dangled from his nose. His nose was red from too much blowing. Benjamin put a hand on Peter's forehead as he had seen his mother do. He was startled by the wave of heat that flowed into his palm. He could not understand why the boy said he was cold if he felt so hot.

"I'll make you a fire."

He went out to get the brazier behind the chicken coop. He shook out the dead ashes and stood it in the open, where there was wind. He put some paper in the brazier, stacked the blocks of wood in it and sprinkled some paraffin over it.

"Stand back," he told Peter, throwing a match into the brazier. The paper burst into flame but the wood did not catch fire. The blocks were too thick.

"Get the axe in the spare bedroom," he told Peter.

Peter brought the axe. Benjamin laid each of the blocks on a stone near the coop and split them. Peter ran around picking up the splinters. Benjamin felt hot. He flung out mightily at one last block.

Suddenly the axe wrenched from his hand. There was an ear-splitting scream. Peter sprawled in the dust, moaning. His leg twisted away from his body and there was blood around his pelvis . . .

With a roar of terror, Benjamin raced to knock on the neighbour's door . . .

They left Peter in the hospital ward with the dead look on his face. His leg was a mass of bloodstained bandages. There were tubes and bottles hanging all over him. The white doctor had come while they were there. The doctor had whistled slow and long and said there was nothing to do but to amputate. He wondered what it meant to amputate. The Overseer had prayed at the bed. Mr Chikwaka had prayed. Mrs Pondokazi had prayed. Oswell's father had prayed. Maria's aunt had prayed. Then the nurses had ushered them out when the bell rang and they had ridden home in the Overseer's station wagon. The church people had sung and prayed in their house. Some of the neighbours were there too. The soldier's wife from next door was there too. The church people left and the neighbours left and his mother howled in the bedroom. She howled the way women did when somebody died. His father walked up and down the house without talking. Outside the wind blew hard. Esther sat in a corner sobbing. He wondered and he wondered what it meant to amputate. His father called him into the bedroom . . .

His father called him into the bedroom and sat on the edge of their huge bed. His mother lay on the bed with her face buried in the pillow. His father still wore his Sunday suit and his Sunday shirt and his Sunday tie. His father sat still like a statue with the Bible on the sidetable. He crouched on the floor as he always did when he was called into the bedroom. His father coughed and sat there for some time. Then he picked up his Bible and read a chapter from it. He spoke to him with the low soft voice the Overseer used in the church closet. His father told him to tell the truth. He read him another chapter and asked for the truth and nothing but the truth. He said only the truth would set him free . . .

He told his father what had happened. He watched his father's face. He saw a cloud of black anger drip down his forehead. It fell over his eyes and his nose and his mouth and his chin. Down his throat his neck his Sunday shirt his hands his legs his feet. It dripped on to the floor. He saw his mother sit up and start crying again. His father whipped off his belt, "Tell the truth, Benjamin," he said. "Tell the whole truth."

"Chopped his brother's leg off?"
  "Him?"
  "*Him*?"
  "Hacked it off with an axe."
  "Clean?"
  "The doctor had to saw it off."
  "*Him*?"
  "Must be something in the family."

One Sunday, he almost opened his heart. He was going to throw himself at the Overseer's feet but something on his father's singing face stopped him.

That night he dreamt of the devil. The devil was black and had a pitchfork, like he was in the books. The devil turned into a snake and bit him. When the snake bit him he died.

"His mother tried to hang herself afterwards."
  "What happened?"
  "She undid the noose."

He thought he had told the truth.

"Him?"

"Yes, him. Poured the petrol over the beerhall, too."

"Him?"

"His friends mocked him into it."

He knew the songs men sang when they marched into the city.

Once, when he was seven, he saw a pool of blood under a hedge near a house. The house was at the corner of their street, next to the school fence. His mother had said they shouldn't go out, but he ran out and looked. A man had been axed to pieces and loaded into a jute sack and dumped on the garbage heaps on the fringe of the town. Axed to pieces, like a block of wood. Arms and legs and head. For selling out, people said. He didn't know what 'selling out' meant then. For a long time he didn't know. He even dreamt about it. He imagined the man had stolen something and sold it. Or perhaps he had sold something outside his house or outside a shop.

He didn't know.

One of his schoolmate's houses had been stoned. The windows had been smashed in. The door had been broken. A stone had carved a huge hole through the asbestos roof. People said his classmate's father had sold out, too.

"Him?"

"Chopped it clean."

At first he tried not to look. But they slept together in the same bedroom. They ate together. They lived together. They were brothers. The only thing he could do not to see was to close his eyes. Or to look away. But he couldn't close his eyes all the time. He couldn't look away forever.

One evening his mother was coming from the church when she met a group of men in the street.

"Whose daughter are you?" the men asked her. *"Uri mwana wani?"*

"I'm a child of God."

"Child of God!" the men had flared. "There's nothing like that! You're a child of the soil, you hear. *Mwana wevhu.* Everybody is a child of the soil. You hear that?"

His mother had told him that story. It puzzled him.

Child of the soil.
   He thought about it for a long time.
   He did not know what it meant. The Sunday-school teacher said Adam
had been made out of clay but that was not what the men meant. Or was it?
   Child of the soil.
   He did not know what it meant. It sounded like you had a mother and a
father but the soil was your mother and father too. It sounded like you had
another father and mother. The men had said everybody was a child of the
soil. That meant everybody had the same father and mother though they had
different mothers and fathers.

The men had said nothing would happen to them. The men had waited for
them at the school gates. All his friends were there. All the children were
there. The men had said all children were children of the soil. The men had
said nothing would happen to children of the soil. The men had given them
the petrol and matches. The men had told them to burn down the beerhall.

He had told his father that.
   His father had said the truth would set him free.

Child of the soil.
   He thought about it. He didn't know.
   One day when nobody was looking he scooped a handful of earth from his
mother's garden and looked at it in his palm. He picked off the pieces of rock
and examined the fine soil in his palm. It was half black, half brown, like
coloured sugar. It flowed in his palm when he breathed on it. He thought of
God breathing into clay. God must have blown hard. He must have mixed
the clay with water first. And Adam must have been fast asleep not to feel
the rib taken off him. He tasted the soil with his tongue. It didn't taste like
sugar, though. It had a dry, gritty taste. Did soil have the same colour
throughout the world? Did soil taste the same?
   He thought about it. He didn't know.

At home there was silence. Nobody said anything. Sometimes he heard only
a crutch thumping on the floor. When Esther left for boarding school there

was more silence.

The axe had flown out of his hands. He had told his father that. His father had said the truth would set him free.

Child of the soil.
    He thought about it.
    It sounded like something from the Bible.
    But he knew if it was, the men in the street would not have shouted at his mother. He knew the Overseer could not like it because the Overseer had nothing to do with men who walked the streets.
    Could the people who marched into the town singing and chanting be children of the soil? What about policemen and soldiers? What about sergeants and superintendents? What about thieves and robbers and murderers and rapists? What about teachers and priests and drunkards and church people? What about Overseers and Prime Ministers and Chiefs? What about white people? What about cripples and beggars and doctors and businessmen? What about mad people and people who hanged themselves?
    He thought about it.
    He didn't know.

Chapter 14

At fourteen he dragged his massive black coffin of a trunk up the concrete path to his dorm, a lean boy with a clean face, knock-kneed, sweating, farting into his 'don't touch' trousers. The dorm smelt of carbolic soap and laundered sheets and floor polish, and in those early term days of plenty there was the additional aroma of home-fried chicken, salted peanuts, peanut butter, cookies and other delicacies packed away at the bottom of trunks by frantic, bustling mothers and brought out for some midnight feast.

The Form Two boys raided his trunk, as they raided the trunks of all other newcomers, with the systematic thoroughness of poll-tax collectors, and that was the last he saw of the biltong, the box of choice assorted biscuits, the six-pack case of tinned beef and the coffee cake his mother had sat up all night baking in the wood stove.

The extortionists were led by a bully nicknamed Chemhere, a tall, wiry fellow, six feet of bone on his bare soles though he was only sixteen and black as a three-legged pot. Chemhere had some kind of nervous disorder, for his hands were always shaking. In spite of this handicap he was the best bread-cutter in the dorm, accurate as a compass: whenever a group of students quarrelled about the way the bread and margarine they had bought together had to be shared out, he was called to mediate.

The raid on the trunks of Form One students was followed by other rituals on humiliation. To Benjamin's surprise on the second night, a group of boys led by Chemhere converged on his bed, laughing and singing, pulling away his bedclothes and ripping off his underwear. An eruption of shrieks and hoots had followed the discovery of Benjamin's clean pubis. The boys taunted him about the cracks on his feet, why he spoke the dialect he did and why he came from a small town at a school where most boys came from the capital.

The worst ordeal was to be made to bark and snarl at a bone while the other boys chanted "Newcomer! Newcomer!" Some of the new boys in the dorm had already been subjected to this, and Benjamin dreaded the day when this would happen to him.

Soon enough, Chemhere brought a bone from the dining hall and flung it on his bed.

"I want you to bark and snarl at that, Newcomer!"

Benjamin backed up against the wall.

"I said *bark* and *snarl* at it, Newcomer!" Chemhere yelled, jabbing at the bed with a convulsive finger.

A crowd of boys gathered round the bed, chanting. Benjamin tried to bolt for the door. Chemhere caught him and flung him back against the wall.

"*Bark*, Newcomer!" he yelled, the tendons in his neck stretched. He grabbed a wet towel from the rail and swung it at Benjamin. The towel hit him on the chest.

"*Bark!*"

Chemhere hit him again on the arms. The towel cracked like a whip as it cut his bare arms, his legs, his face.

"*Bark, damn you!*" Chemhere swung mightily at Benjamin's face.

The spectators around them stopped chanting, suddenly, their voices jammed with fear. Mbombo, one of the bigger boys who had been sitting disinterestedly on his locker, jumped at Chemhere and grabbed his arms from behind, "No, Chemere. Enough!"

"Who does this little stinker think he is?" Chemhere sputtered, trying to break from the powerful grip. For a moment it seemed Chemhere would fight Mbombo.

"Get out, damn you!" Mbombo hissed at Benjamin.

"Grab him!" Chemere yelled to the other boys, but Benjamin had already leapt over the bed and sprinted for the door and none of the boys tried to stop him. He didn't sneak back into the dorm until after lights out.

"Why didn't you just bark and snarl and get it done with?" Mbombo, still awake in his bed near the door when he came in, whispered, with the scornful sympathy of a rescuer of the reckless. To Benjamin's surprise, Chemhere left him alone after that, and would only stare at him and make mild threats, "I'll get you, asshole!"

Besides the dreaded Chemhere, there were other queer boys Benjamin could never have imagined possible – Tawanda, the short foul-mouthed fellow who was always writing home to tell his rural parents to send more money "for photosynthesis"; Tawanda who seemed to have gobbled up a whole dictionary of obscenities and often successfully engaged in slanging-matches with the others. He slept in a bed in a corner of the dorm and the topic he liked to discuss most after lights out was masturbation.

Kainos, the football team's scoring machine who got suspended from school for being found in the girl's dorm at night, trying to visit his girlfriend. Dimpled Kainos, knobby-fingered and pimple-nosed, hopelessly in love at fifteen, always attracting a loyal audience to his long nursed fantasy of making love to his girlfriend while rolling on a long stretch of carpet.

And there was Samuel, quiet as a mouse and tonsil-less, a wizard at Latin, forever helping others with their declensions, expending his vast intellect on a dead language and truant classmates, so timid that though he was in Form Two and as able-bodied as any person of his age could be, he fled even from the mildest threats from the littlest inmates. Samuel whom even Benjamin pitied.

Mbombo, a hefty fellow who charged through the dorm like a baby elephant and yet prayed aloud every night in his bed. Mbombo his rescuer. Mbombo, the epileptic, always telling people to close doors behind them at night, yelling and thrashing his sheets to the floor on full moon nights, always receiving strange sad telegrams from home. Mbombo, accused of having an affair with the old woman who bartered shoe-polish and tinfuls of salted peanuts for the students' weekly ration of blue soap. Mbombo the angry, keeping the dorm awake one night while fighting Chemhere over the allegation. Mbombo, vice-president of the Scripture Union, desperately staving off his affliction with religion.

Chorosi.

Green-fingered and yellow-toothed Chorosi.

Chorosi who took pride in showing off a bottle of vaseline filled with a mysterious creamy fluid . . . .

Masturbation – talked about, imagined and practised – was a major dorm preoccupation, probably taking up as much time as the official school curriculum together. Often when the lights went out Benjamin lay smelling the dorm stench of boy-flesh and sleep and occasionally urine, listening to the sporadic squeak of bed springs and the invariable soft gasp and sigh followed by rolling. For a long time he had wondered ignorantly what it meant to masturbate.

He did not know until the day somebody showed him pictures from a magazine, full page pictures of naked white men and women. Trembling with disbelief, he had hurried away to the bathroom.

Sex was something nobody had talked to him about, an unspeakable act at best reserved for the functional bedrooms of married people, at worst associated with the drunken beerhall couples he and his sister had jeered at as children. Sex was something existing only in these two extreme forms; there could be no mean to it.

His dorm-mates' obsession with it and his pandering to those pictures completely shattered him at first. Whenever he remembered the boys swarming over him, pulling away his bedclothes and laughing at his boyhood, his heart beat quickly, filling him with the sudden strange anxiety to grow up.

He had never imagined children of church-going people, at a mission school for that matter, could behave as his dorm mates did, swearing, lying, smoking, drinking and cheating through their sordid little lives. He had come to the mission school thinking his past would stick out for the whole world to see, fearing that the clawed secret of his childhood would one day seek release and leap out in a furry streak in broad daylight and everybody would know who he was and what he had done. His biggest fear was that one night he would betray himself by talking in his sleep.

But his anonymity surprised him. There were so many people far more wicked than him. Compared to the people in his dorm alone he was a saint. Nobody seemed to notice him. To many he seemed a timid, shy boy. His teachers did not seem to think anything was wrong with him. He got acceptable grades for his homework. He ran for his house in the athletics competition. He did his laundry every weekend, combed his hair and kept his place in the dormitory clean. He did not skip the ninety-minute church service which, compared to the day-long marathons at home, was tolerable. The rituals of the mission church were an easier version of what he had been brought up on. He surprised himself by liking woodwork and metalwork and coming top of class in these subjects. He was not called to Father Casey's office.

He began to think boarding school was not such a trial, after all, and he enjoyed the temporary anonymity it offered him. Though he felt himself unshackled from the fetters of home and his childhood, inside him he curiously felt an allegiance to his religious upbringing, the need to join the Scripture Union. But he was surprised to find how frivolous the members seemed, how they turned it into a matchmaking group and an opportunity for travelling to other schools and places.

At the end of the year he brought home a good report and his parents were pleasantly surprised.

Then came Form Two.

Form Two and its ache, its airs of importance, its vengeance.

Its pubic badge, its broken voice, its swagger.

Form Two and its confidence, its terror, its pathos.

He beat up newcomers and raided their trunks, scribbled in hymn books at assembly, scrawled chalkboard threats to hated teachers, lit up litterbins, carved his name on desks, smoked in toilets, skipped night studies to raid the neighbouring farm of green mealies, drained the wine out of the cup the priest held out to the kneeling line at Mass, laughed to tears poor girls whose ripening bodies betrayed them wetly on classroom seats, fought his enemies with tightly clenched fists, proposed oddly to whimsical finger-chewing girls and when rejected, masturbated fanatically.

And yes, he pushed wheelbarrows for it, dug and filled trenches, scrubbed toilets, wore four pairs of shorts to canings and carried his inflamed butts with the pride of a martyr, cursived thousand-lined pledges of the *I-will-never-jump-out-through-the-window* kind, earned himself the stinging comments on his reports which lost him his pocket money.

"I can't get used to the system," he would moan to his parents, when called, under pain of the belt, to account for his damning school reports. He developed a sinister way of spewing his father's trusted medicine back into his face: "Nobody takes praying seriously at the mission, not even the Fathers. Nobody speaks to God at all. They believe too much in confession and not in fellowship. There is very little control over the boys and girls. They even make us drink wine at Mass. There are discos, film shows. There are too many temptations. Maybe if our church had a mission school . . ."

"You know our church has no schools!" His father would rap back, stunned by the sarcasm his son had acquired in two short years. "We sent you there to get an education. Never mind what their system is like!"

"But I'm all alone there. There's no one from our church I can pray with."

"You can pray alone!"

With the knowledge of this sarcasm came other cunning discoveries. His eyes opened out to the widening world the mission and its inhabitants offered. The unwritten knowledge – garnered in the corridors, dorms, offices, chapel, dining halls, sports tracks, on the graffiti in toilets, scrawled in the margins of textbooks: between lectures, study periods and sleep: among the banter of his peers, the lectures of his teachers, the sermons of the priests – jolted him out of the sense of guilt which heavily saddled his past. His head filled with questions about himself and the world around him.

There developed in his consciousness an ongoing interrogation between an older, authoritarian voice and his defensive, obstinate self:

Do you enjoy causing trouble? *I don't know.*

What if you get expelled from school? *I won't be expelled.*

Why? *I'm just as naughty as any one at this mission school.*

Is that the reason you're behaving so badly? *I don't know.*

Do you realize you come from a poor family? *Yes, I do.*

Do you know one-third of your father's yearly salary goes to your fees? *I know.*

And your mother sells guavas and bananas to raise money for groceries. *I know.*

Don't you want to be educated and get a good job? *Yes I do.*

You hate your parents, don't you? *No.*

Have you forgotten the sergeant's warning when you burnt the beerhall? *No.*

Then why don't you just concentrate on your schoolwork? *I don't know.*

You think you're clever, don't you? *No.*

Are you stubborn because you're bitter? *No.*

Do you know what country you're living in? *Rhodesia.*

And you know what happens to stubborn young black boys who get expelled from school? *I know.*

You don't want to spend half your life in prison, do you? *No.*

You don't think you're a hero, do you? *No.*

Or you believe the devil is making you do the things you're doing? *I don't believe what the Overseer or what my parents think.*

Do you believe in the Church of the Holy Spirit? *Nobody's perfect.*

Why do you say that? *The Overseer stole church money.*
How do you know? *Everybody knows it but nobody talks about it.*
How do you know? *My father is having an affair with the woman next door.*
How do you know that? *I caught them walking in the street together at night.*
How can you be so sure? *I just know so.*
Does your mother know? *I don't think so.*
Do you believe in God? *I'm not sure any more.*
How can you, a boy raised in a Christian family, say that? *I don't know.*
But aren't you afraid of everlasting fire? *I don't know.*
Why are you so stubborn? *I'm not stubborn.*
You don't think you're a hero, do you? *No.*
Are you bitter? *No.*

Six months before he was due to write his 'O' Level examinations, the newspapers reported that the Rhodesian government was considering extending the (previously white) military draft to male black school leavers in order to counter increasing acts of sabotage in the countryside.

There was an uproar in the country. Black students at the University staged a demonstration in the capital. Many schools followed suit. Armies of teenage boys in school uniforms marched by night along farm roads and obscure routes, and trooped into the cities and towns with placards that read, among other inscriptions:

THE BLACK MAN IS TOO HUNGRY TO HOLD A GUN.
GIVE US THE VOTE FIRST.
WE HAVE NOTHING TO DEFEND.

The police met the students with teargas, truncheons, whips and dogs. Some students fled back to schools, some were loaded into trucks and herded into prison and released after a day or two; others were formally charged and released only after their parents bailed them out or their headmasters negotiated their release. Scores ended up in hospitals with broken or dog-mauled legs. Hundreds were suspended from school and sent home with letters blackmailing parents into the customary betrayal of ringleaders.

Benjamin Tichafa marched in the second row propping up one side of the sheet on which he and a dorm mate had painted in bleeding red letters: THE BOYS IN THE BUSH ARE OUR BROTHERS. When the police cut them off at dawn just as they were completing the twenty-five mile march into the

106

little town, he was one of the first ones to be bundled into the truck. At the charge office he was among those who had had their names and fingerprints taken by the time Father Casey rattled into the camp in his Volkswagen Beetle to see the Superintendent. The two men negotiated fiercely in the Superintendent's office while a black sergeant stoically completed the paperwork. After three hours the Superintendent (a stocky middle-aged man with blond hair) came out to announce their fate.

They were all to be formally charged for taking part in an illegal demonstration and were to appear in court in the coming month. Since their particulars had been taken, he was handing them over to their principal, who would decide what to do in the interim. Father Casey waded (in his robes) across the street to the public telephone to send for two mission trucks. (The Superintendent absolutely refused him permission to use government telephones for missionary purposes.) When the trucks arrived at midday Father Casey, pensive as Buddha, thought to make a quick roll call of the group, and it was discovered that three of the boys who had earlier gone to the cafe across the street had not returned.

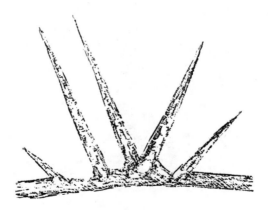

Part Three

Chapter 15

All night the train rattled through places he had never been to before.

He smoked, ate the sandwich a vendor sold him, propped up his head in his hands and dozed, sometimes. The guard charged through the train every hour, rapping his ticket clipper on the sinks, yanking blankets off half-dozing heads, his insatiable pink hand held out for tickets. Behind him followed swarms of vendors loudly advertising their merchandise.

Shivering in his denim shirt, he watched the coal black world outside the window for the first promise of dawn. Sometimes his eye caught a false glimmer, the haze of a farm settlement where labourers lay waiting, the dull shimmer of a star plunging into a plain. Then, yes, the east began to turn purple, then slowly orange and yellow. He began to make out the rugged terrain, the monstrous hills sweeping past in hoary gloom and sudden startling fields of maize stretching out like lakes of khaki in the valleys.

The chill breathed at him through the frosted glass. He prayed for the sun.

Yet when the sun spilled out of its orange puddle, he began to rue the night.

As the train sidled into the mountain station, its last, he began to wish it could go on all day, across hills and the border he didn't know how to cross, into the awesome mountain country beyond. He got out of the train with the crowd, clasping his cigarettes and matches. He let the minutes slip from him, yet clung desperately to every second. He envied the people who had things to do and places to go to.

He stumbled into a company of black and white soldiers in front of the cloakroom. They had just alighted from first-class compartments and were probably waiting for their trucks. Their uniforms were freshly laundered, their heads crisply barbered and their shoes glittered. He hurried past them, past the cloakroom, round the alley into the street. He entered a restaurant and sat next to the window. He still felt as if he was on the train, though music was playing and there were cars washing past the sun-drenched window. He felt numb from sitting too long on the train. He bought a cup of coffee and two meat pies. The coffee made him feel better. He savoured every drop. Then he smoked and read the papers on the tables. As usual, there were military communiques and pictures on the front pages.

After eating he went out to the streets. He was surprised to see how much the town resembled his home town, as if the two had been fashioned from one model. Both towns were framed by the railway station from which the shops and offices fanned out.

But this one was bigger, the roads wider and steeper and of course there were the hills. The business section was perched on a hill like some giant concrete nest. Below him he could see shimmering township houses laid out like thousands of cardboard boxes in the valley, and the plush white suburbs on the hill slopes, out of the pall of industrial smoke.

He walked around the streets, looking at the shop windows.

There was so much time, so little to do, yet he sweated like a student awaiting an examination.

He asked a woman he met in the street to direct him to the terminus for rural bound buses. The terminus was larger than the one in his home town and less crowded. There were three half-full buses waiting.

"Headed east?" a conductor asked him, from behind.

It was only ten in the morning. Benjamin nodded.

"How far?" the conductor asked, opening his ticket book.

"The furthest stop," said Benjamin.

"Which last stop?" the conductor asked, "Kamuti or Zinyemba?"

"Which one is further?"

"Well, they are one place, really, but Zinyemba is where the bus turns back."

"Zinyemba, then," said Benjamin, taking comfort in the fact that it began with a 'Z', as if that last letter of the alphabet could transport him to the borders of his anxiety.

"Got any luggage?" the conductor asked, handing him the ticket and fishing for change in his leather bag.

"No."

"You've been out there before?"

"No."

"Just asking, mate. There've been incidents there and there're soldiers on the way. But you have your papers with you?"

112

"Yes."

"That's the bus there. We're leaving in fifteen minutes."

When everybody was aboard, the conductor gave the side of the bus a bang and they nosed out of the parking bay towards the road.

The bus swept downhill, chugged through the townships, purred past the suburbs and cruised out into the green mountain flanks, into the wind, past breathtaking fields of maize and potatoes and sunflowers, whistling round bends through necks of granite jutting out to the very roofs of heaven.

The passengers gazed at the rich farmland and indefatigable stretches of barbed wire claiming it. They looked out at hordes of blacks toiling in the green, the occasional sunhatted farmer strutting among them. They gazed at the khaki farm compounds of grass and dagga spinning past and the children waving and racing after them.

The bus slowed down when a landrover approached. The landrover was driven by a burly white farmer, flanked by two armed black soldiers.

At the end of the farmlands the tarred road died. They rattled on to the gravel. The green died too, spawning haggard rock and clumps of bush, occasional thickets and trickling streams. Goats nibbled on the unfenced wastes where grass huts timelessly perched and women straddled the paths, backs weighted with babies and necks squashed by buckets of water or bundles of wood.

The passengers became silent, entering the communal lands, like a funeral procession arrived. Only the bus rattled on into that convulsive world that seemed to shrivel from the advance.

The bus rattled and the windows rattled and passengers' teeth rattled. Even the conductor's voice rattled when he lowered his dust-powdered face to speak to a passenger. The dust settled on every head. Dozing men, women and children aged years in minutes of dust.

The bus jerked into heavy gears and slowed down. Ahead was a roadblock. Four black soldiers stood with guns across the road.

"All men take out your *situpas* and hold your hands up!" bellowed a stocky black trooper. In the back of a truck parked by the side of the road three white soldiers sat with their shirts off, drinking bottled beer and watching the scene.

A shiver of panic shot through the queue. Hands dug into pockets as condemned men might fumble for their licences to live. The conductor began throwing down bags and suitcases from the top of the bus. Some soldiers checked the *situpas* and others searched the passengers and the bags. Food, blankets and clothes were tossed in the dust.

"Carrying food to the terrorists, eh?"

"What are you doing with all this meat and sugar? Going to feast your terrorists, eh?"

"Why have you got all these new clothes? Who did you buy them for?"

"What do you need this knife for?"

"Put that bag down, *mfana*! Have you got bombs in there?"

"What's this thing, *ambuya*? Why is it tied up in a cloth? Eat it!"

In the middle of the queue, where he stood thumbing his registration certificate, Benjamin felt a wet trickle in his shoe. There, behind him, stood the culprit – an old man desperately clutching at his wet trousers.

"Is this your first time to see soldiers, *mudhara*?" the stocky trooper bellowed.

"Yes . . . No."

"Do you wet your bed when you sleep?"

"No."

"Do you still sleep with your wife?"

"Yes . . . No."

"Why do you have such a long name? Do you think we have time to read long names? Who gave you such a name, *mudhara*?"

"My mother."

"Your mother is an ass, you hear. Say that after me."

"She's dead, *mwanangu*."

"What! You think I care for that? Say it!"

"My mother was an ass."

"Yah, *mudhara*. Do what I tell you if you want to stay alive. Do you still sleep with your wife?"

"I do."

"Do you know what a terrorist is?"

"I've never seen one."

"Aika, *mudhara*? Who are those young men who came to your village and made you sing?"

"I didn't see them."

"They made you sing all night while they slept with your daughters."

"I don't know them."

"And they planted sweet potatoes on the roads."

"I've never heard about them."

"Don't give that shit, *mudhara*. You know those young men. They think they'll drive out the white man and rule this country."

"I've never heard about them."

"You stay away from them, you hear. And stay away from your wife. You're too old for that. Get back on the bus!"

The line moved again. The soldier took Benjamin's certificate and studied it for a while. He looked him up and down.

"Yes, comrade."

Benjamin looked sideways.

"I said hello, comrade! Can't you speak?"

"I can."

"Then answer me. I said hello."

"Hello."

"So, you're a terrorist, aren't you?"

"No."

"I said hello comrade and you answered."

"I was only greeting you."

"How many sweet potatoes have you laid, comrade?"

"None."

"Or are you a *mujhibha* who carries terrorists' food and weapons?"

"No."

"Where are you going, anyway?"

"To Zinyemba."

"Near the border, eh? What business have you got there?"

"I'm visiting an uncle who lives there."

"Oh, an uncle!"

"I have school fees to collect from him."

"Oh, so we're a student, aren't we? Collecting fees from an uncle who lives near the border. What's the name of our uncle?"

"Gilbert Manzou."

"Why didn't Uncle Elephant send the fees by post?"

"There's no post office near his home."

"Gilbert Manzou. It's so easy to make up names, isn't it, comrade? It might have been Gerald Mashumba or Gibson Man'ombe. Or even Garnet Mashiri. So Uncle Gilbert is paying our school fees, eh? Who's he to our father?"

"He's my father's cousin."

"Our father's cousin eh, and paying our fees. Very kind uncle, eh? What does uncle do? Hold up buses and rob them?"

"He grows cotton."

"So we're going to school on good old Uncle Gilbert's cotton money, eh? How many bales did he make last year?"

"Six."

"Six bales when we had a drought, eh? Can I see your school pass?"

"Yes."

"How come there's no official stamp on it?"

"They don't stamp it. Here's my school identity card."

"Visiting your uncle, eh, and we have no luggage?"

"I'm only staying overnight."

"How old are you?"

"Seventeen."

"What form are you doing?"

"Form Four."

"Why are you wearing a denim shirt?"

"I . . . I just put it on."

"Don't you know that's the comrades' uniform?"

"I didn't know."

"Did you see anybody else wearing denim on the bus?"

"No."

"You think you're smarter than everybody else. Stand there!"

Benjamin stepped out of the line. The stocky trooper checked the rest of the people in the line and then turned back to him.

"Now comrade, you better talk straight. Where are you going?"

"I told you to visit my uncle," Benjamin said.

The soldier struck him hard in the face with his open hand.

"Liar! Don't talk to me like I'm your mother's son!" he shouted, kicking him in the back.

His nose ringing, Benjamin glared at the soldiers gathering around him.

One of the white soldiers came up rubbing the muzzle of his gun over his nipples and said, "Is this monkey giving you any trouble, Corporal?"

"I think he's wanting to go to border, Baas," the black trooper explained in English. "He says he visiting his uncle but I cannot trust him."

116

"Has he got his school pass?"

"Yes, but it have no stamp."

The white soldier looked at Benjamin's papers and tossed them back at him.

"Don't you try nothing stupid, boy," he hissed at him, his face crumpling into a vicious sneer. "You better be going to see a real uncle because if you aren't, we'll get you. We have the whole border area manned, jackass!"

"Should we took him with us, Baas?"

"No, let him off," said the white one. "We've no use for him."

As he scrambled back up the steps a boot smashed into his back and he stumbled. With silent faces the passengers watched him as he staggered down the aisle blindly searching for his seat.

The bus creaked forward. He felt the hot, sweet taste of blood in his mouth.

"They killed a suspected passenger right here last week," the bus conductor told him, with an I-know-where-you're-going look. "You're lucky they let you go."

Benjamin said nothing. He licked his bruised underlip and stared past the heads around him at the long yellow stretch of gravel ahead.

Behind a huge rock boulder, at the foot of a low hill, he waited for the young moon to sink.

The cool evening breeze licked his face. His body was still dull from the blows and his lip was swollen. He ate another of the huge mangoes he picked off a tree in the forest and slowly felt his energy returning.

Dozens of times that afternoon his eyes had swept the narrow neck between the mountains. By the time the moon sank the picture was imprinted on his retina and his mind had scaled the sharp face of rock numerous times. He knew there were no more villages here, that between him and the narrow neck were only rocks and trees and grass and animals and, perhaps, human beings.

An owl hooted from a rocky perch above him. Bats shrieked in dark caverns, crickets shrilled and from a direction he couldn't place some night animal grunted in the foliage.

Something came clattering from the sky and whacked the ground in front of him. He saw it, a dislodged piece of deadwood, but with an instinctive stab of terror he was already leaping forward, thrashing through the bush, flinging himself blindly in the dark. Angry at his reckless fear, he stopped, breathless, his head spinning, to listen. The silence stunned him, as if the world had frozen to his stampede. The neck between the mountains loomed above him. Slowly, he began the climb, tugging at the bushes to help him up, stopping every now and then to cock his ears. As he mounted the slope he saw the neck open out into a grassy plateau.

At last he heaved himself on to the edge of the plateau and paused to catch his breath. The slope spilled into a terrifying tangle below him; ahead of him stretched miles of waist-high grass. Beyond the grass – trees, clumps and clumps of trees.

His eyes combed the wings of mountain flanking him. The slopes were sharp and clean, even in the starlight he could make out their bareness, except for one tree-lined curve.

He combed the acres of wavy grass ahead of him and the clumps of trees beyond.

He knew once he got to the clumps of trees he would be there.

Crouching, he crept on all fours through the grass, stopping after a few paces to listen.

At first he couldn't believe it, but when he listened again he heard it – a shiver of grass somewhere on his left, the irregular crunching thump of feet surging and stopping. Raising his knees, he peered out of the grass, to his left. He saw a dark column of figures scurrying through the grass, towards the clumps of trees where he was going. A gun boomed from the mountain flanks behind. He broke into a run. The column of figures broke up and ran too. Some figures crossed his path and others ran on his flanks. They all scrambled for the trees. The gun boomed again behind them.

Benjamin scurried like a leaf in the wind. He tried to detach himself from the group of fugitives but everyone was scrambling desperately towards the clump of trees. He could not disentangle himself without losing speed. He made out six or seven figures in all. The gun had stopped firing but they ran on until they got to the trees. There they slowed down. In the starlight he made out two females and four males. One of the males had a back-pack and the muzzle of a gun stuck out behind his back. In the trees, they were regrouping. Benjamin stepped behind a tree to let them pass but they had spotted him.

"Who are you?" a voice said.

Benjamin froze in his step. When he turned he saw the group spread out in a semi-circle and the man with the back-pack approach him, his unslung gun in his hands.

"Who are you?" the man asked again.

Chapter 16

By the morning, hunger and thirst had sapped the energy remaining in his body. Here there were no mango trees; the forest stretched out relentlessly, save where it suddenly broke into a river or stream and they went on their knees to drink. They splashed water over their bodies and went on in a straggling line, the man with the gun leading.

His legs had gone limp, then stiff as logs, then cottony and now they were dead like clubs of wood to which his socks and shoes stuck. He looked up at the sun and thought it might be two or three in the afternoon. It could have been night, though the sun was shining: his sense of time was disoriented. The previous afternoon seemed ages away, yet the bus ride still throbbed in his swollen lip. The night was a dull ache at the back of his head and dawn was rocks of sleep hanging over his eyes. The afternoon was a shimmering jumble of sun and green.

Towards sunset, a brusque voice challenged them from a tree. They fell to their knees. The man with the gun seemed to expect it. He stepped forward, under the tree and shouted back a few words, some kind of chant. The man in the tree came down, his gun held in his hands. His clothes were khaki green and he had a crown of leaves in his hair. He looked the group up and down and after exchanging a few phrases in guttural tones with their leader, he beckoned them on and climbed back up the tree.

After another half mile, they were challenged again by another man in a tree and the same process was repeated. Then they were in a clearing, suddenly, facing a cluster of tents among the thinned vegetation. More armed men came to meet them.

In the distance, just beyond the cluster of tents, two figures were cooking something over a fire whose smoke diffused in the trees. From further afield came the sound of an axe chopping wood and the rhythmic grunt of people exercising. A young woman in denim carrying a pen behind her ear and a brown file in her hand came out of one tent, spoke to the leader and asked for their names, which she wrote down in the file. When she asked for Benjamin's name the man with the gun said something to her and she stopped writing and then he and two other men took Benjamin into a tent and searched him. They made him take off his clothes and carefully searched his pockets and the linings of his clothes. They even pried his hair with their fingers and broke open the fountain pen he had in his pocket.

After the search he was led out to where the others were and they were given some food. A large dish of warm sadza and beans was placed in front of them. They ate together, ravenously and when they finished they were led to a corner of the clearing into what looked like a hole in the ground. While waiting his turn to step in, Benjamin saw, in the gathering dusk, a large group of men and women marching into the camp from the trees.

They went down a rope ladder into a large underground tunnel which, because it had beams of timber supporting the sides and the ceiling, looked like a disused mine shaft. In the faltering light Benjamin made out the nooks in the tunnel and his feet kicked things in the dark – a wooden stool, a tin cup that clanked. He smelt blankets and cigarette smoke.

They slumped against the warm earth walls, all six of them, four young men and two young women oblivious of each other in their exhaustion. Sleep soon overtook them and they huddled in that womb, deaf to the bustle and singing on the ground above them.

A shaft of light woke him up. The others were climbing out of the tunnel. He sprang to his feet, beat the dust off his clothes and followed them.

He grabbed the rope ladder and climbed out after the others. The sunlight made his eyes smart.

The man who had brought them across the border was waiting for him, and separated him from the others as soon as he surfaced, marching him off to the largest tent in the middle of the clearing. No people moved in the clearing but there were noises and smoke in the bushes around. The man looked into the large tent, saluted sharply and stepped back to let Benjamin in.

Benjamin stooped and stepped into the tent. Sitting over a low collapsible desk was a man in a camouflage uniform – not the type of camouflage Benjamin was used to, but one splashed with yellows, browns and greens. The man was about thirty. He had a fleshy, clean-shaven face with brown eyes that glazed over the details of a scene before taking it in. He had a digital watch on his left wrist and a ring on the little finger of his right hand. The top of the desk was covered with maps and on the maps sat a small transistor radio, a wad of yellow paper, a silver pen and a pistol. Benjamin instantly knew that the man was the camp commander.

The commander motioned to him to sit on the only other chair in the tent.

"Who are you?" the commander asked, his eyes stilling on him.

"My name is Benjamin Tichafa."

"Why are you here?"

Benjamin hesitated and then said, "I was brought here."

The commander put his pen down, clasped his hands over the table and tilted his face, "Who brought you here?"

"The man who showed me to this tent."

"He just got hold of you and brought you here?"

"No, I met him and the others at the border."

"Where were you going when you met them?"

"I was . . . I was coming here."

"What do you mean *here*?"

"Across the border."

"Why? Why did you cross the border?"

"I wanted to find a guerrilla camp."

"A guerrilla camp?"

"I want to join the guerrillas."

"Why?"

"To fight."

"To fight what?"

"To fight . . . the army. The Rhodesian Army."

"You just decided to come here and fight? Are you trained to fight?"

"No. I came to train."

"Where?"

"In a camp."

"What camp?"

"A guerrilla camp."

"Do you know where that guerrilla camp is?"

"Not exactly."

"So you had some kind of idea where it was?"

"A little."

"How would you know where to find the camp?"

122

"I talked to some people before I left."

" Oh, so you talked to people. What kind of people?"

"Well – people. People who knew . . . people who had some knowledge."

"What kind of people?"

"Some students . . . people who had some knowledge."

"What kind of people?"

"Some students . . . and other people at the border, a bus conductor told me how to cross over."

"And these people told you where you would find a guerrilla camp?"

"They gave me directions."

"How did you meet the people you came with?"

"I ran into them at the border and joined them."

"You mean, the man asked you to come with him?"

"He asked me who I was and where I was going and I told him. We were going the same way so I joined them."

"You mean he let you join them, just like that?"

"I just . . . we just ended up together."

"And he told you he and his group were looking for a guerrilla camp?"

"He didn't exactly say that. But I knew . . . I thought we were all going to the same place."

"Well, Benjamin, we had better not keep you here any longer. Since these people you talked to gave you instructions I better let you go where you were going. You've come to the wrong place, my friend."

"But isn't this a guerrilla camp?"

The commander laughed. "Is this what they told you a guerrilla camp would look like?"

"What is this place?"

"That's not for me to tell you, my friend. You know where you want to go."

The commander called the man who had been standing outside the tent and said, "Take him out."

"I don't know any place here," Benjamin pleaded, looking from man to man.

"You came all this way without knowing where you were going? You'll have to do better than that, I'm afraid. I've heard your kind of story before. Look, I'm willing to help you. It was dangerous for you to cross the border all by yourself and it's even more dangerous to proceed on your own. I'll give you two men to accompany you back to the border."

"I do not wish to go back."

"It's dangerous out here. There are enemies in every square mile and even if their bullets and bombs don't get you there's everything against you – starvation, disease, death. It's no life for a young person like you. You are too young to be risking your life this way. I'll help you get back home."

"I don't want to go back home. I want to stay."

"Well, if you aren't going to take my advice you leave me no other choice."

They took him underground once more.

He sat, alone, in the dark, listening to the confusing noises above him. He was so sure this was a guerrilla camp. He was aware that his meeting with a group at the border might have been unusual, but he could not understand why the commander was trying to send him back.

He took off his shoes and socks and peeled strips of dead skin from between his toes. A thick film of dirt coated his teeth. His breath was sour. He wished he could have a cup of water and a toothbrush – or at least a piece of chewing stick – to rinse his mouth. He put his nose in his shirt and recoiled from the stench of sweat and dust and his unwashed flesh. His crotch smelt like spoiling cabbage. He ran a hand through the jungle of uncombed hair and wiped his mouth on the collar of his shirt.

He thought of the last three days and could not believe what had happened to him – the train and bus rides, the soldiers at the roadblock, the race through the grass and now this underground tunnel. And he thought of the week before those three days, at the mission school, arguing over the newspapers, writing posters – a week seething with anger and fear and hysteria. Now, for the first time, the wreck of that week loomed large and clear in his mind. He seemed to have been catapulted through it all by some force he had not recognized, some force that had pitched him through a blur of crowds and places and events and plunged him, alone, into the dark bowels of this dilemma.

Where was he now and why was he here where he was? Who was he to be here, in this pit? Why had he come here, if only to be down here, in this pit? What was to happen to him? Would anyone out there in the world know he was here, where he was? When would his mother know? What would she do when she knew what she was going to know and had to know? Would she try to hang herself again? Would she wear black and weep? Or would she disown him? What would his father say? Would he rage and roar or would he lock himself in months of silence? Would anyone ever know what happened to him when what would happen happened to him? What would happen to him? Who would know what happened to him when what was going to happen happened? When would they take him out and what would they do when they took him out if they took him out? How had he got here? How could he have come here? Who would have thought a week before he would end up here? What fit of courage could have made him dream of ever ending up here? Why was he now suddenly afraid?

When would they bring him food?

They came for him at dawn. He slumped into the chair in front of the commander.

"Who sent you here?"

The commander's voice thumped like a rock against his mind. He stared at the commander. The commander sat there in his crisp camouflage and digital watch and clean-shaven face and glazed eyes with the transistor radio and the yellow wad of paper and the silver pen and the pistol on the maps spread on the desk. He sat as if he had sat there all night, without moving. He moved his pistol carefully on the map.

"You're a spy!"

The commander's hand balled into a fist and he banged the table. The commander banged the table and his forehead furrowed in anger.

"You're a spy!"

His body was stiff with hunger and his mind blank with shock. He tried to speak, but the words bolted back into him.

"No," he wept. "No."

The commander moved his pistol carefully on the map. He pumped his wristwatch back up his wrist. "What were you doing at the border?" the commander said. "Why did you come alone, without contacting anybody? Why did you suddenly appear when the soldiers started firing? Why were you *alone*? How could you come all the way without knowing where you were going? How did you get through the lines of soldiers unless they helped you across?

"No. No."

The commander moved his pistol carefully on the map.

"I'm giving you the last chance. You were foolish to come here. Because you're a young man I'm willing to help you. I'm giving you the last chance to leave this place. My men will accompany you back to the border. I'm letting you off only on one condition – that you tell whoever sent you that you did not find the information they wanted you to find."

"No. I don't want to go back."

"Why? Because they'll kill you?"

"I just can't."

"You're wasting my time, my friend. Do you know what I normally do with spies?"

"I'm not a spy! I came here to fight. I left school . . . they wanted to force us into the army. I can't go back. Please, let me stay."

"Who doesn't want you back?"

"The police, my headmaster . . . they have my name on record."

"So you're a criminal eh? What did you do? Steal something?"

"When I was a child, I, we burnt down a beerhall . . ."

"Burning down beerhalls doesn't make you a freedom fighter. It doesn't prove you're not a spy."

"We went on a demonstration last week. My school. They already had my name in their records . . ."

"What demonstration?"

"Against black call-up."

The commander leaned back in his chair and moved his pistol carefully on the map. "Tell me about the demonstration," he said.

Chapter 17

At dawn there was the ten-mile run through the forest in a snake formation, along a faintly beaten track through the trees, with the leaves an oily shiver, the grass a yellow breeze and the sky a fling of orange above. Three hundred chanting figures, a fifth to a quarter of them women, in T-shirts, short sleeves, shorts, jeans, khakis and the occasional tracksuit.

The first morning he ran he chugged back into the camp at the tail end, his chest boiling, the blood stabbing through his lungs, pounding in his ears. He plunged to his knees, clutching handfuls of grass, clinging to his consciousness. Then it was over, slowly. The blood and salt were in his mouth, his vision stilling.

"Here we run, comrade," the commander sneered down at him. "Not running from police dogs – real running!"

On the second day he remembered the advice of a former athletics master, and controlled his breath and his pace. He arrived last again, but in an endurable state.

"You still have a long way to go, Mr Politician," the commander said. "You still run as if you are on a demonstration. Forget the goat-butting nonsense of placards. Here we run carrying *rocks* on our back!"

After the run there were press-ups on the grass, the commander chanting through the maze of stretching bodies. Every inch of his body aching, sweat-salt glistening on his body under the drenched shirt, he joined the queue for the ladle of porridge and a tin mug of milkless, sugarless tea.

After breakfast there was the camp to clean and sometimes toilet trenches to dig and bushes to clear, water to fetch in large drums rolled down to the river and back; bathing to do, behind a wall of grass thatch, scooping up the water from a tin bath and scrubbing at his back with the thin cake of blue soap. And then he would borrow a comb from somebody and snatch at his greasy bramble of hair, scrape his teeth with a piece of green stick and, given this temporary reprieve from sweat and dust, soothed by the scent of blue soap on him, he would lie with the others in the shadows of the trees.

Lunch was a lump of sadza and two or three small, salted fish you had to nibble carefully, like a mother pecking at a bit of food to encourage her child to eat, to get you through the sadza. When it became cool in the afternoon there were lectures on bush warfare, sketches made on a piece of portable chalkboard and notes assiduously taken down in little yellow notebooks using stubby pencils.

Afterwards there were practice routines using ropes, large circular shaped rings and logs planted to simulate some aspect of the terrain – chasms to swing over, heights to scale, ledges to cross, slopes to roll down . . .

Shadows stretched and birds flew home to roost and the sun set; darkness swooped from the sky like a conspiracy and another day died, swiftly, so you almost lost count of what day it was and how long you had been in the camp; and if you were on the cooking roster you went down to feed the fire with faggots and make sadza in the large drums, shovelling platefuls of yellow maize meal into the hissing water and stirring with wooden poles, mashing it up smoothly, stirring always, squashing the lumps and grinding the spray of dry meal back into the porridgy mass, stepping back to stop your head popping off into the hot roar and to shake the shower of sweat from your face while your roster mates dug at the drums or tended the beans, and if there was a girl in your roster to know how much water to put in the beans, or how many half tin-mugs of salt to use, or how to turn the fish so it wouldn't turn to mush then it was easier and you soon had it done, and then you would let the sadza sizzle and chortle and hiss and puff for a while before you slapped a palmful of leaves to the edge of the drum and jerked it off the fire, quickly, before the heat melted your fingers; and if you had a girl in your roster and she wasn't too strong and she didn't clutch the drum tightly enough and it slipped she would hiss at her roasting fingers and the drum lurched and landed like a pig falling off a cart, an inch from your feet, almost slicing off your toes and the girl turned and ploughed into you to steady herself and her breasts whipped into your chest and you smelt the blue soap and fresh sweat and girl flesh smell on her and you steadied the drum and tried to grin at her, if you weren't too shaken and then you'd give the drum one last pounding and turn round to serve the waiting queue and after serving everybody you reached with a plate to the bottom of the drum to serve yourself, leaning over and burying your head down into the yellow pit, and you scooped up rocks of sadza, carefully, so that you didn't rake up the sooty cakes at the bottom and you fished into the brown lake in the bucket for beans, and you ate, quickly, knowing there were the drums to wash and the fire to put out ...

And then you ran off, through the darkened tents to the clearing where the others sat having the political discussion session, and you found a place on the grass and sat down carefully so as not to raise too much dust and you folded back your legs and clasped them at the ankles so you didn't toe the back in front of you and you sat there and listened, your fist raised over your head, stabbing the air, chanting slogans and you heard about capitalism and socialism and democracy and equitable distribution of wealth and racism and discrimination and equal rights and injustice and justice and the Land Apportionment Act and segregation and exploitation and neo-colonialism and many other words you had never heard before and you gasped to be told five per cent of the population owned the better half of Rhodesia and earned more than the other ninety-five per cent together, that they had the best jobs, homes, schools, hospitals – everything – because their skin was lighter than yours; you heard it all, sitting there under the grass miles from nowhere and the stars above said yes, yes, and you knew you had grown up quietly with it and taken it for granted all along, you knew it when you left home and left school but you didn't *really* know it, until this hunger and this darkness and these stars and now hearing it made the anger eat you like pepper in your nose and you wondered how you had been so blind and passive; and you sang songs and someone beat a drum and you danced there on the grass and then you felt good dancing with everybody else and you tried not to think about home or what would happen to you or about the ten-mile run at dawn and you danced and sang and stabbed the air with your fist ...

And you heard people talk, some who said they had been thrown out of schools or jobs or denied work or pushed out of their villages and some whose families had been killed or maimed and whose homes had been bombed – their voices filled you with outrage ...

And then you sang and danced again, loudly so you heard the echoes from the sky and you wondered why the soldiers at the border didn't hear the noise or if they did when they would come and then at last you dispersed to your tents to sleep and sometimes you heard the armed people who guarded the camp shuffling through the foliage and you pulled at your scratchy piece of brown blanket and tried to make yourself comfortable on a grass mattress somebody had made and perhaps you heard a girl cough in the next tent and you tried to fall asleep and not to think about her or about home and what the people there were thinking and then perhaps you heard voices muttering in the night and caught the whiff of tobacco on the air that made you think of your last packet of cigarettes on the train and you wondered if a prayer was worth saying and you closed your eyes and tried to sleep and you heard sounds out there in the night like animals moving and snakes rustling in the grass and you looked out through the open end of the tent at the piece of unconcerned sky and the stars nodding and blinking way up there and you slowly slid into sleep and dreamt perhaps about eating rice and chicken on Sunday evenings at the school dorm or your mother baking a cake in the wood stove or people praying in a hospital or a bloated corpse creaking in the tree . . .

Still, you had no gun and you only marched with a wooden model they showed you how to carve out of a block of wood; you had more exercises and more lectures and still you had no gun . . .

Days passed and weeks passed and your body steeled with running. Wedded to river water and maize meal and beans, your stomach lusted for the smells from the fires. Your back jilted memories of mattresses and your skin closed to insect bites. You made peace with your mane of hair or mowed it down, like a chastened bride.

Still, you had no gun.

More people came into the camp, some brought by guerrillas and others on their own and sometimes there was somebody down there underground and some of the guerrillas left and others came and you had different people training you at different times, and the camp grew and grass shelters sprouted on the fringes of the tents.

And sometimes you talked to these people and if you were lucky you found one or two of them who came from your town or had even been to your school but you couldn't talk too long to them and you didn't tell them your real name and they called you only by your war name. Still, you had no gun and sometimes you heard firing in the distance and your heart beat wildly and you were relieved when the guards brought back a buck or buffalo they had killed and you knew it wasn't fighting and there would be fresh meat with the beans.

130

Then, suddenly, one day they told you you would be moving to another camp. You left the camp, as abruptly as you had arrived, with nothing to pack, taking with you only your new war name, leaving behind those people you had begun to know and that girl you cooked with and perhaps flirted with at the dances. You left, marching with the others through the bush to the road. You were surprised to see the gravel of a road again and to think there were still roads, roads leading somewhere to homes and unravaged lives and then you remembered you were in another country, a country that had gone through a similar war and was now helping you. And then a lorry or a truck came, chugging in the blinding heat and you jumped in with the others and you took off, with no time for nostalgia, ploughing up a fury of dust behind you, heading for some new place . . .

Chapter 18

There were over three thousand people in the new camp, two-thirds of them women and children. There might have been eight or ten other camps like that, flung, within several days' walking distance of each other, over that great sweep of country.

Every week the numbers swelled. Combatants, refugees, people caught in crossfire, fugitives whose tongues were clamped by the horror they had left behind, whose muted eyes spoke of suffering.

The crying of babies announced sunrise in the civilian camp, then the camp wrenched to life with a bustle of activities; women tending children, clothes, nappies, blankets and fires, shuttling to and fro with pieces of kitchenware or baggage in their hands, making short, jerky motions typical at crowded railway station waiting-rooms or large country hospitals. The air hung thick with the smell of babies, blankets and smoke.

And on the military side muscles were already aching ...

His new name was Pasi NemaSellout and he lived with the other combatants in the tents on the military side of the camp. From the storeroom he got a green beret and a spotted brown T-shirt, one size too large. The boots he would get if and when the next consignment arrived.

There he fired his first gun.

He fired his first gun in the forest, just outside the camp, kneeling in front of the others, when his turn came.

The machine was much lighter than he had expected. Clutching it firmly with both hands, he carefully coiled a finger round the trigger and pulled. The bullet tossed the block of wood over.

He handed the gun over and stepped back, stunned, his nose stung by the heat of the metal. His hands still shook from the recoil, under the cotton wool muffs his ears were deaf to the soft applause around him.

One day as he was walking to his tent after the shooting practice he met a girl escorting a young boy to the refugee section of the camp.

The girl was slim and dark, wearing a denim dress. She might have been eighteen but looked younger: were it not for the lines over her eyes and the dark hardened knuckles on her hands he might have thought she was fourteen.

"Have you seen Comrade Utano?" she asked him, spreading her dark, slender, fingers over the boy's head like a footballer's hand on a ball.

"Who?" he said, his eyes fixing back at hers.

"Comrade Utano. He's in charge of the medical supplies."

"I don't think I know him."

"This boy is not well," she said, holding the boy's cheeks in her two hands, so that his lower lip fell out, slightly.

"Is he your brother?" he asked, for want of something better to say, trying to evade the girl's fixing eyes, somehow.

"No," she said, with a short, abrupt laugh that left lines over her eyes. "He's in my class. I'm one of the camp teachers. You wouldn't have any pain killers on you – disprin or something?"

She gave him an anxious look, her mouth open, eyes flickering in poised, concentrated sockets. He shook his head. The tightness on her face melted, hung back on the thin sides. Her long fingers kneaded the boy's head again, crushing him to her pelvis.

"Something's happening to these kids," she said, suddenly searching the pockets of her denim dress, as if she had on her somewhere a twist of toffee to give to the child. She fished into the front part of her dress, into the well of her breasts and there it was, a packet of cigarettes.

She plucked one from the box, lit it with nervous, hungry fingers and sucked on it once lit. But she choked on it. It made her cough, as if she was learning to smoke. She looked at him, suddenly, and held out the packet to him, as if it had occurred suddenly to her it was him who had to smoke.

He received it too readily, like a child snatching a precious something denied him a long time. He had not smoked in weeks, his last puff was from a twist of raw farm tobacco rolled up in a piece of newspaper – got from a comrade he shared a tent with once.

"My name is Ropa. What's yours?"

"Benjamin."

"Is that your war name?"

"No. Pasi. Pasi NemaSellout."

"I should have stopped smoking long ago, because it makes my cough worse. I can't believe how it started," she said, as if about to launch into the history of her habit but then suddenly she fixed him another of her abrupt looks, some new urgency biting at her back. "Hey, are you in a hurry?"

"No, why?"

"Come and sit in on my class. We'll pretend you're . . . what do they call those people from the head office of the Ministry of Education?"

"Education Officers."

"Yes. You can comment on my teaching afterwards."

"All right," he managed a laugh.

He followed her and the boy down the leafy path, past a group of women pumping up water at the borehole to water a garden. They walked through another garden where three boys of about twelve were tending a small crop of cabbages and tomatoes.

She said something to the boys, bent over, lifted a handful of grass from a seedbed and flicked at a lump of clay with her fingernails.

"This is our school garden," she told him.

Under the trees ahead there were eighty or ninety children, boys and girls with ages ranging from six to fifteen, all seated on the ground, heads bowed intently over exercise books.

The school is not just some idea flitting through her head, then, he thought.

The children were doing a maths assignment chalked up on a blackboard. Every now and then six, eight heads would look up from the ground, and eyes like birds would go whirring to the board, the little mouths clutching grubs of knowledge for the stubby pencils to peck at. A cough punctuated the silence, and sometimes a ripple as two, three heads consulted, timidly at first, the chirping getting bolder, and then without warning there came a blunt trumpet sound, breaking the silence like old cloth tearing and a chorus of protests and a hymn of boos sprung up and all at once the sacred exercise books were fanning laughing faces.

"Who's that?" said Ropa, taking charge, a laugh flickering at the corners of her mouth. "What did you eat last night? Are the problems too hard? Put up your hand if you need help."

Ten, twelve hands shot up. She went round explaining and when she had finished said, "All right. Let's put the maths books away. It's time for English now. We have with us today Comrade Pasi, who has come to observe the lesson."

One hundred eyes, round with curiosity, veered on Pasi, trained on him for several seconds, and turned back to Ropa. Pasi smiled wryly and fingered his beret, wishing he could have looked more presentable to make his role credible.

"We'll have a vocabulary exercise using the letters of the alphabet. Let's all say that word vo-ca-bu-la-ry."

"Vo-ke-byu-ra-ri!" chanted eighty gleeful voices.

"Good. What is the first letter of the alphabet?"

Sixty hands shot up, fingers snapping. The teacher paced round the class, casting her head from side to side, taunting the shy and undecided.

Arms cracked up, unfurled and followed her like sunflowers.

"Nhamo."

A seven-year-old boy sprang to his feet and said, "Aaaa."

"*Ei*," disputed an older voice, a girl who looked ten or eleven.

"That's all right," said Ropa, writing the letter on the board. "There are two ways of saying it, depending on whether you're speaking English, or Shona or Ndebele. Who can give words beginning with the letter 'a'? Yes?"

"Aeroplane!"

"Army!"

"Against!"

"Apple!"

"Enemy!"

"Enemy?" Ropa quizzed, dropping her hand from the board where she was writing up correct responses. "Does *enemy* begin with an 'a'?"

"It begins with an 'e'."

"Let's have two more words. Two more words beginning with an 'a'."

"America!"

"Yes, but that's the name of a country."

"Among!"

"Good! Now let's make sentences using each of these words. Who can make a sentence using the word '*aeroplane*'? Yes . . ."

"An aeroplane were flying in the sky."

"There is something wrong with that sentence. A little mistake," she pressed finger and thumb. "Who can correct her? Yes, Mabasa."

"An aeloprane was swimming in the sky."

A burst of laughter.

"No, Mabasa. You have made the sentence worse. Aeroplanes don't swim, do they? Who can correct the sentence? Yes . . ."

"An aeroplane *was* flying in the sky."

"Very good. What must you all do if you see an aeroplane flying in the sky? Yes, Sithembile."

"I wave to it."

A chorus of boos.

"At home you can wave to an aeroplane. But should you wave to it here, in the camp? *Ungabhaibhisa ndege muno mucamp*? Kefasi, what would you do?"

"Take cover," said a nine-year-old boy in a torn T-shirt.

"Can you show us how to take cover, Kefasi?"

The boy stepped out of the crowd, ducked under a bush and threw himself flat on the ground with his hands clamped over his head. A burst of applause went up. He stood up, dusted his clothes and returned to his place in the crowd.

"Very good, Kefasi. Next word, *army*. Yes, Vongai."

"The big army . . ." muttered a ten-year-old girl, with a dull stare.

"Yes, go on. Complete your sentence."

"The big army . . ." repeated the girl, her chest heaving as if she were trying to pump out something stuck inside her.

"Yes, what did the big army do? Go on, complete your sentence. What did the big army do?"

"Was burnt a house . . ."

Laughter. The girl stared around her.

"Say that again. Join the two parts."

"The big army was burnt a house . . ." the girl insisted.

"The big army burnt a house. Say that after me."

"The big army burnt a house . . ."

"All right. Next word. *Against*. Who hasn't said anything this morning?"

A forest of fingers snapped at her.

"Muchadei."

"The comrades fought against the army."

"Very good. Another sentence using *against*. Yes . . ."

"The car bumped against a mountain."

Ropa raised her eyes helplessly. She pondered the construction for a moment.

"Is that correct?"

"Crashed," said a voice.

"Yes. The car crashed . . . over a mountain."

The rest of the words were discussed and the class went on to the letters 'b' and 'c'.

"Do you want to teach them for a while?"

Pasi shrugged and shook his head. He did not think he could survive one minute up there, with those eager hands mobbing him. Ropa snatched an exercise book and ticked furiously, as if she had to have the whole pile done in thirty minutes.

"We have no textbooks and the children are all of different ages," she told him. She turned back to the class and said, "Now I want you to write nine sentences in your books, using some of the words we discussed."

Pasi marked half a dozen books. Some of the work was surprisingly good and some was pathetic.

"Sometimes I just put a big tick when I'm too tired to mark any more," she told him, lowering her voice so the interested ears at the back of the class would not hear. "How far did you go with school?"

"I got expelled in my 'O' Level year for demonstrating against black call up," he told her.

"I just walked out of school. Can you imagine that? A group of guerrillas came to our school and talked to us and six girls decided to come over. The guerrillas were so bold, calling a meeting although soldiers were patrolling the area. There had just been a contact in the area and some soldiers had been killed. The army bombed a village in retaliation. We decided to leave. I was one of the six. I was in my 'O' Level year too. I was fed up with our headmistress. She was a blatant racist. Even the other white staff members were embarrassed by her. If I were a combatant she'd be the first person I'd hunt down!"

"Aren't you being trained to fight?"

"A little. Just to know how to react to emergencies. I'll probably stay here teaching or be moved to another camp. Not many girls are being sent out to fight, these days. Do you think this war will ever be over?"

"I don't know."

"When are you going to be deployed?"

"I haven't been told yet. I've only been here three weeks."

"You should be going out soon. People who come here are usually deployed after five or six weeks. Aren't you afraid?"

He shrugged. She ticked at another smudgy book. He had never really thought about going to fight. Not yet. He had been too busy just trying to cope with changes. Now the thought of it made his heart race.

Ropa walked round the class to inspect the progress of the new assignment. "No," she'd say to one pupil, "I want you to write only three sentences using 'a' words," or "This word is wrongly spelt," or "This does not make sense."

Pasi was so sure if he had to do it the talking alone would exhaust him.

"What's wrong with you?" she asked a young girl who kept walking off towards the grass every fifteen minutes.

The girl put a hand to her belly.

"Mabasa, go and look for Comrade Utano. Tell him we need help."

The boy ran off and Ropa came to Pasi and said again, "I'm worried about these children."

Already he felt urges of intimacy towards her. He thought she was slender because of marking books and worrying about the children. Perhaps she had had more weight, once. Her voice and her eyes and her mouth and her long fingernails excited him but her abrupt, restless manner, the lines over her eyes, the way she would laugh one moment and be so quiet the next, disturbed him. He could tell she was about his age. Her age and her younger looks excited him, but this excitement was tinged with fear, that hypocritical boyish fear of blood and saliva – the adolescent male fear of a woman's braided locks.

Months of running and exercise had made him almost forget the little he knew about how to talk to a girl. He had not had a girlfriend yet and he had talked to girls with the reckless banter one used with classmates. He had never talked to a girl in an intimate way before and her openness took him by surprise.

Suddenly he realized how long he had been here with her and her class, how somebody might be looking for him on the other side of the camp, where the combatants lived.

"I have to go now," he told her.

"So what do you think of my teaching?" she asked with anxious eyes.

"You're so good with them."

She smiled, then said, turning to the path, "Here comes Comrade Utano."

Utano was a massive man with a round, fleshy face and huge feet strapped up in black boots. He wore bush camouflage and a machine gun slung over his shoulder. In one hand he carried a first-aid kit. He had given two lectures to the training combatants – on primary health care, with an expertise which had impressed Benjamin. Perhaps he might have been a university medical student or a science student before he came to the bush.

Benjamin stood at attention and Utano responded with a nod. "This is Comrade Pasi," Ropa quickly explained. "He came to sit in on my class and help with some marking."

Benjamin fiddled uneasily with the red pen Ropa had given him. Utano gave him a half officious smile and then turned to Ropa.

"Have you been having any problems with the children?"

"Several of them seem to be having stomach trouble."

"I hope it's not what I think," said Utano, grimly opening his kit.

"What is it?" Ropa asked, peering into his face. "Is it dysentery?"

"It might be. And we haven't had any fresh supplies of drugs from H.Q. I have enough for only the critical cases. A couple of mothers have reported the same problem with their infants. How many have you here?"

Ropa called out the boy and girl who were sick to come and receive tablets, and counted them out into their palms herself.

"Take two right away," she told them, "and two more before you go to sleep."

The two sick children cupped the tablets in their palms and went off towards the borehole.

"Let me know if there's any more trouble," Utano said, shutting his kit. "When do I see you again?"

"I don't know . . ." Ropa muttered.

Utano grinned at her, nodded vaguely at Benjamin and went back the way he had come.

"He wants me, imagine," Ropa told Benjamin, after the other man had left. "He's the one who brought me the cigarettes. But his wife is here, in the camp. She trains the women. I think she knows he's after me but she hasn't said anything to me. If you were me what would you do?"

"I don't know." He gave her back the pen and adjusted his beret.

"I'm giving them a test tomorrow," she told him, and the children at the back who heard her hissed and grimaced schoolishly with anticipation. "Maybe if you have time you can help me mark the papers. If you have time."

"All right."

He hurried back to the other side of the camp. At the garden he turned and saw Ropa's class bustling over pots of food some women had brought.

The children held their plates face high and their teacher, barely taller than half of them, walked about arranging them into groups, pulling a child over, counting heads, like a young Sunday-school teacher supervising a church picnic. The children's voices were loud and hungry and impatient – almost frantic. He could hear Ropa's voice, sharp and tremulous and urgent, touched now and then with a brief schoolmistress anger which broke, almost immediately, into helpless laughter.

When he got back to his camp he was told the supplies officer had been looking for him, to give him a pair of boots. He promptly went to the supplies tent but found all the right sizes given away already, so he had to make do with a pair which was half a size too small and pinched his toes.

That night he limped around in the hurting shoes, knowing that the sooner he started getting accustomed to them the better.

There was excitement in the camp – a truckload of new arms had arrived in the afternoon and the group commanders were busy planning their distribution. Pasi glimpsed a crate of brand-new machine guns and felt a strange wave of excitement. The hot metallic power of the weapon was still alive in his nose.

That night as they sat through a lecture on mobilization of the peasantry, he heard the noises of children singing and playing to a drum over in the civilian side of the camp. He thought he heard Ropa's voice among the excited cries but then it occurred to him that it might be somebody else's voice, one of the mothers, perhaps. He thought about the brand-new guns too. He remembered Ropa asking him what he felt about deployment and suddenly he wondered if after the lecture he could sneak off to the other side of the camp and find her.

He could creep off and look for her, but he wasn't sure where she slept or who he would ask. He wasn't even sure what he would say to her if he did find her – the thought made his heart race. He might run into the camp guards too and get mistaken for an intruder. The more he thought about going to look for her the more ridiculous the idea became.

He sat there on the grass, smelling the tang of his new boots and remembered the quiet shimmer of those guns in the crate. His nose seemed to fill with the smell of metal and new leather. The noises of the children washed up to his ears.

He listened to the lecture, trying hard to concentrate. Sweat trickled down his armpits; he was excited and anxious all at once.

And then the lecture was over and he was going to his tent, going to sleep with the others. The laughing and singing on the other side of the camp had died out, imperceptibly. Out there she must be asleep, with the children, perhaps. The quietness of the trees and the dark orderliness of the tents mocked his plans of going to look for her.

In the morning, they were given guns.

His had his number on it, a number he had to remember like a second name.

Over the next two days they learnt how to break and clean and fix and unfix bayonets to, the guns. They were each given a few precious bullets to test with and after using the guns they returned them to the underground armoury.

When he went down to look for Ropa he found her classes cancelled. Many of the children were down with dysentery and those who were well sat in groups chattering or playing games. Ropa was shuttling to and fro, giving them tablets. She wasn't laughing so much. She looked worried and that made him awkward and nervous. He felt guilty about wasting her time amidst such illness. The sickness around her made her restless, snatched away the promise of her voice.

For days the dysentery raged in the camp, fanned by the shortage of medicines. Some of the combatants caught it too. Two infants died. Pasi's stomach stretched, then shuddered. For two days he waited with dread for the violent purge. Then the pain eased mysteriously, as if he had imagined it all. He was miraculously spared.

He saw his comrades run dozens of times to the trenches and thought himself lucky.

Chapter 19

Once upon a time, every mother was her own household's doctor. Every household had its crushed herbs – its bottled concoctions. Once in a while epidemics overwhelmed the herbs and families would be wiped out, but always there were survivors.

Even today secret powers shake on us strange diseases that scoff at doctors' needles and then, with feeble last hopes, our mothers remember.

Every mother still has a hoe. Sometimes she digs in the early morning, sometimes she digs at dusk. She takes off her socks and high heels and sneaks off into the bush when there is nobody to see her.

When she has a baby, she sneaks off with her hoe, or somebody who knows brings her something.

Every place has a bush, even suburbs. Every metre of earth teems with roots. Bulbous plants curl out of the concrete foundations of houses, dead poles leaf through the mud coating of huts, tendrils announce themselves on doorsteps.

If she doesn't know she asks. She asks quietly, with the low tones of one whose past has been battered by other intelligences.

Now in that camp there were mothers. The epidemic shook them from the slumber and they remembered. Some of them knew, some had forgotten. Others had never known . . .

Some men knew too.

So when the drugs ran out they turned to the forest.

They dug roots from the ground. They crushed them and mixed them with water and drank the potions.

The epidemic raged rebelliously – six, eight, eleven, died – crushing hope in the camp. Then there was a lull, root fighting germ, nature versus nature, while humans waited. Perhaps it was simple, desperate faith.

The deaths stopped.

Five, six days after laughter had begun to return, a man from the resistance radio came to the camp to record a show.

The whole camp came together – women, children, combatants. Songs were sung, speeches were made and greetings and messages were even recorded live, to be broadcast to avid listeners in Rhodesia.

Ropa's class sang two songs and recited poems. After they finished and dispersed back into the crowd, she passed by Pasi, who was standing at the back of the crowd and said, laughing, "We only practised twice."

"They sang well," he told her.

"We missed out a whole stanza of the song," she fretted. "Everyone must have noticed! Didn't you?"

She looked as if she was about to go. A group of women had gone into the arena and were dancing, in a caterpillar formation, jerking their hips provocatively to the drum. The crowd was cheering. She told him she had something to collect from her side of the camp – a copy of the register of the children – for the radio man to take to the headquarters for the records. He offered to come with her.

They left the crowd and shuffled through that darkened camp, and when they got to the civilian side she paused in front of one of the round squat grass shelters and said, chuckling, "This is the schoolmistress's house."

They stooped through the mouth of the shelter. He had to bend so as not to rake the roof with his head. She fumbled on the floor, struck a match and lit a paraffin lamp.

There was a grass mattress, a blanket, an afro comb, a cake of blue soap, a little bottle of vaseline, a small plastic bag of cotton wool and two piles of khaki exercise books.

She fished under one pile of exercise books and brought out a brown manila file.

"There's one name I forgot to strike out," she said, almost talking to herself, running a fingernail over the list of names.

He knelt on one knee and looked over her shoulder, into the file. The first names were written in small letters and the family names in capital letters. The other columns showed dates of birth, names of distant towns and villages which, though familiar to him, somehow looked obscure and distant on that brown paper. Several names, six, seven maybe, were crossed out from the list and now she was crossing out another name.

"This one died last week."

He had seen the women come back from the bush, quietly, with hands clasped behind their backs, and wash their hands, one after the other, in a tin of water.

She closed the file. She showed him another book, and said, "These are my poems."

He flipped through the book – there were scores of poems scribbled out in her bold, galloping handwriting, most no longer than two stanzas, with lines struck out as if they had been hurriedly written. They were all about the war.

He had never had much feeling for poetry but the lines amused him. Her face was hovering near his, flickering, in the yellow light, for approval.

"I haven't shown them to any one. I just write at night, when I have nothing else to do . . ."

Suddenly he knew he would hold her.

Her mouth smelt of cigarettes, but it wasn't the strong smell he had expected. Her tongue wasn't dripping wet as he had imagined another person's tongue would be. It had a half-salty taste, as if she had just eaten a strip of seasoned biltong. Her body smelt of vaseline, with a touch of dust and her hair of blankets, soap and fire. He felt her fingernails on his neck, his face, his chest, her blouse, her hands directing his face to her breasts, her hands holding his face to her breasts.

Her nipples in his mouth.

His hands stroking her, squeezing, pressing, afraid to be stopped, searching for her centre . . .

"I'll be alright in two days," she said, stopping him. She blew out the light and they went out of the hut.

Dazedly he followed her back towards the noise of the crowd.

He woke to an unusual noise.

It was like several loud sirens increasing in noise, bursting into explosions and fading out.

A confusion of cries erupted in the dawn. He leapt through the opening of the tent, into the dust and smoke and scrambled for the trees. In the yellow light there were figures everywhere, bolting, stumbling.

The whine came again, crashing through the sky. A dozen Hunter planes streaked past, leaving mushrooms of smoke in their wake. He was thrown to the ground by the vibration. Coughing in the dust, blinded by smoke, he leapt over a burning tent, stumbling over bodies entangled in the rubble.

In the lull he heard voices shouting, yelling, screaming, feet crashing through the foliage and he ran through the trees.

New sounds converged from the sky – the chugging of helicopters. A ring of helicopters swept over the camp, closing the fugitives in.

An arc of people turned back and ran the way they had come, back to the centre. Bodies were mowed down by the guns in the helicopters.

He scurried through the frantic herd turning back towards the centre. Leaves rained down on him, bullets stitched the rocks on either side of him.

He saw children ahead of him, scattering into the grass. A naked woman passed him, charging through the bushes, arms flailing, her big flabby breasts whipping around her, and, ahead of him, two combatants were swinging an anti-aircraft gun out of the foliage.

The helicopters plunged over the rim of trees ahead, where he was going, spilling into a wider circle, sweeping the people back in. The children turned back to the centre. Ahead of him the big naked woman rocked in the air and plunged. Still he chugged on, past her, over a string of small bodies, away from the camp.

He was in the open, squelching through the garden. Cabbages rocked around him, pumped full of lead. Bullets whined at his ears, and still he ran.

The helicopters converged on the centre, hovered there, spitting fire, and they dived again, outwards, spinning a new, bigger net. Behind him he heard the boom of anti-aircraft guns and the roar of guerrilla AK 47s above the *knock, knock, knock* of Rhodesian FNs followed by the screech of metal. Two of the helicopters spun, belching smoke and plunged into the trees. The guns boomed again and the remaining helicopters spread out, made one last blazing sweep over the camp and vanished into the horizon.

He pumped through the trees, until he got to the river. Breathless, he fell to his knees. Above the roar of his heart he heard noises from the camp – voices screaming and yelling, fires crackling.

The sun had come up and birds were twittering. He stood up and slowly crept back to the camp.

The forest was strewn with bodies and pieces of clothing. A woman wrapped in a blanket ran into him, hands clamped to her head, screaming and stamping the ground with her feet.

A naked boy lay on a rock, clasping an arm half-eaten away by napalm.

He saw two girls crawl out of a toilet pit, completely covered with filth.

At an anti-aircraft artillery post a combatant knelt over his comrade who had been shot in the head.

He stumbled on to one of the smouldering wrecks of burnt-out helicopters. Two Rhodesian soldiers had been flung out of the burning wreck and sprawled dead on an anthill. Their blue eyes gaped, almost alive, out of skins which for some reason had been greased black. The front part of the helicopter looked like the skull of a huge bird. In it he saw two more charred forms, huddled over guns.

The centre of the camp was a hive of fires. A group of men were beating out the flames with green branches. It seemed for every broken, fumbling figure stumbling through that smoke, there was a mangled body, a disembodied leg or hand, a mass of napalmed limbs, a chunk of charred flesh, on the ground, in a bush.

A combatant charged through the smoke with a machine gun raised high in one hand, screaming, "Bastards! Bastards!" A group of men ran carrying crates of undamaged guns and ammunition away from the fires, under the supervision of the commander.

He picked up an abandoned branch and beat out a fire, mechanically, with a frenzied energy. Suddenly he was running through the fires, through the broken clusters of men, women and children. He sprang from blazing hut to blazing hut, ducking his head between tongues of fire, turning up bodies on the ground to look at their faces.

He saw the woman wrapped in a blanket again, darting like a beheaded hen ahead of him, feet stamping. A group of armed combatants came in carrying injured children in their arms.

"Ropa! Ropa!" he shouted.

She sprawled face down, under the tree that had been her classroom, clutching a child in each arm. She wore only a skirt. She must have been caught getting out of her blanket. There were bullet holes in her back, as if she was a piece of cardboard perforated with nails.

He shook her. He turned her over. He turned up her face.

Her eyes were open, staring at him, staring *through* him; her mouth twisted into one last grimace of pain, this girl with lines on her forehead, this child woman whose real name he did not know, who had asked him to wait two days.

Her face terrified him. It spoke a strange language of blood and sudden death. He slowly put her head down, in the dust, and suddenly he too was running, screaming at the sky with upraised fists, running everywhere and nowhere, shouting "Bastards! Bastards!"

Chapter 20

you'll never see these words or hear them because I have no pen or paper on which to write them and not even these trees and rock can hear them

I'm saying these words to myself only because you must be worrying about me though I don't feel now I belong to anything other than this soil on which I sleep

I'm saying this only because they must have given you trouble after they found I'd gone but I think you're OK

I know you worry about me but you shouldn't

I'm not afraid

I'm saying this because I have to say something sometimes because we don't talk about these things among ourselves and even if nobody hears these words at least I can say them

if you saw those little children dead under the trees with their arms eaten away and those naked mothers running through the bush you'd know

if you saw those fires maybe you'd stop chiding

if you saw her lying there clutching a child in each hand then you'd know there's no other way but this

Chapter 21

The old woman knelt on the edge of the well and leaned over to sink her bucket in the water. She let it fill half way, then hauled. Her shoulders creaked at the effort. She tilted the bucket carefully. Some of the water sloshed back into the well. She pulled up the bucket and brought it with a soft thud to her feet. Kneeling cautiously beside the bucket, she dipped into the well with a gourd, each time feeding the bucket, until it was full.

She dipped the gourd one last time, shallowly, skimming over the grey skin of water and, tilting the gourd to her face, drank from it. Laying the wet, gleaming gourd on the grass, kneeling still, she plucked leafy twigs from the bushes around her and plonked them into the bucket, to stop the water swishing out when she heaved the bucket to her head.

She paused to give herself a short rest, to catch her breath before the heave.

The sun was on the crowns of the trees. It would be a swift half-afternoon before it set, yet she was thinking already of the darkness, of her pot of *mfush-wa* frothing on the fire, of the nightly ritual of sleeplessness. She listened to the distant clank of cowbells and the echoing shouts of herdboys rising and falling with the breeze and wondered if her grandson had begun separating his herd to return home. Or perhaps he was still at the dam, fishing, and would come home after dark, with a jug of bream, slipping in out of the darkness like a phantom.

A borrowed child, she worried about him more than she worried for herself. His parents lived away, in the town and they had loaned him, their last child, to her. Loaned him to her, this twelve-year-old boy, together with the five-acre field and the seven cattle and two huts in which she eked out the last years of her life. She worried the way old people weave webs of fear for the young. If he went swimming she feared he would drown. If he came home after dark she feared a fang waited on the path, poised, for his heel. If he ate fish she feared he would choke on a bone. If he climbed fruit trees he could fall down and break his neck. If he dozed near the fire his clothes might catch fire. If it rained and he was out in the vlei bolts of lightning could knock the breath out of him. There were whirlwinds to sweep him away, strangers to abduct him (yes, a child had been stolen once and found dead with his heart carved out of him – there was knowing what the brood of businessmen at the township would do to lure more people into their shops). For her, nothing was safe. The very elements, air, water, land, seemed to conspire against her.

Sometimes she could not believe it, that she could have been an old queen, a matriarch mobbed by fond grandchildren, gloriously telling stories by the fire, living sunnily in a big household with a string of her sons' wives to pay homage to her and ease the path to her grave. The towns had done it, snatched the glow from her last years, leaving her this ash of loneliness, this one child to worry about . . .

The bushes in front of her crackled and seven young men stepped out around her. Their sudden appearance, the way they walked, their chests bent over from the massive weights on their backs, startled her.

A few paces from her, the young men stopped, crouched on their ankles and removed their caps. One of them said, "Greetings, grandmother."

Her shrivelled lips popped open, twitched.

"Greetings, sons," she intoned, cupping one gnarled hand over the other.

"How is your health, grandmother?"

"Well enough, sons . . . as well as life can allow people like me to be . . ."

"And our mothers?"

"They're well," she said again.

"And our brothers and sisters?"

"They're well too."

"And all the little children?"

"They're well, all well. Just the little ailments of human flesh – colds, coughs, but whoever heard of a cure for colds?"

"May we have some water, grandmother?"

"Yes, of course . . . you need not ask."

She scooped up a gourdful from the well and held it at the speaker. He drank up and gave the gourd back to her. She filled the gourd and the speaker drank again, as if he had the bellies of two men. She filled the gourd again and again; the others each stepped out and drank, deeply, like cattle back from a distant dip, like oxen freed from the yoke.

"My old eyes are empty shells, sons," she said, after they had drunk, and

150

the gourd was resting on the grass, while they wiped their weary foreheads. "I am like an old hen which cannot remember its young . . ."

This she said to excuse herself, to allay her doubt and fear, to disguise her amazement at their thirst.

"Do you know who we are, grandmother?" the speaker asked. She wondered at the youthful confidence of his smile, at the attentive silence of his mates that suddenly made her feel they might be people she *surely* ought to know. She squinted deeply at the faces around her, her eyes smoky with doubt.

She shook her head.

"Have you ever heard of *Chimurenga*?"

She stared at them.

"How about Chaminuka and Nehanda? Have you heard of them?"

Now she shook her head, slowly, incredulously.

"We are the children of Chaminuka and Nehanda."

The laughter on their faces puzzled her. They seemed to be bantering with her.

"Thank you for the drink of water. You will meet us again: or if not us, our friends. Goodbye."

With that they rose to their feet and walked away. She raised a shrivelled old hand, and waved, too late, for they were gone.

These could be any people – she thought. There had been many strangers in the village lately. Years back there had been *vanhu vemakandiwa* from the District Commissioner's office who walked up and down people's fields with long coloured poles pushing pegs into the ground which left every field shredded by strips of grass or ditch. To save the soil, they said. (Who had ever heard of soil having to be saved? Who had ever heard of fields having strips of grass for mice to breed in, and ditches one had to crawl across? Wasn't that just another of the white man's ways of making life hard for black people, just like ordering the size of cattle herds to be reduced?) And there had been *vanhu vesenzasi* who came to count the people in each household. (Who had ever heard of people being counted like cattle?) And before that, the year the last of her sisters died, when the groundnuts were in flower and *maroro* fruit was milk-ripe in the vlei, there had been *vanhu vetsetse* who had gone about with little buckets and pipes on their backs, pumping little clouds of white smoke in the trees to kill tsetse flies. Then there had been, the year locusts swarmed over the land, road builders whose monsters of iron and rubber knocked whole trees out of the roots of the earth, loud bustling men who cooked sadza in drums and ate out of the very shovels they used to tear the earth with. (Who had ever heard of men eating from shovels?) That she remembered, yes, and the men in the white trucks who had come to give villagers injections when *gwirikwiti* broke out.

These young men could be any such people, she thought, carrying fresh orders from the white man.

There had been changes in her lifetime, so many new things happening. Too many for her tired old mind to keep track. She had seen cars and radios come to the village; she had seen children born and grow into men who did not rise with the sun to catch the buck in the dewy dawn but sat under the eaves sipping tea with women who could no longer weave mats or baskets or grind peanut butter on a stone – a whole generation of people who could not chant the praises of their totems. Like other members of her generation she had long stopped muttering about the changes and resigned herself to them. She prided herself in having prepared for change.

And yet none of those groups that had trooped into her memory had been quite like these young men who had just asked for water. None of them had been dressed like that, or talked like that. None of them had asked such questions or mentioned Nehanda or Chaminuka.

Those names from the past, on the lips of such babies, (yes, these young men were mere pods of time) had astonished her. The teasing laughter of those young faces made her wonder if they were playing a game on her. Yet they were strangers, yes. The loads on their backs, the grease on their skins, the thirst on their faces spoke of journeys untold. When they turned away she had seen the guns hitched to their backs.

She could recognize a gun when she saw one. She knew them. Her father had had a gun once, ages back, before the forests gave in to roads and human settlement, when white men living in the district could still be counted on the fingers of two hands. Long before towns and cities ate up hills and valleys, when the forest was still so thick that a hunter slipping out of his hut would meet an animal before the pot of water he left his wife putting on the fire started boiling. Her father's gun had been long and thin, unlike the weapons the young men carried. He had used it to hunt buck, though sometimes at the drum and beer feasts after harvest he had brandished it and fired it into the sky at the crest of a war dance. That she remembered, though she

152

had been only a young girl of few summers, dodging the nudging elbows of the elders, old enough only to blow her nose.

Chimurenga. Had the young man said *Chimurenga*? Even that she knew. When she was just old enough to talk her mother had had to hide her in a cave once, with the babies of other women. The men had gone off to fight a war with the white men and the village had been deserted. Many men had died – grandfathers, fathers, husbands of women and young men not yet married, men whose deaths brought months, years of propitiatory ceremonies. And, yes, the names of Chaminuka and Nehanda had been used then, long before the *Roma* fathers put up a church at the township.

That was many years ago – so long ago that men born then had had their children, and these children had seen their children's children. So long ago that three generations of that offspring had left the country to seek work on the farms, in the houses and towns of the white men who had taken their land.

Had those young men said that they were children of Nehanda and Chaminuka?

Why, yes, she had heard about them, about these young men who carried guns and spoke of a new war against the white men. The news came in thin wisps like the smoke of a robber's fire. For years now people had talked about them and once in a while somebody in the village brought stories of somebody else they had met who might have been involved with them. Even the radios were full of the news of them, though the stories sounded like fireside tales that somebody invented. Were these the young men people said could change into lions or chameleons . . . or even vanish into thin air, whose footsteps wiped themselves out as soon as they left?

She thought of what the young men had said and she was filled with excitement.

She wanted to run to the village to break the news to someone. She wanted to tell her grandson that she had met *them*, those boys in the bush everyone was talking about, that she had seen them with her own eyes, and talked to them, and that they had drunk from her very own gourd.

But then a heaviness descended upon her, filling her with prophetic fear. Her sixth sense said, "Caution. Silence." Her mind was spinning new catastrophes already. Suddenly she wanted only to get home, to get home to her grandson.

She weaved through the bush, the bucket on her head spilling water all over her, drenching her dress. She did not see the twist of root thrust out across the path, that hooked her ankle and sent her and the bucket of water on her head hurtling to the ground . . .

Businessman Mlambo finished counting the takings for the day, stashed the money into a little white sack, blew out the candles lining the counter and stepped out to lock his shop. In the darkened verandah he groped for the keys in his bag. The air was stuffy with dust. A lorry had just passed on the gravel road running in front of his shop. He could see the beam of its lights slicing the forest sky on the horizon, the hum and rattle of its engine muffled by the distance. Soon the night noises settled in again – the clanking bell of some cow strayed into the fields, a choir of frogs from the stream, the shrill of crickets, the voices of women, carrying easily into the night, from some household on a hill.

Always he paused on the verandah after locking the shop, to watch the night. He spent the day in the shop, behind the counter, selling blue soap, bread, paraffin, candles, cooking oil and cheap cotton clothes to villagers from the countryside. Every day from dawn to dusk he was in that shop, coming out only to catch minutes of sunlight when the delivery trucks stopped by his shop and he had to go out and check the supplies, or when a visiting friend had to be walked out to the road. For years now, since he had quit his job at an Indian-owned wholesale store to set up his own small business deep in the barren heart of the country where men of his colour were allowed to operate, he had lived in the half light of that shop during the day, and two or three hours of candlelight in the evening, so that when he came out at closing time, the night, with its smells of *muhacha*, and cowdung and fires and elephant grass, was waiting on his doorstep, breathing from the orchard in front of his shop: "There, there, Mlambo, you've been working hard all day, every day, all your life. The day's done, the sun's set. The bats are out, skimming in the grey. The owls hoot in the trees. The cows are chewing slumberously in their pens. Your wife and children are long back from the fields and sit round the fire, awaiting your return. Your stool is empty at the head of the hearth. At least you can stand here a minute and breathe me in, before you go to sleep."

"I'll take a holiday," he would reply, shaking the burglar-barred doors to make sure they were locked. "I'll take a holiday this year. Shut the shop up and go somewhere with my family, visit some place, somewhere . . ."

"I'll take a break," he would tell the crows laughing in the orchard, the crows that shrieked, "Your holiday is to go to your village and plough and plant, Mlambo."

"I'll take a holiday," he insisted, stubbornly, futilely, year after year, walking out to his Datsun pick-up truck parked under a mango tree, every night . . .

"Who are you?"

"Who are you?" he shouted again, as the figure stepped out from behind his truck. "What do you want?"

His thoughts raced, tumbled over each other. This was it. Sooner or later it had to happen. Every businessman had to face it. It had happened to him before, five years back. Three men at closing time. They had stepped out from the orchard and grabbed him from behind. He had not called out, somehow. No one would have heard him, anyway. They had punched him in the stomach, grabbed the bag and raced into the bush with a month-end's takings. People he might have served at the counter that same day, too.

He thought quickly.

He could bolt for the trees behind the store if he dared, charge blindly into the dark and leave the intruder to do what he liked with the car, so long as he got away with the sack and his life.

"Don't be afraid," said the intruder, approaching slowly

"What do you want?" Mlambo panted, suspiciously stepping back.

Other figures moved forward and surrounded him.

"Just open the shop quietly," they said.

He stepped back slowly, the men following him, and unlocked the door.

"Put on the light."

He fumbled with a box of matches, struck one and lit a candle.

"Do you know who we are?"

In the flame of the candle he made out the armed men.

He had never met them but he knew at once. His surprise at recognizing them entangled in the rush of his thoughts. Robbery, murder, fire, the radios had said, looting, death, blood.

"Do you know who we are?"

He looked from man to man. He shook his head.

"Have you heard of the guerrillas?"

Instinctively, Mlambo's hand tightened over the sack of money, crushing it. The paper notes inside rustled. One of the men took the bag from him, looked inside.

Twelve years for not reporting their presence, his mind thumped, *twenty years for assisting them.*

The man folded the sack of money and handed it back to him.

"Don't be afraid. We want you to help us. Just listen, listen carefully . . ."

After they had eaten bread and tinned beef and beans and drunk coke and packed away packets of cigarettes and matches in their bags he locked up again and led them out to the truck. Two of them sat with him in the front, the others climbed into the back.

"Nice engine, eh?" said the one who appeared to be the leader.

He nodded nervously, straining to keep the car straight on the uneven gravel that writhed in front of them. Just a few miles on they ran into the headlights of another car, approaching from the opposite direction.

"Drive straight on, and step on the petrol."

He briefly saw the two men push the muzzles of their guns behind their backs and the other car, whatever it was, whooshed past. The road spat a shower of stones over the windscreen. With a stab of brakes the truck swung though a storm of dust.

"Have you seen any soldiers around here?"

He shook his head.

"Army trucks? Helicopters?"

He shook his head again. His hands were moist on the wheel. He could not keep still on the seat. He heard himself say, "One. Just one."

"One what?"

"A helicopter. It flew over the village, some weeks ago . . . a month."

"Where was it heading?"

"Towards the farms."

Silence again. Just the truck tearing on. Plunging down the darting snake of road, through a blur of shadows. Just the fuel gauge nosing towards a red zero, the last few drops trickling out . . .

"We . . . we're running out of fuel."

"How much longer have we got to go?"

"Ten, fifteen, miles."

"How much further can you go?"

"Three miles perhaps."

"What's that place?" one of them asked, pointing out to the side of the road where things flashed in the dark, like sheets of zinc.

"A road repair station," Mlambo said.

"Do you have a container on the truck?"

"Yes, at the back."

"Take this bend and pull off the road."

The two at the front leap out, get the container from the back, sneak back towards the road station while their colleagues climb out from the back and lurk in the trees nearby. Three minutes later a dog is heard barking, briefly, then there is silence.

Mlambo sits in the midst of the silence, wondering. An owl hoots in the trees; something rustles in the grass. The sky yawns green, a squandered moon makes vague promises in the west.

Mlambo sits in the midst of the silence, hoping, praying: *Oh, my mother lying on an anthill!* Where can they be? Fifteen minutes can be a lifetime. *Such young men I could be their father. Is it really them?*

Then he hears footsteps, sees the shadows converging back. He hears a squeaking at the navel, and then a sloshing deep into the belly of the truck. He sits up, incredulously, as they come back and the truck heaves to the weight of their bodies.

He drops them off at the first farm junction. Barbed wire runs along the flank of the road and at right angles from a silver cornerpost. A charred black board in the shape of an arrow points out to twin car-tracks in the grass. The red lettering on the board shines in the beam of the car.

WHITE OAK
(est. 1907)
(Prop. J.M.P. Mellecker)

He cannot believe they have got off the truck, that he can go back. He cannot wait to go back. He will tear back down the road, he will not stop. He starts when the leader comes to the window to speak to him. He almost does not hear what the man says. He calms himself as he makes a U-turn. The lights glint on the muzzles of the guns, pick at the men's eyes, flash on their boots, leap on to the forest. Then he is swerving back on to the gravel; the trees on either side of the road rush forward and lean in pressing rows to watch his exit. Behind him the figures have melted into the dark, the signpost is a grey blur in the dust. They are gone and he is going, but their last words ring like a refrain in his ear, "You never saw us. You never saw us."

Msindo lies on his back in the dark, smoking a home-made cigarette. When he draws on it his eyes gleam, the zinc roof of his shack lets down a shiver of pale yellow light and a primus stove shimmers in the corner. The room smells of paraffin and farm tobacco and beans.

His wife lies at his side with her head nestling in the crook of his arm. She has been snoring deeply for some time now. He puts a hand on the *doek* on her head and suddenly thinks, "She could easily be my grandchild." She's eighteen or nineteen, nearly one-third his age. Besides, she's a small woman.

Msindo is a tall man with huge hands and a size fifteen foot, one of those miracles of human genetics. He has a hard time shopping for clothes – every Christmas when Baas Mellecker gives the yearly bonus of a pair of trousers to each farmworker, Msindo never gets the right size. His waist presents no problem: it is the legs that are the *skellem;* even the longest trousers are too short, only getting halfway past the knees. He can only wear sandals made out of car tyres, for lack of a right size shoe. He does not mind, though he is the farm foreman. Besides, working twenty-nine days of the month in the tobacco and potato fields leaves his feet too little time for proper shoes.

The farm workers call him *Rangwani,* The Long One. He doesn't mind. He knows men of his measurement are always inflicted with nicknames and the best way to make a name harmless is to wear it with pride. He has a pleasant humour that sometimes allows him to flatter himself with the belief that the nickname is a begrudging acknowledgement of his strength.

His first wife died two years ago, of tuberculosis. She had always had a persistent cough and farm work made her worse. Over the years she had lost weight. When Baas Mellecker finally offered to drive her to the hospital it was too late - she was wasted, a bunch of bone for the young nurses to pedal around.

He misses her, sometimes. Sometimes when he feels sharp pain needling his lungs he thinks perhaps he caught it from her, then consoles himself with the thought that it is only the result of all those years in the barn. She was a good woman, though she had short breath and was stiff and hated his drinking; though she fled from him some nights, a fact she made no secret of to the farm women in whose houses she took refuge. He had beaten her once for it and now feels sorry for doing so, though her frequent complaints to her neighbours had left an ugly dent on his foreman's dignity.

Yes, she was a good woman, obedient and hardworking while her body allowed her to be. She bore him four sons, tall men like him, all of whom are doing well. The first is a tractor-driver on the farm, and has already got a family of his own. He already earns twenty-two dollars a month, five dollars more than the other men, and Baas Mellecker has hinted he might be made deputy foreman on the farm.

The second works on the neighbouring farm, milking cows. Poor fellow, a girl has just eloped unexpectedly to him from that same farm and he might marry her if the girl's parents' demands are reasonable enough. Msindo has met the girl once or twice and thinks he could like her for a *mroora*. She is tall, pretty and seems a sensible person. He really doesn't mind the elopement. It is the order of the day now and all he wants is a quick settlement and happiness for his son.

The third son is a soldier in the Rhodesian army, and, at fifty-eight dollars a month, easily earns the highest salary in the family, whatever the risks of his job. Msindo knows the war has been hotting up, even his boss now walks around with a pistol on his hip. Sometimes he lies awake fretting about his third son. Some people have been telling him to advise him to resign from Ian Smith's army, but he knows many other black men's sons are in the army too. It's the job somebody has to do – like cleaning public toilets and burying the corpses of *bandiets* who die in prisons. He feels the pay is good enough and the perks – the tinned beef, cigarettes, and used underwear he frequently brings home – are irresistible. Besides, where would he go if he resigned from the army? Because of sanctions mines are closing down, and because white people are trickling out of the country and very few replacing them, the domestic jobs once readily available to blacks (cooks, nannies, garden boys) are no longer there. No, let him stay on and make enough at least to buy himself clothes and to save up for his *lobola*. Things will calm down soon, more white people will come and there will be more jobs.

The last boy is in Grade Five, at the local primary school. He probably won't get a place for Grade Six since only a quarter of the black children in Grade Five are allowed to go on to Grade Six. Msindo hopes to arrange for a job for him on the farm – Baas Mellecker has been talking of starting a beef herd and might need an extra hand with the cattle. Yes, he will talk to Baas Mellecker about it. That is one of the perks of being foreman.

The idea of asking for such favours always makes him nervous, though. Like most of the white people Msindo knows, Baas Mellecker is a man of unpredictable moods. He can be seized by sudden fits of kindness, giving away a half a bottle of whisky, extra rations, a soiled shirt, for instance, now and then. But you have to be careful with him – he can lash out like a green mamba when provoked. Over the last few years, since his wife left him, Baas Mellecker has taken on a meaner temper. Msindo cannot understand why people who have lived thirty years together should need to separate. *A man is not a man unless he has a wife to sleep with him at night,* he thinks. He is not even sure if they have divorced or are caught in a long domestic boycott. Madam Mellecker still visits two or three times a year – he hears she lives in a flat in the city by herself. The cook says she comes to collect the cheques when they don't arrive on time and when she visits she sleeps in the spare bedroom upstairs.

If I had to live alone in that big house, without a wife, Msindo thinks, *I'd go mad.* Msindo knows his boss in the secret intimate way only a cook or garden-boy can intuit from the little details discarded around him. Sometimes he dares to feel a tentative pity for his boss, to see this as the reason. Baas Mellecker has become more violent lately. *It all builds up in the loins,* Msindo thinks, *and squeezes up to the head.*

Every time Msindo needs to ask for something, he is filled with apprehension, like a herd boy called up by a farmer whose field the boy's cattle have invaded. He waits until dusk and the workers have gone home and then lopes back past the dairy and across the lawn to Baas Mellecker's house. Baas Mellecker's Alsatian dogs know him well, but they are always on guard. They have been trained to be suspicious of all visitors to the house, even familiar people. At dusk they are in a particularly vicious temper because they know Baas Mellecker is still up, in the house. They bolt up to Msindo, growling. He tells them off, his voice shaky with fear, worried that the farmer might hear him chide them.

"Footsek Spark! Footsek Shumba! Satan wako!"

And yet, cornered by those snarls, he hopes he will be heard, and rescued.

The farmer is already out on the stoep, his pink dome shining in the flood-light.

"That you, Msindo?"

"Yes Baas, me Baas."

"What d'you want?"

"*Mina buyire buza small fevha Baas,*" he snaps into Chiraparapa, stepping out of the shadows, smothering his hat into a ball with a wet hand. He stands wobbling in the blinding light, bowing. He is tongue-tied for a moment, wondering if he is out of range enough, out of the range of the farmer's breath; then the request rattles out of him, the words choke him like urine chokes a drunk stranded at a reluctant toilet door; suddenly the words shoot out in a spray and he has said it – he has said it and hitches up his trousers and steps back and his ears are full of the noise of his foolishness, his fear, and he cannot hear the farmer's banter, almost.

"*You think jobs grow on trees, eh? What about the two dollars I gave you last month? Hini wena enza, Msindo? Wena kumbula fanika pickanniny skati zonke.*"

"No, Baas. Jus' asking Baas."

"*Ho'right. Hamba karokhaya. Mina chere wena tomorrow.*"

Two, three months later, nothing has happened. Msindo holds his silence, works hard as usual, until suddenly one afternoon while they're working at a patch of field the farmer comes by on his horse or truck and says, "Msindo, come here." He swipes down his hat, smacks his jowl with a grey hand-kerchief, plods through the clay and he is told he has been given a two-dollar raise, or one of his sons has been awarded a job with the cows, or that as foreman he has been allowed to build himself a house with a corrugated iron roof in the compound where all the other huts are built of grass.

Thus he has progressed, like a locust leaping in the grass. He has heard years of this banter from his boss and yet has never allowed himself the foolishness to feel at ease with it. He knows self-effacement is the way to get-ting what he wants. His relationship with his boss is survivable – he is pret-ty much used to this cat and mouse act. He has been working on this farm for forty years, since he was a boy and Baas Mellecker was a chubby little fel-low riding a tricycle, frolicking under his mother's skirts round the farmhouse. This farm has been Msindo's life. He knows every square metre of soil on it, every ditch. He cannot think of himself existing separate from it, without it. The very soil clings to his sandals, his skin is bleached reddish with it, grass seeds mat his hair. Every year veld fires soil the blue sky, thunder rumbles from the mountain, rain lashes down and the river gushes with song. The fields have to be ploughed, the weeding teams supervised, the potatoes and tobacco weeded, pruned, picked; the cows have to be milked, fertilizer stored and spread, fireguards cleared, rations given out, poachers apprehended and disputes quelled at the compound. He knows these rhythms as well as a woman would know her cycle. He has grown so used to the farm that it is *his* farm, almost.

"How is your tobacco doing?" he asks the neighbouring foreman he meets at a *shebeen* over a mug of *chibuku*. "You should see mine. It is the best crop my farm has produced so far!"

"My farmhouse needs a new ceiling and repainting," he grins to another, "my floors need new carpets, my lawns need fertilizer. My tractor needs new wheels. I'm seeing to that once I get the potatoes in."

And now with this young woman on his breast, he feels rejuvenated, a fruit tree manured, fertilized, watered for the new season. It is pay-day tomorrow and the thought of the twenty-seven dollars in his hands makes him want to wake her up. Maybe he will buy her a dress - there is a green and yellow one he saw at the farm shop last week, going for sixteen dollars, and probably her size. He will buy her a dress just as he bought her the primus stove and the *doek*, to make her feel she's wanted, that he's as good a husband as any. Not that he feels insecure about having such a young wife; he knows as foreman every woman in the area would give anything to be his wife. He would like to lavish on her the fondness only a man whose children are almost raised and gone from his household and whose first wife is dead can afford.

He will buy her the green and yellow dress so people will see her and know she's the foreman's wife.

His hand strays down over her firm belly. She has not asked for money for cotton wool this month. Already she has complained of headache and nausea. He thinks of a bean, a tiny little liquid bean flowering inside her, watered by her blood.

"Who's that?"

"Who's that?" he shouts again, and the little zinc roof over his head throws his voice back at him, in the dark.

It comes again, a tapping on the thin wooden door, persistently, only just

162

loud enough to be heard. He fumbles for the chair, springs from the bed and pulls on his trousers. His feet kick things – a cardboard box, suitcase, the primus stove. A box of matches explodes under his heel. He crouches in the dark.

"Who's there?" he shouts.

The tapping is now on the window, the wooden board in the gap in the brickwork that's the window.

"Open up," says a male voice, outside.

"Who are you?" he pants. "What do you want?"

"Just open up quietly and stop shouting."

The calm in that voice prompts him to approach the door.

Outside feet crunch the earth. He pulls out a thick stick from under his bed, clasps it behind his back and slowly unbolts the door. A slice of moonlight tumbles through the door and shivers on the concrete floor. Three armed men stand at the door, surrounding him. His stick clatters impotently on the floor.

"Who is it?" his wife shrieks, torn out of her sleep. The men at the door are stilled by the sharp nakedness of her voice, by the warm smell of sleep wafting from the heart of that room.

"Do you know who we are?"

No, he tells them, he does not know who they are. But he knows, almost intuitively, who they are, even before they tell him.

"Come out!"

"Where are you taking him?" the girl wails, clinging to her man in the doorway.

"If she makes another sound we'll . . ."

Msindo calms her with one hand and takes a step forward. He feels brave, somehow, knows the worst he can do is to disobey them.

"Lock her in from the outside. If she so much as makes a sound, if she tries to wake anyone that'll be the end of her."

Msindo locks the door and goes with the men. His house is quiet behind them, its roof gleams pale among the grass huts of the compound. She is whimpering, silently, behind the door. Listening. The men's guns are in their hands and he is stumbling in front of them, plunging through the bush. The farmhouse gleams white on a hill.

"There were seven of them altogether," Msindo is to recount many many times, "seven of them, and three of them came to my house and woke me and took me out to the bush and said how many people are working on this farm and how many hours do you work and how much does he pay you and I told them and they said what is a big man like you doing here getting twenty-seven dollars a month working twelve hours a day and why are you working for him we have heard so many bad stories about how he treats his workers do you think this is his farm don't you know this is our land Cecil John Rhodes grabbed from our people and I did not answer them because I didn't know who Cecil John Rhodes was and I had never heard that name but they looked serious and I just stood there wondering if they meant perhaps Ian Smith and if they were going to kill me or beat me up but they didn't touch me and then they asked me where is the farmer and I told them and they said his name is Mellecker isn't it and I said yes, Baas Mellecker and one of them stamped his foot on the ground and said do you know my name and I said no I don't and he stamped his foot again and said *Baas Die!* and they all turned their thumbs down and said *Pasi Na Baas! Baas!* and they made me say it after them and I did then they said lead us to his house and I did and they said how many dogs does he have and I said four and one of them opened a tin of beef he had in his bag and put something in it and gave it to me and said give it to the dogs and I took the tin and left them standing there behind the orchard and approached the house all by myself looking everywhere all the time afraid the dogs would come rushing at me and then I threw the tin at the kennel where the dogs slept and the dogs came out and sniffed at the beef and ate it and I went back and told them I had done it and they waited a little and then approached the house and the dogs were lying on the grass already and only one was still kicking with its legs in the air and three of the men went into the house . . .

"Seven of them," he says, and something jams his throat and he swallows, his long hands trembling. "And they said afterwards the farm workers should remove all the things from the house and take them to the compound and two of them took me into the house with them and I saw Baas Mellecker there lying on the floor in a pool of his own blood, his throat cut, and we went out again and they said at eight in the morning I should call the police and tell them what had happened, not a minute earlier or a minute later, exactly at eight, and I should tell them the guerrillas had done it and they would do it to every farmer who treated his workers like animals and if the soldiers wanted to meet them they should come to the hills and then they told me to look at the clock on the wall and said I shouldn't wake my wife before then or wake anybody and if I called earlier they would know I was a traitor and come back for me and having said that they left hurriedly towards the farm road.

"It was still dark, two or three hours before sunrise and after they left I sat there not knowing what to do, wondering if I should go into the house and pour water over him or bring him out, but I knew he was already dead and they had showed him to me so I just sat there thinking I should have told them he's away in town visiting or perhaps I should have made the dogs bark to wake him up or I should have let them kill me in his place and the sun was hours coming up and I heard the workers going down to the fields without me and still I sat there on the stoep and at eight o'clock I went in expecting to find him on his feet, walking, or lying in his bed at least, and I said to myself this is just a dream I'm having, it didn't happen, Baas Mellecker can't be dead, it's pay-day today and who will pay the workers and what will happen to the workers, what will happen to the new tractor, to the farm, but he was there, lying on the floor in his blue pyjamas with his throat cut and his eyes open and the moustache on his lip in a pool of dry blood and when I saw him my hands shook so much I could not hold the telephone but I had to, I had to make the call, I can't remember who I spoke to or what I said, I said, *Baas Mellecker is died here, Baas Mellecker is died* and when I finished . . . I don't know what I did then, I tried to shake him, to wake him up but he wouldn't move, he wouldn't move with that gash in his throat and those eyes open and there was blood on my hands, his blood and I went to the tap and washed my hands and went out to the stoep, the verandah, and I kept walking up and down in the orchard, kept seeing him lying there on the floor in his pyjamas, his eyes open, his blood dry on the floor . . .

"I didn't tell anyone, didn't go back to the compound, all the time I was walking round the house, wondering what to do, wondering if I should call Baas Devillers or Baas Van Dyke on the neighbouring farms and if they would drive him to hospital. Then I heard cars, and I knew it was the police. The sun had come up and I saw the police truck coming down the farm road, through the grass, followed by an army lorry full of soldiers. I saw them, through the grass, going across the *donga* where the children sometimes play and I didn't know whether to run to them or run away or stay in that place and suddenly there was a big loud noise, the kind of noise you hear down in the mines when the miners use dynamite and I saw the army lorry shoot into the sky in a cloud of smoke and dust . . ."

Chapter 22

From his post Pasi NemaSellout sees the glint of enamel-ware. A row of heads bob over the breast of the hill and then the figures, hands clamped to heads, come up, emerging out of the rocks in a single file.

Keeping his body still, he raises his head carefully over the wall of rock behind which he stands and peers down into the valley below. An eagle skims over the rim of the forest. Apart from that the afternoon is still. He counts six figures. They are now close enough for him to pick out the colours of their dresses – checked olive, orange, sky-blue, black, red.

Suddenly the girls stop, hands clamped to heads still, so close now he can see the blacks and browns of the pots on their heads. They freeze in a row, as if something has stopped them and then the one in the front steps aside from the line, balancing her pot with one hand and makes motions in the air with the free hand.

Pasi scans the valley again, steps out from behind the rock and slices the air with three slow strokes of the arm. The procession below reassembles, heaves, pads up the slope, fanning out until they have formed an arc ten metres from him. He takes three steps down and stops. He is still above them, higher than they are. His knees are almost level with their raised arms.

"Put them there," he says.

The girls bring down their loads, crouch behind their pots and ask, one after the other, *"Maswera sei, Comrade?"*

He grunts back at each greeting. He feels uneasy, towering above them so he sees the rivulets of skin between the thick braids of hair on their heads, the cupped out necks of their blouses, the light-skinned clefts between their dustwashed toes. Their raised eyes silently train on him. The pots in front of them are hot, wisps of smoke curl out of them and the girls' temples are ringed with sweat from the carrying and the sun.

The silence is awkward but he stands on, stiffly. He scans the hill and says, "Wait here."

He turns round, climbs several steps up the hill and then cuts round the slope to the other side.

Baas Die knows already and stands there waiting but Pasi steps in front of him, clicks his heels, his hands straight and stiff along his flanks and says, "The girls are here with the food."

"Send them off and tell them to come again tomorrow," Baas Die says.

Pasi climbs back. The girls are still crouching behind their pots.

"Did anyone see you coming here?" he asks.

They shake their heads, wondering if something is amiss. Suddenly he remembers what it is he wanted to say to them.

"Next time you come put on dark clothes – green, or brown. No bright colours, eh. Come again this time tomorrow."

Each girl opens her pot, eats a handful of the food she has brought and closes the pot. The girls know they have been dismissed but they do not immediately rise. The one in front clears her throat. She has something to say.

"Some of the women in the village are not sure if the *pungwe* is tonight or tomorrow night."

He concentrates on her face for the first time. His eyes have been skimming over them, avoiding their faces all along but now he has to give a reply. He bunches his brow and chews his lower lip in an attempt at impatience.

"Tonight," he says, curtly, and jerks away his head. The girls still crouch there. "You may go now."

They rise crisply, brushing the sand off their knees and climb down the hill. One of them turns round and catches him staring after them. He looks quickly away but they are already snaking through the rocks, out of sight.

Baas Die comes out first, a lanky, straight-limbed man with a face like a knife and a thin goatee which, combined with a sparse and receding hairline, seem to add half a dozen summers to his twenty-one years. His hands are small but finely cut – one thumb is hooked at the shoulderbone to the strap of the machine gun at his back. The other thumb rakes the soft groove running down his ribcage to the peach-like navel. The short-sleeved blue 'Sting' shirt is flung open, the white collar stained with sweat. The pocket bulges with a *chipako* he keeps there – every now and then he takes snuff. His voice has the sniff of one who seems to have a perpetual cold. Only one button is clipped on, exposing the almost femininely hairless chest. His limbs shuffle easily in 'Bootlegger' jeans of a cloudy blue colour which has been preserved from fading by the grey dye of dust and grease which has ground into the coarse fabric and stiffened it. The waistline is a size too big, so that the jeans inch down over the curve of his butts every now and then, exposing the red band of his pants and threatening to flop to his beige farmer shoes unless hitched up by a quick flash of the wrist. Normally he would wear a green beret tilted over the right hemisphere of his head and dangle a pair of binoculars over his chest but today his eyes – unshaded – look a glazed brown.

The leader is followed by Mabunu Muchapera and Torai Zvombo, both slim and seventeen, the youngest in the group. By some coincidence these two look like brothers. Their even heights match up in brown 'Sting' shirts. The jagged angularity of their faces seems to have been sculptured out of the same rock – both noses lifting off a jutting upper lip, the nostrils flared with just a hint of arrogance. The difference is in their voices. Mabunu Muchapera's is a loud whine that leaves his thin lips panting wetly for breath while Torai Zvombo's sand-papered mumble is dry and monotonous. The bushes chatter as the two, side by side, and yet apart, each cutting his own path, charge down the hill.

Shungu Dzangu bounces round from the other face of the hill, a dark fleshy nineteen with a round head and a blotched skin. His clothes are full of him – the armpits of his shirts are torn and the insides of his green corduroys are worn with the rubbing together of his thighs. His skin is a patchwork of *nyora*, there are dozens on his wrists alone. He is a round man and yet he is not fat – the short neck and round arms suggest the bulging tight power of men used to lifting hundred-kilogram sacks of mealie-meal on their heads. His face is drawn into an interminable smile yet his jaws seem to ponder over his thoughts before the wet tenor voice uncoils. He speaks slowly, the words wafting from him like a tiny worm of smoke, his lips smiling so if you stop him he dispels the wisp of his words with a painful, abrupt laugh; yet you get the impression of something coiled up and poised down deep inside him.

Gidi Ishumba is a dark, diminutive man who walks with quick short strides and outstretched hands, his head thrust up to make up for his size. He gives the impression of a small but tough and angry bull charging ahead of gigantic but less emboldened peers. His head is a little too big for his body. The wide forehead beams over a piercing pair of round brown eyes, a wide squashed nose and impressive teeth reminiscent of ears of R200 seed maize. Viewed from afar he might be mistaken for a boy, yet he is probably twenty-two – the oldest in the group. His small gnarled fingers which remind you instantly of spanners and nuts and bolts – a mechanic's hands – and the way his head shifts make him out to be a trouble-shooter.

Last comes Sub Musango, light-skinned, pimple-faced with a moody face made worse by his having just got up from a siesta. His body is almost perfectly formed – the limbs proportionate, the hair thick and long, hands effeminate. He wears a solid green T-shirt and camouflage pants of chocolate and veld yellow. He is a fidgety man, given to long vacant stares and sudden spurts of speech.

Pasi is soon surrounded by his comrades. The men crouch on the ground, guns cradled between the knees. They open the pots and attack the food. They have not eaten in twenty-four hours, the elimination of hunger needs no formalities. Hands throw off the lids, dip into pots, criss-crossing, scooping out loads of rice, sadza and chicken. Veins of fat drip down arms. There is enough food for twenty men here but soon the pots are nearly empty. There is a redivision of food, ripped chunks of meat changing hands, rocks of sadza and avalanches of rice tipped over. Each man stands up and steps back, pot in hand, eating more slowly. Soon the pots are abandoned on the ground. Hunger, time's taskmaster, thwarted in minutes.

Pasi crushes each bone, sucks the marrow out, grinds the sharp splinters into a smooth pulp and then swallows everything.

Afterwards he collects the pots and puts them in the cave.

Sub Musango dawdles to Pasi's former position, Shungu Dzangu bounces to the foot of the hill, Gidi Ishumba skips up to the anti-air post; it is now Pasi's and Mabunu Muchapera's turn to sleep.

Another rotation is complete.

Pasi's watch is over now, he will sleep until the sun sets and the moon rises. He belches softly and scratches at the hint of sideburns on his face. Grains of rice and meat come back up and he crushes them between tongue and palate. His fist is loaded with bones. The crowns of *mpfuti* trees form a basket of blue sky above. He sprawls lankily on his back, chewing, feeling the breeze lick his face. His jaws grind more slowly now, the birds twitter in the boughs, his eyelids blink. The smooth oily fullness inside him sucks him into sleep . . .

Even when he was a child, the rising moon startled him, bursting over the flickering township lights, beyond the trains that rumbled all night into the mysteries of distance.

Out here among the hills, where there are no lights to compete with, the event is a ritual. First there is the incredible haze in the east, as if a portion of the world is on fire, then it spills out, round and reddish yellow, from the dark peak of land. He looks at its face and tries to read the picture on it. A deserted husband carrying his own pots to the fields? A woman punished with a hunched back for working on a Sunday? A bull charging into a hut? There are stories he remembers about the face of the moon. He remembers the day when Neil Armstrong first walked on the moon – a howling July morning and how his Grade Four teacher had spent half the morning pacing the classroom panting, "And what is it they had to run away from on earth to go to the moon?" and he has never ceased to wonder why the teacher had said that, though the teacher died years back of a swollen liver.

He loathes the darkness, when the trees and the land blend into one blind mass of impenetrable black. Even the air presses around you like a cloth held up by large, invisible hands. The only thing you can make out is the glint of your bayonet. He loathes the darkness because the only thing you have is your ears. Even a twig falling in the dark can make you swivel suddenly.

And now, from the fork of the tree in which he nestles, gun between knees, wrapped up by the leaves around him, the valley below is a flood of light. Across the valley the hill – their hill – looms above the pinched curve of horizon; he knows some of his comrades are out there. Every now and then he lifts the curtain of leaves and peers out below him. If a rabbit scurried out there in the grass he would see it, he thinks.

Earlier in the evening, he has seen the villagers trickle in for the *pungwe*. The ones from the hills he hasn't seen, but those from the valley, whose edge he is guarding, have passed just under the tree where he is stationed. Sitting there in the fork of the tree he has seen them come in solemn groups of twos and threes, their bodies squashed up from above so he can only see their heads and feet, moving slowly, anxiously looking about. He has seen them – the men and women, boys and girls, children. He thinks he has heard Headman Sachikonye's voice. He has felt a strange satisfaction sitting in the tree with his gun slanted towards where they came from, hearing their whispers as they passed, unaware of his presence.

And now from behind the hill, where they have gathered, he hears Baas Die's voice begin. He cannot see behind the hill where they are, but he has been there with them before and the picture is not difficult to imagine.

He sees in his mind the two half moons of people. The women, girls and children form one half while the men and the boys form the other. The younger people are on the insides while the older people form the rind. The women and children sit cross-legged, the men and the boys squat on the ground or against the rocks. Some of the women have babies tied to their backs, others breastfeed infants as they sit. Some of the men hold on to walking sticks planted in front of them, their beards shining in the dark. The faces are awed, attentive. Even the infants are quiet.

Baas Die struts in the bare centre of the gathering. Gidi Ishumba probably paces the fringes of the gathering. Mabunu Muchapera, Torai Zvombo, Sub Musango and Shungu Dzangu weave, with him, at a quarter-mile radius, a rough fence round the hill.

This is how he sees it, sitting in the fork of the tree at his post. And now Baas Die's voice booms from behind the hill, echoes of his voice carrying easily in the night.

Pasi feels he is there, almost, in the midst of the gathering.

"*Icho*!" Baas Die chants.

"*Charira*!" the crowd shouts back.

"*Icho*!"

"*Pamberi neChimurenga*!"

"*Pamberi*!"

There follows a score of slogans, the night reverberates with the response of the crowd. Then there is silence.

"*Ndichambokuitirai ngano yangu,*" Baas Die says, "I'm going to tell you a little story."

Once upon a time – Baas Die says – once upon a time, a long time ago, there came to a certain village a group of visitors. These visitors did not look like anyone the people had seen before. They stood at the stockade of the *musha*, peering in.

The children who were tending the goats saw them first and fled, yelling, and buried their heads among their mothers. The mothers beat off the children and stepped out to look but they too were terrified by what they saw and they ran back into their huts and hid behind *maturi*. Then the men who were sitting at the *dare* picked up their axes and went out to see what it was had come to their homes and frightened their wives and children so, but when they saw the strangers at the stockade, they too were seized with fear. Some wet their *nhembe*, some dropped their axes, others sneaked back and hid behind the huts. The strangers at the stockade smiled and waved their hands, and suddenly the remaining band of men scrambled back to the *dare*.

The women and the children saw the men run and the men were ashamed for if they were men and they ran, who would protect the women and the children? The men talked among themselves, saying, "Who are these strangers outside our homes with the skins like the skins of newly born babies and hair like the hair of maize cobs? Who are these beings without knees or toes? Are they people or spirits?" A new panic swept through the *musha*, for the strangers were opening the gates of the stockade and walking in.

The women and children froze in the huts and the men bunched like chickens which have seen an eagle in the sky. Not a dog barked, for the dogs huddled with the men; even the whimper had gone from their throats. The strangers walked slowly across the *ruvanze*, turning their heads from side to side, smiling. Then the villagers saw that though the strangers' skins were like babies' skins and their hair long like the hair of maize, their knees and toes were hidden in their clothes, and they had heads and arms and hands and feet like them.

One of the strangers picked up a child who had strayed from its mother and was tottering in the doorway. The people hissed with fear, but the stranger gave the baby something to eat from the pockets of his clothes, and put him down again on the ground. When they saw this the mothers were no longer afraid of the strangers, and they came slowly out of the huts, holding back their children. The men were ashamed of their fear and their bad manners and they ran about getting stools for the strangers to sit on, and water to drink.

When the visitors were seated the people drew closer to examine them. Children touched the shoes on their feet and felt their hands with their fingers. The visitors fished in their coats and gave children little things to eat, and talked and smiled, and the people laughed because when the visitors spoke their voices seemed to come through their noses, but the visitors laughed back. Then the women brought food for the visitors, who ate and drank a little, and their hosts thought they did not take much because they were not used to the food. And after the visitors had eaten they opened their bags and gave presents to the women – beads, trinkets, cloth, looking-glasses. For the men they had tobacco and clothes like the ones they themselves wore, though there were only enough for a few of the old men there.

Everyone was happy with the presents. The women clucked over the sight of their faces in the looking-glass and cooed over the cloths spread out on their knees. Men hitched their new clothes and sampled the tobacco. The excitement took a long time to die down and when it did they sat waiting to see what the visitors would do and when they would say where they came from and were going, but the visitors sat there, speaking little, laughing with the children. Because of the silence the young people decided to sing and dance for the visitors. But the visitors turned their faces away. The dancers moved further off, thinking they were too close, and the dust might make the visitors cough, but the visitors shook their heads and hands wildly. The dancers stopped singing and took off their *hosho* and put away their *mbira* and packed away their drums. Then the men began to wonder what they should do to drive away the silence, but the visitors began singing, and the people thought it queer that when they sang they did not dance, but each stared at a thing like a bunch of thin dried leaves packed together which he held open in front of his eyes, and between songs they knelt on the ground and crossed their hands over their chests and touched their breasts and foreheads, and closed their eyes and spoke to the sky with slow, grave voices. And afterwards they took the children and made them kneel in front of them, and dipped their hands in a shiny vessel of water and touched their foreheads and mumbled words over them. The people had never seen this before and were surprised. The visitors had been kind to them and given them presents, but they did not understand what the strangers were now doing to the children – if this was some custom that was practised in the land they came from, or some new way to stave off illnesses, perhaps. So the people sat and watched, and a few of the older ones among them even stepped forward and had their foreheads touched with water, and words mumbled over them. Afterwards the visitors spoke for a long time, again looking at the bunch of leaves in their hands. They spoke with eager voices. The people did not understand most of the things they said, but they heard words like 'peace', 'friendship' and 'love' and they nodded their heads for these were good words, and they thought it was the custom where the strangers came from for visitors to speak like that, and they let them speak.

The sun had by then long set and it had grown dark. The young people were asleep, snoring, and the heads of men and women were drooping one by one into their laps. The fires burnt low. They began to wonder when the strangers would stop speaking. At last the strangers finished their speech, and the old men who were still awake thanked them and showed them the hut where they would sleep, for it was clear that they would not be leaving that night since it was late. Afterwards everybody went to sleep, and the *musha* was quiet.

A very strange thing happened in the morning. When the men went to greet the visitors and ask how they had slept, they found the hut empty! They waited, thinking the visitors had perhaps gone into the bush to relieve themselves, but the visitors did not appear. Then they thought perhaps the visitors had gone to the river to bathe and they sent boys to check but the visitors were not there. The men began to panic, thinking perhaps their guests had been eaten by some beast during the night; but what animal, to eat a whole group of people like that, without leaving a bone or a trace of blood or marks of struggle or even a sound in the night; or who knew what evil spell had whisked them away in the dark, the spirits forbid! They searched around the hut for a spoor but saw only the strange footprints of the visitors, going away from the hut, towards the forest! Then they thought perhaps it was the custom in the land where the visitors came from for travellers to leave early in the morning, without eating or bidding their hosts good morning or farewell.

The villagers were greatly surprised. Girls placed *matende* on their heads to go to the river and boys opened the pens to take cattle, sheep and goats to the pastures. Men and women stood with hoes in their hands, talking aloud on the paths while their fields waited, unweeded. Before long the girls came back from the river running and spilling water over their shoulders. The people crowded round them to ask what was the matter. The girls said they had seen the visitors walking in the forest. Soon afterwards the boys who had gone to the pastures came running too to say they had seen the visitors walking up and down the fields, and round the gardens in the valley.

Then the people began to think the visitors had gone hunting (but had they any weapons besides the shiny sticks they carried on their shoulders?) or had been seized by a wandering spell during the night, for how else could strangers walk up and down like that in the morning dew, unaccompanied, at that unhealthy time when the things of the night, their roaming errands completed, were returning to their nests? How could visitors walk, unescorted, through the fields and forests of people they had only met the day before? Who would show them where to step and where not to? Or perhaps it was the custom where the visitors came from to inspect the hosts' field early in the morning. Who knew if they, secret suitors to some belle in the village perhaps, had been working in the fields and gardens to impress their

174

hosts? Anyway, the people were relieved to know their guests were still alive and walking and in the area, that they had not been eaten by beasts or whisked away by wicked spells during the night. Who would know how to appease the visitors' ancestors if anything happened to the visitors here, in this village? Who knew where they came from or what their totems were, to unknot the secret wraths of their pasts?

The people agreed to go out and meet the visitors. They went in a group, and met the visitors coming out of the forest. The visitors carried a dead buck on their shoulders! The women brought down pots of *maheu* from their heads and knelt by the side of the path, men squatted on their haunches and began clapping their hands and asking their visitors how they had slept. The visitors laughed and spoke something that the people did not understand, and the people laughed back because when the visitors spoke their voices came through their noses, and they did not kneel, but spoke standing in the middle of the path, but they drank the *maheu* and gave the slain buck to the men to carry and let the villagers lead them back to the village.

The villagers were puzzled as to how the visitors had killed the buck without spears or arrows – for, apart from a small wound on the neck, the buck showed no serious marks of injury. Anyway, the men thanked their guests for the kill, skinned it and gave it over to the women for cooking. The women cooked the meat and everybody ate and left for the fields. Later in the afternoon the men got together to discuss the situation. They sought the advice of the *svikiro* and were told, *"Beware of the visitors. Beware of them but do not try to harm them."*

In the evening the visitors, who had spent the afternoon resting under the shade of the trees, sat on stools outside the hut assigned to them, and called the children over with little things to eat and laughed with them. And after the visitors had eaten they began to sing and talk as they had done the night before. Interested by their voices and strange speech, the young people gathered round them to listen, though they understood nothing of the visitors' language. The men sat at the *dare* watching. They tried to call the children over with signs, but the children, who were expecting presents from the visitors, refused to come.

For several days, the same thing happened. In the morning the villagers would wake up to find the visitors gone. Sometimes they were out in the forest, sometimes they were walking through the fields or the pastures or the gardens. They were even seen inspecting the cattle pens and the graves behind the huts.

Sometimes during the day they would emerge from the forest to the edge of a field and watch the villagers at work, and one of them would ask for a hoe and make a few strokes at the weeds, and the villagers would laugh to see that the strangers sweated heavily in the sun, and that their hands quickly blistered. And if there was a child among the women who had a bad cough the strangers would give it medicine from their pockets and then move on to the gardens, where it was said they gave a man seeds for a new kind of vegetable; or they would go down to the river to watch the herdboys catch fish. Sometimes the strangers fished too, and their lines were different, and the boys laughed when they caught bullfrogs and did not throw them away, for the strangers ate frogs. Once they helped the boys pull up a calf stuck in the mud.

Occasionally when they returned from the forest in the morning the visitors brought back a buck they had killed. The men of the village, who were themselves skilled hunters, did not understand how the visitors killed their game until the day an ox struck badly on the neck by a slaughterer broke free from the ropes tying him and charged, with blood raining from its neck, across the yard. The people fled into nearby huts and the unlucky slaughterer ran after the ox. One of the visitors who happened to be watching the scene merely took one step back, lifted the shiny stick from his shoulders and pointed it at the charging ox. There was a thunderous noise that made every villager dive for the ground and, miraculously, the ox fell down, dead. The visitor who had shot the ox went up and kicked the dead ox, and waved his gun, and laughed to show them everything was all right. After that the villagers, who had never seen anything like this before, were very much afraid of the visitors' weapons.

In the evenings the visitors sang and talked to the young people, and the older ones joined in too, and soon the new songs were known and sung in the village, and this did not worry the old people at first because the visitors seemed good-hearted, helpful people.

And so the days passed. One evening the strangers did not return from the forest. They had left at dawn, as usual, but nobody had seen them during the day, though one man who had been chopping wood in the forest reported hearing the sound of axes deeper in the forest. By the time the villagers went to sleep the visitors had not returned. The next morning a group of men from

176

the village went out to the forest and were surprised to find the visitors had cleared an area deep in the heart of the forest and put up three rough huts!

The strangers did not come back to live with the villagers. They lived in the huts they built, and began to clear a field round the huts. The villagers were surprised. They consulted the *svikiro*.

"*Burn the huts in the forest,*" the *svikiro* said, "*burn the huts and the strangers will go away.*"

There were loud arguments at the *dare*, much anger and swearing and plucking of beards and fist-shaking and calling of names, but they could not agree on one thing, and it was clear that some of the men would not be willing to give back the presents they had received from the strangers, and that in fact they were eagerly awaiting more. Who was to obey the *svikiro's* command? Who was to brave the dark in the forest, creeping up on the strangers? The men could not agree on what to do, but they would have to obey the *svikiro*.

Then the men made a shocking discovery! Their own sons were working for the strangers! First, they noticed that the cattle, goats and sheep were roaming unattended during the day, and some of the boys were wearing shorts similar to the ones given to the men by the strangers. When asked the boys admitted getting the clothes from the strangers in return for work. The men were angry. They beat up their sons. Afterwards they made them take the clothes back. But the strangers only sent the boys back with more presents for themselves and for their fathers.

Some of the men accepted the new presents. Others burnt them. Again there was much arguing and shouting.

The *svikiro* repeated: "*Burn the huts in the forest. Burn their huts and they will go away.*"

Five brave men agreed to take on the task.

The five men left after supper, carrying axes and spears. One of them carried a faggot of hardwood with live coals in its hollow centre. As they drew closer to the heart of the forest, they saw a ball of firelight over the trees.

They cautiously approached the clearing and peered through the foliage. The strangers sat around a big fire. Their figures shone white like ghosts in the light. The wind brought the smell of roasting grain and meat from the fire and behind them lay the skinned carcass of a beast.

The men crouched in the shadows for a long time, listening to the voices of the strangers which carried to them in the breeze. The air was sweet with the smell of meat but the fire made the strangers look terrifying. At last the strangers rose from the fire and went into the huts to sleep. Suddenly the men's hearts were filled with worry. They wanted only to burn the huts and not hurt the strangers, and now if the strangers were sleeping in the huts, how were they to do that? Their hands went cold with doubt. They wanted to go back. But one of them who was bold sneaked up to the fire which the strangers had left burning, picked up a brand and tossed it at one of the huts. The grass roof of the hut popped into flames, but almost immediately, the strangers came rushing out of the huts.

The men fled into the dark, thumping into the bushes. Behind them they heard a thunderous noise – a noise they now knew, followed by wild screaming, but in their fear they charged blindly through the dark. Only when they reached the gardens in the valley and regrouped did they realize that their friend – the one who had set fire to the hut, was missing. But they were too afraid to go back and went to the village to sleep.

The strangers came to the village early the next morning. They were very angry. They kicked the chickens out of their way as they marched up the *ruvanze*. The villagers saw them come and they ran away. Women ran away with babies on their backs. Men ran away. Children ran away. The strangers tore the roofs off the villagers' huts. They went to the kraal and shot three bulls. Then they went back to the forest.

The villagers reassembled when the strangers left. They saw the dead bulls, the torn huts, the chickens lying dead on the *ruvanze*. They had heard the sound of the guns shooting. Now they knew the strangers were really angry. The men sat at the *dare* and talked. They did not know what had happened to the man who had been shot in the night, if he was injured or dead. They consulted the *svikiro* and were told, "*He is alive. Do not fight the strangers now. Appease them only.*"

To show that they were sorry, the men sent their sons to rebuild the burnt huts. They even built more huts for the strangers. But the strangers were not satisfied. They made the villagers chop more trees and enlarge the clearing around the huts. The villagers made a huge field for the strangers. They destumped the field and planted maize and groundnuts and millet. The strangers made them do more work. The strangers appointed the man they had shot in the night their supervisor. He had been shot in the leg, but the strangers gave him medicine and he soon recovered. They gave him a gun and taught him how to use it. They made him live in a hut on the edge of the field. Whenever they wanted anything from the villagers they sent him. They made him report everything.

The strangers' field grew and grew. It ate up the whole forest. It ate up the valley. It ate up the graves. It ate up the pastures. It ate up the children's playgrounds. It ate up the gardens. It ate up the paths to the kraal. There were good rains and the crops were excellent. But in the villagers' fields the crops were choked by weeds. There were problems in the village. Because the boys were away working for the strangers, the men had to look after the livestock. And because the men had to look after the livestock they could not spend much time on what they were supposed to do. Weeds grew waist-high and choked crops and vegetables in their fields and gardens. Baboons and wild pigs raided their fields. Women had to repair fences and walls.

The strangers' supervisor guarded the crops. Some of the boys helped him. Any livestock that came to the strangers' field were impounded. Soon the strangers had large herds of cattle, sheep and goats built from the impounded beasts. The pasture shrunk and shrunk. The villagers had to take their livestock to the hills, as the strangers grazed their herds in the valley.

After the rains the villagers built granaries for the strangers and brought in the harvest from the field. They reaped little from their own fields. Because the stalks of their millet were hard and thin, it was like a harvest of thorns. They expected to share in the harvests from the strangers' fields. But the strangers made them buy back the food they had themselves grown. The villagers paid with cattle, sheep and goats. The strangers' herds grew.

The villagers' food ran out. They were hungry. They were angry. All along they thought they would get something from the strangers' fields. Their cattle grew thin. Their babies wailed in the night. One night three men went to steal food from the strangers' granary. The guards caught them and shot them. One of the men died and the other two were seriously injured.

Now the villagers were really angry. One of their men had been killed by their own people – guards appointed by the strangers. They gathered axes, spears, bows, arrows and knobkerries and sang war songs. Nobody went to work in the strangers' fields. They burnt the guards' huts and slaughtered their beasts. They tried to raid the granary.

The guards ran off to the strangers' huts. The villagers followed them there. But their weapons were no match for the guns. Five men were killed. The villagers fled to the hills.

There they consulted the *svikiro*.

"Poison the wells from which they draw water," they were told. *"Poison the wells from which they draw water and they shall die."*

Before the villagers could obey the *svikiro's* command, the news got to the guards through some of their relatives in the village. The guards told the strangers of the plan. The strangers placed guards at the wells. So the plan did not work.

The strangers came down to the village. They burnt down the huts. They destroyed the gardens. They drove off the abandoned animals. They extended their field over the area where the village had been.

The villagers stayed on the hills. They built new huts there, but the land was steep and barren. There was not enough land to plough or enough pasture for their livestock. They had lost their land and their livestock to the strangers. They could no longer grow vegetables in the valley. They could no longer fish in the river. They could no longer collect firewood or logs or grass in the forest. They could no longer hunt.

The villagers needed food. They slowly started working for the strangers again, to obtain food. First the men sent their sons then the men themselves went. Even the women went too. They worked all day in the strangers' fields and gardens and homes. The strangers brought their families and built more houses.

The strangers made new rules now. The villagers' wives had to be counted. Their children had to be counted. The marks on their bodies had to be counted. Their cattle and goats and sheep had to be counted. No villager could hunt without the strangers' permission. No villager could chop down a tree without permission. No villager could cut a roll of grass without permission. No villager could build a hut without permission. No villager could marry without permission. The rivers were given new names. The mountains were given new names. The valleys were given new names. The animals were given new names. The birds were given new names. The flowers and the trees were given new names. The children were given new names.

They were taught new songs. They were taught new dances. They were told new stories. Drums were no longer allowed in the village. *Bira* was no longer allowed. *Chisi* was removed. The children were taught to speak the strangers' language. The children were taught to worship the strangers' ancestors.

"Cut the throats of the strangers' children," the *svikiro* said. *"Cut the throats of their children and they will go away."*

The strangers came and took the *svikiro* away and hanged her. Now the villagers had no shrine. They were afraid to touch the strangers. They were the strangers' slaves...

"That is my story," Baas Die says. "That is my little story."

The sniggering initially punctuating the narration has given way first to sympathetic mournful sounds, then a deep silence. Baas Die pauses to feed his nostrils. Baas Die's voice scrapes gravely at the bottom of the silence.

"That is my story," he says. "You may think it's funny or you may think it's sad. You may think it's a story for children round the fire over a pan of *maputi* or you may think it's a tale I made up, but you all know it's the story of our country."

"*Pamberi neChimurenga!*"

"*Pamberi!*" the crowd roars.

"We were bought off with bits of cloth and mirrors. And here we are now..."

Pasi listens from the tree. He knows almost every word Baas Die is going to say. The imagery of it is terrifying. The symbolism of it is vivid as blood pounding from the nose. He has been stirred by speeches like these dozens of times before, but from out here, in the fork of the tree, a quarter-mile from that huge, ultimate audience, the situation is bathed with a terrible significance. Things take on the desperate clarity of this full-moon light. An urgency throbs in his wrists.

Out there Baas Die's voice laughs and starts singing. The crowd joins in, the valley erupts into song. The hills blindly echo back the sound. In the fork of the tree Pasi sings. He sings inside himself, in his head, only his lips move. He feels a mixture of elation and nervousness at the singing in the valley. His eyes scan below, around, beyond – daring, almost, the dangers of the haunting sharp dark profiles of the hills, daring them over into the light, where he can see them.

The moon is half-way up the sky. Pasi looks at its face again and decides the figure on it is a man carrying a sack of maize.

The voices out there are only warming up. The night is very young. Baas Die hasn't really started speaking. His voice isn't hoarse yet. The slogans have only been chanted once. This is only the first song. The drums haven't barked yet, the dancers' feet are still strapped up in their shoes.

Baas Die hasn't started yet. His story has to be paraphrased – the visitors and guests have to be labelled, the presents from the strangers exhibited, the guests' actions weighed and rationalized and the strangers' trickery condemned; the tyrannies have to be enumerated, grievances solicited from the crowd; the protests have to be parallelled with historic events. Then, still, there'll be the mechanics of the war to explain, the role of the villagers, the sacrifice, the vigilance, the traitors to be warned. The goals have to be specified and the spoils glimpsed and, of course, the promised new code explained.

There'll be more singing and dancing.

There is a breeze in the air now. Pasi NemaSellout's head is clear. He has slept in the afternoon and he knows his watch will be easy tonight.

He knows out there by the time the second cock crows and Baas Die's voice is raspy as sand and Gidi Ishumba will have taken over perhaps, the responsive chants of the villagers will be slurred. Fisted arms will not snap into the sky but will rise feebly over drooping heads; the audience will have to be prodded with song. There'll be a hundred battles with sleep out there; the children will be sprawled in the dust and the heads of young men and women will be nodding in the moonlight. Only the wizened heads of the old, sleep burnt out in decades of fretful nights, will stay erect, coughing, wheezing, grunting, scowling, propped on knees or walking sticks.

His head will still be clear then. The sky above is awash with light. He waits. It will be some time before the first cock crows – before that there'll be owls hooting and crows shrieking and maybe a hyena calling. It will be hours before that first flap and tearing cry is taken up in a rippling echo over the land; the moon will be orange, the head of the deserted husband carrying a sack of maize will be tilted towards the trees.

Pasi NemaSellout shifts in the tree. He wishes he could smoke a cigarette, but the smell drifts deeply in the night. He likes the sound of the crowd out there. Their presence uplifts his spirits – something always gnaws at him when, sleep frayed, they straggle back up to their homes along uncertain tracks, leaving the hill to silence.

Something gnaws at him when the group is left alone.

Chapter 23

The Rhodesian soldiers were not deaf. They heard the nightly singing from Sachikonye's village. The singing stung their ears. It made their fingers itch in the crooks of their FNs.

One afternoon an army truck rumbled up to the village shopping centre at the 'township'. There were six soldiers in the truck, two whites in the driver's cabin, and four blacks sitting at the back. The soldiers jumped out, marched into the shops, grabbed four youths, ordered the shops to close and took the youths to their camp for questioning. The youths returned the next day with swollen faces and black eyes. One of them had a broken jaw.

The news got to Baas Die and his group.

"Deny our presence utterly," Baas Die told Headman Sachikonye. "Admit only if you are extremely tortured, and then give misleading information." Sachikonye went away cow-faced. He knew he was like man carrying a sack of grass full of live snakes on his shoulders. He had to be very careful.

The soldiers' interrogation continued. Women returning from the maize mill were charged with feeding terrorists and had buckets of mealie-meal confiscated. The mill was closed. The headmaster of the local primary school and three of his teachers were taken away for three days. The school was closed. The soldiers came to the township and the village, but never ventured to the hills or the forest. They knew the people they wanted were in the area – they did not even need the forced confessions of the villagers to confirm this, but without knowing the exact location of the base or the whereabouts of their enemy, it was too risky for them to go out.

Baas Die and his group kept a low profile for a while. They suspended the *pungwes*. Sometimes they would send for food from the villages, sometimes they wouldn't. Sometimes when the girls brought food, concealed in bundles of wood and grass, there was no one on the hill to meet them. Sometimes the guerrillas would be seen on one hill, sometimes on another. At other times when the *mujhibhas* were bringing them information about the soldiers' movements, one of the guerrillas would intercept them before they got to the pre-arranged place.

One morning at dawn a lorry full of soldiers drove up to Headman Sachikonye's homestead. Sachikonye heard the truck arrive and came out of his hut tying the bark-string belt of his frayed black trousers.

The soldiers, black and white, scrunched through the confusion of huts and squawking chickens and saw the shrivelled, old white-haired headman cowering on the doorway of his hut. They stood around him, glaring down at him.

"Where are they?"

"You were singing with them every night. Where are they?"

"Where are they?"

"Where are they? You're feeding them!"

The barrel of a gun rammed into the old man's chest, digging between his ribs.

"This is your last chance, *mudhara*. We've let you off too long. If you don't tell us *now*, where they are, we're setting this whole village on fire!"

Sachikonye knew what he was going to say. He had been thinking about it every night since the start of the *pungwes*. He cringed under the weight of his secret rehearsal. His face was flashed with sweat. He broke wind and relieved himself into his trousers. The soldiers bunched and wrinkled their faces. One of them kicked him on the side.

Sachikonye staggered. Then he raised a gnarled old finger and pointed to the hill. "There," he said, "their base is behind that blue hill. That's where they live."

"You know what will happen if you lie to us?" A barrel jabbed again at his chest.

"You . . . you'll find them there."

They got back to their truck, voices swarming over walkie-talkies, and drove off in a cloud of dust.

Sachikonye picked himself up and banged on the door of one of his huts.

Musa and Cheukai, his two teenage sons, were already awake to the noise and rushed out.

"Run to the comrades, " Sachikonye panted, "tell them the soldiers came and that I sent them to Mvuri Hill. Run as fast as you can. Run like the whirlwind, you hear me?"

The two boys bolted into the bushes, in the opposite direction from where

184

the truck was going. Soon, all his wives were clamouring around him. He gazed at the rope of dust in the sky, at the shimmering blue hill and then gripped his trousers, bunched his feet together and hurried off through the crowd of his wives and children towards the bushes behind the huts. He had not finished cleaning himself when the guns started firing in the forest.

The lorry swerved off the twin track road and crashed on its side, in the grass. The firing was brief. When the soldiers jumped out of the smoking truck to haul out the injured, and others scrambled into positions round the carnage, the forest was quiet. The only noise was the growl of voices over walkie-talkies and the echoes of the villagers fleeing. And, in the distance, the drone of approaching helicopters.

They set off as soon as dusk set in. There was no moon, darkness clamped its hand over the eye of the land. Weighted down by the heavy arms they carried, they moved slowly.

Pasi NemaSellout concentrated on breathing deeply and steadying his pace to save his energy. He had slept that afternoon and the day before that and he knew it would be some time before sleep started tugging at his temples. The line kept rearranging itself. Sometimes it was Baas Die leading, at other times Gidi Ishumba; and he was in the middle or near the end, slogging behind Sub Musango.

The line stretched and compressed as the terrain swept them up and the narrow necks of rock squeezed them together and sometimes they would bunch up when the person at the front stopped to review the directions. The night sucked them deep into that dead world where shadows stooped to the weight of darkness and lunged after them.

They passed a stream where fireflies squirted sparks of feeble light, wading through acres of waist high grass, and then sometimes they stumbled on to the edge of a homestead and a sheet-white tombstone shot up, out of the bush, in front of them, like a bed somebody had made and left out there unslept in, behind the blue ink stain blotch of huts where the people seemed dead too – strangled by darkness and sleep so even their dogs didn't bark.

The milky way swung like a great white crocodile in the sky. His eyes swam and he was only his two dead feet slapping in the dust after Gidi Ishumba and there were others groping behind him . . .

Just before dawn, they sat down to rest.

He flopped against the trunk of a tree and fell asleep. He woke up two hours later to the sound of a cow lowing nearby. The sun was up and in the distance, a mile away, the sky was full of the sound of cattle running and cowbells clanking. He sprang to his feet, thinking the herd was coming towards them. His mates were nowhere in sight. He looked around him carefully, listened.

The noise was receding, going away from where he was. The stray lowing came again, closer now and a brown cow stepped into view, between the trees. It stood ponderously, its ears poised towards the bushes on its flank.

Pasi heard a very low whistle from the bushes at which the cow was gazing. The cow grunted and took one step back, its big eyes bulging with curiosity. Gidi Ishumba carefully stepped out from behind the bushes, whistling low to keep the cow still, and tossed a belt round the cow's hind legs.

The cow spotted Pasi. It kicked out wildly. Gidi Ishumba sprang back from the flying hooves and snatched up the belt in the grass.

"Don't move." Gidi Ishumba flipped the belt at the cow's legs, coaxing it, whistling softly. The cow stood still for a moment. Gidi Ishumba nimbly locked the belt round its legs and pulled the thin end.

"Hold this," he said, holding up the end of the belt to Pasi.

Pasi stepped over, planted his feet at a safe distance just behind the cow and grabbed the belt. He tugged lightly at the belt, stooping against the weight of the cow's back.

"I had forgotten you *born-location*s are afraid of cows," Gidi Ishumba chuckled, crouching under the cow's belly. The cow's udder was big and swollen like a football and the teats hung down like huge, cream-coloured bananas. Gidi Ishumba's small black fingers dug into the udder and pulled at the teats. The milk squirted out into his open mouth, the flow growing thicker, foaming over his pink tongue. The cow stood still and grunted a little. After a while Gidi Ishumba stood up, wiped his milky mouth on his sleeve and took the belt from him.

"Don't you need a drink?"

Pasi crouched timidly under the big hot flank of the cow. The cow turned its head slowly and looked down at him. Its eyes were big and round and dark, like plums dipped in oil. It grunted inquisitively and turned away and then he tugged at a teat. A few foamy drops splattered over his face.

"Squeeze slowly from the top of the teat, downwards," Gidi Ishumba laughed. "*Hei*! Have you never milked a cow?"

The dust from Gidi Ishumba's fingers was still on the teats, soaking in the foam. Pasi locked his fingers at the base of the slippery teats and pulled slowly. Two arrows of milk darted into his shirt and dripped down his chest. He lowered his gaping face, pulled again and the milk rained into his mouth, pinging on to his palate. His nose filled with the hot dark smell of the cow's underside – the smell of hide and cud and urine – the warm creamy milk oozed into him as his fingers slid confidently over the supple teats.

"Is this our breakfast?" he heard Baas Die's voice from behind him, and Mabunu Muchapera said, "Where did you get her?"

Pasi closed his eyes and drank until Gidi Ishumba laughed and said, "Don't you ever have enough? There's a line waiting!"

They all laughed. He squirted a few more mouthfuls and then stood up.

After they let the cow loose it turned round and grunted at them, as if it was still expecting its restrained calf to burst out from their arms to claim its rightful teats.

"I think it strayed from the herds going to the dip," Gidi Ishumba said, beating it off. "It probably left a young calf at home somewhere . . ."

The cow backed off angrily, its empty udder swishing from side to side like an old woman's breasts.

They rested there throughout the morning, taking turns to sleep and keep watch. At midday Baas Die took off his shoes and his bazooka and exchanged his shirt for Torai Zvombo's ragged T-shirt. He slipped a knife and a grenade into a secret pocket in the inside of his trousers and rubbed some dust in his hair.

Barefoot, ragged, carrying only a cattle whip – disguised perfectly as a herdsman – he went off alone to inspect the district office, now just two miles away from where they stopped. He did not come back until late in the afternoon, sweating profusely.

The district office consisted of three white buildings with neat roofs of grass thatch. Two of these were long like classrooms, with wide verandahs. The rooms in these buildings served as offices where villagers came to pay poll, cattle and dog tax, to apply for registration certificates, building permits and so on. The third building was the District Commissioner's house built in the Dutch style popular among the early colonial whites. A high pig-wire fence topped by four strands of barbed wire and backed up by a two-metre high wall of sandbags enclosed the buildings. Two floodlights lit the area and a narrow perimeter of bush. There were three sentry posts on the sandbag walls and four military trucks parked in a corner behind one of the office buildings.

West of the District Office, separated by a thin bush, outside the fortification, was the shopping centre – half a dozen small shops, a grinding mill and two bottle stores. Beyond, on the stretch of denuded land was the dip tank where cattle from the district came for the weekly dip.

By nightfall the whole area was quiet. Before the war, the hubbub of voices and screaming juke-boxes from the bottle stores and shops would have filled the night. The bush around would have been alive with the abandoned singing and humming of drunkards straggling home. The kerosene light would still be blazing in the shops, and youths would be idling and flirting under the eaves. The grinding mill might still be pounding away at one last bucket of maize, rocking the earth and filling the night air with the familiar township smell of diesel.

But now, tonight, the area was dead. The closed shops glowed dully in the moonless night – only the two floodlights blazed like incongruous suns on the fortification. The only sound was the soft thud of the feet of the dozen guards shifting round the sandbag wall, marking time to the shrill of crickets, and, occasionally, muffled gusts of music from the District Commissioner's house.

The attack lasted exactly five minutes.

First they cut the telephone lines.

Three bursts of shellfire crashed through the two administrative buildings. A rocket tore down a section of wall on the District Commissioner's house. Grenades exploded through the windows. The grass roofs of the buildings popped into a blaze as incendiary arrows hit them.

There was a shudder inside the fortification, a few seconds of paralysis, followed by shouts and running feet. Camouflaged figures darted in the searing light of the fires. The machine guns roared from the darkness, sweeping the sandbag walls and raking up the middle.

Five minutes – and there were thrashing sounds in the bush, drowned by the roar of sky-licking fires as an angry quartet of FNs started a blind stutter into the night.

He had run for two hours through the dark bush and now his pace slowed down to a quick march.

After the attack the group had broken up and fanned out in concentric spoors. He had laid his trail on a mile of sandy forest, away from the scene. Losing his footprints on to a stretch of stony slope, he had swung back in the direction of the camp so that the haze of the burning camp was half behind him and half to his left. For two hours, alone now, he had run on that course.

Now the hunger of two nights sent a wave of nausea through him. The ball of his throat stuck into his pipe like a chiselled stone that cut at him with each attempt to swallow. A tightness wove around his eyes.

Let me not lose my way . . . he repeated to himself, peering out into the horizon for a sign of the hills. His eyes were accustomed to the darkness now – the two nights had dovetailed into each other squeezing the thought of day into a thin blur.

The forest thinned out and he was facing a stretch of winter-ploughed fields. They had not passed these on their way the night before; he realized how far south he had gone. He followed the razor strips of forest on the edge of the dark furrowed acres, down the undulating slope, until he made out a grey belt of mushroom huts backed by a thin bush. He scanned the line of huts for a while, looking for breaks in it. The line ran almost evenly, except for two wooded points where the land lifted like a pair of hairy breasts. He made for the nearest of these points.

A dog bayed at him from the line. Soon another joined in, and then the night erupted into a far-flung cacophony of growls and yelps. As he approached, crunching through the tall grass of an unploughed stand, this noise swirled to a pitch and he saw two dark forms dash at him from the huts. Suppressing the urge to curse and run, he slinked on, and then he was in the bushes, over the hill and the line, past kraals of cattle. He stumbled through the backyard night smell of that village, cutting across a tangle of tracks, through the stink of cattle and cowdung and human refuse and crumbling graves, through mournful *mpfuti* trees to the valley.

He smelt the damp clayey smell of the vlei ahead. He swallowed thirstily, his throat hurting again.

There were gardens in the vlei, fenced in by rough walls of logs and dead tree branches. At first he did not recognize the gardens – the walls might have looked to him like a stockade round a home. Then he made out the tasselling heads of the maize sticking out above that fence. He walked up to one of them and heaved himself over. He landed on a damp patch and his boots squelched in the mud. His nostrils were filled with the dampness. Green maize stalks brushed his face. He lumbered through the mud, parting leaf blades with his arms, his eyes searching for water.

It was only a dark gleam in the corner, framed by logs, so thin he could have mistaken it for a sliver of light. He knelt in the mud, cupping his hands.

The water stabbed into him so that he swayed dizzily over the well. He clamped a hand over his head and drank more slowly from one palm, until he felt the water almost coming up to his chest inside him. The mealies were only tasselling and had no cobs. He searched for pumpkins among the tendrils snaking at his feet, but there was nothing there either. Then he found a bed of sweet cabbage and ate the white hearts of two balls. He put three cabbages into his back-pack and climbed out of the garden.

Up at the line the dogs were barking again, in another direction. He decided they were not barking at him. He wondered if perhaps they were barking at one of his comrades. Munching up the cabbage in his hands, he crossed the vlei. The water swished heavily in his belly. A frog croaked timidly in a ditch, all around him the grass glowed pale khaki. A tiny purple hint of dawn streaked the eastern horizon.

He waddled into the dark trees to find a place to sleep.

The sun woke him up, burning red through his eyelids. His skin and clothes were damp with the dew. The black vlei mud had caked thickly on his boots. He ran a hand through his hair and ripped out grass seeds. He rubbed the corners of his eyes and mouth. A dove cooed in the boughs above. He sat up, stretching and yawning in the warm sun.

He stood up and scanned the land around him. Across the vlei in the east, he could see the line of huts and brown fields he had crossed, clear now in the daylight. He looked out to the west for the hills. His eyes met only rolling forest. Then he moved his eyes slowly, northwards. There was a point on the horizon, a shimmering blue swell of land, just visible from where he was.

The sun seemed to be out of place, somehow. At first he could not believe it, but when he slowly retraced his course he realized he had gone too far south, so far that his destination, the shimmering hill, was now north, and not east of him. A faint tremor ran down his spine.

He saw two women with buckets on their heads coming down the vlei towards the gardens. He was seized by the momentary impulse to go down to them and ask for food, but remembering the cabbages in his back-pack and the ugly footprints he might have left in the garden, he suddenly wanted to get away from the place. He walked up the forest, close to the edge of the vlei until he heard the cattle herds coming. He hid behind a tree. The cattle passed him in a swirl of dust, cowbells jangling, the trotting little herdboys' whips cracking behind them.

Further on he skirted a man chopping down a tree. It was hot now, getting on towards midday. He sat down and ate another cabbage. He had just finished eating when he heard the chug of a chopper.

A few paces away from the tree under which he sat there was a bushy *nhengeni* tree whose thick bows hung down to the ground. He scrambled towards it, dragging himself through the thorns and sliding on his belly to the dark base of the tree, just as the chopper thundered past, almost over him, so that its huge shadow streaked over the perimeter.

He lay there for a while, until he heard the echo of the chopper, now in the west, fading out.

It didn't come back. He decided it was unsafe to walk during the day. It was dark and cool under the trees. He spent the afternoon there. He would sleep for some time, and then wake up abruptly when a twig snapped and then fall slowly asleep again.

He resumed his march after sunset. The rest had refreshed him, but with the last cabbage gone, hunger was now a nausea gnawing up from his belly. His arms were torn where the thorns had slashed at his bare skin.

He didn't reach the first huts in Sachikonye's line until after midnight. It was a small compound of one round and one square hut, surrounded by mango trees drooping with unripe fruit. On one corner of the clearing was a granary, perched on large rocks. He picked his way through the orchard, towards the huts. A dog growled at him from the granary. He paused to brush off nests of *chidongi* thorns from the hem of his jeans. He walked straight at the dog. For a moment the dog stood its ground, thin head reared, growling, but when it saw he wouldn't budge it backed off. The skin of his ankles crawled as he passed, inches from its sniffing snout, his hands gripping the barrel of his gun, ready to smash down on the creature's back if it leaped at him. But the dog knew better; it crawled off with a gruffy, superstitious scowl and side-looked him as he crept up to the door of the square hut.

He knocked twice. He heard movements inside – a bed squeak, the soft thud of footsteps – and then a man's voice.

"Who's that?"

He knocked again.

"Who are you?" the voice inside asked again, shakily.

The door cracked, squealed an inch and the gleam of an eye peeked from the dark thin gape of doorway.

"Who are you?" said the voice, hesitantly now. The door squealed another inch and the half face peered at him, at the gun and the shiny bayonet.

"Come out," he said.

A lean man, naked except for a pair of shorts, stepped out in front of the bayonet. The man's arms were held out at his sides like the wings of a hen about to bolt.

"I'm hungry," Pasi NemaSellout said. The man stared at him for a while, his eyes dropping over his clothes, his gun, timidly climbing over to his backpack. He made an unintelligible sound, half gasp, half greeting. Then, with one hand held up and out at Pasi, he ducked his head into the hut and summoned his wife. She was awake already. She promptly came out, a short, plump woman, swishing a cloth over her waist, behind her husband, and they strode towards the round hut, in front of him. He stood in the doorway, watching and listening to the dark, while they fumbled inside the hut. Then he heard a match struck and he saw a tiny wisp of flame curl at the fireplace, in the centre of the hut. His eyes swept the orchard once more, and the trees beyond, and then he went into the half-lit hut, stooping in the doorway. The man planted a stool for him at the head of the fire, opposite the door, but when he saw the visitor remain there, near the door, he approached with the stool held out in his hands.

Pasi took the stool, set it behind the door and sat down on it, his gun held between his knees. The woman went past him, her head bowed slightly, at a polite distance, through the door, into the night. His head shot up instinctively and peered after her, listening to her footsteps. The man watched him uneasily, squatting on his ankles against the wall. Pasi heard thin wood snap, grass rustle. He sat up when he heard the footsteps return and then his eyes met the man's eyes and he coughed quickly.

The woman crouched at the fireplace, cracking twigs and carefully laying them over the ball of grass. The hut filled with smoke, and then a strong flame burst out of the turf and she planted the faggots symmetrically round it. Pasi's eyes smarted from the smoke. The man squinted his eyes and held his lips open. The woman breathed heavily, her breath rasping like an asthmatic's, her eyes unblinking.

192

Pasi's eyes watered. His chest felt stuffy and his nose stung, but after a while the smoke cleared and a draft of fresh air breezed through the door.

At the head of the hut there was an earthen shelf full of brightly painted plates and mugs and pots. At the base of the shelf, against the mud wall, stood three buckets of water. In one half of the hut, he noticed suddenly, a stride from where he sat, a sleeping figure lay wrapped in a blanket. The snores came in low gusts, below the crackle of the fire.

The woman worked nimbly, cutting up ropes of dried meat and loading the pieces into a pot, next to another pot of water already on the fire. Every now and then the man would reach over and shove a faggot deeper into the fire, making the flame hiss and leap, and then sit on the earthen bench against the wall, his hands listlessly hooking up his heels.

The hut got hot, the air moist from the frothing pots on the fire. The woman's small, corpulent face shone red in the firelight, her forehead laced with sweat. Her cheeks looked healthily puffed out, white grains of sleep stuck in the corners of her eyes. Her hair was short without a head-tie and she kept tugging at the printed cloth wrapping her legs.

Her small bust heaved and swung under a faded white T-shirt on which the words RHODESIA IS SUPER stuck out in bold blue print over a faded picture of the Victoria Falls.

Pasi looked at the tongues of firelight flickering out of the hut through the open doorway and he stood up and closed the door. The man glanced at him when he closed the door, and shoved a faggot into the fire. The woman's mouth twitched as if she was going to say something but the man stretched and smothered his fingers with his hands and stared darkly from the bench.

The woman in the T-shirt glanced at him, her eyes colliding with his. She was older than she seemed, one of those small, plump misleading bodies that, especially in the half-light of a *pungwe*, could pass for thirty when they were forty-five. The man had hair on his chest and some of it was white. His face was thin and smooth and beardless, but his hair was grey.

The woman's mouth moved as if she wanted to speak. Then she said, *"Hatizi kuzobvunza kuti munotamba here."*

She spoke with a heavy accent, her voice just above a whisper, clapping her hands in quick courtesy. It took him a while to work out what she had said, to realize that she was half apologizing for not having formally greeted him earlier. The man joined in immediately, clapping his hands too, but making a shallower clapping sound expected of men. Pasi responded briefly to their greetings, nodding his head towards them. The man said, as if to ward off the silence, "*Ndimi munebasaka iri.*"

"*Yaa,*" Pasi nodded, his face almost a head above the level of theirs, from where he sat.

The pot of water was boiling now. She stirred the mealie-meal into it, smoothing it with a stick. She closed the pot and then turned the frying meat and put onions and salt in it. She tasted the soup with a small quick tongue, added more salt.

The man coughed, brought out a tin of snuff from his shorts. He tipped a little on to his palm, pinched it into his nose and then offered the tin to Pasi.

"*Mazvita,*" Pasi said, shaking his head.

The man gave a small, puzzled smile and put the tin away.

The figure on the floor moved. The blanket slid down and the upper half of a face appeared.

The woman's hand worked nimbly at the pot. The *sadza* was thick now, heavy on the stick, puffing at her. Meal powder sprayed into the fire and burst, filling the hut with a sweet pungent smell. She fetched a plate from the shelf, dusted it with a cloth and then scooped the *sadza* out on to the plate with expert sweeps of the stick, shaping the steaming hot layers into a conical white hill.

The figure on the floor stopped snoring. Braided locks appeared under the blanket. The man coughed on the earthen bench, hands fidgeting. He ducked at the fire and pulled two faggots to the edge of the fireplace to disperse the heat and smoke.

The woman turned the meat again while the sadza cooled and then poured some water into a tin dish made out of an empty oil can for him to wash his hands. She tipped the meat into a bowl, knelt and put the two steaming plates in front of him. She clapped her hands quickly, squeezed her right hand in the water and took the customary cook's taste of the food she had prepared.

"*Mongodya zvichipisa,*" she said, retreating to her place at the head of the fire.

He ate quickly, his hands waiting impatiently, loaded, at his mouth. They watched the shadow of his face on the wall. His face was flushed with sweat, his eyes still squinting in the thin smoke. He saw them watching him. The woman's mouth twitched. She wanted to say something. The figure in the blanket moved again, wakeful movements, breath coming in slow, cautious sucks of air.

194

The man coughed, and said, "You must be very hungry . . ."

"*Yaa*," Pasi grunted. The man looked back with a hopeful smile.

He was eating more slowly now, licking the soup off his fingers, scraping at flecks of sadza with his teeth. The conical white hill was reduced to a small fist, the lake of soup to a quarter-moon-shaped pond; the meat gone. He dunked his hands into the tin dish and wiped his hands on his sleeves.

"Did the soldiers come?" he asked, at last, sitting up on the stool.

A face peered from the blanket, a girl's face with braided locks.

The woman looked quickly at the girl and stared into the fire. The man hesitated, then he said, "We don't know."

"You don't know?"

"No."

There was something the man was hiding. He didn't want to talk. He peered through the dim light at Pasi, at his boots, his gun.

The woman looked up at her husband, her eyes transmitting secret messages. Pasi caught her gaze and she looked away. Then she said, "We are not sure . . . Do you . . . are you part of the group?"

"What group?" Pasi cut in.

She looked into the fire, her eyes trembling. Her husband stared open-mouthed at the wall.

"The group," she said, "*vana mukoma* who were here."

Pasi stared into the fire and laughed, a long loud puzzling laugh. "Why did you cook for me if you didn't know who I was? Do you cook for *mapuruvheya* too?"

The couple protested vigorously by shaking their heads and stared dully into the fire.

A pair of eyes peered from the blanket.

The man looked up hopefully and said, slowly, "We only wanted to be sure."

"Who do you know that you are sure of?"

The couple did not answer. The embers sputtered in the fireplace.

"Which others have you cooked for?"

"We've never cooked for anyone . . ." the woman jumped in, agitated now by the man sitting on the stool laughing, this man who had come out of the night and closed them in behind their own doors, this young man who hadn't said a word until he had eaten, and was now cradling his gun between his knees . . .

"We only know of Comrade Baas Die and his group," the man said, boldly avoiding his wife's remonstrative looks.

"Who is Baas Die?"

"He's the leader."

"How many men does he have in his group?"

"I don't know."

"Is he still around with his men?"

"We haven't seen them for a week."

"Would you know any of his men if you saw them?

"No."

"Then how do you know them?"

"We only heard their names."

"What are their names?"

"Can I . . . may I ask you who you . . ."

"I asked you a question. Does a question answer a question?"

The man scratched his temples.

Pasi laid his gun carefully on his knees. "Who is Pasi NemaSellout?"

"He's one of the comrades in the group. Baas Die mentioned his name."

"Have you ever met him?"

"No."

"Would you know him if you met him?"

"No."

Pasi laughed again. *"Kudzidza hakuperi nhai*! You'll never stop learning in this war . . . it's all right. Yah. You should never answer questions unless you know who you're talking to. And even if it's a comrade don't be too keen to show you know him or her even if that comrade is your own brother or sister. Vigilance! *Pamberi nekuchenjera muhondo!"*

"Pamberi!" the couple responded, raising their fists in the dim light of the hut.

"Now answer my question," Pasi said to the man.

"About the names of Baas Die's men?"

"Aika, baba, we finished with that one. What was the first question I asked you?"

"You asked about the *mapuruvheya*."

"Yah."

"Three helicopters came after the lorry crashed. Two of them landed where the crash occurred and then flew off again, but the third one – it flew over the village, for a long time, like an eagle . . . The people were hiding in the bush and in the fields. Two herdboys were shot. They ran away when they saw the helicopters and then they were shot."

"They shouldn't have run. We told you never to run when you see the helicopters."

"One of the boys – the grandson of Makwande, an old widow who lives up the slope, she has two huts next to a clump of rocks near the *ruware* – this widow's son, the boy, he was running through the cows, Ephraim is his name, he was shot here, in the head, just above the ear, and the women who went to the hospital to see him yesterday, Mai Mahamba and Boki's aunt – the men are not going out since – these women who went with his mother to see him, they say any morning he could be gone . . . The other, the *sabuku*'s son, Sachikonye's second son with his third wife, the one who had started at the big school this year, Cheukai is his name, they say he and his brother had been sent to alert the comrades when the helicopters came, his brother escaped, but he, this boy, the *sabuku*'s son, he was shot in the shoulders and legs. He's in hospital too, and they say the nurses took seven bullets out of him . . ."

"Did the soldiers come again after that?"

"We haven't seen them."

"Have any of my comrades been here?"

"Not one of them. Did they . . . did you go away, then?"

"That is not for you to know," Pasi snapped, and the man's face sank in the shadow of the wall, a thin man's face just finished telling news of death, cowering in the shadows, wilting to the stare of an eighteen-year-old.

"You realize you must not tell anyone that I came here?" he said, hitching his gun over his shoulder. "Nobody."

The man and his wife nodded. Pasi pointed to the face peeping out of the blanket, "Her too."

The man and his wife nodded again, frantically. Then he said, "*Pamberi neChimurenga!*" and they responded, "*Pamberi!*" He sprang to his feet, opened the door and strode out, without another word, without a goodbye, into the darkness.

He thought about the woman's small plump face while she made sadza, of the face with the braided locks in the blankets, and the man's eyes wilting when he spoke sharply to him and he wondered too about the faces of the boys who had been shot and if he would ever remember them and if perhaps he should have said something kind or sorry about them to the man and his wife, but he could not concentrate on that yet, he was full of sadza and biltong and the thin dog was snarling again under the granary and soon the night would erupt into growls and yelping and he had to pick his way swiftly through the dark, through kraals, through nests of crumbling graves and fields of *chidongi* thorns to where he had to go . . .

Chapter 24

Torai Zvombo sprawled in the pale morning light of the cave with his back against the wall, half propped up on his elbows.

Gidi Ishumba knelt over him holding a tin mug to his face.

"What happened?" Pasi gasped.

Nobody said anything. Baas Die chewed on the inside of a cheek and plucked at his goatee. Gidi Ishumba pressed the tin mug to Torai Zvombo's face.

"Drink," said Gidi Ishumba, tilting the cup.

Torai Zvombo moaned, a low moan echoing in the tin mug. He pressed a feeble hand to his stomach. He moaned again. Then he retched.

Gidi Ishumba leaned, with a contorted face, over him.

He tried to drink again. The milk washed over his lower lip and dripped to the ground.

"Don't you have anything in the first-aid kit?" Baas Die asked.

Gidi Ishumba pressed the tin mug to Torai Zvombo's face. Torai Zvombo made a quick harsh sound in his throat. His head fell again, his eyes squeezed tight. Gidi Ishumba held his head down by the neck. He threw up again, through the mouth and the nose, a slimy greenish yellowish liquid. His breath scraped through blocked nostrils.

Gidi Ishumba wiped the vomit off his arm with a bunch of leaves. He wiped Torai Zvombo's face and laid him against the wall. He picked at the stuff splashed on a rock and said, "Yes, mushrooms."

Torai Zvombo's breath steadied, but his eyes were closed.

Then they heard the chopper.

It came from the east.

Baas Die and Pasi NemaSellout scrambled deeper into the cave, cradling their guns. Gidi Ishumba swung his rifle over his shoulder and faced the light. Torai Zvombo's sunken eyes snapped open.

The helicopter drew a wide circle round the area and then came towards the hill, a big screaming green and black iron dragon-fly. It chugged over them, whipping wind and dust through the mouth of the cave. Then it rolled away, crashing into the distance.

Mabunu Muchapera and Shungu Dzangu scrambled into the cave.

"We could have roasted them," Mabunu Muchapera panted. "They flew right over us! Sons of bitches!"

Sub Musango stumbled in.

Torai Zvombo sat up, inching away from his vomit.

Gidi Ishumba loaded a new magazine into his rifle.

Shungu Dzangu gazed out at the sky with moist, tremulous eyes and shook his head.

Pasi NemaSellout leaned on a rock to quell the hammering in his chest.

"We're staying under close cover today," Baas Die said.

"But one bit of fungus can poison a whole load of mushrooms," Shungu Dzangu said.

"We can't let her get away with this," Mabunu Muchapera said.

"Even if it were a mistake, it'd be unforgivable," Gidi Ishumba said.

"Why did she give them to *him*?" Sub Musango asked.

"She can't get away with this," Pasi nodded.

"She'll have to be a lesson for all the others," Mabunu Muchapera hissed. "The *povo* could turn against us."

"What more do you want?" Mabunu Muchapera ranted. "She has poisoned one of us – what more proof do you need that she's a sellout?"

"She has to go," said Sub Musango.

"What if it had been in one of the pots the girls bring? We'd all have had it!" said Pasi.

"She has to go."

"She's a goner."

"She'll have to go, fast, before she does us all in."

"Today . . ."

"Now!"

"What do you say, Chef? I say, let's search her home! I wouldn't be surprised if she had guns hidden in her roof!"

"Yes, that's an idea," said Gidi Ishumba.

"What if we don't find anything?" Shungu Dzangu said.

"We still have enough proof," Sub Musango said.

200

"You don't want her *ngozi* after us. We don't know any of these people . . ."

"They don't know us either," said Gidi Ishumba, "They don't know our names or our totems or where we come from. They couldn't harm us."

"What do names and totems have to do with this?" Pasi asked.

"You don't mess around with the blood of people you don't know," Shungu Dzangu shook his head admonishingly.

"What about *mapuruvheya*? Do you care for those too?"

"Soldiers are soldiers. These people, the povo, they see us and know us . . ."

"What's wrong with you?" Mabunu Muchapera flared. "She's a traitor! Forget the *ngozi* nonsense. We're digging our own graves if we let people like her off! I'd bet my sub she's an informer. I say she has to go, now!"

"Make a lesson of her for the others . . ." said Sub Musango.

"But how do you get the villagers together with a curfew on and the whole sky full of choppers?" Shungu Dzangu continued.

"To hell with the curfew! Smith's soldiers never move in the dark. You know that! I wouldn't be surprised if she brought the choppers."

"How?"

"She knows we're back. She knew when Torai Zvombo went to her place to ask for food. What do you say, Chef?"

Baas Die coughed. He took a pinch of snuff. Then he said, "Mabunu Muchapera may be right. There is something fishy about this. There haven't been any soldiers here since that ambush. And now the morning we come back the whole air force is after us. There must be an informer in this village."

Torai Zvombo sat up and closed his eyes, with a hand on his belly. Gidi Ishumba fixed his hard round eyes expectantly on Baas Die. His lips were clamped shut. They all looked at Baas Die.

Baas Die cleared his throat and examined a piece of hair on his fingers. Then he said, "All right. So far we are only suspicious. The poisoning may have been intentional. It may have been accidental. When I was a child me and my sisters got sick from mushrooms my mother picked. Obviously my mother didn't mean to kill us. It's difficult to decide if this case was accidental or intentional . . ."

"She shouldn't have taken the risk," Sub Musango butted in.

"Feeding mushrooms to a . . ."

"Don't interrupt me!" Baas Die continued. "We'll question her and search her home. Any volunteers?"

"I'll do it," said Mabunu Muchapera. "It was my idea."

"You'll need one other person to go with you."

"I will," Sub Musango offered.

"No," said Baas Die, "you stay behind, Sub. Shungu Dzangu will go with him."

"It was in the grass thatch of her hut," Shungu Dzangu said.

Baas Die took the walkie-talkie from Gidi Ishumba. He flicked the switch on and off, pulled the antenna up and down.

"Where did she say she got it?"

"Her son gave it to her. He's in the police reserve."

"What?"

"She confessed."

"Where is Mabunu Muchapera?"

"He stayed behind, guarding her."

"Well," said Baas Die, "who's going to stay behind with Torai Zvombo?"

"You go," Torai Zvombo said, sitting up against the wall, "I'll be all right."

The villagers came quickly in the dark. They sat under two large trees in a grassy area behind Sachikonye's compound. A fire burnt in the middle of the gathering, bathing their faces with an orange light. The whites of their eyes shone expectantly in the firelight. Only the fire made a sound as the twigs crackled and popped in the blaze.

Baas Die paced round the fire. Mabunu Muchapera and Pasi NemaSellout stood at the edge of the crowd, out of reach of the firelight. The others were in the bush, patrolling.

"Tonight you have gathered to see a *m'tengesi*," Baas Die said. "Do you all know what a *m'tengesi* is?"

Tension rippled through the crowd.

"*Vahandzvadzi*," Baas Die pointed to a young girl in the crowd, "can you tell us what a *m'tengesi* is?"

The girl stammered confusedly and Baas Die picked on the young man sitting next to her.

"A *m'tengesi* is someone who sells out," said the young man.

"What does he sell out? Tomatoes? Pumpkins?"

"He passes information to the enemy."

"That's right," said Baas Die, almost like a teacher in the classroom. "A *m'tengesi* passes information to the enemy. What do they call a *m'tengesi* in

202

English? Hey? Aren't there any schoolchildren here? Or is the word not in your syllabus? Heh? A *m'tengesi* is a 'sellout' in English. 'Sellout'. You get that?"

Baas Die brought out the walkie-talkie and held it up to the crowd. "Have you ever seen *chiover-over*?" he shouted, pulling the antenna up and down. A low buzz began in the crowd.

"Mai Tawanda," a low woman's voice hissed, from the crowd.

Baas Die turned on the woman sitting alone in front of the others and said, "*Amai*, can you show us how this thing works?"

She was a big boned, light-skinned woman with a wide face and long dark hair swirling out of a white *doek*. She wore a grey nylon blouse, a blue skirt and white tennis shoes. A pair of yellow earrings shaped like half peaches plugged her earlobes. At first her face had a defiant upward look but when Baas Die thrust the black thing into her lap her face sunk and stared glumly into the fire.

"Mai Tawanda! I've said so many many times," the voice hissed again, with gleeful vengeance, and other voices took up the cry. The crowd broke into shrieks and hoots.

"Mai Tawanda," Baas Die repeated. "I said can you show us how this thing works?"

Mai Tawanda looked up briefly, and then broke into a loud wail.

"*Aika, Amai*, don't waste our time."

The crowd laughed.

Mai Tawanda picked up the walkie-talkie from her lap and held it in her trembling hands. The crowd shrieked and hooted.

"I've said so many times before," the voiced hissed again.

"Forgive me, *vanangu*," she sobbed. "I didn't know, *vanangu*."

"Don't call us *vanangu*. We are not sons of *vatengesi!*"

"It was just given to me. I didn't know . . ."

"Who gave it to you?"

"They came to me and gave it to me . . ."

"*Who* gave it to you? Have these people got no names?"

"The men from the camp."

"What relationship have you got with *mapuruvheya!* Are they your *vak-washa*? Why did they come to *you*?"

"They said, 'You have to do this for your son.' They said, 'If you don't tell us where the boys are we'll shoot your son'."

"Where does your son work?"

"He is a policeman."

"He's a *puruwheya!*"

"No, *mwanangu!*"

"*Aika, mhamha,* we are not playing *nhodo.* Who doesn't know that even policemen are carrying guns and fighting against us? Isn't your son in the police reserve? Isn't your son on patrol at this moment?"

"I don't know, *mwanangu.*"

"Your son gave this thing to you. Don't deny it! What did he tell you to do with it?"

"They said . . . he said . . . if the boys came . . . I should speak to them with this thing . . ."

"So you were telling them about every meeting we had?"

"I only used it . . . once."

"When?"

"The first *pungwe* we had."

"What about the lorries and helicopters that came to the township? What about the helicopter that flew over the village this morning? You told them we were back, didn't you?"

"No, *mwanangu.*"

"*Footsek, mhani!* You'll make me call you things you'll never want to hear again! We are not at a women's club! We are not at a *ndari.*"

"Forgive me, *vanangu.*"

"What about the poison you gave to one of us last night?"

"Poison?"

"Yes, the mushrooms you cooked for our friend."

"He came to my hut and said, '*Amai,* I'm hungry.' I said '*Mwanangu,* I have only mealie-meal and no meat or vegetables and I can't go to my garden at this time of the night and if I try to go out to the pen to catch a chicken it might make noise and bring the soldiers.' I said to him, 'I only have these dried mushrooms my aunt gave me' and he said, 'Cook them' and I did. I even tasted the food for him before he ate . . ."

"Those are just stories you're making up. We wouldn't know what you drank to protect yourself. You'll be glad to hear our friend is ill because of what you gave him."

"I'm very very sorry, *vanangu.* I didn't know. Honestly, honestly, honestly, I didn't know . . ."

"What did you put in the mushrooms? *Dhibha*? *Rogor*?"

"Honestly, *mwanangu*, I didn't know. The mushrooms were given to me by my aunt. I didn't pick them myself. There might have been poisonous ones among them. I told you I even tasted the food myself . . ."

"Why did you have this thing in your roof if you didn't want to kill us? Why were you telling the soldiers about our movements?"

"They made me do it, *mwanangu*. They made me do it for my son's safety."

"Your *son's* safety! Aren't we sons, too? Haven't we got mothers too? You think we were born by animals, don't you? You are worried about your son's safety, your son who is doing nothing except keeping you and me and everyone under the shoes of *mabunu*. Is your son fighting for your freedom?"

"It's just a job he's doing, *mwanangu*. His father died . . ."

"Listen to her! 'Just a job' she says. Running in front like the white man's dog. Does he earn a *tenth* of what the white man who sends him gets? And what about *us*? Are we paid? Do we get a cent? Your son's safety!"

Baas Die paused. There was silence in the crowd now. Only Mai Tawanda's sobs could be heard.

"There's no case here," said Baas Die. "Mabunu Muchapera, Pasi Nema-Sellout, teach this woman. Don't waste your bullets on her."

Mabunu Muchapera and Pasi NemaSellout stepped through the crowd to the centre of the gathering. The crowd shrank back.

Mabunu Muchapera broke off a low branch from one of the trees under which the crowd sat. He stripped off the leaves until he had a thick, green stick about the size of a hoe handle. Pasi NemaSellout looked on the ground around him and found a long piece of dry root half buried in the ground. When he pulled up the free end it snapped up in a puff of dust, causing a commotion among the women sitting near him.

Brandishing the root, curved and supple as a stick a ploughboy would use to beat an ox, he stepped out to the fire.

The crowd scrambled back, away from the victim, the way a group of seated people would scramble from a snake hurled into their midst. Mai Tawanda sat there, next to the fire, sobbing, peeking through tight fingers.

Mabunu Muchapera struck her first. He took two steps towards her, swung his hand suddenly and the stick smashed across her back, knocking her flat on the ground.

She screamed.

The crowd hissed.

Pasi NemaSellout gripped the root in his hand and approached her from the other side. In the corner of his eye he saw Baas Die watching him, and the wall of frightened villagers gaping. The woman's legs were sprawled towards him. Her calves were fat and shiny in the firelight. Pasi took another step forward and raised his root. The root came down with a sharp whistle. It caught the woman's waist with a whack. She gripped her waist and writhed.

The crowd hissed.

Mabunu Muchapera struck her across the shoulders, close to the neck. Her arms flew forward, hands clawing into the ground.

The *doek* fell loose from her head and flapped into the fire, exposing her wildly tangled hair.

She let out a low moaning sound, deep in her throat.

A dog howled in the grass.

Pasi NemaSellout took a step forward and struck her again, hard, on the waist. She writhed. Pasi lifted the root. It was broken in the middle.

A baby howled.

The nylon *doek* hissed in the fire, melting into a sheet of blinding white light. Pasi held the broken root in his hand. The woman's calves were fat and shiny. His eyes swept through the blur of the crowd. Baas Die stood alone on one side of the fire, watching. Pasi stepped back.

A voice spoke from the crowd. A man's voice. A figure pushed through the dark mass of limbs and heads. A man's figure. He was crouching and clapping his hands with a hollow sound. He was speaking with a shaky voice. His grizzled hair shone in the firelight. The fire glowed in the wells in his cheeks. He was talking to Baas Die. He said, "Have mercy on her, *vanangu*, have mercy on her."

Other voices joined in from the crowd. The voices said, "Have mercy on her . . ."

Pasi NemaSellout clutched the broken root. Mabunu Muchapera leaned on his stick. Mabunu's lower lip was wet. The woman's calves shone in the firelight. One leg was exposed to the knee.

Headman Sachikonye spoke again. He said, "Have mercy on her, *vanangu*." Baas Die did not turn his head. He looked straight ahead. He did not look at anyone. He said, "There is no mercy for traitors."

Headman Sachikonye spoke again. He spoke with a low, soft voice. He said, "Have mercy on her, *vanangu*."

Baas Die did not turn his face. He looked straight ahead, into the fire. He twirled his beard. He did not look at anyone. He spoke with a rising voice. He said, "There is no mercy for those who sympathize with traitors, either. You should be rejoicing."

Baas Die did not turn his face. He said, "Anyone here with a relative in the army should tell them to resign. They should resign now."

"Give her another chance, *vanangu*," Sachikonye said.

"There are no second chances," Baas Die said. "There are no second chances in this war."

Baas Die did not turn his face. He stared into the fire. He stared beyond the sprawling woman, into the fire. "Mabunu, Pasi, finish your job," he said. "Finish your job."

Pasi NemaSellout threw down the broken root. His hands were damp. He walked towards a tree. The crowd scrambled back. A woman pulled up her cloth from his boot. A woman snatched up a child from his boot. He walked up to a tree and reached up with his hands to a branch.

He swung the branch sideways until it broke and fell to the ground. He put his foot on the branch and stripped off the leaves.

Women cried in the crowd, muffled mucous cries.

"You should be rejoicing," Baas Die said, staring into the fire. "You should be rejoicing we caught her before she finished us all off. You should be clapping hands and ululating."

Pasi NemaSellout picked up his new stick. It was a thick stick, almost as thick as Mabunu Muchapera's. The bark smelt fresh. The juice of the bark stained his hands. He clutched the stick with both hands. His hands were damp.

Mabunu Muchapera stepped forward. He took two steps forward and whipped up his stick. It smashed across the woman's shoulders.

There were cries in the crowd. There was sobbing in the crowd. There were tongues clicking in the crowd.

"You should be rejoicing." Baas Die said. "You should all be rejoicing. You should all be clapping hands and ululating."

Nobody said anything. Nobody did anything.

"Don't women have voices in this village? Don't men have hands?" Baas Die's voice was rising. His eyes were looking round the crowd.

A thin ululation started from somewhere in the crowd. It rose and died.

"Is there only one woman who can ululate in this village?" Baas Die said. "Is there only one woman who can ululate?"

Other voices joined in, ululating. The voices were tremulous. The voices joined in the ululating.

A man started clapping his hands. More men clapped their hands. More men joined in the handclapping.

"That's right," said Baas Die. "You should be rejoicing. Mabunu, Pasi, finish your job."

Mabunu Muchapera clutched his stick. His lower lip was wet. He flung the stick sideways and caught the woman on the back of the head. It made a sound like the soft liquid burst of the shell of *mutamba* fruit knocked against the trunk of a tree.

Baas Die jabbed the air with a down-turned thumb and chanted, *"Pasi ne-Vatengesi!"*

"Pasi navo!"

"Pasi nemaSellout!"

"Pasi navo!"

Pasi NemaSellout clutched his stick and took two steps forward. The woman's calves shone in the firelight. The women were ululating. The men were clapping their hands. The woman did not move. She did not make a sound. Pasi raised his hand and struck her on the waist.

"She's not even worth the soil she's lying on," Baas Die said, spitting forcefully on the ground. *"Pasi neVatengesi!"*

"Pasi navo!"

Mabunu Muchapera hit her again. He hit her on the back of the head.

"People like her don't deserve a proper burial. *Pasi neVatengesi!"*

"Pasi navo!"

Pasi NemaSellout clutched his stick. His hands were damp. His eyes swam round the crowd. The chants rang in his ears. The woman sprawled motionless in front of him. She did not move. There was a dark stain at the end of his stick where the green bark had shredded off, where the exposed wood shone white. The woman's calves were fat and shiny. Her canvas shoes were still on her feet. He did not want to look at her legs. He did not want to look at her head. The hair stretched out in wild wings over her face.

The crowd was chanting. Women were ululating. Men were clapping hands.

Pasi NemaSellout clutched his stick. His hands were damp. He did not look at Baas Die. He did not look at Mabunu Muchapera. He did not look at the crowd. He did not look at the fire. He looked at the woman sprawling on the ground. Her hair was wild. Her earrings and shoes were still on. There was a dark stain on the grass near her head. He looked away from her legs and her head and fixed his eyes on her waist. He clutched his stick in his damp hands.

He clutched his stick and stepped forward.

Chapter 25

Gidi Ishumba, who was keeping the early morning guard, saw them first, a column of twenty soldiers bolting out of the trees, bent low, approaching the hill in the pale light.

He shouted, *"Masoja!"*, swivelled his gun and started firing wildly at the arc of men fanning out at the bottom of the hill. The soldiers dived low to this initial burst, spread out, darting among the rocks, and opened fire.

From his flanks Baas Die and Shungu Dzangu started firing. Pasi Nema-Sellout and Mabunu Muchapera responded moments later, from higher up the slope, and then Sub Musango stumbled out of the cave, firing as he emerged, arms stretched far out in front of him, his machine gun rocking.

Two choppers streaked over the horizon and screeched towards the hill.

Baas Die yelled and scrambled to the anti-aircraft, swung round the muzzle and jammed his eye into the view lens. The choppers were nosing low on the hill. He rammed the anti-aircraft into action. The hill shuddered as four explosions rocked it.

Baas Die trained the anti-aircraft on the choppers as they dipped, and fired again.

In the billowing smoke and dust the FNs paused. Then they opened up again.

The choppers banked. Baas Die swung the anti-aircraft round.

Bullets whistled over his head. He saw, above him, Sub Musango – upright, tall on his feet, firing wildly – fold up and plunge headlong on to a rock.

Pasi slammed a fresh magazine into his gun and swept off a camouflaged soldier half-way up the hill. Mabunu Muchapera fired in wide, angry sweeps, shouting insults at the advancing men below.

The choppers turned back. Baas Die steadied himself. He saw Gidi Ishumba slap a hand to his shoulder and fire crazily with one hand. The choppers roared past and Baas Die released the anti-aircraft. The hill shuddered again and the air rushed with a hot, sucking sound. A huge gash smouldered in the earth between him and Gidi Ishumba.

"Run!" Baas Die shouted suddenly. "Run!"

He took a last crack at the choppers and scrambled towards the other side of the hill. Gidi Ishumba was already racing like a buck in front of him, a hand clamped to his shoulder. Pasi NemaSellout was chugging through the bush. Shungu Dzangu stooped over Sub Musango who sprawled on a rock.

Mabunu Muchapera was still crouching behind a rock, pumping lead on to the rocky slopes.

"Run!" Baas Die shouted. He grabbed Sub Musango by the legs. Shungu Dzangu heaved him up by the arms and they weaved through the rocks, coughing madly in the dust.

Pasi NemaSellout somersaulted over a bomb-carved crater, tore through the mask of smoke and charged into the grass, across the valley.

The choppers banked, swung towards the hill.

Still, Mabunu Muchapera's machine gun roared from behind a rock.

Baas Die and Shungu Dzangu lugged through the bush, their backs bent to their heavy load.

The hill thundered again in blind mushrooms of smoke and fire.

The roar of Mabunu Muchapera's machine gun momentarily drowned in the echoes of the explosion.

Shungu Dzangu chugged on like a runaway ox dragging a plough.

Gidi Ishumba clasped his blood-soaked shoulder with both hands, his half-hitched gun slapping his thigh.

Pasi NemaSellout reached the trees first, and when he shot his head back to the hill he saw Mabunu Muchapera outlined against the white morning sky, hung in a thin corridor of air between black walls of smoke, his legs bunched together and arms stretched out against the hill, like a long-jumper frozen in the middle of his leap ...

Chapter 26

Now many stories have been told about that battle on the hill in Sachikonye's village.

Many many stories, some true, some not so true, some highly-coloured by the terror and imagination of the people who heard about what happened from those who saw it happen.

Stories about a witch called Mai Tawanda who poisoned a comrade who came to her home to ask for food in the middle of the night, and her death when the comrades found out she was a traitor. Some people say she gave him rat poison, some say *rogor*, some dip-tank fluid, some say mushrooms, some say she put ground glass into the mealie-meal she made sadza with, others say no, she tried to hack his head off with a matchet while he sat in her hut, eating.

It is said by some that the comrades knew all along she was a traitor, that they could read it on her face, through the secret powers they had, that she was a traitor and only waited to catch her at her act. And it is said by others that the spirit of Mbuya Nehanda came to the leader of the comrades in a dream and said to him, "*M'zukuru*, I see a traitor in this village – a woman with long dark hair and green things on her ears. This woman has a son in the white man's army and is their spy. Find her and kill her before she destroys you." But some say no, the comrades saw her flying in a helicopter with the soldiers, showing them where the base was, and they did not shoot down the helicopter because they knew she was in it and they wanted to punish her in front of everybody. Yet some say they caught her in the forest talking to the soldiers on the *chiover-over*. Some say two comrades went up to her home and straight away pulled the *chiover-over* out of the grass thatch, some say the *whole* group went and dug up guns from the floors and hauled up baskets of bombs from her granary, others say things exploded in her heart and some comrades were killed. Some say she passed out in her hut when the comrades came and was already dead when the people gathered round the fire, others say she was heard screaming and struggling in her hut before that.

And some stories have it that when the people gathered round the fire Baas Die showed her the *chiover-over* and asked her about it and made her eat it, every bit of it except the metal horn, and that they started beating her when she couldn't swallow the horn. Some say it was the comrade with the thick stick who killed her with a blow on the back of the head which spilled her brains, some say the other comrade killed her with a sharp blow which broke her spine. Some think the comrade with the thin stick did not really want to kill her or was afraid, and that he had to do it because his leader would have killed him for sparing the life of a traitor. Others say it was all planned, that they wanted the woman to take a long time to die so that the people would know how bad it was to be a traitor.

Some of the little children who were there say they beat her until she was only a dark stain on the grass, some say every bone was crushed to pulp and only her legs were left, some say they burnt her in the fire and left the ashes of her body there for the wind to blow away. Some say the woman would not die even after all that beating and they had to hack her head off with their bayonets, and that her tongue wiggled for a long time after her head had been severed, others maintain her head rolled down to the river and was lost.

Some people say Headman Sachikonye was going to be killed too for asking them to spare a traitor's life; that he was struck on the back with a gun. Others say the comrades forbade them to bury her body because she was a traitor and that her body lay there under the tree for days, under a cloud of flies, until the whole village reeked with the smell of her and the dogs went wild and tore her up piece by piece. Others say her relatives came and collected her by night and buried her in a secret place. And it is said strange noises were heard afterwards, noises of a woman screaming and groaning and that a fire without a shadow was often seen burning between the two trees, and that the dogs in the village sneezed and howled for many days.

And it is said people began to talk about the dead woman, saying that her husband had not died of tuberculosis five years before as was generally supposed, but of poisoning, that she had poisoned him and that even the doctors at the hospital had not detected this; and some even said the woman was a witch and not a traitor, that her witchcraft drove her into poisoning the comrade, and the comrades had killed her because they intended to clean up the land of witches too.

213

And many things were said about the comrade who had been poisoned. Some said the poison killed him there in her hut, straight after he had eaten the food. Some said he crawled back to his comrades and died in the caves. Some said no, the poison went to his head and he became mad and began shooting at his comrades, who had to kill him. Some said his comrades prayed to the spirit of Chaminuka and Mbuya Nehanda to make him well and that he became well again. Some said the comrades had medicines and they treated him. Others said he was killed in the fighting on the hill.

And even stranger stories are told about that battle on the hill. Some people say the soldier whose mother had been killed knew about his mother's death in a dream and that he brought the white men with whom he fought to avenge his mother the very next morning. Some say the comrades brought the people together that night just to lure the soldiers to a battle. Some say half the comrades were killed by the bombs on the hill, some say it was only two, some say it was the sick poisoned comrade who was killed because he could not get away, others say it was another comrade.

And many tongues have it that the fighting lasted the whole day – that there were thousands of soldiers at the bottom of the hill and dozens of choppers in the sky, fighting only a handful of comrades, that the choppers dropped bombs like eggs from a basket, that the bombs flattened and hollowed the hill, squeezed the broken rocks up and then flattened it again, until the hill was completely moved to a new place and a maze of craters hollowed the place where it had stood, that the sun was blotted out by the smoke and soot. Some people say the comrades caught the bombs on the nozzles of their guns and exploded them in the air, above their heads, before they landed. Some people say when the battle got unbearable the comrades changed into hares and vanished into the bush. Some say the smoke and dust of the bombs provided a screen through which they escaped. Some say they rolled down the hill, firing their guns. Others say they dug in their guns on the hill and left them firing on their own, while they fled from the place.

And it is said when the soldiers saw their mates die at the bottom of the hill they turned round and fled, and that the choppers continued bombing for a while then vanished over the horizon and did not return until that afternoon, to collect their dead; that when the choppers returned and landed on the hill there was wild firing from a single gun and the choppers took off again, as quickly as they had landed, before they could load a single corpse. Some say it was one of the comrades in the cave who fired at the returning choppers, the poisoned comrade lying sick in the cave when the fighting started. Others say it was one of the dying injured soldiers blindly firing at his colleagues – but whoever it was, it is said he kept them off for two days, and that the unclaimed bodies went bad in the heat, and the wind blew the smell up to the village, that crazed dogs dragged disembodied arms and legs, black and white, still covered with twists of torn camouflage and sometimes with rings on the fingers and watches or bangles on the wrists, to the village. And it is said a man from the village sneaked up to the hill at night and picked wrist watches, sunglasses, cigarettes, binoculars and money off the dead soldiers, and even collected scattered and abandoned rations to sell them.

It is said that on the fourth morning the hill was clear of bodies, though nobody had seen the soldiers return to collect their dead. Some say the soldiers returned in the night to collect their dead, others say the leaders of the soldiers and the comrades met and talked, and agreed to hold fire while they collected their dead.

It is said the comrades were not seen in the village for several weeks after that, that some people thought they had all been shot dead and taken away by the soldiers to be dragged in the dust or dangled from helicopters, as slain terrorists, in the sight of village schoolchildren herded out of classrooms, and it was thought by others that they fled to another village or even crossed the border. And it was said by some that the comrades had buried their dead and were hiding in the forest, that their bullets had run out and they were secretly sending for mealie-meal and dried meat and salt and soap from the village and preparing their own food. Some have it a visitor to the village saw four or five men bathing in a river ten miles from the village, others that a man going after a strayed cow saw the dead guerrillas' grave – a strange patch of ground on the side of a hill, newly dug and framed by large stones, and that his dog sneezed and howled when it passed by the place.

And it is said by some that Headman Sachikonye knew where the comrades were after that battle, and that he met with them frequently when they wanted him. It is said by some that he knew some of the comrades had died but the comrades would not allow him to help in the burial. It is said then he asked to be shown where the dead had been buried, so that he could say a few words over the grave, the words people say over a grave, to ease the dead person's passage into the other world, since they were all boys and had probably never buried anyone before, and he was the headman, an old man at least, even though he was unhappy about the way they had killed Mai

Tawanda and even though his own son was sick in hospital, though he wasn't the dead comrade's father or uncle or relative, he was the headman and he was an old man and he knew how people ought to be buried, even if he did not know the dead's real names or totems or where they came from or the secret rites of their ancestries, he was an old man and they ought to show him to the grave and let him say a few words at least, that the dead could not just be laid in the ground like that, like animals, that a dead person not properly buried would always be uneasy and his spirit would wreak blind vengeance on them all but it said the comrades said no, only comrades could bury comrades, that they had said what had needed to be said and they could not tell him who had died or show him where they had laid them.

And it is said Headman Sachikonye returned with tears on his face, saying what young men they were to say that, what young men not to cry or flinch or show signs of pain, what young men to bear the weight of death on their own, how sad it was that the dead were just lying there, with nothing said to ease their passage to the other world, how it had never been done, how in the seventy years of his life he had never heard of such a thing . . .

216

Chapter 27

if you took away the earrings and cut the hair and lengthened the skirt she might have looked like you

strange but I remember the time I used to look up from under the table and you were cutting bread and I saw you and your calves might have looked like hers looked

or perhaps we were out near the factory working in that rice field near the ash hill where the little train dumped the slug and Esther and I were catching locusts in the grass and you were bending over in the mud to plant the rice and your legs must have looked like that

her voice was like your voice in the bedroom after we came back from the hospital when the doctor said there was nothing to do but to amputate

he was light skinned too but it was different, we never knew when we brought him down from the hill nobody would make him get up

it's different if it's a blast a hundred metres away or it's somebody at the bottom of the hill whose face you don't know and can't see but if it's one of you then it's different

there was that girl under the trees with the children and I thought I'd be used to it

I didn't think it would be like that

the only thing was that stiff cat we found that cold morning in the woodpile I went to dig down under the gum trees near the green grass and you had said the caretaker might find out

and there was the red clay in the shower that evening you came back in your white and purple church uniform and you didn't answer when Peter asked where you had been

it was brown rocks and black soil where we put him and we had to dig with our bayonets and I didn't think it would be like that, him there with the roots brushing his pimples, lying there where his mother didn't know, without a blanket

I didn't think it would be like that

Chapter 28

At first the rain was no thicker than the flirting showers and thin grumble of October skies.

Then November whipped in with pounding pebble rain and vengeful lightning.

December was a deluge.

March, April, May, June and July had surprised him too, in the training camps, warm, cool, and passing without any of the cold cutting draughts he had expected. August, September and October had been fine, on the hills, sometimes hot, but the sky had always been stunning blue and the air dry and clean.

November he had watched the yellow winter stubble flourish after the first showers. On the ground mushrooms burst out of the earth in jaunty clusters, tendrils curled up the trunks of trees, twists of wood that had seemed dead spurted into leaf. And then with hardly a month's warning the grass had marched up to the line of trees and embraced the forest and hills in a swishing skirt of green. The trees had closed up with an incestuous thickening of leaves. Mangoes, *maroro*, *mazhanje*, and *nhengeni* ripened in squelching riots of purple, pink, white and brown. The ripeness had oozed into the damp earth, poisoning the air with the madness.

December, Christmas December, was a deluge. For days on end the skies frowned. Listening to the humming of the storm and the relentless hymns of thunder he thought he might not see the sun again.

He had watched his comrades through the months, noting the scraggy beards creeping over their faces like lichens on rock, the cuts and bruises on their hands he knew like his own, the dark sour lines over their emaciated faces. He had seen the glint in their eyes, heard the edginess in their voices, felt the silence hardening.

They had waited for the rain, waited for the flower of vegetation that would hide them from the eye of the choppers, for the deluge that would wipe away their tracks, flooding rivers and making roads impassable, dismounting the enemy from their mud-ambushed vehicles to the primordial challenge of feet. But when the rain came, bringing with it flu and malaria, it soaked through their clothes and skins to their bones, washing the patience out of them, exposing their brittle longings.

It might have been the rain that fermented it.

It could have been sparked off by anything.

Anybody could see it was coming, but when it happened it happened like this: A man in the village complained that a comrade was having sex with his daughter. The man complained to Baas Die, charging the comrade with rape. This comrade was identified as Mabunu Muchapera.

"I didn't force her," Mabunu maintained. "She did it willingly."

Baas Die considered what to do.

No sex with civilians, ran the rules, *Pay for what you buy, Return everything you borrow, Treat the civilians with respect* and *Be firm in handling traitors.* They were straight-forward rules: they made sense. But how to deal with infringements? No óne had written *specific* directions.

Depending on the nature of the offence, a fellow comrade could be confronted, face to face, like a peer, for indiscipline. His rations could be cut. His gun could be taken away from him for some time; he could be assigned extra duties; his privileges could be withheld. He could even (with luck) be physically punished (get two others to grab him? flog him? with a stick or whip?).

But no one had written, *If a member of the group rapes a girl in a village (or is accused of raping a girl or forcing a girl to have sex with him) and this comrade is identified by (i) the father of the girl (ii) the girl herself and you can't talk the complainants into dropping the charges do (a) . . . (b) . . . or (c) . . . and (1) if there are members in the group who have girlfriends in the village and the accused knows it do (d) . . . or (e) . . . or (f) . . . and (2) if the commander of the group is among those in the group known to have girlfriends in the village and the commander knows the accused knows it do (g) . . . or (h) . . . or (i) and (NB) (3) if the accused comrade has distinguished himself in the latest battle by saving the group members' lives do (j) . . . or (k) . . . or (l).*

Mabunu Muchapera carried himself superciliously, giving Baas Die unrepentant looks that said he would know how to hit back if rebuked.

Baas Die maintained a dignified restraint. Taking the silence for cowardly guilt, Mabunu Muchapera grew more arrogant, as if he was itching for a confrontation. When he was given orders he responded tardily. One morning he simply did not go to his post. Baas Die thought that this was enough. He called a general meeting.

"Am I still the commander of this group?" Baas Die ominously began.

They crouched around him, cradling their weapons, their faces blank with surprise.

"What do you mean?" Gidi Ishumba's hard brown eyes searched the commander's face.

"I asked a question," Baas Die said.

"Of course you are, Chef."

"If I am then why are my orders not being obeyed?"

"What orders, Chef?"

"There was nobody at the anthill yesterday morning."

"Pasi NemaSellout is supposed to have been there . . ." Gidi Ishumba said.

"I was off duty yesterday morning," Pasi NemaSellout cut in.

"Was it you, Torai Zvombo?"

"But I was at the *muonde* tree."

"You see, none of you seem to know where you ought to have been."

"I was off duty too," Gidi Ishumba defended himself.

"I was in the valley," Shungu Dzangu said.

Mabunu Muchapera raised his head and said, "I was supposed to be there. I forgot."

"Forgot?"

"Yes, I forgot."

"Since when have any of you started forgetting your posts? If *mapuruvheya* overran the base would you be saying so calmly, 'I forgot'?"

"I *just* forgot."

"Don't talk shit! I've been watching you, Mabunu. There's something you're after. First you go out and rape a village girl and earn us all a bad name and now you refuse to do your duties. Is this your way of telling us you are tired of the war? Is this your way of showing us you want to desert?"

"I'll do no such thing."

"Or are you planning to join *mapuruvheya* or the Selous Scouts? The *povo* is confused and their patience is running out. You know our honeymoon with the *povo* is over, but you're behaving exactly like the Selous Scouts who are out to destroy our image!"

220

"What's the matter, Chef?"

"You all know what Mabunu did. He's planning to break every rule . . ."

"You know the rules too," Mabunu Muchapera blurted and everybody looked up.

Baas Die clicked his tongue and swung his gun at Mabunu. Gidi Ishumba dived at Baas Die and wrestled him for the gun. The two rolled fiercely in the mud. Gidi Ishumba pinned Baas Die down by the shoulder. Baas Die writhed on his back, kicking out with his knees. His arms tore free, jerking up the gun. Gidi Ishumba clawed blindly at the air and pushed the muzzle into a vertical position. A shot rang out, slammed into the trunk of the tree above. A chunk of dead bark fell from the tree and landed, smoking, at their feet. The bang echoed through the forest and crashed from hill to hill.

"No!" Gidi Ishumba gasped, "Baas Die, no!"

Gidi Ishumba snatched the gun from Baas Die and sprang to his feet. He turned round and snatched away Mabunu Muchapera's gun, unslinging it from his shoulder and then backed off with the two guns. Baas Die leapt from the ground, hands balled into fists, and charged at Mabunu Muchapera.

"Come," he hissed, "I'll show you with my bare hands!"

He swung out with a fist that caught the younger man on the jaw, making him reel blindly. Shungu Dzangu threw his arms round Baas Die's waist and dragged him back. Mabunu Muchapera stumbled round, fingering his jaw, but Pasi NemaSellout and Torai Zvombo grabbed him and blocked his advance.

"Enough!" Gidi Ishumba gasped, "Baas Die, enough!"

Pasi NemaSellout took Baas Die's binoculars, climbed a tree and swept the landscape to see if the shot had caused any commotion. Gidi Ishumba sat with the two captured guns between his knees. He kneaded his shoulder with his hand. The struggle with Baas Die had wrenched the not-so-healed wound where a bullet had hit him months ago, in the battle on the hill. Baas Die rubbed black mud off his elbows while Shungu Dzangu and Torai Zvombo sandwiched the still dazed Mabunu Muchapera between them.

"We have to discuss this like men, Baas Die," Gidi Ishumba said. "Everything has to be said here, today."

"That's all right with me," Baas Die said, "as long as we stop shitting on each other's feet."

"You have to let Mabunu Muchapera speak."

"Shit!" Baas Die snatched his snuff from his pocket and thumbed a pinch into each nostril. "Shit!"

"Get down from up there," Gidi Ishumba told Pasi, who was still up in the tree, scanning the forest with binoculars. "We have to settle this once and for all."

Pasi NemaSellout scrambled down the tree and sat down next to Mabunu Muchapera.

"Anybody who has anything to say must say it here, now, or forever keep his mouth shut," Baas Die declared. "Well, Comrade Mabunu Muchapera, you seemed to have plenty to tell me about the rules."

Mabunu Muchapera stared at his boots and said nothing.

"Speak!"

"You have to say what you wanted to say," Gidi Ishumba told him. "Don't be afraid."

"I'm not afraid," Mabunu Muchapera said.

"Then get on with it. What are the rules *you* wanted to tell *me*?"

"It's about the girls . . ."

"Oh, the girls eh?"

"Let him speak, Baas Die."

"It's just that I . . . I . . . I'm not the only one . . ."

"Aha! Are you accusing us of being rapists, too?"

"Let him speak, Baas Die."

"Damn it, Gidi Ishumba! Are you supporting him? Are you going to listen to this cowdung?"

Mabunu Muchapera shot his head up and said, "Everyone here has been involved."

"What do you mean?" said Gidi Ishumba.

"You and Baas Die have girlfriends in the village and . . ."

"Leave me out of this," Shungu Dzangu cut in, his face, for once, unsmiling, furrowed with irritation, "I haven't messed up any man's daughter."

"I've seen Torai Zvombo and Pasi NemaSellout talking to girls too."

"Now, Mabunu Muchapera," Gidi Ishumba turned on him, "you're making a big mistake . . ."

"Are you accusing us of rape, too?" Baas Die rapped.

"You're making a big mistake, Mabunu Muchapera."

"Did anybody come saying they had been raped by us? If, as you say, we have girlfriends, or you saw us *talking to girls,* does that make up rapists, like you?"

"But you know the rules. You are not supposed to have any relationships with the girls."

"Now you are being childish, comrade," Gidi Ishumba laughed, waving a hand at Mabunu Muchapera's face. "You couldn't charm the girl you wanted so you decide to rape her."

"I didn't rape her!"

"What happened then?"

"Her father got to know about it and was angry about it. He force her to accuse me of raping her."

"The girl wouldn't have admitted it you hadn't forced her. That's your problem, comrade. Don't drag us into it. We never *raped* anyone. We proposed to the girls just like any other men and we were accepted."

"But you had sex with them! That girl, Marita and that other one, Chenzira, I've seen you with them and I know you slept with them."

"Don't be stupid, Mabunu," Gidi Ishumba said. "We are all men here. Even when the general commander himself spoke against sex to us in the camp he knew we would need women. We are talking about *rape,* comrade, not normal relationships."

"Rape or no rape, we shouldn't be messing up people's daughters," Shungu Dzangu butted in.

"If you are a castrated ox there's not much we can do about you, Shungu," Gidi ishumba laughed.

Shungu Dzangu's eyes glowered. He swallowed hard.

"I was a fool to you off, Mabunu," Baas Die said. "I was lenient with you, and don't think it's because I have a girlfriend in this village. I have nothing to hide. Don't think I didn't punish you because I was afraid of you. I'm not afraid of any of you here. Not *one* of you, and I want to make that clear. I don't care if you all go off and team up with the *mapuruvheya.* You can even join the Selous Scouts or *madzakutsaku* if you want. I'll hunt you down. I know why I'm here. Let me tell you. I had a job before I came here. I wasn't at school or at home looking for a job like you were. I know why I'm fighting. I didn't leave home for this nonsense. I didn't survive those bombs to bicker like this. We're all men here and I want us to be fair to each other. If I made all kinds of petty rules and said 'Don't do this and Don't do that' all the time would you respect me as your *Chef*, eh, Mabunu? All I want is that we fight and fight well, finish this war and go home. That's why I ignored your case. I even tried to persuade the girl's father to drop his charge. And for that you took me for a fool. We have enough trouble from soldiers and Selous Scouts and traitors. What I can't work out is why you, Mabunu Muchapera, are choosing to be difficult. Don't think I haven't noticed it. There's something you are hatching. I *demand* to know it now!"

"The Chef has a point, there, Mabunu Muchapera," Gidi Ishumba said.

"That goes for you, too, Torai Zvombo."

"Me?"

"Yes, you. You two are trying to form your little clique in the group. I know what you and Torai Zvombo are up to. I've heard your little discussions . . ."

"I never said anything . . ."

"If you allow yourself to be fooled by Mabunu Muchapera you're making a big mistake, Torai Zvombo."

"What did they say?" Shungu Dzangu demanded.

"*Aika*, Shungu Dzangu," Baas Die snapped, "don't pretend you joined this group yesterday. You know what our hero has been saying about the battle on the hill. You know how he thinks that battle *ought* to have been fought!"

"All I said is we shouldn't have left Torai Zvombo behind, in the cave," Mabunu Muchapera sneered.

"But did we *know* he was still in the cave?"

"That's what we should have checked!"

"I asked about him! I thought he had already escaped down the hill. How was anybody to know he was still in the cave? How many things could I do at one time? So I ought to have worked the anti-air, fired my own gun, looked for Torai Zvombo, run down the hill, helped carry Sub Musango . . . How many hands do I have? How many pairs of eyes do I have? Am I a machine?"

They all looked down. Nobody had referred to the deceased guerrilla by name since his death.

"You think I am a coward, don't you?"

"I never said anything about cowardice!" Mabunu Muchapera shouted, his voice edged with a badly-masked glee.

"Yes you did! I heard you. You were standing right here, under this tree, last Wednesday after those *mujhibhas* came to say there had been a convoy

224

of *madzakutsaku* on the road. I was sitting there against that *muzhanje* tree. You must have thought I was asleep. Torai Zvombo, didn't Mabunu Muchapera say, 'He's just a coward . . .' Answer me!"

"He only said you should have looked for me in the cave before going down the hill," Torai Zvombo looked sideways at Mabunu Muchapera and shrugged.

"Now let me tell you one thing, Mabunu Muchapera. That battle on the hill was yours. You won it. You were a damn good fighter. If I didn't say that before I'm saying it now. You too, Torai Zvimbo. You were bold to stay in the cave and fire at the soldiers when they came back for their dead. We've all said that. But don't let that go to your heads. Suicide never won a war, and anybody who wants to win this war has got to learn to stay alive first . . ."

"What the *Chef* is saying is you endangered your life unnecessarily," Gidi Ishumba explained. "You should have run when he gave the order to run, and I agree with him."

"You should thank your spirits you're alive, Mabunu Muchapera," Baas Die wrested back his point. "I bet even *you* can't imagine how you escaped those bombs and bullets without a scratch. You could very very easily have been killed. *You* could be dead. We'd have had two graves in this forest, and what good is a dead comrade? Did you want us to stay there and use all our ammunition, and bring the whole airforce down on ourselves?"

"No, but the anti-air . . ."

"OK, OK, so we lost the anti-aircraft. But what good is a weapon without a person to operate it? There were two choppers in the sky and twenty of them on the hill. I gave the order to run because I knew they'd get us. I was playing safe. That's *my* idea of this war and that's what I was taught, and as long as I'm the commander that's how this group is going to fight. If you're going to fight like you're competing in school athletics then I'm afraid you're in the wrong group. As for you, Torai Zvombo, if you slurp up the poison Mabunu Muchapera is trying to feed you, that we didn't care about you, then you're lost too. Sub Musango had already been hit when I gave the order to run. Shungu Dzangu and I had to carry him. Gidi Ishumba had been hit in the shoulder. You know that. There was simply no time to check on you."

Baas Die's voice sounded over-anxious, somehow, in spite of his anger. "I asked Shungu Dzangu about you. I thought you had run. Shungu Dzangu, didn't I ask as we were carrying Sub Musango down the hill?"

"He did," Shungu Dzangu confirmed. There was momentary silence. Mabunu Muchapera and Torai Zvombo backed down.

But Shungu Dzangu's face remained furrowed. He said, "I have something to say. Something about that woman, that traitor ..."

"What about her?" Gidi Ishumba muttered, expressing the group's common distaste for the topic.

"The way she died," Shungu Dzangu said.

"What about it?"

"Just the way she died. She could bring all kinds of bad luck on us."

"You want to bring up your *ngozi* nonsense again," Gidi Ishumba interrupted.

"A person doesn't just die like that, like a snake or animal."

"This is war, Shungu Dzangu. Forget those village taboos."

Shungu Dzangu cut his breath with a sharp, mocking sound and said, shaking his head almost imperceptibly, "All kinds of bad luck ..."

"Are you saying we shouldn't have killed her?" Baas Die asked.

"No."

"Then what are you mourning for? Was she a relative of yours?"

"We could have taken her away and shot her in private, at least."

"I think we should have made the villagers *themselves* beat her!" Pasi NemaSellout interjected.

"Is that why you whipped her with that piece of root like you were punishing your little sister?" Baas Die laughed.

"You didn't strike a single blow yourself!" Pasi NemaSellout retorted, stung by the laughter. Long-harboured thoughts tumbled out in a choking rush.

"Why did you pick on Mabunu and me to do it?"

"Yes," Shungu Dzangu echoed Pasi NemaSellout, "forcing things like that on others ..."

"Why didn't you beat her *yourself*?" Pasi NemaSellout demanded, thrusting his face at Baas Die.

"Me," Baas Die laughed, a weird, surprised laugh. "Why? Is this another accusation? Are you teaming up with these two, Pasi NemaSellout? Has Mabunu talked to you about this?"

"I'll crush traitors' heads any time you ask me," Mabunu Muchapera said, cracking his knuckles against his thumb.

"You shouldn't force things like that on others," Shungu Dzangu repeated.

Baas Die jabbed a finger in the air, "So the commander should have picked up a stick and beaten Mai Tawanda! Who do you take me for? You people are getting into my pockets. Do you think I'm the same rank as you?"

"No, Chef."

"Shut up, Gidi Ishumba! I'm sick and tired of you 'Chef, Chef-ing' me and playing peacemaker while you support them! Shows what kind of deputy I have. Now I know. There's not one among you I can count on . . ."

"That's a dangerous assumption," Gidi Ishumba retorted.

"You're all snakes in the grass, harbouring evil thoughts. You, Pasi Nema-Sellout! You are the very last person I expected to join in on this!"

"But you said we should all speak our minds, Baas Die," Gidi Ishumba said.

"Not one of you," Baas Die fumed bitterly. "Shows you what I have for a group. Not a single one. All smiling to my face and plotting behind my back. You think this is a boy-scout picnic, don't you? You forget why we are here. I'm older than you four. I was working before I came here and wasn't at school like you. As for you, Gidi Ishumba, you are old enough to know better. This is like making a bonfire in a grass hit, that's what it is. *Mahumbwe chaiwo!* Wiping your backs with razor blades. Thankless bastards. You need a Hitler of a commander to shake you back to your senses. You've lived with white oppression for so long you can't recognize fairness when you see it."

"No, Baas Die," Gidi Ishumba said, "that's no way to talk. You're taking things too far."

"You need a leader who's some empty-headed young fool who will get you all killed. And then you can all become heroes and not live to see the Zimbabwe you're fighting for. That's what you all want, eh? Don't give me that grin, Torai Zvombo . . ."

"I'm not grinning," Torai muttered.

"Show some respect," Gidi Ishumba snapped at Torai Zvombo. "This is no laughing matter!"

"Let me tell you something. You may think I'm a bad commander but if I should go this group is finished!"

"Enough, Baas Die."

"I know it! I can see it. This group will have no direction whatsoever! Everybody will be pulling his own way."

"The day I get killed maybe *then* you'll appreciate me."

"Shut up, Baas Die."

"We never said we don't appreciate you . . ." said Shungu Dzangu.

"Oh, you do?" Baas Die laughed, a bitter, almost crazy laugh. "You do?"

Everybody was quiet now, reflecting on the sombre depths of the situation. Shungu Dzangu's brown eyes were cloudy and moist. Even Mabunu Muchapera held his face in his palm and stared pensively at the ground.

Pasi NemaSellout grabbed the binoculars, raced up the tree again and swept the terrain.

"Why bother?" Baas Die cynically said to him. "They wouldn't even need an ambush to catch us bunched up here like lizards in the sun!"

"Sometimes people have to speak, Baas Die," Gidi Ishumba said. "Silence can breed all kinds of tension."

"You've all made your point," Baas Die said, fetching his snuff, and the way his palm brushed his tobacco-stained nose was sad, somehow, like a bitter old man's last words to his wayward family, though his eyes shone in a way that still moved and silenced them.

"You've made your point. From now on everything we decide we will decide together, and I mean it, and you're all going to tell *me* what you think we ought to do before we do it."

"That's not the point Baas Die," Gidi Ishumba began again, but Baas Die hardly gave him a glance.

"We'll see what fine planners you are, for a change," he went on. "But make no mistake about one thing. I haven't forgotten who I am here and anybody who makes the mistake of thinking I might at any moment forget will get it in the head, and if that means a shoot-out I'll be ready for it!"

With that he sprang to his feet and snatched back his gun from Gidi Ishumba. Above them, in the tree, a startled bird shot out of the boughs and skimmed off towards the setting sun.

Chapter 29

Later that night as he sat at his guard post, under the *muonde* tree, Pasi NemaSellout thought of the night they had woken up Msindo at the farm compound. He remembered the hot smell of sleep that had wafted out of the door when the foreman had stepped out, bare-chested, his fearful wife screaming behind him.

He remembered too, the couple he had woken up to cook him food after they shelled the district office, that musk again, of nestling bodies stirred from sleep, of blankets: the surprised man stumbling out, nervously, smelling of snuff; the maternal odour of his small, plump wife, her face sweating and reddened by the fire, the smoky reek of blankets on the floor where their daughter had lain and the drenching, hunger-dazing aroma of meat cooking.

There were the smells of the girls who brought them food, the girls standing paces from him, at an awed distance, with hot pots on their heads, and sweat on their temples – the smell of flesh and hair and food and soap and perspiration – and, sometimes, in the darting shadows at the *pungwe*, the sudden, cruel, sweet stab of perfume.

And always, there was, mingling with the dusk smell of grass and fruit and clay, the odour of Ropa, Ropa in the kerosene lamplight of her hut, the smell of vaseline, hair, cigarettes, soap, children's books and blood.

These smells settled like a growth in his nose, as if the forest had reclaimed him – outcast from the huts and houses where humans dwelt – to its kingdom of leaf and claw, and restored to him the prehistoric animal capacity for smell. On nights like these, these smells and odours visited him, fleshed up into vividly haunting bodies, pressing upon him in a throng, pricking his body into a desire bigger and more terrifying even than the thought of death.

But when he closed his eyes, that night, and saw an imaginary picture of Mabunu Muchapera's face, open-mouthed, wet-lipped, panting, eyes clenched shut, legs astride, arms gripping in front of him, his gun jostling at his back, this longing flared into hate and disgust and shame.

He had not been there when the girl, led by her father, came to the camp. He could not recognize her from the sketchy descriptions he heard.

Before that, he had seen Marita and Chenzira, Baas Die and Gidi Ishumba's respective girlfriends, sneaking in and out of the base. At first he had not suspected anything, and then, slowly, it had dawned on him that everyone carried on their faces the furtive looks that said they knew. It had shocked him at first, then filled him with the despair of one who discovers *he* has left *himself* out of something big and dangerous and exciting. He had looked closely at the faces of his comrades and seen that secret, triumphant look which mocked deep into the seat of his body – the seat of his body battered by the daily ritual of self-love.

And then, one day, he had stumbled upon Shungu Dzangu sitting under a tree with his head thrown back and his trousers open . . .

Driven by the sight of that sad, blotched, *nyora*-riveted face under the tree, Pasi had sought someone.

She was sixteen or seventeen, a creature of a certain hard, birdlike beauty – darting eyes, small, sharp nose, bright, pointed teeth, short, slender fingers with long, hard nails, spare, supple waist, thin, tapering ankles. She had thick braids of plaited black hair and an unusually big bust which combined to give her otherwise slight features a provocative, precarious femininity. He had singled her out at a *pungwe*, for her stirringly sharp voice as she sang *Zimbabwe NdeyeRopa*, dancing, to much cheering from the crowd, at the head of waist-jiggling column of girls. The sound of her voice, lurching dangerously from her small body, decided him.

For two, three weeks, he had secretly watched her, his claim staked, waiting for a chance to corner her. And then one morning when she and four other girls brought food he had kept her back, to give her clothes to wash for him, another chore the girls did for the comrades.

"What's your name?" he snapped, handing over a pair of dirty jeans and a greasy grey shirt, his only other clothes besides the ones he wore.

"Tunhidzai," she said.

"When do you think I can have them back?"

"This afternoon."

"Are you sure?"

"I'll wash them straight away and press them in the afternoon."

"I'll be over there, under the *muonde* tree near the valley," he said, pointing. "Bring the clothes to me there."

"*Zvakanakai*, comrade."

"And look out, eh."

"I will," she said.

She folded the clothes, clutched them to her chest and skipped off into the forest.

Five hours later, she returned, darting expertly from bush to bush, with the clean clothes pressed and neatly folded.

"That was quick," he smiled, taking them from her and sniffing them. "How do I know you didn't put chemicals that eat into the skin?"

She stared at him for a moment then her lips broke into a smile.

"Where did you learn to wash and press so well?"

"At home," she said, and he thought she *chirped*, "and at school."

"You go to school?"

"I did, until the school closed."

"Was it closed because of the war?"

"Yes."

"What form were you doing?"

"Form Three."

"You look younger than that."

"*Kutsonga*," she said, and he laughed, his finger playing with the muzzle of his gun.

"We're going to win this war, soon, and all schools will open again. And when we take over this country there'll be many schools and *all* children will go to school, not just white children or the children of rich people. No one will be too old to go back to school, see?"

She nodded.

"You don't have to keep kneeling," he told her. She rose to her feet and stood two paces from him, with grains of sand on her knees, her eyes fixing on to his face with an ease which made *him* nervous. He said, "What did you say your name was, again?"

"Tunhidzai. Tunhidzai Tanaka."

"We had a boy with a name like that at school," he lied.

"What school was that?"

"I can't tell you," he shrugged, with a wink that promised a few secrets. "Comrade Tunhidzai Tanaka," he said, rolling her name on his tongue, trying out the sound of it. "How would you like to carry a gun and fight for your country?"

"I'd fall down just carrying it . . ."

"Did you know there were girl comrades, fighting this war?"

"I've heard about them, but never seen them."

"You'll meet them," he said. "And they're tough! Girl comrades don't like staying in the bush long so when they fight they fight to *finish* a war. Anyway, we can't all carry guns. Some of us have to fight. Some have to cook and look out for *mapuruvheya*. Others have to go to school so that Zimbabwe can have educated people to take over those jobs the whites are refusing to give us now."

She listened to him with awed absorption. Even he surprised himself by this, but it felt good to talk to her like this, to talk to *somebody*, and besides, he liked the way she joked, boldly, with him, the way her voice erupted so easily into laughter.

"So what were you going to do after school, comrade Tunhidzai?"

"I wanted to be a typist or secretary."

"Why typist or secretary?"

"I like working in an office. I like typing and talking on the phone."

"Why not something else? Wouldn't you like to be an accountant or even a manager?"

"I don't think I could do it."

"Or you think those are positions for whites only?"

"No. I'm not sharp enough. *Ndakawoma musoro*."

"If you all become secretaries then who'll *plan* and *organize* things?"

She was nodding resignedly, waiting to see the drift of his conversation, making him nervous again, giving his voice the hectoring tone behind which he hid his nervousness from village girls.

"Comrade Tunhidzai Tanaka," he heard himself say, his eyes a pendulum on her bust, "you'll come and see me again . . ."

His voice trailed, hovering obstinately between command and request, question and command. His right boot smothered the grass at his feet, the lip of loose sole biting into the red soil underneath.

"We'll be bringing food again tomorrow," she said.

"I mean, you, alone . . ." he blurted out, standing there in front of her, rubbing a finger into the muzzle of his gun, a combatant stripped finally to the searching gaze of a sixteen-year-old country girl, swaying awkwardly, with a wavering smile that said 'Now-I've-said-it-and-you-know-what-I-really-want-don't-you-and-you'd-better-not-be-mean-to-me-because-that-could-make-things-very-awkward . . .'.

He expected surprise, shock, but she was looking up at him, smiling still, with just a hint of tremor in her eyes, the two rows of her small, sharp bright teeth barely separated, showing a pink flash of tongue.

She said, "When do you want me to come?"

"There's a *pungwe* tomorrow night," his voice caught and broke into a rasp. "After the *pungwe* . . ."

She patted her braids and stared sideways at him, considering.

"Who do you live with?"

"I stay with my sister."

"Is she married?"

"Yes."

"Can you make it?"

"I can try."

"After the *pungwe* you'll stay behind and wait for me . . ."

"All right."

"You won't tell anyone, will you?"

She shook her head and laughed and he laughed back, with her.

She skipped away, back towards the village.

It had been too easy, he had thought after she left. Far too easy.

Suddenly he had been seized by a massive premonition that something would go wrong.

He had wanted it to be difficult, to feel himself overcoming each problem as it cropped up, but she had agreed readily and rushed him.

His anxiety grew during the *pungwe*, the following night. What would he do to her, his heart had thumped, as his comrades melted to their posts and the villagers dispersed quietly to their homes after the *pungwe*. His heart had erupted into a tom-tom of self-doubt when he found her waiting for him at the agreed place.

She had been ready and eager to please, the way girls like her burned to please young men who had left home for this danger in the bush. And this eagerness, fuelled by her own keen adolescence into a loud, clinging heat, lit up his despair in himself.

They had kissed for a long time, large, wet, blundering kisses, during which his hands like dubious guests hovered, trembling, over the threshold of her body, his mind savagely fighting to convince his body that *he* would not let *himself* down.

She had grasped him frantically and just when he had begun to hope that she had done it before – this bold, bird-like girl gasping to death in his arms who should surely know how to help them both – her unexpected virginity had dashed his hopes.

Ashamed to face her, he had not talked to her again, or asked to meet her, though at times when she brought food with the other girls or brushed past him at the *pungwe,* she had seemed to want to step back to talk to him. Imagining that she talked about the incident, he had read all kinds of ridicule on the blank faces of the village girls, hearing mockery in their silence, dreaming tongues of their abuse. This shame had grown and grown and grown, self-eating in its secrecy, until it seemed to him he had not only let himself down, or the girl, but the whole group, and the whole village would know that a comrade had failed.

He had decided not to talk to another girl in that village.

And then in the wake of his shame, he had heard of Mabunu Muchapera's alleged act of rape.

It had shocked him. He had not even allowed himself to consider that Mabunu Muchapera had been driven by a variation of his own despair. For days, he had not talked to Mabunu Muchapera.

And now, sitting at his guard post, under the *muonde* tree, after the argument, the tensions within the group became apparent to him for the first time.

It struck him that though they, as a group, shared the common fate of having been wrenched from their youth by the war and united in the bitterness of having survived together the savage bombings in the training camps – each comrade was really on his own. The nature of the war itself – the relentless routine of guarding the camp, eating, sleeping, conducting *pungwes*, reconnaissance, ambush and retreat seldom allowed them to be together for any stretch of time. In the face of constant danger, the differences of their backgrounds and characters blurred into insignificance. Social conversation was rare. Though he could claim certain intimacies it was futile, if not foolish, to expect friendship.

He remembered with surprise Baas Die saying he, Pasi Ne· aSellout, was the last person whose opposition the commander had expected. This hurt him, made him feel weak and tractable. He was alarmed by the possibility that he had accommodated his comrades until perhaps they had all, like the commander, grown to regard him as a weakling.

He had not held any ill feelings against Baas Die, whose manner, apart from a few eccentricities, he had regarded as more than tolerable. But now, embittered by the accusation of disloyalty, he began to pick at the commander's faults.

It enraged him to think Baas Die had, without striking a single exemplary blow, picked on him and Mabunu Muchapera to kill Mai Tawanda. Mai Tawanda's death had not at first worried him. She was a traitor and she had to die. The horror of it he could suppress; he never allowed himself prolonged thoughts about it, though the incident had sought out a corner of his mind and pitched a little tent there. And now Baas Die's laughter had triggered off his anger. That the older members of the group had not taken part in the killing, that he himself had been hurtled into that first act of punishment filled him with bitterness.

He thought Gidi Ishumba had been slick about it. Gidi Ishumba, who had frequently called him a *born-location* and ridiculed his ignorance of the country, his poor sense of direction, his timidity towards girls – why had he not done it?

He did not mind Gidi Ishumba's taunts, yet he thought now the deputy commander was slyly playing the role of peacemaker while keeping his hands clean. Why had Gidi Ishumba not done it if he was so experienced? Why had they chosen him, whom they chided for being raised in the townships? And why was Baas Die worried about Gidi Ishumba? Had he recognized his slickness too?

What would happen if the group split? Would Gidi Ishumba team up with the fiery Mabunu Muchapera and Torai Zvombo or stick with Baas Die? And where would Shungu Dzangu stand? And where would *he* stand?

He felt both admiration for and dread of Mabunu Muchapera. Always it was Mabunu Muchapera urging the most daring operations, taking on the most risky tasks, trapping the more cautious commander into a dangerous exhibition of audacity. It was Mabunu Muchapera who had cut Farmer Mellecker's throat, after all, and he had wiped off his bayonet on the curtains and dipped his finger in the pool on the floor to scribble slogans on the wall, though any of them, yes, in that mood of raw, unrequited rage, could have done it. And after he had come down from the hill after the battle with his pack empty, every bullet gone, his eyes were *red* and he had not said a word. He, the scourge of the Boers – lived up to his name.

If he, Pasi NemaSellout had to choose who to stick with, it would surely not be Mabunu Muchapera, or Torai Zvombo. It would not be Baas Die even – the commander had a sad earnestness which reminded him uneasily of a young teacher who had just left college and had taught him science in Form One. Shungu Dzangu was earnest too, though the secret, quiet strength beneath the haunting silence, the superstitious caution, reminded him of an overworked, long-suffering animal – yes, a mule.

And Torai Zvombo, what lurked beneath the silence and the sneer?

The deputy commander, on the other hand, seemed to him neither coward and nor fiery headed hero; he was handy, reliable, practical, mocking sometimes, but always laughing. His recovery from the shoulder wound in spite of the depleted first-aid kit had impressed everyone.

If Gidi Ishumba had perhaps been the commander . . .

Damn it, Pasi NemaSellout! When it comes to contacts, it really doesn't matter who's who. Everyone reacts instinctively. Grab your gun. Fire. Load. Fire. Pump the lead. Throw grenades. Zap them. Blast them. Bloody soldiers. Bloody racists. Selfish bastards. Bloody murderers. Give it to them. Farmers or soldiers or whatever. Keeping you in this rain. Making you leave school. Shit! Flush them out. Stuttering, bloody FNs. Blast Baas Die. Blast commanders. Who was the commander anyway? In a contact he was just another bag of flesh. You want to go back home alive. You want to go back home. Alive. You want to go back. Home. Alive. Blast Mabunu Muchapera. Blast Torai Zvombo. Blast the squabbling. All that matters is scorching the enemy. Like bees. Blasting them. One by one. Bullets, grenades, knives. Blast them. But stay alive. Blast traitors. Blast rapists. Blast cowards. Blast heroes. Blast *mapuruvheya*. Scare the hell out of them. Scaring the hell out of the enemy is what you ran away from school for, isn't it? It's what you survived those bombs for, isn't it? It's what those children died for, isn't it? It's what Ropa died for, isn't it? Blast Tunhidzai Tanaka. Blast the village girls. What matter! Wriggling little bottoms. Safe in huts. Warm. Dry. Running off to towns to live with relatives when things get hot. Blast *mujhibhas*. Getting rounded up in trucks. Getting shot in crossfire. Being paraded as terrorists.

Blast this bickering! You have to get back home. Blast this rain. Blast this thunder. Blast this mud. Blast speeches. Blast oppressors. Blast politics. Blast *politicians* talking forever in posh hotels. As if they can tell the muzzle of a gun from the butt. Sending their children to schools in the USA and UK. Chanting slogans. Blast schools and education! There's enough to worry about without having to sing the alphabet. Getting the next meal. Staying dry. Keeping eyes peeled. Every second. Always. Even when asleep. Ready to run. Wondering when you'll get hit. Who'll die next. When this war'll end. When supplies'll come. When the ammo'll run out.

Blast the ammo!

Blast! Blast! Blast!

Chapter 30

The district commander came with two new groups passing through the area and, communicating through the local *mujhibhas*, was able to arrange a meeting with Baas Die's group.

The district commander was escorted by four members from the groups in transit; Baas Die and his men met them in the forest and after a passionate but brisk exchange of greetings they got to business. Baas Die gave a report of his group's operations and informed the DC of Sub Musango's death. (Later, they showed him the grave.) He briefed the DC on the situation in the area, and explained how their activities had been all but halted by the shortage of ammunition following the battle on the hill, in which they had lost several weapons. The DC was not impressed about the loss of the anti-air, but he was relieved that only one combatant in Baas Die's group had died so far. (Another group of six had been wiped out in a surprise attack, he grimly warned them.)

The DC explained that he had not been able to meet them earlier because of dense enemy patrols in the neighbouring sub-zone, then he briefed them about the situation in the training camps and in the operational zones. There had been more bombings in the camps, they were told, but the casualties had been minimal because of changes in camp sizes and locations and deployment of recruits. The offensive had been broadened and virtually every district infiltrated; enemy numbers were strained and the internal government was relying heavily on military call-ups, thus weakening the economy of the country and the morale of the whites. New mine-detectors had been brought in from the South, but these were few and sometimes unreliable – one of them had been destroyed by a mine. He also stressed the growing threat from the Selous Scouts and the *madzakutsaku*, and the need for more co-ordination between guerrilla groups to keep won-over areas firmly in control. To ensure this the DC mapped out plans for more regular contact between groups in the area and more co-ordinated offensives. A review of supplies revealed Baas Die's group was dangerously low on ammo as the DC had anticipated and since it would take time for requisitions to be relayed and supplies ferried through from the difficult border zones, the DC decided Baas Die and his group should leave directly for the supplies base, and that one of the two new groups be deployed in their former zone.

The group were to march to the base, collect ammunition and medical supplies and then redeploy south of the area, where they would be under a new DC.

And so they left the area. They left at night, without a goodbye to anyone. A *mujhibha* from the village accompanied them, showing them a route through the farms. They marched at night, keeping to fences and avoiding roads and buildings. During the day they slept. They fed on strips of biltong and sometimes melons or mealies filched from the fields and roasted over a carefully guarded fire.

On the foot of the hills they passed a mission school closed because of the war. From two trusted white nuns who had remained behind they got anti-malaria tablets and a portable radio and they learnt that a platoon of the infantry had passed through the area two weeks before.

Beyond the mission school they began the ascent into the bewildering tangle of mist-capped, mystical hills that looked so alike that without the *mujhibha* they would have spent days going round in circles. An athletic eighteen-year-old with a sombre face, the *mujhibha* knew the area as he did his own village. He had escorted another group to the supplies camp before and moved with the sure-footedness of a mountain goat, guiding them through the mists and the showers and great blue whales of rock. Every so often he would kneel precociously before a mountain pass, clap his hands and speak to the breeze, invoking the spirits of the land to give them safe passage through that area where it was said travellers who had not heeded the laws of the soil had wandered in a trance until they were driven to death, or if they were lucky and their people followed advice from the village elders and went through established propitiatory rituals, the strayed traveller re urned, blank-eyed and speechless, from the ordeal.

The arms depot was situated on a plateau of high land ringed in by three sharp peaks. A shrill female voice challenged them as they began the final ascent. Baas Die shouted back the code-word given by the DC and identified himself and his group, and then a woman comrade armed with a bazooka emerged from the foliage and came up to meet them. She brusquely shook hands with them and, leading them up through the opening between the peaks to the base, delivered them to another comrade and went back to her post.

On the plateau the dozen girl comrades who manned the arms depot came out of the trees to meet them. They all wore denim shirts and trousers and caps and were armed with bazookas. They shook hands with them in the same brusque manner, grunting slogans with guttural voices, brandishing sturdy, bangled arms in the air. Pasi thought he recognized the dark-skinned comrade with close-cropped hair who greeted him last. He racked his brains, trying to think where he had met her. Had he gone to primary school with her, perhaps, or was she somebody from his home town? She herself seemed to show a flutter of recognition when she shook his hand.

Baas Die and Gidi Ishumba were talking to the depot commander, a buxom girl with a startlingly well shaped face and striking brown eyes. Mabunu Muchapera and Torai Zvombo talked briefly to the two girls who brought them mugs of water, and then went off to sleep, already Shungu Dzangu and the *mujhibha* were reclining under the trees. Pasi NemaSellout stretched out languidly against a rock and pulled his cap over his eyes.

Two girl comrades shook him awake three or four hours later in the afternoon.

He pulled his cap into place, wiped his mouth with the back of his hand, and sat up. He splashed water over his right hand, wiped it on his shirt and picked up the tin plate of meat and beans. The girls sat with their knees to their chins and watched him eat.

"The others have gone," the girl with the close-cropped hair said. From somewhere in the trees he heard Baas Die cough, and he grinned, still trying to figure out where he had met her.

"Is this buck meat?" he asked, between mouthfuls.

"Just eat quietly, comrade," the other girl said.

"I've been trying hard to think where I met you."

"*Aika*, comrade," she said, "*munodirei kudada so?*"

He explored her face.

"You can't be serious," she said, shaking her head, "didn't you train in the same camp as me for a while?"

Suddenly he remembered her, the girl he had sometimes cooked with in the first training camp.

240

"I must have changed a lot, then," she said.

"*Tashataka*," said the other girl, laughing. "We are now unlookable."

"He might have thought we were men, *nhaika*. And *hondo iri mayazi, sha*."

"I was eventually going to remember . . ." Benjamin began, but she cut him off.

"I think your comrades are waiting for you."

He rose and went to where Baas Die and Gidi Ishumba were, watching, with the buxom commander, the girls bringing up crates of ammo from the secret underground caches.

"These are all the grenades we have left," the depot commander was saying. Shungu Dzangu and the *mujhibha* were already there. Mabunu Muchapera and Torai Zvombo came up shortly.

Baas Die and Gidi Ishumba divided belts of bullets, small rockets, incendiaries and grenades into seven piles. There were two landmines. Baas Die signed in the khaki manilla file and then his men started loading the arms into their backpacks . . .

"We leave at midnight," Baas Die told his men. "If you want to sleep again you can do so."

"If anybody's stomach starts complaining again let us know," the depot commander said and everyone laughed.

They heaved their packs and drifted off to separate sleeping places – even in the base they never stuck in a group. Pasi went back to the place he had been and soon fell asleep.

When his eyes wrenched open it was dark, the sky was ablaze with stars. The mist had mysteriously cleared and the peaks ranged out round the plateau, their edges sharp and solid against the sky. He had been having a bad dream he could not recall and this and another sound in his ears had made him wake up. He knew from the position of the milky way it couldn't be long after nine or ten at night.

He looked carefully round him, scanning the dark. He heard movements behind his back. He grabbed his gun and swivelled.

"It's only me."

She bounced from the rock and stepped out in front of him.

"I was going to let off the whole magazine," he said, breathless.

"*Tairidzirana!*" She sat next to him, hitching her bazooka over her shoulder.

"You scared me."

"I just thought to check on you before going to sleep," she said, pulling off her cap so that he made out her profile; flattish scalp, cascading forehead, gleaming eye, furrowed nose, twin swell of lips.

He rubbed his eyes and killed off a yawn. Surprise still tugged at his sleep-dulled senses.

"I'm sorry I woke you up."

"It's OK."

"Can I sit here with you?"

"Sure," he said, "sure."

A mist was settling on the mountain tops when they left at midnight. The air was damp but not too chilly. Weighted down by their loads, they moved slowly down the slope. The *mujhibha* was tired now, panting to keep to the combatants' accustomed pace.

Pasi NemaSellout marched in a daze. His body pitched itself forward with a force and will of its own. His limbs tingled, his mind was outside his body, somewhere; he still felt a hand, hard fingers brushing his chest and kneading his back and clawing at his spine and a mouth breathing hotly at his neck.

Dawn cracked in the sky. The hills washed out of the mist and towered blue grey. Below them the valleys twisted out in an untidy splotch of greens to where sky and land met in horizons and the world crouched, waiting.

In the morning they made a brief detour and followed a meandering valley in search of water. They found a well among thick reeds, but were hit by a putrid smell around the place.

"Something died here," Gidi Ishumba said. He shuffled in the reeds and found what he was looking for: a dead monkey, bloated and rock-stiff; he kicked it into the open with his boot.

"The well is poisoned."

They drew back.

"Keep your eyes skinned," Baas Die said as they trudged back up the valley. "They've been here."

They found mangoes in the forest and after carefully inspecting the fruit, loaded their bags.

Pasi sucked at the mangoes until the seeds were clean. The juice dripped down his arms. He licked his fingers, rubbed his sticky hands together and remembered her saying, afterwards, "*It gets so lonely out here sometimes we wish we were out there at the front.*"

242

He had wanted to tell her about the contacts he had been in and to ask her what had happened to her since she left the training camp, but there hadn't been much need or time to talk and she had said, *"Sometimes we get so crazy you wouldn't believe the things we talk about."*

This, then, was sex - two bodies meeting on a rock.

This then was the act you had idolized, Benjamin - a faceless meeting in the dark, totally unplanned, banishing forever the foolish maidens of your longing. This was your initiation. You traced the terrain into your memory, clung to its every detail. This was your initiation on a rock, in the forests of hoary mountains, with a girl who smelt of blue soap and beans and gunpowder, who wore denims and boots and carried bazooka on her back; a girl who cut her hair short like a boy and whose fingers were stone-stiff from hauling crates of ammo. You were surprised when she said *"Thank you, I needed it,"* never having thought a woman could say that and you tried to say something nice back, wondering is she knew this was your first time. You didn't want to think she had done it to somebody else before because she had been good to you, this daughter of some father with a gun on her back. You had heard girl comrades didn't do it, that doing would suck the fire out of their guns, that they didn't handle their weapons during their time of the month even, and now she had done it to you and delivered you from your fear, this girl you almost forgot where you had met; and she had said, *"I wish you were spending another day here,"* but you had left her there with your seed in her and would she have your child? Or had she already had someone else's before? And what is she had your child? Would she deliver here in the camp? Would she carry the child in a strap together with her bazooka? Would the child look like you?

Or did she know how not to have . . .

Torai Zvombo, who was on the far right, fell first, yelling and kicking in the grass and then the *mujhibha* next to him let out a bellow like a young ox, flapping his arms over his chest like a man mobbed by a hive of bees.

"Spray!" shouted Baas Die. "Move back!"

The other five took cover, diving behind bushes.

The *mujhibha* staggered before them. His hands clawed at his body wildly, ripping out strips of bleeding skin.

Torai Zvombo thrashed in the grass.

The *mujhibha*, face bathed in blood, fell and was quiet. In he grass Torai's noises faded to a whimper, then stopped.

Their clothes were eaten away. Torn flesh bled through holes in the cloth. They lay close together. Torai Zvombo's face was buried in the grass, the *mujhibha* gaped at the sky. The grass was soaked red.

Mabunu Muchapera crawled on his elbows and knees and roared. Gidi Ishumba stood upright, hands supporting belly, tears streaming down his face.
Pasi NemaSellout leaned forward over a rock and moaned.
Baas Die squatted, vomiting.
Shungu Dzangu knocked his head against a tree, moaning, *"Kufa takangotarisa here?"*

They cut branches and tossed them over, across the three metres of safe ground.
First they threw small leafy branched over the bodies and when they were completely covered by leaves they threw bigger ones. Some of the branches landed in the sprayed area – there was no way of reclaiming those. Their hands blistered and bled from breaking boughs. Splinters of wood stabbed their flesh. After the big branches they tossed dead logs and rocks until they had built a rough stack three metres high. Gidi Ishumba wanted them to burn the stack to prevent wild animals digging to the bodies but the others objected.
So in the end they left the stack there, a grotesque mound of rock and wood on the hill slope.

Deprived of a guide, they walked for three days in confused circles, moving in broad daylight and resting at night. They checked the bushes carefully for signs of aerial spraying, poking through forbidding mountains mists. The biltong ran out and they fed on mangoes; once a warthog chased them out of a dense bough and they scrambled up a rocky hill.
At last they found a pass through the mountain and went down into the village where they met a group of women carrying large calabashes of beer to the fields where there was a *humwe*.
They made the women leave the calabashes in the forest and sent them to round up all the villagers. As soon as the women turned their backs they fell upon the beer. They drank and drank – and on their empty bellies they soon were all fiercely drunk. When the villagers came they made them sing, hitching up their guns to dance with them, and during one of the songs Mabunu Muchapera fired twice into the air and caused the crowd to scramble for cover.

Baas Die, who was tottering in the middle of the crowd, quickly recovered from the shock and seized the opportunity to announce momentary silence for the dead comrade. The singing and dancing resumed and continued into the night, by which time the seven-day brew had achieved its full effect.

Shungu Dzangu crawled off to sleep first. Mabunu Muchapera ranted for some time and crashed out unexpectedly under a bush just out of sight of the crowd. Pasi NemaSellout stumbled off retching into the dark when the trees began to swim and plunge in his eyes. Baas Die tottered bravely on his slender feet, wrenching his slurring voice awake with sporadic shouts. Only Gidi Ishumba contained the power of the brew, ducking every now and then for the calabash behind a tree and returning with a renewed vigour; but neither he nor Baas Die could remember the next morning, when they all woke up scattered in a field, how or when they had got to the places at which the woke up, or who had brought the *pungwe* to a stop or how or when the villagers had left.

They stared dully at each other, reeling from the hangovers and the bronze mid-day sun striking their brows; miserable, ashamed, baffled at the recklessness which might have cost them their lives.

No one said anything. They heaved their packs and fled from the place.

Chapter 31

The *svikiro* came to visit a week after the DC of the zone left their new base. The *mujhibhas* and the *sabuku* accompanied her from the hill on which she lived. She came disguised as a sick old wife; the *sabuku* played husband. The *mujhibhas* drove a cordon of cattle in front of and behind them. They did not meet any of the *madzakutsaku* who had been seen in the area or the Selous Scouts whose presence had been rumoured. The sky was clear of helicopters and, apart from a honey-bird which winged their course, they travelled without a hitch.

Their arrival had been revealed to her, she said, and she had asked to be brought to them. She wanted to see them together at the same time so Baas Die, rather against his wish, sent out for his comrades and dispatched the *mujhibhas* to scout the area while the meeting took place.

When the group assembled the *svikiro*, who had finished putting on her headpiece and black cloth, began to burp and hiss, tossing her head from side to side.

"*Svikai zvakanaka sekuru,*" the *sabuku* pleaded, clapping his hands. The *svikiro* sneezed, fetched her *chipako* from her skirts and tipped snuff into her palm. She fed each nostril carefully and then offered the headman a pinch. Then the *svikiro* turned to each of the comrades. Baas Die refilled his *chipako* from hers.

Pasi NemaSellout, who was nearest her, squatted and held out his open palm – the left one, he remembered, and when she shook the oily, black, horned container over his palm with her sinewy hands her smoky man's eyes were staring into his; he squeezed the snuff into each nostril and, with tears burning in his eyes, stepped back to let the others through.

"*Makadii sekuru?*" Shungu Dzangu and Baas Die addressed the *svikiro* and the others followed suit. She responded to each greeting with her gruff man's voice, "*Takatarira m'zukuru.*"

She shook her head over her lap, making clucking noises. A shiver ran through her body. She lifted her head. Tears were streaming down her face. She dipped her head and wept, then suddenly squeezed her eyes dry and crinkled her face.

"Those two you left in the forest," she said, in a sad old man's voice, shaking her head over her lap, "those two you left there, under a mountain of rocks and leaves . . . those two children . . . their bodies are cold but their hearts are still breathing."

The comrades looked at one another, at the *sabuku* and back at the *svikiro*. Tears sprung down her cheeks again but she flicked them off with the back of her hand. She blew her nose loudly and wiped her fingers on the grass.

"Those two you left there, lying in the forest . . . no one turned their bodies or touched them . . . no one folded their hands or legs or closed their eyes . . . those two children . . . their bodies are rotted but their hearts breathe still and it is a bitter breath . . . That one who carried the gun on his back . . . he knew it could happen to him one day and he understands . . . his people are scattered over the land and they cannot know . . . the time will come for them to know about his departure . . . but this other one, this boy that was given to you to guide you through the mountains . . . logs lie on his neck and rocks sit in his wounds, his voice is choked with leaves . . . but he speaks . . . he says, 'My mother and father sit awaiting my return' he says, 'Why have my people not been told?' . . . Jackals sneeze around him and the shadows of vultures fill his eyes with darkness and he weeps, 'Who shall pick my bones?' . . . he is a young man like you and his spirit perches in a tree over that place, his spirit moans, 'Who shall throw stones here where I lie and wish me a safe journey to the world of my fathers?' . . .

"The soil is not happy and the skies are frowning," the *svikiro* paused, then began again with a low voice, her eyes sweeping round them. "And there are things you did in the mountains and the soil says, 'No, this is not the way, boys and girls who carry guns on their backs must not meet' . . . it washes the power off your weapons and the scent of it brings the enemy to your trail and then you get caught in your enemy's snare . . .

" 'The end of the war is near,' the soil says. 'Too many of my children have died . . . the land flows with blood . . . but this land cannot be free while my children roam the forests, naked and hungry like beasts,' the soil says. 'The black men who sit with the white men on the hill of Harare sending wings of death to my sons and daughters shall be removed and *I* shall choose whom I want . . . the war will not be long . . . a wet season and half another and the

247

sons and daughters of this land shall go home to rest . . . but it will be a wet season and a half,' the soil says. 'Blood shall flow and black hands shall spill black blood and black blood will mingle with white but black will flow over white and blot it out, and the sky will send heavy rains to wash away the filth . . .'."

The *svikiro* paused. Baas Die looked at the headman and said, "Can we ask the *sekuru* a few questions?"

The headman clapped his hands and relayed the request to the *svikiro*. The *svikiro* grunted permission.

"Is there anything *sekuru* sees in this village that we need to be made aware of?"

"Beware of the men whose clothes are the colour of ripe grass in May and those that shall come to you with faces painted with soot."

"Is there anything you would like to ask *sekuru*?" Baas Die turned to his comrades, but none of them said anything.

"I see blood," said the *svikiro*.

"Among us?" Mabunu asked.

"I see blood only. Plenty of blood."

"Is there anything you can do to strengthen us?" Shungu Dzangu asked.

"There are things I see about some of you that may need to be cleaned up – things from your homes that could open doors to problems if left unattended . . ."

"Do we need to know these?" Gidi Ishumba blurted.

The *svikiro* glared at Gidi Ishumba for a while, then her voice broke suddenly into an old man's cackle. "Let it rest then, let it rest."

His blotched face trembling with concern, Shungu Dzangu put a hand on Gidi Ishumba's shoulder, but Gidi Ishumba slapped the hand down. The *sabuku* nervously looked on.

The *svikiro* extracted an old razor blade and a small pouch from her skirts.

"If any of you want her to give you *nyora* she'll do it," the *sabuku* explained.

"I already have those," Baas Die said, turning to his comrades. "I don't know about you."

Shungu Dzangu crouched in front of the *svikiro*. Pinching folds of his skin with her gnarled fingers, peering with her foggy eyes at the ghosts of earlier incisions, she nipped deftly at each wrist, each ankle, at his neck under the collarbone and his chest where the heart throbbed. Shungu Dzangu did not flinch. She let the blood squeeze out then rubbed the sooty black powder from the pouch into the incisions.

"What about the others?" the headman said.

"I was worked on when I was a child," Gidi Ishumba said.

"It doesn't matter if someone did it to you before," said the *sabuku*.

"And you *muzukuru*?" the *svikiro* turned to Pasi NemaSellout.

Pasi NemaSellout stared at the *svikiro's* sooty hands and the stained razor blade gripped in her fingers. He stepped out and crouched in front of her. He closed his eyes as she pulled up his skin and nipped with the razor blade. He felt a faint itch as she rubbed the powder into his bloodstream, but it was over sooner and easier than he had thought and he was stepping back, watching the darkening clots.

The *svikiro* calmly packed away her tools and wiped her hands, and then she shivered the sudden big chest-heaving shiver of the old man inside her going, leaving in a whoosh of salivary breath and she was still, emptied of the other being who had sat heavily inside her. The *sabuku* helped her take off her black things and she was a woman again, a quiet old woman waking slowly from sleep . . .

"So the deacon's son finally got *nyora* today!" Gidi Ishumba laughed.

"Shut up, Gidi."

"And you Shungu, how many dozens of them have you got now?"

"Just leave us alone Gidi Ishumba. If it's the *ngozi* in your family troubling you, don't take it out on us."

"But why did you say that to her, Gidi?"

"You shouldn't listen to everything these people say, Baas Die. Who hasn't got things that happened in their family?"

"But it does no harm to listen."

"I'm not just going to let any old woman I meet open my veins or tell me about my past. That is for my *mudzimu* to tell me. Do I know who she really is or what she's dabbled in? Does she know my *mutupo* or where I'm from? Why didn't you let her give you *nyora*, Baas Die?"

"My grandfather took care of that."

"And you, Mabunu? You've never had any, have you?"

"The soil will protect me."

"What was she saying about, about . . . the two who left us?"

"The *mujhibha's* people have to be told."

"We can send a *mujhibha* from this village with the news."

"His people will still want to be shown the place ..."

"But how can we go back there, Shungu? The spray is still active ..."

"And besides, can we spare anyone?"

"Pasi has a point."

"What do we do if the boy's parents insist?"

"We can't start worrying about that, Shungu. What do you think Mabunu?"

"They'll just have to accept what happened. We lost one of our own comrades there."

"What do you think, Chef?"

"You decide. You said you want to make decisions."

Chapter 32

now they have burnt down the grass and leaves to smoke us out

they have burnt down the crops in the fields in the hope that they can starve us

the land lies bare

if they had enough dynamite they would blast away the rocks and hills that hide us

they have poisoned the natural wells from which people drink

everyday we meet dead animals at the side of the wells, their eyes frozen and their limbs stiff

a few wells in the village are free of the cyanide but the river runs free and like our anger cannot be dammed

schools, shops, dip tanks, churches — everything has been closed

cattle roam untended in the fields licking the ash

people are prisoners in their own homes, the curfew lasts from dawn to dusk

young people defy the curfew and race across the blackened fields, bearing messages and arms

we've driven away most of the white farmers from the surrounding farms and the people feast on beef

we hit the soldiers in their camps, mortar their farms, cut telephone wires and landmine their vehicles

they come out like swarms of angry bees, stinging everything in their path and the povo suffers from their wrath

we hear there are talks to end the war but we know we are going to be at it for a while yet

Chapter 33

Ahead of them the fires loomed larger as they approached the burnt out village. The acrid smells of the carnage – of burnt cloth, baked enamel-ware and roasted grains in the bins – swept up to their noses.

They skirted the fringe of firelight, keeping to the shadows and when he thought she pushed on too fast, he pulled her back and they stopped to listen, trying to distinguish from the soft crumble of molten roofs caving in, the muffled pop of tinpots and the sudden spluttering flare of twists of nylon any sound or sign of danger.

Pasi NemaSellout wondered how much further she had to take him into this seething trap of fire, hating why her parents had had to be caught in the ill-fated village.

They were there, suddenly, a compound on the curve of a hill and he knew they were there because she veered from the bush and made towards the blaze at the centre.

"Wait!" he hissed, grabbing her hand and pulling her down. He looked around, listened. Two of the huts had been reduced to roofless rubble, the circle of stumps glowed like red teeth. On the edge of the compound clearing, tilted back into the indifferent bosom of the sky loomed a small hut and a grain-bin balanced on rock, both untouched by fire.

"Mother! Mother!" She banged on the door of the smaller hut. "Father! Are you in there, Father?"

She rushed out and searched the grain-bin. He heard her feet plunging in the groundnuts, her hands groping among the bags and the thin mud walls.

In the rubble, Pasi saw the rim of a three-legged pot and the red hot frame of a bed. The glow lit up the prints of boots on the sand – soldiers' boots coming and going.

"I can't find them," the girl sobbed.

"Maybe they got away."

"My mother can't walk. She's paralysed."

"Perhaps he carried her off before they got here."

"They've both been killed," the girl wouldn't be consoled, "I know it."

Two or three compounds away, in the gloom, a fresh hut burst into flame.

"Into the grain-bin!" he ordered the girl. "Quick! And don't move!"

He sprinted towards the new fire. In front of him was a kraal and the cattle milled about, large, round, fearful black eyes flashing. In the leaping light he saw a glint of metal as a camouflaged figure slipped into the shadows.

Pasi let out a volley of shots with his AK. The figure stumbled, his gun tumbling from his shoulder, and plunged into the bush.

Pasi charged after him, running in short bursts and sinking to his haunches, to listen. His feet kicked the abandoned FN. He felt something warm and moist and sweet-smelling rub off the leaves on to his arm. Blood. He had hit the soldier all right. He had seen the soldier stiffen and plunge. But he had to be careful. The soldier could be hiding or leading him into a trap.

Come out, soldier boy and let me drill a nice big donga in your face.

He listened carefully, peeled his eyes.

No sound.

Where was the soldier? Who was stalking who?

Show your hindside and let me roast your civet cat bottom.

He heard loud breathing ahead, somewhere very near, saw a dark shiver of movement and a snorting beast thrashed off through the foliage.

Squeal, Smithy's dog, so I can grill your snout with my AK!

His eyes hurt. His finger ached on the trigger.

Carefully, he climbed up a tree and scoured the forest.

More than half a kilometre away, in the sparsely treed grounds of the mission school, he saw a slow blur of motion creeping towards the ruins of the classrooms which had been gutted earlier and the mission church with the corrugated iron roof which had somehow survived the carnage.

He scrambled down the tree and thrashed off towards the mission. He searched the orchard, squashing guavas with his boots and peered through paneless windows into the empty classrooms. Nothing there, either.

Then he knew the fugitive must be in the church. The church had no doors, just open doorways. One Sunday afternoon he and Shungu Dzangu had crunched in from the orchard in the middle of a sermon to address the villagers and the visiting white priest, visibly shaken, had flailed about in his robes, fearing the soldiers would come.

He slipped in through a side doorway. The rough, hard, backless benches stood in tidy rows. In front was a crude table and the pulpit.

Where are you?

He heard soft breathing noises from the front, from somewhere near the pulpit. Gun held at the ready, bayonet gleaming in the gloom, he stepped out.

The figure sprawled inside the pulpit, almost hidden away. Pasi flashed a torch at the man. The man's head and shoulders rested against the panel of the pulpit, the rest of him stretched out on the floor.

The man's face was black as soot but, when they caught the torchlight, his eyes were blue!

"Finish me off," the man said, in a perfect, white man's English.

Pasi flashed the torch slowly down the man. His face was black, yes, but his eyes were blue and he had a sharp nose and his lips were very thin. His neck was black too, and his hands and arms were black and his hands clutched at something silvery and snake-like tumbling out in shiny coils from a dark patch at the side of his stomach.

"Kill me, please," the man said. "Please finish me off with your bayonet."

Under his beret, his close cropped hair was dyed black. He was a young man and underneath the soot or dye or whatever he had applied to his skin he couldn't have been older than nineteen or twenty. Under the dye his hands were slim and the fingers were long and light like a young man's hands. He was a young man and he couldn't have been older than Pasi.

"So you are a Selous Scout," Pasi said in English, standing astride over the man.

"Won't you finish me off?" the man pleaded. Some shudder seized him and he moaned. "So stupid . . ." he gasped, "so stupid to die . . ."

The man's head dropped to his side and he was still.

Pasi rifled the man's pockets.

Two photographs. One of a white, middle-aged couple posing in the driveway of a large white suburban house. Another of a white girl with blonde hair smiling from behind a typewriter.

Money.

Cigarettes.

A twist of dagga.

He slipped the photographs back into the man's breast pocket and tossed the rest of the loot into his own. He took one last long look at the man's face, pulled the cloth off the pulpit and covered as much of the body as he could, then stepped back slowly. He paused in the doorway. In the village the fires had subsided and were now glowing like scattered lamps.

A soft wind was breathing through the orchard. Out in the forest, a lost calf bleated plaintively. Hitching his gun, he shambled into the gloom.

When he tapped on the wall of the grain-bin, the girl screamed.

"It's me," he whispered through the narrow window hole.

"I heard the firing and thought you had been killed," stammered the girl.

"I got him," he said, dryly.

He could feel the heat in the girl's hands, the heat fanning up from the glowing rubble around them. The heat in the air.

"I know my parents have been killed," she started sobbing again.

"We'll find them in the morning," he said. "We'll find them."

He felt tired and empty. He let her cry and hold on to him. He felt tired and weak and empty and he clutched her and let himself stroke her face and they hung together, swaying together at the centre of her razed homestead.

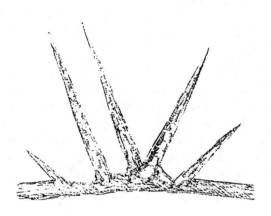

Part Four

Chapter 34

The battered red Zephyr Zodiac swung off the road and bumped up the narrow stone path to the house. Peter, who sat against the wall reading a tattered magazine, dived for his crutch and scrambled out of the way as the car nosed up to the wall.

The driver, Clopas Wandai J. Tichafa, opened the door a little, careful not to bang it against the wall, and squeezed out. He wore faded blue jeans and an old leather jacket, high-heeled black shoes and a yellow golfer's cap.

"Surprised?" Mr Tichafa grinned at his son. "Yes, I thought you'd be. It's a 1962 model. Can you believe it's been on the road eighteen years now? It looks almost new, doesn't it? I got it for just six hundred dollars from a white man who was emigrating to South Africa!"

A yelping from the back seat of the car reminded Mr Tichafa of something he had forgotten to bring out.

"Sorry Dingo," he said in English, fishing out a young Alsatian cross from the floor of the car. "Sorry, doggie, so sorry."

The dog licked his face furiously and he patted it off, "OK, Dingo, OK, Doggy. Enough now, Dingo. Right, Dingo. Stop it, Deeeengo!"

He put the dog on the ground and hissed, "*Zids!*" Instantly, the dog folded up at his feet and was still. "It understands German," he said. "Its previous owner was German and he gave it to me because he was going down south too and there'd be no one to look after him. Good dog, Dingo. Good dog. Are you hungry, Dingo? Do you want some food, Dingo? All right, Dingo. All right. Get him some milk, Peter."

Peter went into the kitchen and as he was coming out with the bottle, the dog dashed at him, grabbed a mouthful of his shorts and held on, growling even as Mr Tichafa pulled him off.

"Bad dog, Dingo! Bad, bad dog! Here, Dingo. *Zids,* Dingo! *Zids*! Are you hurt, Peter?"

"No," Peter fingered his mauled shorts and poured out the milk. After slurping it up, the dog decided to be friendly.

"Where's your mother?" Mr Tichafa asked as he sagged into the green sofa.

"She's not back from the market place."

"And Benjamin?"

"He went away in the morning."

"I heard he came back. So he lives here?"

"Yes."

"What is he doing? Has he got a job yet?"

"No."

"Is he in the army?"

"He had a problem – something to do with his papers."

"So what does he do with himself?"

Peter shrugged.

"Has he changed much?"

Peter shrugged again.

"I don't suppose you'd know or notice. I don't suppose you knew enough about him before he decided to leave."

They sat together for a while, then outside Dingo started barking and growling again. Peter stumped out to look.

"It's mother," he said. "Stop it, Dingo! *Zids*, Dingo!"

"Whose dog is that?" Mrs Tichafa demanded, slinking sideways through the door. She stopped when she saw Mr Tichafa stretched out in the sofa. She shook hands with him and parked herself in the sofa opposite to him. Moments later Nkazana followed in, slowly, careful not to lean over too heavily, dropped to her knees, shook Mr Tichafa's hand and shuffled on her knees to the floor next to Mrs Tichafa's seat. From that safe distance she asked after Mr Tichafa's health and discreetly disappeared into the kitchen.

"I almost failed to recognize you," Mrs Tichafa said, glancing at his clothes. "Did you bring the dog too?"

Mr Tichafa picked a thread from his jeans and stared at the floor.

"And the car?"

"I bought it last week from a white man who was emigrating to South Africa."

"Lucky you."

"It was only six hundred dollars. A rare bargain, these days. Did you look at it?"

"How could I, with the dog waiting to leap at me?"

"It's a 1962 model but it's been very well looked after. White people look very well after their property."

"I didn't know you could drive."

"I've been taking lessons. I'm going for a road test next month."

"Good for you. You're doing very well for yourself. And how were the others when you left them?"

Mr Tichafa picked at his jeans again, his eyes shifting uneasily. The door opened and Peter's face popped in.

"Where's the needle and thread, Mother?"

"In the tray in the kitchen cupboard. What do you want it for?"

"Dingo tore my shorts."

"Dingo?"

"The dog."

"Take the shorts off and I'll mend them for you," said Nkazana.

"So Benjamin's back?" Mr Tichafa resumed.

"We sent word months ago. Peter left a message with Muchaneta. Or didn't she tell you your son was back?"

"I was tied up. And besides, he, as a son, should have taken the trouble to let me know he was back."

"So what made you come today?"

Peter's face popped round the door again to ask for money for milk.

"But we left a bottle on the shelf in the morning," said Mrs Tichafa. "What happened to that?"

"I gave the milk to Dingo."

"A dog indeed!" snorted Mrs Tichafa, fishing into her skirts and counting some change into Peter's palm.

"And who's that pregnant young woman?" Mr Tichafa asked, once Peter and Nkazana were out to the shops.

"Don't pretend you don't know."

"As the owner of this house I have the right to know and hear from *you* who is living in this house."

"What's that supposed to mean? But didn't you get the message? I told you Benjamin had brought somebody with him."

"You said he brought a friend, not a pregnant woman."

"I thought you'd have guessed what that meant. What was I supposed to say? Anyway, I thought you'd come and find out for yourself."

"You mean he brought that girl with him, from the bush? He brought her here with him, to my house, without my knowledge, and you let her stay, without consulting me?"

"What was I supposed to do? She followed him here, came the very next day after he arrived. He told me she was his girl and he was going to marry her."

"Marry her? Just like that? Without telling me? And who is she? Was she a . . . was she in the war?"

"Don't ask me."

"Do her parents know she's here?"

"No they don't."

"How can that be? What if something should happen to her, in the condition she is in?"

"Her parents died in the war."

Over and over again, in his mind, he had wondered what the reunion would be like. Thousands of times he had wondered what they would say to each other. He would write the script of his speech in his head, practise it, churn it in his mind and discard it for another. Anger, remorse, embarrassment and shame had gripped him in turn until he had taken refuge in procrastination.

He had wanted to tell his son how much they had suffered after his departure, how the police had harassed them, how the whole township had talked about his truant son who had burnt down a beerhall, cut off his young brother's leg and run off to the war to escape the shame. Shutting his ears to any suggestion of the heroism of his son's departure, he had seen his son's act as the ultimate defiance of his authority. And then he would hear first hand accounts by people fresh from the operational areas, people who talked endearingly about the brave boys in the bush who were fighting the war to free the country. The fact that he was a father of one such son would startle and stab him in the night, making his soul bleed with remorse. Then he would think of other things – the wife and the house and the children he had forsaken, the church he had turned his back to – and he would try to stave off the drab hypocrisy of his existence with brash material acquisitions. Once or twice when the tension got too much for him he prayed for his son.

When he heard his son was back alive and safe the remorse had worn off; the weeks of procrastination had gradually hardened him again.

And yet, when Benjamin came home later that evening, when he had already threatened twice to leave, when his son crunched in with three litre-packs of 'shake-shake' beer and shook his hand and flopped into the sofa opposite him and lit a cigarette and slipped off his cap in his old theatrical way and asked him casually how he was, when they ate together – sadza and vegetables and bones – from the same plate, Mr Tichafa's rehearsals came apart.

"So you've bought a car?"
"It's a 1962 Zephyr Zodiac. I bought it from a white man who was emigrating to South Africa."
"Did you pay cash for it?"
"Yes."
"Did you borrow the money?"
"I used my pension."

"So, you're married now."
"You could say that."
"And the child the girl is carrying is yours?"
"That's right."
"I'm sorry her parents died."
"It's over now."
"But how did it happen?"
"What would it help if you knew? What would it help if you knew anything?"

"I meant no offence . . ."
"Very well."
"She can stay here. You can both stay here."
"Where else could I go? This is my home, isn't it?"
"But what will you do?"
"About what?"
"About getting a job?"
"I'll do what I can."
"Are they going to take you into the army?"
"Can't say, yet. I'll take what I can get."
"I hear you had trouble with your papers."

263

"Who said that?"

"I meant no offence."

"I didn't mean for you to think your mother and I didn't care when you left. It hurt us so much when we knew what you had decided to do. We worried a lot about you. We feared for you."

"What about all those others who went too? Didn't they have mothers and fathers too?"

"I don't mean to say you shouldn't have gone. I don't mean to belittle what you did. All I'm saying is, had you been in our shoes, you'd have found it very hard."

"You don't live here now. You don't look after mother or Peter. You don't buy anything."

"Are you judging me?"

"I'm merely stating facts."

"Are you judging me?"

"A man can go and live with another woman. But a man must never forget his first home."

"Are you accusing me?"

"You broke all the rules you set for us."

"Don't say that in my house!"

"I can say anything I want anywhere. You have to admit your mistakes."

"I meant no offence, really. I came back to see you, to show you I'm glad you returned alive, not to argue. I'm sorry it's turning out this way. I think I should be going now."

The car wouldn't start. It sputtered, grumbled, hummed but it wouldn't start. He opened the bonnet and struck a match, pushed and squeezed and tightened among the maze of wires and tubes, but it wouldn't start. On the back seat, Dingo whined and wriggled restlessly.

"Are there any taxis at this time of the night?"

"Why don't you just put up for the night?" his wife answered from the window. "Huffing and puffing and getting mugged in the streets looking for a taxi at this time of the night as if your own house is a witch's lair to run away from?"

Eventually he locked up the car but when he went in Peter was asleep in the sitting-room and his wife had locked herself in the kitchen. The main bedroom had been vacated for him.

He was at the car as soon as it was light enough for him to see, poring over the bonnet with a screwdriver and a spanner. Later, Benjamin, shirtless and yawning, joined him.

"It must be a very small problem," the father said. "The oil and the battery and the water are all right."

Benjamin inspected the frayed seats, kicked at the worn tyres with his heel and opened the boot. The boot was full of empty beer bottles. He closed it and grinned when he saw his father look up uneasily.

"You have to be careful what you buy these days," he said. "They'll try and squeeze dollars out of every bit of scrap they can before they go."

Mr Tichafa tried to start the car again, without luck.

"Do you want another push?"

"No."

Benjamin went off to the shops to buy a packet of cigarettes. When he got back there was nobody outside and the excited voices from the house told him there were visitors. In the sitting-room were his sister Esther and a bearded man.

As soon as Benjamin set foot through the door Esther rushed up to him, wrapped her arms around him and wailed. He held uneasily to her until his father said, "Enough, Esther. No need to do that."

"The dreams I had about you, Benjamin," Esther broke into sobs again. "Three years, my brother. I thought I'd never set eyes on you again. Oh, Benjamin. Are you all right, Benjamin? Stand up and show me you are all right, Benjamin. Weren't you shot at or injured, Benjamin? Have you got any scars? Oh, the dreams I had."

"He's all right, Esther," Mr Tichafa said.

"Let her cry her fill," Mrs Tichafa said, touching the corners of her eyes with the point of her head-cloth. "She's a woman too. She's got a womb and she knows the pain of childbirth. You men don't feel the pain of anything."

Esther was slim and looked taller, somehow, in socks and high heels.

A slight bulge on the belly hinted of something on the way. Her hair was permed, she wore lipstick and eyeshadow and nail polish.

"I left home too, Benjamin," Esther dried her face carefully with coloured tissue paper. "Some time after you left for the bush I ran away . . . I ran away with a man, Benjamin, and he is sitting next to me. I was young and foolish and didn't know what I was doing, but I was lucky because the man cared for me and looked after me very well. I knew I had wronged our parents and didn't dare set foot in this house. Then I got the message you were back B . . . B . . . Benjamin, back after those three long years and I said to Dickson, I said 'I'm going home to meet my brother even though I ran away like a fool and lived with you against their wish.' And Dickson said he was coming with me . . . even though he knew we had wronged our parents . . . And so here we are, Benjamin, and if I have done or said anything worse than I already did, if I have been a rotten sister to you, Benjamin, if I have done anything to make me a worse daughter than I already am, then I ask you as my brother to forgive me and I ask you to ask our parents to forgive me . . . and Dickson. And if I haven't properly introduced Dickson to his *ambuya* your wife, I apologize, Benjamin; his name is Dickson Mhungu and he's a good man and if you and father and mother allow him he'll make up for our wrongs . . . and marry me."

"Do you know anything about cars?" Benjamin asked Dickson.

Dickson looked up with a startled nod and said, "A little."

"We can't get the old man's scrapper in the yard to move. Maybe you can come out and spot the trouble."

Dickson followed Benjamin outside, discreetly bending his back and clasping his hands together as he wormed his way through the women.

"Just a way to get us away from the sobbing and to some fresh air," Benjamin winked. "You'll get used to this sort of thing around here if you don't take it too seriously. You're a long distance driver, aren't you?"

Dickson nodded.

"The old lady told me. She's on your side, so long as you handle Esther well. So am I. As for the old man, he's too worried about getting this thing of his back on the road. You better get started at it, and if you get it going the old man might forget about the fine and even knock a beast or two off your *lobola* list."

Dickson laughed politely, warming up to Benjamin's manner, and opened the bonnet.

From the kitchen tempting smells of liver, chicken, onion and tomatoes drifted into the yard. The three women bantered and bustled, swopping roles,

266

work changing hands. Every now and then Esther would dig into her hand-bag and send Peter on a new shuttle for something – pepper, flour, cream, custard. Even Dingo made himself useful by keeping away from people's ankles and dragging old newspapers into the garden.

"Don't strain yourself, *mroora*," Esther told Nkazana. "You are not your-self yet. When you have recovered from your burden, later, we'll check you out."

"She passed the test the very first week she got here," Mrs Tichafa vouch-safed her. "I don't know what I'd have done without her around and me at the market all day. You don't look well this morning, Nkazana."

"Must be all that pushing we did last night."

"Did you push too, Nkazana?"

"I wanted some exercise."

"Goodness me. You mustn't overdo it!"

"What did they push?" Esther asked.

"Your father's car. Don't know how many times they went up and down the street trying to get it started."

"But what's wrong with the car?" Esther asked. "Have you spotted the problem, Dickson?"

"I can't say," said Dickson from under the car, his hair and beard white with dust.

"It must be a very small problem," said Mr Tichafa, wiping his fingers with a piece of newspaper.

"Leave it, *mwanangu*," Mrs Tichafa told Dickson. "Get a wash and come for breakfast. *Baba* can get the car towed out to a garage and checked up later. Leave it, now."

Mr Tichafa acquiesced, resenting the way his wife had been, purposely or not, pushing him up for judgement all the time, hating the way she had suc-ceeded in making him spend the night and then cut the ground from under him by keeping her cool and refusing to share the bedroom with him.

Just then Peter came up the path, leading along a two-year-old boy. The moment Mr Tichafa saw the boy he stiffened.

"Where did you get him?" he demanded, snatching up the boy.

"I met . . . I met . . . Mainini Muchaneta at the shops."

"Muchaneta! What is she doing here?"

"Who's the child, father?" Esther asked.

The boy buried his face in Mr Tichafa's shirt.

"Can't you see?" Mrs Tichafa said excitably. "Can't you see it's your father's child?"

"Mainini was looking for you," Peter tried to explain. "She wanted to find out if you were here . . ."

"She was looking for him here, eh?" Mrs Tichafa snapped. "She was looking for your father and you helped her find him. And she made you bring her child here to hurt me!"

"*Jeeeesus*, Shamiso!"

"That woman has the nerve to come looking for you here, Clopas! And why shouldn't you be here? Isn't this your home? Am I not your lawful wife? Selfish bitch! She can't spend one night without you, her borrowed husband. She can't survive one night without a stolen man. What about me? What about all the nights I've spent alone in this deserted house? Have I ever gone to her house in the morning looking for you? Am I not a woman? Don't I have my needs, too?"

"Stop it, Shamiso! *Jeeeesus!*"

"Muchaneta!" she spat savagely. "Devil-snake-bitch-Muchaneta! Babbling at my babies in the cot and wriggling, her bottom at you behind my back. Don't think I didn't notice, Clopas. I knew the day that woman came to live next door you were after her. Don't think I didn't notice how you secretly rejoiced when her husband died in the accident."

"Mother, enough," Esther pleaded with her but she would not be restrained.

"And you, Peter, calling that bitch, *mainini*. Letting her lick you up with her serpent tongue like that. So that's what she does every time I send you down there with a message for your father. Feeding you all kinds of poisons to turn you against me. As if stealing my husband from me is not enough, she'd like to steal the only child I have left."

She fled weeping into the kitchen. Esther and Nkazana rushed after her. The baby let out a terrific scream. Tears rained from his little round eyes, his hands balled into tiny flailing fists of fright. Mr Tichafa could not calm him and handed him back to Peter.

"He looks like you, Peter," said Benjamin, pinching the boy's cheeks and making faces which made the boy catch his breath and stare. "What's his name?"

"Takunda."

"Why would she give the boy such a name if not to spite me?" Mrs Tichafa yelled from the window and in no time she was out again, resolutely drying her face. "She's boasting in front of me, laughing at me for being weak. Today she'll know I'm not going to take it lying down any longer. I'm done with forgiving people who dance on my toes. Yes, Clopas. I'm going to fight her at her own game. Everything is going to be equal between Muchaneta and me. If you spend one week with her you'll spend the next one with me. You'll split your pay equally between us. Whatever you buy for her you'll buy for me and if you refuse I'll go to court. I've been meaning to do so but my pride wouldn't let me. Don't think I don't know my rights. This is not the old days any more. We women have laws to protect us now. And if she dares to have any more children with you, I'll see about that. I'm not past child-bearing age yet and if you think you can go filling this town with children like a stud bull your pockets will call you to the reckoning."

"We have visitors here, Shamiso. We'll talk it over later."

"What visitors? You call your own children visitors? What is there to hide from them? What is it they don't already know? Go and bring Muchaneta over. She hasn't been in this house for a long, long time. Tell her I'd like to have a long friendly chat with her. If she wants to be respected by my children and called the *mainini* she so desperately wants to be, she'll have to come and meet Esther and Benjamin and their spouses. She *wants* to meet Benjamin, doesn't she? Or has she no sense of shame at all, or is she a woman of the shadows? Bring her over. The food is ready. We'll eat and talk like women. I won't harm her or her baby. All I want is some respect."

"Mother's right," said Benjamin.

"Bring her over, father," said Esther, taking the baby from Peter and hitching him on to her back.

Mr Tichafa knew he had no choice. He slouched off to the shops. A long while later he was seen coming back, leading behind him a hesitant Muchaneta.

"Now you know what kind of family you are marrying into," Benjamin told Dickson in a corner of the beer garden, hours and several rounds of lager later. "You could say Esther, father and me are all versions of one song, the common tune being that we all ran away from home and from mother – each for different reasons, of course. Not that mother deserved it."

Dickson offered Benjamin a cigarette.

A big plump woman with a banana complexion splashed opaque beer on Benjamin's shoulder and began a profuse apology.

"Forget it," Benjamin cut her off, then turned to Dickson. "Sorry, am I being rude?"

"No, *tsano*."

"Perhaps I've lost faith in common manners, got to the point where, if I have to say something, I just say it. You don't have to agree with me all the time. I like a person who says what he thinks. Anything goes, really, except cheating and abusing another person. That I can't stand. Are you serious about Esther, Dickson?"

"I am, *tsano*."

"Because if you aren't and you ditch her tomorrow I wouldn't like that. But we'd still be friends. What happens between you and her is your business and I've no right to even be talking about this. I bet if everyone made a policy of not sticking their noses into other people's affairs this world would be a much healthier place. But as it is this world is full of noses . . ."

Dickson laughed.

"Am I talking too much?"

"No, *tsano*."

"Stuff a bottle down my throat if I'm boring you."

"No, no."

"And call me Benjamin. You could be my brother, you know. I mean, real brother. I've sometimes wished I had an older brother. Tell me about yourself. All I know at the moment is you are Dickson the gliding cobra who ran away with my sister."

"There are seven of us in our family, five girls and two boys. I come second and am the older boy. We were raised in the country looking after cattle and goats and working ourselves to death in the fields for a few bags of maize. Father had a job in town and came home every month-end."

"What did he do?"

"He was a policeman."

"One of those people who hunted us down in the bush, eh?"

"He retired last year."

"After shooting his quota of comrades?"

"He didn't go on patrol much, really."

"What difference does it make? Hustling political activists and throwing demonstrating schoolboys into jail was just as bad."

"We had trouble at home when the war started and the boys demanded his resignation from the police force. When he didn't resign, they burnt down our home and my mother and some of the children had to go and squat in his two-room shack in the police camp. I had already finished school and was working as a truck driver. We didn't dare set foot in the country until after Independence."

"Everyone had to have a job to fend for their families. But we couldn't forgive policemen because they kept the system going. But when you look at it more closely, it makes no difference what job one had. Life couldn't just stop because there was a war going on. People had to eat and wear clothes and go to the hospital. The food and clothes we got in the bush came from salaries from the system. We knew that. Take my father. He was a messenger at the District Commissioner's office for years and years. Carrying files from one office to another and making tea for the 'Baas'. I didn't know until I was much older that that's all he did. I thought he was some kind of officer or clerk. But he ran a family on the pennies they paid him. Amazing, how our fathers managed on their pathetic budgets. I sometimes think if you took somebody like that, somebody who fed ten mouths and sent four children to boarding school at the same time and paid the rent and still afforded a *doek* for his wife all on a teaboy's salary, he'd make a very fine Minister of Finance. But what was I saying about my father – oh yes, that he, in carrying those files, in making the tea that wetted the baas's throat so that the baas could harass our people better, he too was propping up the system."

"There were so many ironies in this war."

"The man whose wife my father married was a soldier. He died in an accident before I was old enough to go to school. I don't remember much about him, in fact all I remember was his camouflage kit hanging on the line to dry at weekends. That was before the war got hot and Rhodesian soldiers were having a good time. You know I used to look at the camouflage kit almost with envy. Something about the colours – the greens and browns – always intrigued me."

"Perhaps that was the war instinct speaking even then."

"I hate talking about the war."

"Why is it so difficult to talk about it?"

"How do you know it is?"

"A cousin of mine was in the bush for five years. He's a captain in the army now. When he came back he wouldn't say a word about his experiences. He wouldn't be drawn out at all."

"There's nothing to talk about, really. If the bush could speak then it could tell the story. When you are trying to piece together the broken fragments of your life it hurts to think back. The worst thing is to come back and find nothing has changed. I look at my father and mother and brother and sister, at the house in which I was born, at the township in which I grew up – people prefer to call it suburb now – and I see the same old house, the same old street and the same old faces struggling to survive. We won the war, yes, but it's foolish to start talking about victory. All this talk about free schools and free medical treatment and minimum wages is just a start. The real battle will take a long, long time; it may never even begin.

"Of course, when we went out we thought our guns could change things overnight. And then we came back to find the whites could still shout at us because they still have the money and the ex-combatants have to scrounge for jobs just like everyone else. I worked for a day as a hand at a construction site last month but when the white foreman heard that I was an ex-combatant I was told the company had employed too many casual labourers by mistake. Is that fair? You come back and find you are years behind your classmates who didn't leave school. Some of my classmates are at the university now. It's not the gap that I regret – that was part of the sacrifice. It's not being given the chance to catch up that makes me bitter. What is there to talk about when people are too busy to listen and too quick to forget? Five years from now the war will be totally forgotten. The truth of it is that those of us who went out to fight will carry the scars for the rest of our lives. We were heroes during the heat of the war, but now we have been left to lick our wounds. You think we consider ourselves heroes? When you wake up every morning and hitch your gun and go out in search of death it's idiotic to talk about heroes. Out there it was kill or be killed."

He paused and reached over the sea of bottles for a fresh pint. The way Dickson listened attentively, urging him on with his silence, somehow annoyed him. He had not talked like this to anyone, had not *wanted* to talk but now he could feel himself sliding towards a confession. He wanted to be told he was wrong, some violent disagreement that would help him sort out his conscience and force him to salvage some belief in the heroism of his past.

"I grew up in an exaggerated Christian family, Dickson. My father and mother were exaggerated Christians and I knew that even as a child. I was absolutely terrified of God. We were not allowed to dance to the radio and if Esther had been seen with make-up, she'd have been slaughtered. The church came first. While other people were marching into the city to demonstrate for majority rule my father had us scurry off to church. But now, of course, he belongs to The Party. Now everyone has a card and is a comrade.

"I grew up with God breathing down my neck and it made me hate my parents. I tried to be a good son. I was unlucky. At school there was always talk about our family being sellouts. I tried to fight that down by joining school demonstrations. Once I helped burn down a beerhall and I got into trouble with the police.

"Esther must have told you about Peter's leg. It was an accident, but they believe I did it on purpose. The Overseer made the church people believe some kind of demon possessed me and made me do it. A demon trying to destroy the church. They had a special service to cleanse me. That made me hate God even more. Then at boarding school I got caught up in demonstrations against black call up. That's when I had to cross the border. I went because I was caught up in a crisis and leaving was the only thing to do. Had I stayed on the system would have crushed me. I found myself in the thick of things and struggled to make the best of it and survive. That happened to a lot of other people. And that's how this war was won. I never had the chance to experience what other young men experienced. The church robbed me of my childhood and the war took away proper school, friends, holidays and all that. One day I was a teenage student doing prep in the dorm. The next I was a guerrilla shooting Smith's soldiers in the bush. And before I even knew it, I was bringing home a wife. I can't say when or how all that happened. Sometimes I can't believe it *happened* to me; I think it happened to somebody else. That pregnant girl we left at home had her full supper of the war. There's not one girl in this town who has seen half of what she has. If she could speak she could tell you how the soldiers burnt out her village and how her parents were found floating in the river with their throats cut. She could tell you about her friends who were dismembered in bomb raids while at the *pungwe*. She could teach you how to wrap up a bunch of grenades in a bundle of grass and carry the load through a cordon. I couldn't stay in the assembly points after the ceasefire was announced. And this I've never told anyone, Dickson. And that's why I couldn't get proper discharge papers. I couldn't stay there, not with those British and Canadian troopies politely bossing us about and the Rhodesians waiting in the wings to shoot us. Rhodesians walking free while we were herded into the points like prisoners of war, as if we had not won the war! I tell you, Dickson, a guerrilla is only a hero while the war is raging. Once it's over the regular soldier in the smartly pressed camouflage kit takes over."

Benjamin lit up a joint, smoked, and offered it to Dickson. Looking uneasily around, Dickson declined.

"How do you think we survived the war?" Benjamin closed his eyes and released thin wisps of smoke through the corners of his mouth. "My group lost three comrades. The first one died in a contact soon after we crossed back on deployment. The second stumbled into chemical spray. The third shouldn't have died at all. He was the youngest and boldest guerrilla this war has ever seen. He was a born guerrilla. His gun was like a third arm. His eyes were telescopes – when he looked out at a tree or hill or building, they seemed to be taking sights. He was not afraid of anyone or anything and if he felt like going to blow up an enemy truck he did it, and then he would come back with his eyes red and so quiet you'd know he had done it. His death was a stupid, stupid mistake. Stupid! Stupid! Stupid!"

He smashed his elbows against the table.

"Stupid! Stupid! Stupid! Went out alone against a military camp, just a few weeks before ceasefire and got himself riddled with bullets. They flew him dangling from a rope over the village. Just weeks before ceasefire! Stupid! Stupid! Stupid! Oh, Stupid!"

He buried his face in his hands. When he looked up his eyes were moist.

"I think we should go now, *tsano*," Dickson said.

Benjamin stood up slowly, bracing himself against the throbbing pressure at his temples.

"I have to mourn my comrades," he said.

Chapter 35

Benjamin and Dickson get home to find all the doors ajar and lights ablaze. Dingo rushes at them, flings himself at their knees. Peter stumps into the sitting room with Takunda at his heels.

"What's up?" Benjamin squints in the yellow light. "Where's everyone?"

"They took *Maiguru* Nkazana to the hospital. We had to call an ambulance."

Benjamin and Dickson turn back to the road.

The night is quiet, a soft wind blows balls of paper down the road. The township houses crouch darkly in fatigued rows. In the yards banana leaves shiver; tall, thin stalks of choumoellier nod. Somewhere on the edges of the town a drunk croaks home. In the south, a shoe factory drones on. The police camp glimmers blue on the side of the road, ahead the abattoir breathes offal and singed hide. In the solemn acres of a white cemetery planted next to black townships, a lone cyclist's light slices through the brooding pines.

A dog knocks down a street bin and snouts the rubbish.

A taxi swings down from behind them. Benjamin leaps into the road and flags it down.

The battered Renault creaks through the emptied city, shudders along mirrored pavements, rattles at the slow, crimson robots and coughs up suburban curves. The hospital leaps out of the grove.

The car park is deserted. No one meets them at the entrance. The corridors are long and brightly lit, the tiled floors sparkle with polish. Ahead a nurse pushing an empty bed darts into the passage.

At the maternity ward, the sister can't find her name.

"She was brought in this evening, by ambulance," Benjamin repeats, peering over the list.

"Is she a fee-paying patient?" the sister asks.

"No."

"We had only one ambulance delivery this evening but with a different name."

"What name do you have?"

"Mrs Tichafa."

"That's the one."

"But why didn't you say so?"

"I had given you her maiden name."

"But aren't you her husband?"

"I am. Is she all right?"

The sister points out a room at the corner of the ward.

Nkazana lies pale and exhausted, surrounded by Benjamin's father and mother, Esther and Muchaneta. A cot stands near the bed. They open out to let Benjamin and Dickson through. Benjamin steps forward and peeks at the little bundle of whites. The face is a mess of red skin and black hair – a tiny round ball of a head, a half of it forehead, bumps for eyes, a little hill of a nose, a pink line of pursed lips and two brown leaves of ears.

"It's a boy," his mother says.

They all beam at him.

He touches the tiny face with a finger and turns to the bed. Nkazana smiles weakly at him. Her face is very pale. She looks small but her breasts bulge round and firm through the hospital vest.

"She didn't take long to deliver," says Esther.

"He's just like you," his father tells him. "He's got your nose and forehead."

"His mouth is his mother's," says Muchaneta.

"He's going to be dark," says his mother. "You can tell by his ears."

"Not rough dark, but smooth dark," says Muchaneta.

"And he's big, for a child born three weeks early," says Esther.

"Must be all that car pushing she did last night," says his mother. "Something good came out of that car, after all!"

They all laugh.

"What are you going to call him?"

"Zvenyika," says Benjamin.

"Did you decide that with Nkazana?"

Nkazana nods.

"Zvenyika Clopas Tichafa," says his father.

"Nobody gives children European names any more," says Esther, "especially Jewish ones."

276

"But as the first grandson, he'll have to carry his grandfather's name," says his mother, "even if the name doesn't appear on the birth certificate."

"Zvenyika Clopas Tichafa," says Esther, poking gently at the whites, "wake up and see your father."

In the doorway a nurse stands waiting with a trolley. Benjamin peeks again at the white bundle.

"Zvenyika will use his head and hands and grow up to be somebody," he says.

He's only twenty and he has no job or house of his own yet but he tells himself he'll do all he can to raise the little bundle of humanity in the cot. He'll do all he can, even though all he has is a pair of chapped hands.

He tells himself he'll do it.

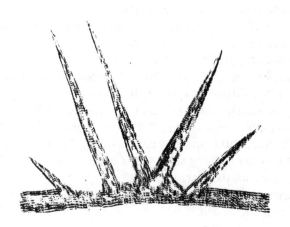